THE SPACE
BETWEEN WHENS

BLUE BOX BOOKS

THE SPACE BETWEEN WHENS
WICK AFTER DARK
BOOK ONE

Published by Blue Box Books
www.blueboxbooks.com

ISBN 978-1-932461-49-7

Printed in the United States of America

THE SPACE BETWEEN WHENS

MAX THOMPSON

Also by Max Thompson

The Emperor of San Francisco: The Wick Chronicles, Book One
Ozoo: The Wick Chronicles, Book Two
Forked: The Wick Chronicles, Book Three
The Psychokitty Speaks Out: Diary of a Mad Housecat
The Psychokitty Speaks Out: Something of Yours Will Meet A
Toothy Death
The Rules: A Guide For People Owned By Cats
Bite Me: A Memoir (Of Sorts)
Epistle: A Love Letter
There Once Was a Cat From Nantucket

Visit Max online at his blog, The Psychokitty Speaks Out
http://psychokitty.blogspot.com
or on Facebook
http://facebook.com/thepsychokittyspeaksout

Books one of his people (K.A. Thompson) wrote

The Charybdis Novels:
Charybdis
As Simple As That
Finding Father Rabbit
The King and Queen of Perfect Normal
The Flipside of Here

It's Not About the Cookies
Rock the Pink

Visit K.A. Thompson online at her blog,
Thumper Thinks Out Loud
http://kathompson.blogspot.com

For my real-life Jays...
I hope I got it right.

THE SPACE
BETWEEN WHENS

WICK AFTER DARK

THE STUFF BEFORE THE STORY

My name is Wick. The year is 2416. The place is San Francisco, capital of Pacifica, North American continent. In case you didn't already know.

I've told a few stories along the way, but if you're just now coming to the party—well, not a real party, I'm not serving snacks or anything but I wouldn't object if someone showed up with some dead delicious things to share—there are a few things you might need to know. Just to ease your confusion.

Pacifica is a country born out of the demise of the United States of America, encompassing the western quarter of the old U.S.A. and ruled by monarchy. When the U.S. opted to fracture rather than engage in a protracted, unquestionably bloody Civil War, Pacifica waged a five-year election cycle. At its culmination, the people picked the candidate they thought would be most fair and named him King.

That was King Norval Blackshear. He didn't want the job and hadn't even campaigned on his own behalf, but a few million other people decided he was wrong and that he was perfect for the job. He would treat the people fairly, choose his heirs wisely, and thus was the House of Blackshear born.

A couple hundred years later, here we are. Pacifica is governed by King Jackson, known as Jax to his family and friends. He rules as well as reigns, his word being law. But he's fair, so there are no dictatorial temper tantrums going on. He has several advisory groups and listens to them carefully, but the final decisions are always his. He rules with logic and kindness and relies on his closest friend to pull him from the abyss of stupidity when needed.

They met when he was six years old, the day he tried to climb a tower on the Bay Bridge and got stuck partway up. A dozen adults stood below and watched him cry as he dangled with his backpack caught on a piece of metal; their notion of rendering aid was to yell at him to get down. When no one else would shimmy up after him, a fifteen-year-old who called himself the Emperor did, and over the years they became friends so deeply bonded that they consider themselves brothers.

Jax has synesthesia and can see sound, which is a secret because he can use it to his advantage when negotiating deals on behalf of Pacifica. The sounds you make when telling the truth and lying are different; lie to him, and he knows.

There's the Queen, Aubrey. She teaches fifth grade in the public school system, loves to cook—if you're in her house, there's a good chance you won't leave unless you've been stuffed—and she's dedicated to her family. Jax rules the country, but she totally rules the home. And if you're hurting, she has an amazing capacity for empathy. A touch from her is genuinely healing. She loves people first; they have to earn her antipathy.

That's an amazing thing, by the way. She has every right to not trust anyone.

She was a fourteen-year-old runaway, bolting from theocratical Florida and her father's abuse—and yeah, let your head go there because it was *that* kind of abuse—after he'd arranged for her marriage to the pastor's seventeen-year-old son. With some help from her older brother, Red, she made her way to San Francisco, and once there she figured out how to support herself, even getting a college education without help from anyone else. While Jax knew the story of her past, their kids didn't, and they had no idea that her father was Levi Munson, the First Minister of Florida and titular head of the Church of Florida.

Aubrey met the Emperor first, but there was never a chance he would fall for her. His first impulse was to introduce Jax to her because he knew they would be perfect for each other, and he was right. Jax knew within an hour that she was the one. She was twenty-three and he was eighteen, but he knew. They married two years later, and with over two decades together, they're still so adorably in love that it makes me want to hurl.

There's the oldest of their offspring, the Princess Oz, whose real name is Australia but you'd better be prepared for a swift kick to the junk if you call her that. She's the heir to the crown, and like the King, she can see sound. Lie to her, and she'll know it because all the colors around you change. She has plans for her future on the throne: she wants to bring back the United States. As part of that plan, she fully intends to marry Midlam's Prince Andrew, something he's totally on board with. Oz is smart, funny, and tough, a second-degree black belt in karate, and she has a taste for adventure.

All the toughness and skilled fighting didn't help her when war broke out and she was abducted from the safe house where the Emperor had hidden her, along with her brother and Prince Andrew. While Drew and the Emperor were on the roof making repairs, the underground bunker was infiltrated by a few dozen of Florida's military. It was a brutal fight, but she killed several of them before they grabbed her and ran, and she took out several more as they spirited her to the man who wanted her taken. She was straight up tortured: First Minister Munson had her beaten, battered, nearly drowned, legs broken, flesh flayed, and he used electric shock to punish her for having the gall to exist. But she throat punched him in the end and dropped him like a rock.

There's Zed, her brother, younger by almost two years. He's a typical teenager, though he has a serious mature streak, cultivated by his work at the mortuary on Alcatraz Island. He tends to the dead and takes it seriously, so much so that he's slowly changing how the dead are treated. Before your body is cremated, he will speak to the truths of your life, he will read to you your favorite stories or poems, he'll sing to you—whatever it is that he knows you would most want. And before he sends you off on your next journey, he will very gently bath you with warm water, and he will wish you well. He will shed tears, and will truly, sincerely mourn your passing.

Oh, he can also smell your feelings. If you're confused, he can tell you that you smell like old gym socks. If you're sad, he can tell you that smell like salty tears. If you're feeling, well, horny, he can tell you that you have an aroma of onion rings and desperation. He tries to not be rude about it.

There's Andrew, better known as Drew, the Crown Prince of Midlam, another country born from the demise of the U.S. From age five or six, he began spending summers in San Francisco with Oz and her family, and when he was home in Chicago, he and Oz either video chatted or texted each other daily. He's two years older than Oz and is sweet and smart and sees details other people miss. He totally saved the world once, and when Oz was missing, he willingly walked for days on end to get to her.

Seriously, when Oz went missing from the safe house, he was determined to get to her and no one could have stopped him if they'd wanted. He and Zed and the Emperor set out on foot to find her, and while they battled blisters and body odor, there was no complaining. Oz was missing and there was no question: they would find her. He soldiered on and got super close to the Emperor, which was a good thing because a few months later he totally screwed up when being taught how to use the time portals, and because they're close, the Emperor wasn't too upset. He was supposed to head for 1980 but he let himself think about how spiffy it would be to jump forward 1000 years, and *boom* we found ourselves helping a sword-wielding teenager and a grumpy old wizard lead elves into battle against the dark wizard who had enslaved them.

I suppose at this point, I should mention that time travel is involved.

And there's the Emperor. Like I said, when he was fifteen, he saved the life of six-year-old Prince Jackson when he was stuck on a tower of the Bay Bridge. After that, he popped in and out of Jax's life, and when he was seventeen, he decided to stick around.

By that time, Jax was just a bit shy of being eighteen years old. Time travel. It does funny things.

For over two decades, the only name he was known by was *Emperor*. He kept his past hidden and true name to himself, and when he was near the end of his life—well, he thought he was near the end; boy, was he in for a surprise—with his life's mission complete, everyone finally learned his name.

William.

Will to his friends, Dash to his father.

The Emperor did not touch people. Period. He never offered an explanation, but once Oz and Zed hit puberty, the hugs and kisses stopped. He'd never touched Jax or Aubrey, but they respected him enough to not examine that quirk too closely, and the kids knew not to push him for personal information. They weren't sure why; it was a given: you don't ask him personal things.

He was there to help his father, Finn, who popped up in an egg-shaped time machine with no memory of who he was or when he belonged, get home. He was there even though he knew he would die at forty-two, because the thing about time travel is that time is super picky and doesn't like people messing around with it. Without the right someone to hold a guy in place? Well, he gets super sick and croaks.

I'm the someone who held the Emperor in place, and I was supposed to go through a portal to see if the world had ended or not. There was a meteor headed for it in the 27th century, and Finn was the one working the hardest to save the planet—he allowed his seventeen-year-old son to move to the 25th century to be there to help him regain his lost memory. It's complicated, but there's a building with a time lock on it, a place where they can check data from time lines lost to the meteor, so they know what's already been tried. In every history noted in the Old Mint, the Emperor died at 42, because his anchor went through the portal and never came back.

This might be a good time to mention that I'm a cat.

It might also be a good time to mention that Will understands everything I say.

Long story short, the world didn't end, I stayed, and with me still here, he got to live. That meant he was there when the war broke out, and he was able to take the kids to the safe house. He marched with Drew and Zed to find Oz, and while we camped one night, he admitted to Drew that he was Oz and Drew's great grandson, which helped them become extra close. He was there for Drew's time portal training gone wrong and battled Shedu warriors to free elfin slaves, and he rode on a baby black dragon named Jeff that I created from a wish. He let me keep a giant cat I created named Fluffy. And he fell in love, so deeply in love, with the woman whose heart he'd once broken.

He'd broken her heart because he would never be able to touch her. When he touched people, he could hear their thoughts, and they could hear his. After he didn't die, when the future did not end with the destruction of the planet, Oz patiently helped him learn to control what happens when he touches people. He learned to close a window in his mind, to not listen and not be heard, so when Aisha Salazar Okuda kissed him on his birthday, he stepped into a whole new world.

And that's where we are. At the end of Drew's time traveling hiccup, having just come out of the lab to tell Finn that his failsafe worked. We hadn't gone forward 1000 years, but instead wound up in a simulation, playing a game of good versus evil that was all too real. Aisha Okuda had a good hold of his hand as he walked her home, and she warned him: he was never running away again.

PART 1

THE FLAPPING OF WINGS

1

My life was a lot more comfortable before everyone around me paired off and started touching each other. I could sit on someone's shoulder and enjoy the view from up high or ride in the pouch of a sweatshirt and steal warms, and I especially didn't have to worry about a sudden change in balance or swinging back and forth because of bumpage caused by horny people needing to walk closer together than should be possible. Before the touching started, if I was on someone's shoulder and they were changing gait, they reached up to make sure I wouldn't fall. If I were in the pouch, they'd slip a hand in to make sure I didn't slide around too much.

Those days were over.

There was a lot of touching going on, and with it far too much kissing, and I was on the short end of everything.

I rode in the pouch of the Emperor's sweatshirt as he escorted Aisha home after a time-traveling date gone wrong (as wrong as one might consider an *awesome* time spent with a wizard and elves, a giant cat named Fluffy and a baby dragon named Jeff, fighting Shedu warriors while chasing an evil dude named Tobias.)

(Time travel is tricky.)

(We wound up in a holographic simulator 200 years in the future instead of jumping ahead 1,000 years, which was the whole going-wrong of it.)

As I swung back and forth and bounced against Will's crotch, I fathomed that my days of comfortable travel were behind me. He was holding Aisha's hand and not paying attention to me—which was fine, really, I just wanted him to brace me a bit and perhaps adjust the sweatshirt so I wasn't damaging his virginal fun bits—and it was obvious that the whole touching thing was not going to end.

All right, truth. I didn't want it to end. He deserved a chance at all the fun kinds of touching he could get. A little help in the whole sloshing back and forth thing would have been nice.

Will—the Emperor, who was not really an Emperor but, hey, you grab a title when you can, I suppose—had spent forty-two years with a brain that could suck up the thoughts of other people when he touched them, which meant they could hear his, too, if they were paying attention. When he learned it was possible to control it, that he could touch people and close off his mind, it opened up everything to him. He could hug Oz and Drew and Zed. Aubrey could kiss him on his cheek without advanced warning. He didn't have to take steps away from people when it seemed as if they might be reaching for him.

More importantly, he didn't have to run when Aisha Okuda decided she was damn well giving him his first kiss.

He'd done that—he ran—just before his twentieth birthday when he stood with her in the middle of Union Square and lied through his teeth, telling her that he didn't love her and never would.

He broke both their hearts that day. He broke mine that day because there was nothing I could do to help him. I sat on the bathroom floor of his tiny apartment in the South of Market neighborhood and watched as he stood in the shower with the water as hot as he could stand, and then as he broke, sliding with his back against the tile until he was sitting under the spray of water, his gut-wrenching sobs echoing in the small bathroom, until he began to dry heave and the water ran cold. He'd broken her heart so that she would move on and find someone who could love her without reservation and give her the things she most deserved—a life with passion and intimacy and secrets that she could keep to herself—everything he would never be able to.

I couldn't help him. There was nothing I could say that was going to make him feel even a tiny bit better, and I couldn't purr for him while he was soaking wet, so I curled up on the bathroom floor while he grieved until he was literally sick. I wanted to go get Aubrey because she could help him if he would allow it, but she and Jax were several blocks away doing official royal things, and I wasn't allowed to cross the street.

Aubrey had told me specifically, "Stay here with the Emperor, and we'll pick you up the day after tomorrow. I promise." So I had to stay, even though he was falling apart and there was nothing I could do.

He went to bed in the middle of the afternoon but didn't sleep. He laid there with his pillow over his face and stayed like that until the next morning. He didn't move until his doorbell rang, and only then to pull the pillow away and moan. He didn't get up when Jax unlocked the door and came in, yelling, "You'd better have pants on, Emperor," because he was coming in and Aubrey was with him.

He didn't have pants on, but he didn't care. He pulled the sheet over the things she didn't want to see and stayed in bed while they came in to check on him.

That was probably the last time anyone saw him without a shirt; he began getting his entire torso tattooed after that, images he didn't want displayed, and he kept them hidden for another twenty-two years.

Aisha was leaving for Las Vegas. She asked Aubrey to tell him but didn't elaborate. He wouldn't tell her anything, either, other than to whisper that maybe it was for the best. Aubrey urged him to go after her—she wasn't leaving until late afternoon; there was still time, and she clearly wanted him to stop her—but he refused. Going after her wouldn't change anything.

His life was woven around secrets that he kept shoved down deep. He couldn't tell Aisha that he wouldn't be born for another 200 years, or that his refusal to touch anyone wasn't owed to a religious belief, as she assumed; it was because he could hear their private thoughts when he did. He wouldn't risk gifting her the burden of the things that simmered in every nook and cranny of his brain: the world was going to end in two centuries' time, unless his father could find a way to save it, and he was waiting in this When to protect the man from his own amnesia.

It's all a bit complicated, and I've told the story before.

The simple gist was that he could tell her none of it, and when she confessed her feelings, that she loved him and would be patient for as long as he needed, he ripped her heart out, stomped on it hard enough to make her hate him, and then walked away. After he walked, he ran; he threw his sweatshirt onto the ground and took off, running as hard as he could for as long as he could. When he couldn't take another step, he took a taxi home and hid in the shower.

He thought he would never see her again, but there she was on his forty-third birthday, floating from the elevator like a wish he'd waited nearly twenty-five years for.

When the elevator doors opened, he was doomed in a happy way; she was no longer the confused twenty-year-old who let him run away rather than hold him in place to demand answers. She was confident and collected, and once she knew why he'd intentionally hurt her, she was determined to get what she'd wanted back then. She even warned him, as we left the elevator of Finn's lab, that she wasn't letting him get away.

He had no intention of running this time. He took her hand and they walked across Union Square, toward her apartment a mile away. On a slow stroll, it took twenty minutes. They took their time, wandering down streets that headed away from her building, and the longer they walked, the less tense Will became.

You seem happy right now.

"I am happy, Wick." They were still holding hands, swinging their arms back and forth. "It's a beautiful day."

"Not to mention we didn't get eaten by Jeff the dragon or blown up by a deranged wizard," Aisha said with a bit of a laugh.

Jeff was awesome. And it wasn't his fault Drew screwed up and tried to go a thousand years forward.

Drew's stray thought about how spiffy it would be if we could jump forward one thousand years tripped a failsafe in the portal and dumped us into a simulation filled with elves and wizards, and we stayed because it gave Oz a chance to work through some anger issues left from the war. She felt like having been taken from the safe house in Denver by Florida's megalomaniacal First Minister's military was her fault, that she didn't fight hard enough, and a week battling simulated evil allowed her to come to grips with it. It wasn't her fault, and she needed help.

"Indeed," Will said. "I will admit that Jeff was magnificent. If you begin to miss him or Fluffy too much, I might be convinced to take you for a visit."

Fluffy was a Clydesdale horse-sized cat; Jeff was a twenty-foot-tall baby black dragon. I created them both from wishes while we were stuck inside the simulator because they were useful, and why not? Will hadn't been happy that I brought them to life, but he couldn't deny their effectiveness.

I might want to.

You have other things to worry about, though.

"I'm not worried about anything. Why would I be?"

Because Aisha said her reward for getting through the battle was murdering your virginity. She got through it, dude. Pay up.

"I think for the moment Aisha would simply like to go home and see her son."

"The son who has no clue I was gone in the first place," she said. "I'll want to hug the stuffing out of him, and he'll think I've gone nuts. How the hell do I handle this?"

"What would you do if you'd simply gone out to lunch?"

"Ask him if he cleaned his room, most likely. It's the current ongoing battle."

"Then do that."

"Will, I haven't seen him for nearly a week. I don't want to butt heads with him right now."

"He saw you this morning, remember that. Don't turn it into a battle. If you ask and he says no, sigh and tell him if it's not done by tomorrow, you're doing it for him. That includes cleaning up his browser history."

She laughed. "That's mean, Will."

"Little bit, yeah."

What's in your browser history, dude?

"I haven't searched for anything untoward, Wick. She can look at my browser history if she wants. The worst thing she'll find is a string of searches for a discontinued ointment that I would *really* like to find."

Jock itch again?

"Dry, cracking feet."

Sure.

"Arguing again?" Aisha asked.

His balls itch.

"Wick knows what buttons to push," he said.

And it's so easy.

"So does my son," Aisha sighed. "I'm having a hard time wrapping my head around the idea that I worried about him and missed him, and he has no clue that I was gone. As far as he knows, you and I went out for coffee a couple of hours ago. He won't know about Shivan and his quest to free the elves, or the wizards, or the fighting we went through. No hint of the things Oz endured when we finally caught up to Tobias. Even the dirt on my clothing stayed behind. I have bruises, and he won't see those, either."

Will could relate. There were dozens of times as a teenager that he left his home to visit Jax, spending days, sometimes weeks here, and his parents never realized he was gone. "I sometimes found it difficult. These huge things happened to me, things that began to fundamentally change who I was, but to them I was still the boy they'd had breakfast with. Sometimes I was the boy they'd yelled at five minutes earlier because he'd told his mother he would shave off his beard when she shaved hers."

"Oh, no, Will…you didn't."

He rubbed a hand over his beard. "This has been a point of contention since I was fifteen. Half the time I think I keep it out of spite, even through the years when she wasn't here to be upset about it."

"You've shaved it off before. Jax and Aubrey's wedding. And a few other times. I've seen pictures."

"Jax's mother was quite adamant, and I acquiesced because of the wedding. Once, Oz asked me to shave so that she could see what I looked like without it, and then promptly told me to grow it back. Another time I shaved because the child of a visiting dignitary was terrified of men with beards. Other than that, I've kept it in one form or another."

"Remind me of that once Jimmy gets facial hair. He wants a beard so badly, and I want him to not grow one so badly."

"Not a fan?"

"Not on my sixteen-year-old, no. I'm not ready for all the grown-up things."

"And on me?" he pressed.

We were across the street from her building, near the entrance to a small park where kids were running around, squealing at high volume. It was surrounded by a short retaining wall that was capped in smooth stone all the way around. Aisha gestured to it and nudged him to sit.

"You're a grown man." She turned toward him, reaching out to slide a finger over his cheek. "It fits you. There's nothing about this that says, 'hey, I want the world to think I'm an adult even though we can all see I'm pretending.' But I never would have guessed it was a middle finger to your mother."

He shrugged lightly. "Mothers and sons. It gets complicated."

"Oh, sweetie, you have no idea." She set her hand on his leg, absently rubbing his thigh. "My son's entire life is complicated. Though I haven't found his middle finger yet."

"It's coming." He set his hand on hers. "If this is the new normal, I'm going to have to switch from carrying a backpack to a messenger bag. Or wear very long sweatshirts, to hide the evidence."

She had to think about it, then leaned in to kiss him.

That's not going to help. That's going to make it worse.

He ignored me.

Dude, I'm sitting right here. *I'm hiding the evidence. Stop it.*

He didn't.

And fine, it's not like he was full-on happy, but there was twitching and I was not in favor of it. They didn't stop kissing until Will caught sight of Jimmy from the corner of his eye and even then, it took a couple seconds before he pulled away.

Aisha pretended they hadn't been doing anything, even though she was a little flustered. Jimmy crossed the street, hands in pockets like he was annoyed, and she asked him what the problem was.

"No problem. It's just that Dad wants to talk to you and I get to be the messenger, like he doesn't know how to work a phone."

"About?" she prodded.

A teenaged-size sigh huffed out of a twelve-year-old sized kid. "Zed's spending the night, right? And Dad just got this wall-sized video monitor and says it's okay with him if we use it for video games, but also if we're going to we might as well spend the night with him since we'll probably stay really late playing and he knows you would wait up for us, and that's not fair to you."

"And he needs to tell me this personally?"

"I think he just wants to be sure that you're really okay with it and that I'm not just saying you said it's okay just so we can use the monitor. Especially since this is your weekend and not his. He doesn't want to make you mad twice, I guess."

She started to say yes but then stopped. "Wait. Why did he buy a wall-sized monitor? The eighty-inch monster wasn't big enough?"

"Work stuff, I think. But he also wants to see how well it handles game graphics. He's working on a virtual reality combat training thing. Something about using the games to check the refresh rate and simulation lag."

"And he wants to play, too," she ventured.

He nodded. "George is out of town tonight, so we can, you know, actually have fun."

She turned to Will. "Before I tell him yes, are you free for dinner tonight?"

"Absolutely."

She kissed him again and then got up to kiss Jimmy on the forehead. "Let me talk to your father, but I don't see a reason why not."

"Your weekend," Jimmy started.

"It's technically not the weekend yet," she said. "He can owe me a day or two either way." To Will, "I'll call you in a little while, after I talk to James."

They watched her walk across the street into the building. An awkward silence formed; Jimmy wanted to leave but didn't know how to do that politely, and Will was perfectly willing to let him stand there and squirm. It went on for nearly a minute, until Jimmy exhaled hard and said, "Look, she really likes you, you know. She's never let me see her kiss anyone, and I've only met one guy she went on a date with and that was by accident."

"Does it bother you?" Will asked. "I was aware you were unhappy when she kissed me at the party."

Jimmy sat next to him on the wall. "I just didn't expect it. I mean, I thought she had *just* met you and all and I'd never seen her kiss anyone except my dad, and that was like a million years ago. I didn't know that she knew you when you were my age. She never said anything, even when Zed started hanging around."

"That doesn't really answer the question. Will it bother you if I'm seeing your mother?"

"Nah, doesn't bother me. It's about time she had a social life, you know? I mean, as long as you're serious and she's not one of a dozen other women you're dating."

"She is not. There's no one else. And my intentions are quite serious."

"Hurt her and I'll nut-punch you."

"I would expect nothing less."

He folded his arms. "Yeah, empty threat, I know I'd never get a shot in even if I wanted to. Zed says you fight like a crazy motherf—well, at least I'd want to."

"Jimmy, if I hurt her, a line will form. After you, then comes the King and Queen. Especially the Queen."

"Mrs. B wouldn't hit you," Jimmy snorted. "She'd just give you that look and say, 'I am *so* disappointed in you, Emperor.' And it would make you feel really bad because she does that look like a pro."

"Indeed. There is no one who can take me to task as well as the Queen. That includes my own mother."

Jimmy leaned forward, his hands pushing against the top of the wall. "I dunno. Moms know where all the panic buttons are." He took a deep breath. "Has my mom told you about me? I mean, my...stuff."

"I've known you since you were eleven, Jimmy. I'm not sure there's much she needs to tell me."

Jimmy pushed off the wall and stood up. "Yeah, there's a lot. And if you stick around she's gonna tell you sooner or later, but I gotta ask you...don't let it freak you out. It's kinda big."

Will pretended to consider it. "Are you wanted in Las Vegas for outstanding gambling debts? Smuggling alcohol into Florida? Or did you kill someone?"

Amused, Jimmy said, "No, not big like that."

"That's not a deal breaker, you know. It would depend on whom and why."

"Yeah, no one has pissed me off that much. Yet."

"Then I don't see a problem."

Jimmy contended that he might want to reserve that opinion. "I'm not, like, you know—" He fumbled, searching for the right words. "A lot of people would walk away, that's all. I mean, even George…"

Will crossed his arms. "Clearly, you're not ready to discuss this. But keep in mind, I don't rattle easily. Whatever it is, I'm sure it's fine."

"I hope so. Because if I'm the reason—"

"I promise you," Will said. "If there are ever issues between your mother and I, none of them will be because of you."

Jimmy glanced toward the building. "Good. Because she's got enough crap to deal with."

I think Will wanted to press for more, but instead he fished me out of the pouch so that I could ride on his shoulder. We watched Jimmy go inside, and then we headed the short way home.

There was no point in taking the long way. I sure as hell wasn't going to hold his hand.

2

Drew's feet thundered on the stairs as we neared the door to Will's apartment. He was in the same clothes he'd worn for the week we were in the simulator, minus the dirt that stayed behind when we stepped into the portal to come home. Will listened to the rapid popping patter descending from above, and waited until Drew was all the way down before saying anything.

"I thought you were headed to shower and then off to eat half of San Francisco."

Drew nodded toward the stairs. "Waylaid by Mrs. B and furniture she wanted moved. And then she and Oz started talking…"

"Ah. So the next sound I hear will be the massive vacuum as you inhale your entire kitchen?"

"I wish. But no. Mrs. B decided that we *all* need to go out for pizza tonight because she wants a beer on tap and Mr. B wants to shoot pool. That includes you and Aisha so you might want to turn off your phone and hide if you made other plans."

"Aisha and I have dinner plans," Will said as he punched in the code to unlock his apartment. "Pizza is dinner."

"Yeah, but do you really want to spend your date with her hanging around the rest of us?"

"I'm fairly sure you had other plans as well, Andrew. Plans sweatier than mine."

"Not really. As long as someone feeds me, I'll be happy. I just thought you might not want to get tied up with family tonight. Just in case."

"It's our first actual date. I'm neither counting on nor planning anything."

"Yeah, no, you just had a week-long date with her and half of it was foreplay. But sure, try to get through dinner with that planted in your head."

Will paused. "I think I hate you."

"Sure, you do, old man. But you know I'm right. You two aren't exactly on the normal-people-dating time schedule. And I'm betting that there was a lot more going on than just sleeping in the lab over the last week."

"Truly, that's all that happened," Will said as he shoved the door open.

"Fine. What about when you two took that long walk without Oz and me? I didn't buy for one minute that all you wanted to do was check out what was left of the Embarcadero. We weren't going in that direction. It didn't need to be checked out."

Will sat on the sofa, running his hands through his hair, but he couldn't keep the corners of his mouth from turning up.

"Thought so." Drew dropped onto the sofa next to him, ignoring the fact that Will had pulled out his phone and was texting her. "Come on, I know she dragged you here to make out like a couple of teenagers on Zed's birthday. She probably groped the hell out of you on your so-called walk, and it all got just hot and heavy enough that the little emperor was begging to come out and play, and she was hyper aware of that. She was willing to wait before, but now? After spending a week with you and *literally* going to war right beside you? That was probably more intense for her than a few awkward dates ending with inappropriately long showers in different bathrooms."

With a chuckle, Will asked, "What makes you think I'd have waited for a shower?"

Drew pointed to me. "No witnesses."

I stretched from my place on the back of the sofa to look at Will's phone. Whatever he might prefer to do, Aisha was fine with going out for pizza with the Queen, and she was going to meet him here.

"He's truly not interested in watching. Kissing sometimes fascinates him, but he finds sex to be a little disturbing."

"So he says. It's not like he actually leaves the room."

"My pursuit of Aisha will be respectful, Drew," Will said. "I am so far out of my element with her, and I have no idea what to do. Moving forward…I suspect that I will truly have no idea what to do once the clothes come off. Or even before. My imagination will bolt from my head like a frightened little girl."

"Tell her that."

"I can't imagine that would be a comfortable conversation."

"It doesn't have to be awkward. Oz and I talked about it a lot when we decided it was going to happen sooner or later. And I warned her it was probably going to suck for her at first. I was pretty sure I'd be done before she even got started."

"I've considered that."

Drew shrugged lightly. "And I was right. Like, literally ten seconds after she got my shorts off. I swear, she got, like, three fingers on me and…" He splayed his fingers and made a whooshing sound. "Never even got into the bedroom."

"I'm sorry," Will said, and he sounded like he meant it.

"That's the thing. I was so worried about *exactly* that happening, but when it did? She was more like, that's fine, now we can fool around and I'll get there, too, and by the time I do you'll be ready again."

"I'm not sure she would want me to know that, Drew."

"Yeah, she would, under the circumstances. Oz didn't expect me to be all that great at first, and I wasn't. I struck out the first time at bat and there was a mess to clean up. But she wasn't done with me, she wasn't upset, and we were able to relax and then just let it happen. Give Aisha a chance. She'll help you."

"You are absurdly excited about the idea that I might finally lose my virginity."

"Sex is fun, Will."

"After you get over the initial nerves," Will guessed.

"You're overthinking it."

"Andrew, I feel like I've waited twenty-five years for this woman, and I can't bear the idea of losing her again. If I'm too—"

"She knows she's the first. That's not stopping her."

Will held his phone up. "And she's coming here before we leave for dinner. I should clean up."

"You're not a slob." Drew got up and looked around. "It's clean enough."

"I know I left dishes in the sink and I have a bad habit of piling things on the counter. I don't recall cleaning the litter box or making the bed. And the dust—"

"She won't care."

"I do."

"Fine." Drew pushed himself up. "Go check the box and change your sheets, then jump into the shower because you stink a bit."

"So do you."

"I'll take care of the dishes and clear off your counters, and run a dust cloth over the stuff that shows."

"You don't need to."

"Great grandpa wants William to get the girl," Drew snorted as he headed for the kitchen.

I jumped from the sofa to the fireplace and pawed at the switch.

"It's not cold, Wick."

I pawed at it again, and he sighed. "Fine. But it will be half an hour before it's as warm as you like."

He turned it on and headed down the hall. I followed him as he checked the litter box—it was fine until I saw it and realized I needed to pee—and I helped him change the sheets on his bed, which consisted mostly of me chasing the top sheet as he flicked it across the mattress.

"You could go help Drew, you know," he told me.

I might accidentally say something to him.

"And he would appreciate it if you did."

But it's not four in the morning. I'm waiting until four in the morning to see if he can still understand me.

"Drew is always very nice to you, you know. It wouldn't hurt you to give him this one thing."

I will. At four in the morning.

"That's not very nice," he said as he peeled his shirt off. "What would the Queen suggest you do?"

Interrupt Drew at four in the morning, because it would be funny.

"I don't think so."

I waited on the bathroom floor while he showered, rolling onto my back to enjoy the warm, moist air as it lifted over the glass door.

I was almost asleep when he slapped the water off and slid the door open, sending a wave of warm wetness over me.

"Wick, what the hell?"

It's like a sauna. I think. My useless fun bits enjoy it.

"All right, that's fine, but you need to move so that I can shave."

I thought he just meant he was going to scrape off the extra hairs above his beard line, or maybe trim it up a bit, but he ran a little comb through it, and then pulled his razor out of the drawer and turned it on.

The razor had a smooth, oblong head with dozens of little holes in it, and when he turned it on, a glowing blue light poured from the mesh. I had a vague memory of him using it once before, but it had been years, and I didn't remember how the hair just fell away from his face as he slid it over his cheeks.

This was worth not waiting for four in the morning. I ran down the hall to get Drew because he was not going to believe it.

Drew. Drew. Drew. Drew. Drew.

He was rubbing dust off the end table and stopped suddenly. "Wick."

He's shaving.

"Holy shit. I can still understand you."

No. Really?

"What the hell was that outside the portal? You literally meowed at me."

I was messing with you.

He dropped the dust cloth and scooped me up. "Cat, I want to be pissed off at you right now, but son of a bitch, we can still talk."

Yeah, that's spiffy, sunshine. Did you hear me? Will is shaving.

"He probably wants to be pretty for Aisha."

Not just trimming, dude. All of it. His whole face.

He finally got it. "Wow. I've never seen him without a beard."

His mom is going to be so pissed.

"Why?"

Because she's been asking him to shave it since he was fifteen. And now he's doing it for a girl.

"She'll get over it. The real question is how Aisha will like it."

We were about to find out. He set me down to finish dusting, and there was a soft knock at the door. She looked confused when he answered, but he picked up the cloth and said, "Uh, I needed to borrow his dusting stuff."

Tell her what Will is doing. Oh, wait. Don't. He probably wants it to be a surprise.

"He'll be out in a minute, Wick."

"Ah." She broke into a grin. "He's talking to you."

"Little shit thought he was funny, making me think that was over with."

It was funny. It would have been even funnier if I had waited until you were busy with Oz and I interrupted to give you directions.

"I don't need directions, Wick."

I've watched. Yes, you do.

He sighed and said to Aisha, "He really is a furry little asshole."

I am not.

I would have defended myself further, but I heard Will in the hallway and wanted to see Aisha's reaction to his naked face.

"Personal question, Andrew," he said halfway down the hall. He was holding a small pair of scissors, and when he realized Aisha was there he stopped, but the words were still falling out of his mouth. "Trim or—"

All he had on was the towel.

Aisha looked at Drew and said, "You need to leave now."

Without a word, he dropped the cloth onto the end table and left, closing the door with a quiet click.

Her voice had a musical lilt as she asked, "What are we thinking of trimming?"

Will set the scissors down on the end table next to the cloth. "Hair."

"And you shaved!"

The hand not holding the towel in place went to his face. "Mistake?"

"God, no. I can't wait to kiss you without all the prickly hairs."

He took a step toward her, but she held a hand up to stop him. "Stay right there, mister. I'm enjoying the view."

Breathe, dude.

I ran over to the fireplace and hopped up onto the hearth. He had no idea what to do or say but I was pretty sure what came next and wanted to get out of their way.

She kicked off her shoes and then whipped off her shirt. "Drop the towel, Will."

He was still clutching it when her jeans came off. "The rest of this comes off once your towel does," she says.

Her undies match and they're pretty. She was planning this.

Will dropped the towel.

Aisha's eyes crinkled at the corners as she grinned. When she spoke, it was half breath. "My god, Will, you have a beautiful body."

His mouth opened, then closed, and opened again. "I think, wait, I think that was supposed to be my line. Because you do. Goddamn, you do." His breath hitched and he stepped toward her, still uncertain, trying to keep his eyes locked on hers. She unhooked her bra and let it drop to the floor.

"You can look, Will. I'm sure as hell going to."

He was close to her, one hand on his chest and the other on his stomach, and he swallowed hard. She peeled his hands away and still holding onto them, leaned in and kissed him. Against her lips, he muttered, "I honestly have no idea what to do."

"No worries. I do."

She let go of his hands and slid her arms over his shoulders, pressing up against him. They kissed for a long time, until I thought one of them was going to suffocate from all the heavy breathing.

She must have thought so, too, because she pulled away a step and took in a deep breath. "You already have a fire going, and there's a fur rug. No reason to go anywhere else."

"It's Wick's. The rug, I mean. It's fake. I thought he would enjoy rolling around on it."

"And I think we will, too."

I hope you plan on washing that.

I curled up in front of the fire, knowing this might take a while. But I had to give Will points; he wasn't fumbling around as much as I thought he would and he wasn't shy about touching all the things he never thought he'd be touching. He let her guide his hands and his mouth, but he didn't lay there like a dead fish, which seemed to make her happy. I thought he was doing fairly well, right until he was practically on top of her and said, "Point of law."

Dude.

"Seriously," she chortled.

"Consent." He was laughing along with her. "Do I have it?"

"Sweetie, I have my hand on your *extremely* hard penis and you're less than half an inch away from finally having sex. Do you really want to talk about consent laws?"

"Well, technically, you need my consent, too."

"Have me arrested. I'm not stopping."

His sharp intake of breath kept him from saying anything else or calling one of the royal guards and made me wish I could laugh out loud. I had to give him bouncing points, too, because it wasn't over in five seconds like he was afraid of and he didn't fall off. He might have when her back arched suddenly, but he was bracing pretty well.

"Did you just—"

"God, don't stop, Will. I did and I might again."

She probably shouldn't have told him that, because that was all it took, and from the look on his face, it caught him by surprise.

Before he could even catch his breath, she looped her arms around his neck and pulled him down for a long kiss, until she realized he was still bracing himself up. "I can take more of your weight on me," she whispered against his lips. "The closer you are, the better." She wrapped her legs around him. "But if you get uncomfortable, pull out. I know it can get a little sensitive."

"Right now, I feel like I could stay like this forever. Goddamn, I love you."

Stay like that and you'll get stuck when all the sweat dries.

"Damn, Wick."

Aisha laughed and asked if I was trying to help.

"He's mocking me."

Her hand went to his face, stroking his newly-shaved cheek. "There's not anything to mock. For someone who said he didn't know what he was doing...oh my god."

"One of us knew what we were doing, and it wasn't me."

"Come on. If I hadn't known this was the first time, I never would have guessed." He pulled away, laying on his side next to her. She grabbed the towel he dropped with her toes and tucked it under them. "Leakage."

"Huh. I never considered that."

That's why I want you to wash the rug now.

"It's messy fun, Will. Sweaty, sticky…should I have warned you?"

"I guessed about the sweat." He set his hand on her stomach and began tracing small circles with his fingers. "And even though you beat me to it, I meant it. Everything about you is beautiful."

Barf. Here we go.

"Worth the wait?"

"Indeed."

She grabbed his hand and pulled it to her lips. "There's my stuffy Emperor."

"I am honestly making an effort there."

"I've noticed." She set his hand on her chest. "And don't be shy. Touch what you want. I could feel your fingers twitching like you weren't sure it was all right."

"I wasn't."

She rolled onto her side, sliding her hand across his hip. "Trust me…if you learn my body, it does us both good. I won't have any problem playing with yours."

That's gonna hurt if she squeezes those too hard.

"I tend to get clinical about things. I'm sure there would be nothing erotic about me allowing my curiosities to lead to an examination of your individual parts."

"Will." She lifted up on an elbow. "Take my word for it. You can touch and taste and look and it will definitely be erotic. I don't care how stuffy you are, if you're examining my nipples with your tongue, it'll be erotic." She guided his hand between her legs. "If you're learning your way around by feel, it will be erotic."

"I would have enjoyed biology so much more if you'd been my teacher."

"Ah, but you weren't touching anyone then."

"Fair enough. You'll tell me if I do something that makes you uncomfortable?"

"Will you tell me if I say or do something that feels like I'm making fun of you?" She set her head back down, nearly nose to nose with him. "It's too easy for me to make light of everything. If you promise to keep me from being too much of a smart-ass, I promise to tell you if you get too clinical, or touch me in a way that hurts."

"I don't mind being made fun of a bit. I know this borders on absurd."

"It's not. I love you just like this, Will. And you have no idea how badly I wanted to be your first. And my god, you're hard again already."

"Sorry?"

"At our age? It's impressive." She pushed him to his back, and before he could figure out what she was doing, she straddled him. "Tell me if you think I'm too pushy."

"Someone needs to tell me what to do." He lifted onto his elbows, half sitting, happily surprised when his face lined up with her breasts. "Oh. Hello." He tilted his head back to look at her face. "Are we not doing the whole foreplay thing? Because I've thought about it quite a bit. Hoping this would happen sooner or later. Trying to figure out what I would do. Should do. I'm still not sure."

"Foreplay is for getting you almost there, I think. I've wanted this my entire adult life, Will…we'll get to the foreplay, but holy hell, all I want is you inside me."

"I won't argue that." He laid back, running his hands over her ribs, fingers brushing over her nipples as she reached between them and then settled on him.

"Let me control this, all right? You're a bit on the large size and if you thrust too hard…"

She'll choke.

He laughed when he heard me, and she made him repeat it. "We'll go slow, then," she said. "Give my gag reflex a chance to relax."

He was breathing hard and fast and told her there wasn't going to be anything slow about it this time. "Jesus…"

It didn't matter. She was begging with God at the same time he was talking to Jesus, which made them both start laughing.

"I think we might be compatible," Aisha snorted.

"Good. Then you won't have to suffer for the next three or four decades."

Dude. Was that a proposal?

Spent, she stretched out on top of him, her lips on his, until his stomach growled. "Another country heard from," she said lightly. "What time is it? We're supposed to meet everyone."

Will contended that he didn't care and if they didn't show up, oh well. Drew was probably well aware of what was going to happen; he'd make excuses.

"And you'll still be hungry. We have all night, Will. I told Jimmy that I'd be out late, and he's staying at his dad's all night, anyway."

"All night?"

She nodded.

"I predict chafing."

3

The Queen's choice for pizza was two blocks away, just past Fuzzy's, the bar where Jax and Will often went for drinks. I'd been in Fuzzy's once before; on the night of Zed's seventeenth birthday, after Will sent Aisha home in a taxi and Zed was on his way to work, Will and Jax dragged Drew to the bar to grill him on his plans for the summer. He thought the King wanted him to stop being a mooch and to get a job; Jax really just wanted to talk to him about convincing Oz to see someone for help with her post-traumatic stress issues—being kidnapped and tortured during a war can mess a person up—and while he was at it, he forced Drew to promise he would get a degree. It didn't matter in what; the King thought it was important for the future Prince Consort to be reasonably well educated, and he intended to press the matter until Drew agreed.

Drew didn't have a problem with the idea; he had a problem with the cost. His education stipend as Midlam's crown prince evaporated with its monarchy. No stipend meant he needed to work for a year or two to afford a single semester's tuition, and in order to support Oz once they were married. Oz still had an education coming to her, and since they planned on marrying soon, he intended to be the breadwinner.

Jax refused to accept that; Drew and Oz had a roof over their heads and food on the table no matter what. He made it a condition to his ongoing blessing of their wedding—go to school, or you're not marrying my daughter.

I doubted that he meant it, but Drew was flustered and he didn't know what to do or say. Will listened while they came close to an argument, and then calmly informed Drew that his tuition wasn't an issue. An education account had been opened a few days after he was born; there was more than enough to finish his degree, and if he chose to pursue it, enough to get a post-graduate degree.

"I suggest you choose that," he said.

"The account was opened a few days after he was born, when?" Jax asked, dryly. "Last week?"

"January," Will answered. "Still, the money is there, Andrew. And I will not allow an argument about it. I'm investing in my own future, you understand that."

He understood. He was, after all, Will's great grandfather. If he refused the offer, Jax might get between him and his marriage to Oz, and then Will might not be born.

No one brought up the notion that Aubrey would put her foot down and tell Jax to mind his own business. In her heart, Drew was already her son; he wasn't screwing that up.

As we passed Fuzzy's, Will nodded to Peter, the muscle-bound giant who stood at the door and granted entry to the bar. Every now and then Peter refused to let someone in, and on rare occasions that resulted in fast fights that he won with a single punch. I wanted to stop to say hello, but Will and Aisha were talking and not listening to me, and he wouldn't have understood me anyway.

"This is going to sound somewhat childish," Will said to her, "but unless you have a serious objection, I would prefer that we don't mention to anyone what just happened."

Dude, no one over fifteen walks into a room and announces HEY I JUST HAD SEX.

It's rude.

Besides, what are they going to do? Applaud? Give you a trophy?

He ignored me and went on. "Perhaps it's overly sentimental, but for now I want this just for us."

Maybe they would give you a cake instead. The kind that people write on with frosting. Yours would say 'Happy Bouncing Day.'

"Drew—"

'Congrats on not falling off.'

"I'll ask for his discretion."

"Sweetie, chances are they'll take one look at us and guess. I won't be able to keep my hands off you."

"They may think we're getting close, but knowing me, and how rigid I can be? We haven't been seeing each other long enough for Jax or Aubrey to assume. And I really do want this to be something that's between us and not laid bare for their inspection."

She leaned into him. "That's kind of cute. I won't say a word."

I am nearly dead from the cute.

"You whine too much sometimes, Wick. No one said you had to stay in the room."

Well, no one said I could leave, either.

Aisha reached up and tucked a finger under my chin. "Taking notes?"

Someone needs to be able to run for help when he falls off after you choke half to death.

"Holy hell, Wick, I am not going to fall off."

"You might," Aisha snorted.

"He also thinks you might choke."

"I might."

We were the first to arrive; there were a few people at tables across the room, but there were several open booths near the pool tables toward the back, and Will headed for those. He tossed his sweatshirt onto a table to save it and asked her to place hers on the one near it.

"And be warned. Half the people in here are probably guards, so if you feel pressed to hit me for something I say or do, they'll react."

"What happens if I just grab you inappropriately?"

His eyebrows arched. "I'm willing to find out."

I'm gonna start hanging around Drew again.

"Fine, Wick. Become Drew's appendage. See how Oz feels about that, especially when they're…alone."

Fine. The King and Queen, then.

"Really? Haven't you proclaimed them gold medal winners in the bounciest old people Olympics?"

I'm starting to hate you all.

"He says he hates human intimacy," Will said to Aisha, "but not enough to leave when it starts, apparently."

"Don't worry, Wick. No one will be taking their clothes off in here."

"One would assume. It depends on how drunk we can get Jax."

"Please, not that drunk." Amused, she led him over to the closest pool table. "Aubrey would not appreciate it, and I have no desire to see a re-enactment of the fountain of vomit."

"To be fair, he didn't fully disrobe," Will said.

"Sweetie, still, there's only one man I want to see naked tonight." She racked the balls. "Eight ball?"

"I am not a skilled player," he said as he nodded.

"It's all geometry. Find the angle, take the shot." She went first, and three balls sunk on the break.

She's going to murder your ego and there are no witnesses.

She took solids. Will went to the opposite side of the table as she bent to line up her next shot, and she glanced up at him. "You might not want to stand right there, just in case. I'd hate for the ball to jump the rail and hit you. Besides, it's distracting. Your groin is right in my sight line, and now that I know what's behind the zipper—yes, it's distracting."

"Come on. You knew."

"Not in my wildest dreams."

"You don't have to do that. My ego is not wrapped up in the size of my penis."

"You don't really know, do you? Getting that towel off you? It's like Christmas, asking Santa for a kitten and getting…Fluffy."

"I doubt—" He glanced down. "Really?"

She set the stick down and went over to him, grabbing his belt loops to pull him closer. "If I didn't already love you, I'd have to consider keeping you just for that."

Dude, you are so pink right now.

"What about the whole assertion that size doesn't matter?"

"It doesn't. You could be below average and it wouldn't matter to me, but the fact that you aren't? There's no reason I can't enjoy the hell out of that."

She's challenging you. See if you can make her gag.

"I'm not making her gag, Wick."

"Oh, honey, you definitely will sooner or later. Just not the way Wick thinks."

Damn. You're beet red right now.

Also, close your mouth.

He was spared the bouncy details because Oz and Drew arrived, and she reminded him he wanted to talk to Drew before anyone else showed up. He told them to toss their sweatshirts onto the tables, and as Oz headed for Aisha, he pulled Drew aside.

"A moment, Andrew. What happened before you left—"

"I know. Keep it to myself. It's no one's business, not even mine."

"Thank you. Did you tell Oz—?"

"She was getting into the shower when I got there and honestly, I pretty much forgot that your girlfriend ordered me out of your apartment. Soapy boobs and an invitation, you know."

Will pretended disdain, and said he didn't need any details.

"Screw that. I do. Did you—?"

He tried to look annoyed at the question, but couldn't hold back the grin.

"Great grandpa is so proud."

"Shut up, old man."

He didn't even fall off.

Drew laughed, but Will poked at me. "Stop it, Wick."

I thought you'd be proud of that. Tell him what she said about Fluffy.

"No. And you will no' either."

"Dropped your t again," Drew said.

"Damned cat. I take it he already informed you that the two of you can still understand each other?"

"He was oddly excited that you shaved."

"Fine." He picked me off his shoulder and held me close to his face. "You will show me the discretion you show the King and Queen. Understood?"

Fine. Do I have to do that for Oz and Drew?

"Not at all."

"Hey." Drew grabbed for me. "I feed you dead things. Be nice to me."

I am nice. It's not like I actually told Will when you dropped Oz after trying that weird thing with the whipped cream.

"You really are a furry little asshole." He handed me back to Will. "And for the record, I didn't drop Oz. Exactly. It was more like a slow slide."

"And I don't need the details."

But it was weird.

"Is he like this all the time?" Drew asked as they made their way to the pool table. "Snarky?"

"You haven't begun to experience the snark," Will said.

Aisha had already done with the game; he lost without ever taking a shot. Will looked at the table and warned them to not play with her unless they didn't mind having their egos wounded.

"I've never played," Drew said. "Besides, I lose to Oz all the time. My ego is used to it."

"You're getting better," Will told him. "When we last sparred, I noted that you're finding openings where you failed to, even a few weeks ago. You're also not afraid to hit her with more than a tap."

"If I don't hit a little hard, she threatens to kick me in the nads."

"Wear a cup," Oz said. She picked a stick from a rack on the wall and pointed it at him. "I've never played either, so we're on the same level here. All I know is you hit the white ball with this, and make the other balls go into the holes."

"Oh, I'm playing you for money," Will warned.

"I have about twenty bucks," she said. "I hope all you intend to buy afterward is a candy bar."

"It's not the amount, it's the winning and then making you feel bad when you have to pay up." He started pulling balls out of the pockets, but Jax and Aubrey came in, and with them two more guards. He rolled one of the balls across the table and told her she was saved by her father, but sooner or later, he was taking her candy money.

"He's being mean to me, Dad," she called out.

"What'd you do to deserve it?"

"If anyone deserves it," Drew said, "it's me." He turned to Will. "Have you told him? About the simulator and how we got there?"

"We got back only five hours ago. I've been busy."

Jax folded his arms and leaned against the pool table. "What did you do now?"

"They were trying to show me how to use the portals." He shrugged. "I screwed up. Oz said to only think of nineteen-eighty, but I stepped in and had this quick thought that it would be seriously cool to jump ahead a thousand years."

Jax was not amused. He twitched away from the table and said, "You are not fucking serious. You know better, Drew. I *know* you know better."

He does now.

"Relax," Will said. "It was a mistake, but we didn't wind up in a post-apocalyptic Pacifica."

"Nah, just in a place with elves and wizards gearing up for war," Oz said. "And there were dragons. And a massive cat named Fluffy. Like, taller than a horse."

Jax sighed. "All right, you're screwing with me. What really happened?"

"That *is* what happened," Will told him. "We spent roughly a week with a wizard named Hagar and a boy warrior named Shivan." He went on to explain Finn's failsafe, a program that redirected people attempting to go too far forward through the portals into a simulator. It was brilliantly crafted, and that we wound up there gave Finn invaluable data that he otherwise wouldn't have had.

"You're never using a portal again," Jax said to Drew.

Will disagreed. "He simply needs practice. And the mistake truly is beneficial for my father. His tests were limited to brief excursions by his lab technicians and were fully controlled. Now he can tweak the program to accommodate the weaknesses in the scenarios he coded for. What he's done is incredibly inventive, Jax. It's an immersive experience and with enhanced protocols, quite safe."

So we're not telling him Drew got shot. Or that Oz flew on Jeff and had to be naked in front of everyone. Okay.

Jax wasn't appeased. "My daughter—"

"—is fine," Aubrey interrupted.

"If anything had happened to her," Will added, "it would have been on me. We both know that, Jax. I bear the responsibility for anything that happened in that simulator. If I'd ordered them to leave a minute after we arrived, they would have."

"Bullshit." He took a deep breath. "They would have turned around and gone back if you'd forced them home."

"I know I would have," Oz said. "Drew would have fought me on it, but I would have gone back. It's not worth getting upset over, and admit it, you wouldn't mind seeing the whole thing for yourself."

"Oz."

"Come on. We could create things by *thinking* about them, Dad. Wick coughed up a massive cat he named Fluffy, and then a baby dragon named Jeff. They were amazing. You'd have loved every second of it."

"Finn needs to test it again once he's worked out the kinks," Will said. "I'll take you. Jeff will even take you for a ride."

Jax sucked in another deep breath, and let the anger go. "You're all insane. And your father needs to focus on the transporter, not a simulator. What the hell is going on with it?"

"Still turning things inside out," Drew said. "My dad tried sending back a bowling ball that Finn had sent through, thinking he'd get the ball back, but it just kind of…crumbled."

"Explain to me how he can transport a human from point A to his ship, or even within the portals, but not from here to Dayton."

Will tried to explain it. "It's the difference between sending someone through time versus sending someone through space. He utilizes small tears in the fabric of time to push people through portals. It's less transporting and more like bubbling time around them. To get the transporter to work the way he wants, he needs to truly move every molecule in an item, and reassemble it on the other end."

You also think he's overthinking it.

"I'd ask him when he gets here," Jax said, "but I wouldn't understand it any more than I did when you tried to explain how you planned on sending Finn through the gate. I just want an evening where I don't have to think very hard."

Will pulled Jax away from the pool table, and motioned to Drew to play with Aisha. "My parents are coming?"

"Aubrey assumed you would want them here."

He hesitated. "Of course, I want them here."

"But?" Jax prodded.

"But, tonight started as a date that turned into a group dinner, and now my parents will be here."

Jax glanced at Aisha. "Then why the hell are you even here? Aubrey would have understood if you'd told her you had a date."

"I am far more familiar with saying yes to the Queen's requests than I am with dating."

"You're an idiot," Jax said. "Nights like this aren't requests from the Queen, they're invitations from your family. You don't get to say no to the Queen, but you do get to tell Aubrey when you have other plans, especially with Aisha. You have no idea how badly she wants the two of you to get together."

"You have no idea how badly *I* want that."

"Order of the King, then. Make it happen."

"That will certainly go over well. 'Aisha, you have to be my girlfriend because the King said so and what he says is law. So there.'"

"Ah, she doesn't need a royal decree. She spent a week stuck with you in magical fairy town and is still here, so there's something there. What did you do while you were in there? I mean, when the kids weren't around."

"I didn't sleep with her in the simulator, Jax. Even if you set aside the short amount of time we've been in each other's lives—that was essentially one giant room, and if the program had failed? I was not willing to go there."

Jax nodded toward Oz and Drew. "Did you tell them that?"

"Eventually. Although by that point, we were spending all our time together, rendering the issue moot."

"I'm not happy about it," Jax said. "Anything could have happened, Will."

"You allow her free access to the portals. Anything can happen every time she goes through one. This time there was a purpose to it and when I realized that, I chose to stay."

"How so?"

"By the time we were home, she realized that she needs to talk to someone. She faced several of her issues and reached the understanding that she cannot heal herself. I would expect that sometime soon, she'll ask you for help in finding a therapist, and I'm not sure that would have happened otherwise."

"She is a stubborn one," Jax said softly.

"She is also innately compassionate." Will went on, and told Jax about Tobias, the dark wizard who was the ultimate target of the simulation. In the battle of good versus evil, he was the Big Bad, the thing they needed to eliminate. Yet in the end, when all the facts were laid at her feet, Oz chose to set him free. She had Will code a pocket program, an alternate simulation where he could live out his existence with his wife and children, and she let him go. "He wore Levi Munson's face for a time," Will added. "Oz wanted to destroy him, and yet in the end, in his words, she showed him grace."

Jax watched his daughter lean over the pool table, purposely nudging Drew's cue stick. Her laughter mingled with his, and when his ball went only an inch, she kissed him on the cheek. "I don't think I would have. I'd have killed the bastard."

"She wanted to, Jax, and I would have let her. But ultimately, she grasped that her anger was not directed at Tobias for using Munson's face. She understood that her anger is mostly self-directed and she needs to deal with it."

"But you could still take me to a place within the simulator where I could kill the son of a bitch myself."

"I could. If you wish to engage a replica of Munson, it can be arranged."

"God, don't tempt me."

Finn and Jo arrived at the same time the pizzas came out, interrupting Jax's revenge fantasy, but more importantly, the food gave Will a buffer. He had time before dealing with his mother, who was clearly thrilled that he had shaved, right up to the moment when she witnessed Aisha brushing her fingers over his newly-bare cheek and then as she kissed him.

"High chair," Will said to me before I could jump onto the bench seat. "You know the rules."

Or I could stay on your shoulder.

Drew was already dragging the high chair across the floor, and patted the seat when he had it snugged up to the table. "Come on, ya big baby. I'll sneak bits of meat off my pizza to you."

Fine. I can snoopervise everyone from here anyway.

What I saw from my perch in the high chair was how annoyed Jo was when she wound up next to Aubrey instead of Will. She tried to hide it, but every time Aisha touched him, or their shoulders bumped, the little muscle at her temple twitched. I don't think anyone else noticed, because they were talking over each other; Oz told Jax and Aubrey about the simulator—avoiding mentioning the bloody bits—and Drew babbled excitedly about seeing a holographic computer display in the lab.

Don't forget you promised me I could have a birthday.

"Indeed," Will said. "I promised Wick he could pick a date that would be his birthday. He wants a cat of his own as his present."

And a hover cart.

"And a hover cart."

Jax grunted. "I'm not cleaning up after another cat."

"Really, Jax?" Aubrey said. "When have you ever cleaned up after Wick?"

"Right up until I married you."

I didn't care. Someone was cleaning up after me, and there was food in every apartment. Aubrey kept the best kinds of canned food, Will had that and cheese, and Drew was always willing to feed me with whatever he had on hand. Jax pretended to not notice as he snuck bits of bacon and sausage to me, and he didn't say anything when Drew went to get a little bowl so that I could drink some water.

Finn, on the other hand, snorted, "No, he's not spoiled."

"He has to drink," Drew said. "Let's see you get through dinner without touching your glass."

"The points are mutually exclusive of each other," Will said. "We spoil Wick because he's an old man and deserves it. That doesn't change that he does, indeed, need water, and I appreciate that Drew realized it, because I did not."

I would have said something sooner or later.

"Sure about that?" Drew asked. "You didn't tell me you were thirsty while we were hiking through Colorado. You were dehydrated before I noticed."

That's different. We were busy.

Finn leaned forward, squinting at me. "Drew understands you. How?"

"We think the computer running the simulator triggered something between their transponders," Will said. "At least, that was the only thing that seemed to make sense. It may explain why I can understand him, as well."

Jo shook her head. "I don't think you'd been exposed to the portals then."

"But I had a transponder and it was active. And Wick had been exposed."

"Possible," Finn said. "I used to think Wick chose the people who could understand him. He had you, and didn't need anyone else."

"He needed Drew at the time," Oz pointed out. "Will was otherwise occupied."

You can stop staring at me.

Everyone was looking at me, and it made me uncomfortable.

Will did bouncy things with Aisha. Maybe you want to talk about that.

"That's fine," Will said. "Dinner is over. We'll stop looking at you. We can shoot pool and you can chase a ball or two."

Drew was the first to get up. "Come on, Mister Wick. You can chase my balls."

Ew. No.

I sat on the edge of the table while Aisha helped Drew determine the angles he wanted while losing a game to Will. Finn and Jax were at another table, and Aubrey and Oz wandered back and forth, talking to everyone, but Jo sat on a stool against the back wall and watched quietly. When Will bent close to Aisha and whispered something into her ear that made her laugh, the little muscle at Jo's temple twitched again. When Aisha touched a finger to Will's chin, she closed her eyes for a few seconds, pretending like it wasn't happening.

Unhappy mom at three o'clock.

"I know," Will said quietly.

I thought she liked Aisha.

"She does. Just not with me."

I don't get it. Aisha is awesome.

He set up to take a shot, and as the balls connected he said, "I don't get it, either. She's not giving her a chance."

Bothering you? You're playing worse than Drew.

"I'm playing worse than Drew," he said, loud enough for him to hear, "because Aisha is helping him."

"You don't need help, sweetie," she said. "He's never played before."

Will pointed his stick at Drew. "Next game, no help. Beat me, and I buy you a root beer."

"If I lose?"

"You buy me a shot of whiskey."

"All right." Drew set up for his next shot, scrunching his nose as he tried to find the angle he wanted. "Let me win this one first."

"A little to the right," Aisha told him. When Will frowned, she said, "It's not the next game yet."

She guided Drew through each shot, until the only balls left on the table were the eight ball and three of Will's. Before Drew could celebrate, she patted him on the back and said he had to make that one himself; call the hole and make the shot, and he would win. He grumbled under his breath, and she headed for Aubrey at the next table, taking a breath to kiss Will as she passed him.

Drew crouched down to look at the ball from the edge of the table, and while he was putting off taking the shot, Jo got up.

"All these years, and you finally shaved."

"I did," he said. "I thought you would like it."

You didn't shave for her, dude. She knows it.

"Will. You know this is a bad idea."

"Nah. Next game I'll beat him easily."

"You know what I mean."

"I do, and I'm choosing to not address it."

Drew took his shot and scratched, and then begged off the next game long enough to grab another slice of pizza. Will gestured to his abandoned cue and suggested they play a game, and as he racked the balls he said that he understood her concerns, but he had everything under control.

"William, how could you possibly have this under control? Reining in your thoughts when you kiss her is one thing, but you have no idea—"

"Maybe I need to find out."

"At what risk? Every thought you've ever had. Every memory."

Will moved very close to her, and sat against the edge of the pool table with his back to everyone else, but where she could see his face. "If I choose to assume the risk that she'll learn every single thing about me, that's my decision. She knows my abilities, and it doesn't frighten her."

"Think it through. It might all seem terribly romantic now but down the road? How many times have you looked at your father or me and had that 'Oh please shut up and die' thought? Everyone does, but it's not something you want heard."

"We're adults. We'll deal with any unkind thoughts as they come up."

Jo folded her arms and huffed out an exasperated breath. "Kids, William. What if you become intimate, and she gets pregnant?"

Will shrugged. "Haven't you ever wished to be a grandmother?" When she became flustered and stammered that grandchildren weren't the point, he asked, "Was I a mistake? Do you regret having me?"

"No! Not for one minute."

"Then why would I regret bringing a child into this world, even risking that he or she would inherit this?"

"You were horribly lonely as a child, don't forget how miserable you were and how other children treated you."

Will nodded. "As much as I would like to forget that, I can't. But the difference is that I would surround my child with the people who would never think she was a freak, and would never treat her like one. Until I came here and stayed, I honestly thought I was one, Mom. And I thought you believed that, too."

She tried to protest, but he stopped her. "I know you don't, but I didn't then. But I will be sure that *if* I procreate, my child will know with absolute certainty that she is normal, and she is special, and that there is never even a moment when I think she's in the way. I won't isolate her from the world, but I will protect her."

She had no answer for that—she had isolated him and couldn't deny it—and before she could think of anything else to say, Jax interrupted them.

"I have to leave," he said. "Will you make sure Aubrey gets home all right?"

Aubrey protested; she had a guard and was perfectly capable of walking two blocks by herself. Besides, if he was leaving, she was, too. "You go do whatever it is that requires your attention. There's a book and a hot bath waiting for me at home."

"One of those can wait for me," he grumbled.

"We'll see."

He turned to Finn. "I have a car outside, and I'm going past your apartment if you want a ride."

Will bent his head to whisper in Jo's ear. "Mom, stay. I've hardly had the chance to talk to you tonight."

She patted his arm. "That's all right. It's getting late and we need to be up early."

Finn shrugged, as if that was news to him, but he followed her out to the car without protesting. Will remained at the pool table, his back to the room, and took a moment to compose himself. When he turned around, Oz and Drew were sitting in the booth together, and Aisha waited to see what he needed.

"Shaving may have been a mistake," he said to her.

"She doesn't like it?"

He pushed away from the pool table. "Bad timing. She asked a thousand times, and I did it without her prompting."

"Ah." She leaned in and kissed the tip of his nose. "She's unhappy that I didn't have to ask."

"It would seem so."

"Remind me about this when Jimmy brings home his first serious crush. I'm sorry, Will. She should be happy for you."

He agreed, but they stopped talking about it and slid into the booth across from Oz and Drew. They couldn't leave yet, Drew said, because he had ordered dessert and it wasn't ready.

"Where are you doing to put it?" Oz asked. "You nearly ate an entire pizza by yourself."

"Three of my toes are still empty," he said. "You guys don't have to stick around to keep us company. Oz is pretty good about telling me how gross my eating habits are all by herself."

"I'm sure," Will said, amused. "But I'm getting a bottle. Who wants a drink?"

Aisha said she did, and Oz said she would, if not for the whole age issue and no parents around to say yes or no. Will told her to call her mother and put her on speaker phone; if she said it was all right, he'd get her a glass.

"The Emperor wants to get me drunk," Oz said when Aubrey answered.

Aubrey laughed and asked if that was a direct quote or not.

"Just a drink, Aubrey," he said. "One shot of whiskey. Something relatively newby friendly."

"A couple of drinks won't hurt her. But don't get her sloppy drunk, Will. Just a mild buzz, all right? I'd like her to learn to drink before she gets drunk."

He went to the counter and brought back a bottle of booze, a bottle of root beer, and four glasses filled with ice. Drew twisted the top off the root beer and was about to pour when he caught a whiff of the whiskey.

"Cinnamon?"

Will nodded. "You can try it if you want. No pressure. Oz will still respect you in the morning if you stick to root beer."

"Well…" Oz sniffed.

With a shrug, Drew decided that one drink wouldn't hurt, and it smelled like something he wanted to try.

Will mused that this was an event, and there should be a toast. "To finally feeling like adults." Then he adds, "And I don't mean because you're drinking something with alcohol."

Drew snorted. "Fine. To adulting. Especially now that you're finally a real man."

Oz was confused. "What?"

Drew's eyes went wide. "I'm sorry, I wasn't thinking. I mean, you *just* asked me to keep my mouth shut. Like, three hours ago."

"*What?*" Oz insisted.

"I ravaged the man," Aisha said.

"Oh. Congrats." She looked at Will. "I'd high-five you, but I'm pretty sure I know where your hands have been, so, no."

"It's fine, Andrew," Will said. He was more amused than irritated. "It's mostly my parents I want to protect from that slice of information. Well, Jax and Aubrey, too, for the time being. I swear, she would use it as an excuse for some odd hallelujah coming-of-age party and I'm not ready for that."

Seriously, dude, no one announces their bouncy things. It's rude. Ask the Queen.

Drew took his first sip and grinned. "This is actually good. I thought it would burn."

Oz leaned into him. "We'll make a man out of you yet."

"I'll get better," he said. "I swear."

Will clinked his glass against Drew's, "Indeed. To goals."

"Dorks," Oz chuckled.

Will nodded. "Forward thinking dorks. The future awaits." He considered that. "Truly. A year ago, it did not."

"I can't imagine how afraid you were," Aisha said.

"I made a concentrated effort to not think about it. But I watched these two on Oz's last birthday and witnessed their first kiss, and felt incredibly sad that I wouldn't be around to see them wed. And I couldn't let on."

Drew's eyes reddened, and he took a long sip of his drink.

"I'm still here, Andrew," Will said gently.

Drew set the glass down. "I know. But you almost weren't. And every now and then it occurs to me that there are versions of us who grow old and die, believing that you died when you were still young. I'm sorry, but it hurts. Because I can imagine how they feel."

Will, gently, "If it helps…that Emperor and that Andrew likely did not become as close as we have. They never endured the war and the safe house, nor did they make the trek across Colorado with Zed. He probably did not have as strong a connection."

"But Oz did," Drew argued. "That Oz loved you as much as this one does, and her pain would tear into that Andrew every bit as much. It doesn't seem fair that those people not only lost you but thought the world would end before their great grandkids were done living."

"They might have mourned the world, but you two would have never known who I really was. That Emperor did not give Oz his memories, and he didn't take Wick's place in the portal."

Oz let out a long breath. "Your parents were stranded here. Surely at some point, the truth came out." Will wasn't sure; Oz was. "Either way, there's a timeline where my heart was broken. And my parents, oh my god. What did it do to them?"

"Your own parents," Drew said. "I sometimes wonder how long they survived after losing you."

"They knew when I was a teenager that I would die. There was time to come to terms with that."

Aisha slid her arm across his shoulders and rested her chin on his arm. "Will...there's no way to come to terms with losing your child. You could give me a lifetime knowing it was coming, but if something happened to my son, I would shatter. You wouldn't be able to pick up all the pieces."

Will sighed and slugged back the rest of his drink. "Well, thanks, until now I was perfectly happy with how things turned out." He refilled their glasses. "I would try to convince you that those people no longer exist, but knowing that my father regularly pops back to his own When will refute that."

Drew wanted to know which timeline that was. Will wasn't certain, but he suspected it was the exact one he left, in which case his ancestors are the people Oz and Drew worry about.

"I know you keep saying we can't go into the future, but is there any way you can?" Drew asked. "Just to tell them that it worked and you're all right?"

Oz piled on. "Just so they know before they die, that's all."

"We don't have to go. I know you think that's a bad idea."

"Indeed."

If you go forward, can you be sure you'd come back to this now and not the other now?

"My father comes back to this When, Wick, so I don't think that's a problem. The other timeline will erode as this one progresses, I think, but as long as I stick to specific dates, I wouldn't get lost in time." As Drew took another long sip, he added, "It's not a promise. But I will think about it."

They were interrupted by the server placing Drew's order of two dozen tiny donut bites on the table. Oz took one look and blurted, "How freaking hungry did you think you'd still be?"

"I thought there would be more people. I planned on sharing." He looked at Will. "I know you don't eat a lot of junk, but you guys have to help me with these."

I'll eat one.

"You'll have a tiny piece of one," Will said, breaking a bite off for me. "Drew, you need to learn about leftovers."

Drew contended that Will never had to fight Carter for the last piece of chicken at dinner. "There were no leftovers. It's a foreign concept."

"Learn, then. You're not going to be young forever, and trust me, it's harder to stay lean when you're older."

"Says the guy with zero body fat," Oz snorted.

"And I work hard for that, harder than I'd like most days. You can be sure that once I retire, I won't."

"Like you'll ever retire," she said.

"A month ago, I might have agreed with that. Things change, Ozzie. I want a life of my own now."

"Yeah." Her smile was a mix of warmth and alcohol. "You deserve one."

Drew said, "I'll drink to that," and then slugged back the rest of his glass. Will asked him how much he'd had, and Drew said only a couple. "I'm not drunk."

"All right." He refilled Drew's glass, but specifically didn't refill Oz's, looking at her with a smirk.

"Take it easy," Aisha told Will. "I have plans for you that don't include being too drunk."

He raised an eyebrow playfully. "Whisky dick is not on the agenda."

Oz snorted a laugh, hard, but Drew was horrified. "That's a real thing?"

"It doesn't matter," Oz told him. "Drink if you want. I'll survive any repercussions."

"My lips aren't numb! I could still—"

"Stop talking."

"But—"

"Stop. Talking."

"He's young," Aisha said. "Don't worry."

Maybe she'd like it more if he was drunker.

"Furry. Little. Asshole," Drew said.

Will reached across the table and took Drew's glass. He scooped up the bottle and glasses and got a box for Drew's tiny, uneaten donuts. "Truly, you don't want to eat much more. Just in case."

While Oz boxed them up, Aisha leaned toward Will and asked how many Drew really had.

"Five. New drinker. He's drunk."

"This probably isn't the way to cultivate a drinking buddy," Oz said. "If he gets a hangover he'll never want to drink again."

"Indeed."

"I am not drunk," Drew said. "Am I?"

"Little bit, yeah."

"Oh. Wow. I'm sorry."

Will looked at Oz. "You?"

"Not even buzzed."

"You sound a little disappointed," Aisha said.

"Might be."

Chuckling, Will told her she might want to hold off on the declaration for a minute. He watched as Drew struggled to get out of the booth and then as he tilted toward the nearby table, where he sat down, hard, and then apologized to the chair for tipping back a few inches. Oz got up easily, but once she was on her feet she blinked rapidly a few times, and then decided she might be at least a little bit buzzed.

"Just a little?" Will asked.

She reached for Drew's hand to help him up. "Okay. Maybe a bit more than little."

"Can you walk?"

"Probably not in a straight line," Aisha whispered to him. They followed Oz and Drew down the sidewalk, amused at the volume of their laughter, and how they were intentionally bumping their shoulders together and then stumbling to find balance. It was Ozoo at twelve and fourteen all over again, but this time with random kisses thrown in.

Will watched them for a bit and then said, "I really hope I haven't ruined the rest of their night by letting him drink that much."

"He's young and it wasn't *that* much. If it numbs him up a tiny bit, Oz might be grateful."

"Ah. Maybe I should have belted back a couple more."

"Stop. You've had sex twice, that's not enough to decide—"

Drew spun around. "Twice? *Already?*"

"Damn, Drew." Oz grabbed his hand and yanked him back around. "None of your business."

Will was amused but apologized to Aisha anyway. "We might have an oddly complex relationship. He brings out my inner eighteen-year-old."

"I knew your eighteen-year-old self. You were not that open."

"And now?"

"Oh, I'm going to make sure you're a lot more open soon."

Yeah. You're gonna fall off.

In the hallway, Drew stared blankly at his door when it didn't open after he pressed down on the handle. He tried again, and then rattled it back and forth, as if force alone was going to unlock it. Oz was content to let him try to figure it out, but after the third "dammit" Will reached over Drew's shoulder and tapped in his passcode. "Risking your father's ire," he said to Oz, "stay with him tonight. Just in case. And put a bucket by the bed."

Drew turned and sagged against the door jamb. "Please go tell me you're not dead. Maybe the other me didn't get that close to you, but this one did and I know he needs to know."

"I'll seriously consider it."

Drew threw his arms around Will. "I love you."

"All right." Will hugged him back. "I love you, too. Now go inside and do whatever the hell Oz tells you to do."

Once they were inside and the door was closed, he showed Aisha the passcode for his apartment. "In case you ever need to get in when I'm not here."

"That's a pretty high level of trust, Will."

"You've seen me naked and didn't laugh," he said as he closed the door behind them. "If I trust you with that, the entry code to my apartment seems rather insignificant."

"Sweetheart, my ex has seen me naked plenty, but he still doesn't have the code to my place."

"Honestly, that surprises me."

"There's a staircase that leads directly from his apartment into mine, but unless a switch is flipped on both sides, the door won't open. It's an odd and uncomfortable arrangement, but it works for Jimmy. If for not for him—" she shrugged lightly "—I damn well wouldn't be living there."

"You've lived a lot of your life for your son," he guessed. "I admire that."

She appreciated that, but living where she did wasn't her choice, and once Jimmy was out on his own, she wanted to move. "Understand…I love James, there's no question. We settled into a very warm friendship, and I'd like to keep that. But I don't want to live *that* close to him, especially with his husband as part of the package."

"Jimmy's almost seventeen?"

"Another week."

"Then a year or so and you're free of the obligation. Though by now isn't he old enough to manage a few city blocks of distance? Zed has free rein for the most part."

"Technically. Can we leave it as something that's complicated for now? Because it is, perhaps more complex than your relationship with Drew." She stepped very close to him and slipped a hand under his shirt. "It's late, and you've been tormenting me all evening with the tight jeans and t-shirt, and all I've wanted to do is get them off you again."

At least get her into the bedroom this time. My poor rug is ruined.

"I need to feed this monster before I forget."

Breathe, dude.

She told him that was fine, she needed to use the restroom first. He directed her to the one in the master bedroom and then rushed to feed me. "Don't feel obligated to spend the night with us, Wick."

You still need adult supervision.

"Fine, but no critiquing. Or complaining."

While I ate, he ran into the guest bathroom to do whatever pre-coital things a guy needs to do—I don't know, I was robbed of that choice not long after Finn rescued me—and then met me coming down the hall.

Is she staying the night?

"I hope so."

Aisha's voice came from the bedroom, "What are we hoping?"

She was already stretched out on the bed, in her underwear. I jumped up to sniff her face. *He can't answer. There's no blood in his brain.*

She scratched between my ears. "Are you making fun of him again, Wick?"

"Ah, no, he's not," Will answered for me. "And I was just answering him. He wants to know if you're staying the night."

"I did say we had all night."

"Yes, but it would be rude of me to presume—"

She scooted to the side of the bed and told him to take his shirt off. While he pulled it over his head, she slowly unzipped his jeans, brushing her fingers over the fabric, teasing him. When his jeans were halfway down his hips, he gently pushed her back, and as she scooted toward the middle of the bed, he followed, trying to kiss her.

I got out of the way.

She snagged the waistband of his jeans with her toes and pushed them over his hips as he crawled onto the bed, but she left his underwear on, which made me wonder if she knew as much as he thought she did.

You're supposed to get naked. Or at least expose the dangly parts.

I jumped onto the headboard and curled up. This was going to take time, while they figured out that all those underthings were just going to get in the way, though I supposed they could have planned on just grinding against each other the way Oz and Drew sometimes had before she let him touch her boobs for real.

"I still have no idea what I'm doing," he said, kicking his jeans off the rest of the way. "But I'm damn well going to try."

I wanted to close my eyes and go to sleep, leaving them to their horny aspirations, but if he really did fall off, someone was going to have to go get help. Aisha would probably be too busy laughing to pick up the phone and get Jax or Aubrey. I could always run across the hall and get Drew. He'd laugh, too, but at least he would run to help.

"I'll try to not rush it," Will said quietly.

"Whatever you want."

He was half on top of her. "Just this."

She kissed him, long and deep, then said against his lips, "You taste like cinnamon."

"So do you. Almost makes me wish I'd kept the bottle. Though I'm glad I'm not drunk."

"Ah, but you could have dribbled it all over me and then licked it off."

He slipped fingers under her bra and popped it open. "I can pretend."

As his mouth slid to her neck, she said, "Play all you want."

"Don't let me do anything stupid—"

A soft moan escaped her when he ran his tongue over a nipple. "I can't imagine that."

He might bite you, you know.

Oh, wait. You might like that.

She was squirming, but he wouldn't let her touch him. As he worked his way down, he caught his fingers in the waistband of her panties and pulled them off, very slowly, trailing kisses down her thighs, all the way to her feet, and then back to her knees. He stopped long enough to pull his own underwear off, dropping it to the floor. Her breathing was fast and she reached for him, begging him to come back and kiss her, but he chuckled, and then ran his fingers over her skin softly, teasing, and with her hands in his hair he moved between her legs, licking gently, testing, tasting, until her back arched off the bed and she was moaning his name.

When she relaxed, his kisses moved upward, over her belly and between her breasts, and he slid his torso over hers, still kissing and licking. She reached between them and guided him in and then pulled his head to hers to kiss him, moving with him. As he got closer, she pulled her legs a little higher and told him to go harder, fingers digging into his back.

Breathlessly, she said, "Come. With. Me."

He couldn't speak. He lifted more onto his hands, breathing hard, until his face contorted and a moan escaped him with a *holy shit* riding on it.

"My god, you play well," she said after a long, quiet moment while he caught his breath. "Next time I'll try to participate more."

"That was exactly what I wanted," he said against her lips.

"Bloody scratch marks across your back? I'm pretty sure I drew blood."

"I didn't notice. I was too busy being completely amazed at what I can feel when I'm in you."

She looped her arms around his neck. "What, my tonsils?"

He laughed with her. "No. I was surprised—well, honestly, I didn't expect just how warm you would be inside. And how soft. All the little spasms, I never stopped to think that I would be able to feel those."

"It's called an orgasm, Will. And I quite enjoy them."

"I'm not opposed to them. But I think I enjoy yours more."

"For now," she said, nudging him onto his side. "And honestly, I am going to enjoy every second of your curiosity. I thought you'd be a little shyer, but you went right for it, didn't you?"

"You have no idea how badly I wanted to do that. If I didn't—"

"Nope, don't do that. No criticizing yourself. You're damned good in bed already, Will. If you get much better I might explode. I'll certainly have issues walking afterward."

"Or perhaps the men you've been with…sucked."

She fell quiet for a moment and then kissed him gently. "I'm not comparing. But if I ever do, if you ever think I am, or if I say something about someone else that rubs you the wrong way…tell me."

He thought he was comfortable with the idea that she'd had an active social life; he would find it odder if she hadn't. "You like sex. Why wouldn't you act on that?"

"Understanding that and hearing about it are two different things. Promise me, if I step over a line, you call me on it."

"All right. As long as you promise me to show me what I can do to be better at this." She started to tell him he was doing fine, but he stopped her with a kiss. "I want to be better than good for you. I'm truly not shy, nor am I especially modest. There's nothing about human biological processes that embarrasses me. Just tell me what you want me to do sometimes."

"Nothing embarrasses you? Let's see about that if I ever throw the bathroom door open while you're peeing."

Amused, he said, "I will respect your wish for privacy, but it wouldn't bother me. If I'm willing to ejaculate in front of you, urinating seems rather tame."

She reminded him that technically, she hadn't seen him do that yet, but, "I am leaking the reminders."

He started to sit up and said he'd get a towel, but she reached under the pillow and pulled one out. "I took it out of the bathroom. I *really* hate lying in the wet spot."

"Well, if I'm honest, I'm not a fan of the sticky spots, either. I usually have a hand towel nearby."

"What, no socks? Isn't that the stereotypical standard?"

"Not since I was a young teenager. My mother finally asked me to stop, because it was leaving stains. She handed me a giant box of tissues and told me to have at it. They flush."

"How mortifying was that for you?"

"Not at all. My parents were extremely open about that. I was told long before puberty that it would happen, it was normal, I should absolutely do it…just privately."

"Kudos to your folks. I had no idea it was normal. Oh my god, the shame." She laughed. "Not that I stopped. I just lived with the shame and was positive I was the only person alive doing things to myself."

"If you had any idea how many tissues and hand towels I went through when we were not-dating before…"

"If you had any idea that you were the reason I bought my first toy."

The idea intrigued him. He thought it was probably better he hadn't known. If he had, he might have broken himself thinking about her using it. "Then again, that might have been my breaking point. I would have forgotten every reason I was here and tried to skip right over the first date, first kiss…the first time I touched you, you'd have been shouting 'get off me.'"

"Not a snowball's chance in hell." She lifted his hand from her side and placed her palm against his. "I just wanted to hold your hand. That would have been enough."

"I know." He pulled her hand to his mouth and kissed her fingers. "You were willing to wait for even that small thing, all the way to marriage."

She could feel him sliding into the sadness of that memory, and yanked him hard in the other direction. "Not anymore, Emperor. I don't need a commitment. I will hold your hand, put my arms around you, kiss you without a damned good reason, and if there's no one else around, I won't have a problem groping you through your clothes."

"I don't think I'll have a problem with it, either," he said with a laugh. "Spare the Queen, however. Her sensibilities are easily offended."

"Bullshit. Aubrey would laugh her ass off if she caught me grabbing you."

"Fair enough. She wants us together."

"So do I." She lifted up on an elbow to look at him better. "Can I ask you something beyond personal? Because I'm selfishly curious."

"You can ask me anything."

"You could have gotten yourself a personal 'bot. No emotional attachment, but it would have felt like the real thing. A warm body, arms and legs and lips…inside and out, it would have felt the same. I know it's not a relationship, but you would at least have been able to satisfy your curiosity."

The idea never appealed to him, and he didn't understand people who used them. "Isn't the greater purpose of sex to be close to someone, and to make them feel good? I never could have been emotionally attached to an artificial, robotic device made to look like a woman, and the only purpose would have been for me to get off. I could do that on my own. And it seems to me that someone fucking a doll would end up lonelier than they were when they started."

"All right, hearing you say 'fucking' just made my night."

"That's all it would be, though. And that's not something I ever want."

She stroked his cheek with her hand. "Oh, hon…trust me, there are going to be times when that's exactly what we're doing. Not a thing wrong with it, if it's what we both want."

"I'm truly not certain about that."

"This, what we've been doing today? Not that. But sooner or later we're going to have been apart for longer than we like, and we're both going to just want to get down and dirty and *do* each other. And that's all right."

"I'll take your word for it. But you and I, right now? This isn't just sex for me."

"I know. It isn't for me, and it won't just be sex later, either."

"It might be a while. The little emperor is letting me know loud and clear he needs time."

That made her laugh. "Little emperor. Oh my god. And it's fine. Right now, all I really want is to do exactly what we're doing, and I think I could do this all night."

"Until you fall asleep."

"If I do, wake me in a few hours. Or I'll wake you."

"I rarely sleep," he reminded her.

"Stay in bed? If you can."

"If you wake up and I'm not here, I've only gotten up because my tossing and turning would wake you. I'll stretch out on the sofa with a book. Just come get me."

"Good. Because the idea of actually sleeping with you is as appealing as making love with you. Which I want to do again tonight, after the little emperor has had some rest."

Their voices became a lull, and I let myself drift off. If they weren't doing anything else, no one was going to need my help in case of injury, so I took the chance to snooze. When I woke later—it could have been an hour, it could have been three—the lights were off and they were propped up with pillows, cuddled up together, her head on his shoulder.

I thought I'd probably slept through more bouncy gymnastics, and worried about it. They were old, and old people have greater coital falling risks. I mean, I'd seen Jax fall out of bed, though not after the third time that Aubrey pinned him to the mattress. Those days were fewer and far between, but they did happen, but she was pretty good about not flinging him across the room.

"What do you think about taking another portal trip with me tomorrow morning?" he asked her.

"You want to find Oz and Drew when they're older?"

"It seems like a simple enough request. And I know the ideal moment to approach them."

"You don't want to meet them alone?"

"I want them to not only see that I live, but that I also have love in my life. That will matter to Oz, especially."

"As long as we're back early enough to get home before Jimmy and Zed are done abusing James' video game system."

"Time travel. We'll return a minute after we leave."

"No dragons or giant cats or teenagers swinging swords they have no business handling?"

He laughed. "No promises, but I can say with some certainty that the worst of it will be wrapping our heads around the idea that we're seeing Oz and Drew when they're older than we are."

"I can't imagine that."

"I have no clear memory of them when they're older, but I did spend time with them when I was a toddler. Something you cannot tell them. I want to say they were spry, but three-year-old me might be unreliable."

"Any chance we'll see three-year-old you?"

"A glimpse. You won't be able to talk to him."

"All right. Let's go find them and hopefully make their day."

"I hope they'll be happy. If we tell them and they're not, my feelings will be hurt."

She pressed her chest against him and kissed him: "If your feelings get hurt, I promise to make it up to you."

"Well, then. I kind of hope they do."

If it'll help, I'll hurt your feelings.

"You're a good man, Wick." He reached up to scratch my chin, but couldn't quite reach with Aisha lying half across him. "Sorry. I'll pet you later."

That's fine. I saw where your hands have been. I'd prefer you washed them first.

"Understandable."

"You think I'd be used to the way you talk with each other by now," Aisha said.

"I'm sorry, I know it's rude. I translate for him when it seems as if I should."

"When you don't, I just assume he's making fun of you."

She's sharp. You need to keep her.

"Indeed."

4

Drew swore he didn't have a hangover, but he kept trying to press his brain back into his head through the crease on his forehead, and he kept furrowing his eyebrows together like they were mad at everyone in the world for daring to breathe the same air. We waited on Union Square while Will went down into Finn's lab to borrow money from him—he had cash for several different time periods, but had never bothered with future funds—and Drew was nothing but surly and four kinds of unhappy.

"He says it's a bad mood," Oz told Aisha. "I think we all know better."

"I'm allowed a bad mood, Oz. You fucking kept me up half the night arguing about the damned wedding."

She didn't let him get under her skin. "See? We talked about it for maybe twenty minutes, until he fell asleep."

"That was more than twenty minutes. I wish—" he pressed fingers to the bridge of his nose "—just make up your mind, all right?"

She ignored him. "The entire conversation was more like, 'your dad said no to a wedding on Union Square. How about the roof?' 'How about the beach?' 'Ugh, sand everywhere.'"

"A beach wedding would be lovely," Aisha said. "Sand washes off."

"My parents are urging us to pick someplace indoors. Dad is worried about security."

"Ah. I can see that."

"It's *our* wedding," Drew grumbled. "The guard can figure out the security issues. Just pick something, Oz."

"I did. You don't want sand crawling up your royal ass."

Aisha hid a smile behind her hand and watched as Will exited the elevator and walked toward us.

"Fine," Oz said. "The beach. Pick the date."

Will raised an eyebrow. "Still?"

"Is this all women?" Drew asked Will. "Like, none of them can say what they want without it turning into an argument?"

"Keep me out of it," Will said.

"Be nice," Aisha said, reaching for his hand. "He's in a bad mood."

"Bad mood my ass." Will leaned closer to Drew, and said loudly, "Are we hungover this morning?"

"I'm entitled to an answer," Drew said. He looked at Oz and went on. "Goddamn, just fucking make up your damned mind already, and I'll go—"

That was as far as he got before Will grabbed him by the arm and yanked him close. "I don't care how badly your head hurts, Andrew, you will no' speak to her like that. Never again. Do you understand?"

Drew swallowed hard. "Yeah, got it."

I don't think it bothered Oz because when Will let go of Drew, she slipped her arms around his waist and squeezed.

"We'll be back in a few minutes," Will said. "Try to pull your shorts out of a wad by then, all right? And apologize to her."

He started toward the new portal in the center of the Square but Drew stopped him.

"Before you go…it's been bugging me and if it's bugging me, then he might have spent time chewing on it."

"What?"

"Aside from it being weirdly funny to you, what was the point of making me afraid of you when I was little? You said that the other Drew never got close to that Emperor. But he could have. Even me…I mean, when I was little, we could have gotten close then."

Will agreed, they could have, which was exactly why he didn't allow himself to engender that kind of familiarity. "I know more of you than I perhaps should. I grew up on fantastical tales of my great grandfather, and I know how deeply you love. It was hard enough knowing I would leave my best friends and the children I loved as my own behind…but I also knew that with time they would rebound, if not recover. My heart told me that you would break."

"I get it. I don't agree, but I get it."

"Andrew. I have seen an extraordinary capacity for love in you since you were a little boy. You've always been incredibly forgiving and willing to reach out even when someone hurts you."

"Like every time I stole your toys," Oz reminded him. "Every time I said mean things or got you into trouble, you wound up being the one to apologize."

Will nodded. "Exactly. I knew I would die at a time when you were especially vulnerable. It would come when you were wrapped up in the blush of new love and trying to be strong for Oz and her family. I knew from several accounts that Oz credited you for getting her through what was, at that point, the hardest time of her life. I needed you to not love me, Drew. You needed to be detached enough to be there for her, and if we'd been close, I didn't think that would happen."

Oz squeezed him again. "Drew, it was damage control. He knew that you'd be as close to him as my dad."

"Indeed, but now?" Will grinned. "I will relish tormenting you every opportunity I have, but instead of you being the boy who feels like Zed, a son to me, I've been gifted the opportunity to have you as my friend and my brother. I'm sorry if your feelings were hurt when you were younger, but I wouldn't trade this—" he gestured between them "—for anything."

Teary-eyed, Drew nodded. Will kissed him on the forehead, then kissed Oz. "We'll be back in a few minutes, and with any luck, we'll unbreak your hearts."

= = =

"Oz and Drew's firstborn is my grandfather," Will explained as they stood on Union Square, nearly two hundred years in the future. "He spent his adult life bouncing between the When of his birth and the When of his marriage. I've never been clear on why he made the leap forward, but he met my grandmother not long after and he didn't want to leave. They married, had babies, and for a time

Oz and Drew occasionally ventured into a portal to visit."

"So you knew them when you were little?"

"I vaguely recall them, but I'm uncertain if those are true memories or remnants from stories that were told to me when I was younger. And I'm now positive that they learned who I would become." He pointed across the Square, to a restaurant on Powell street. There were tables outside, lining what was once the sidewalk, and spilling out into the now-nonexistent street. "This night was the last time I saw them. My third birthday."

He'd taken us from mid-morning to evening, when the sun was beginning to fade and the air was beginning to cool.

"They came to see me one last time, and chose that restaurant because it was close to the portal."

"Why was it the last time?"

"My best hunch? They'd known the man I was and had learned who their great grandson would become. If they kept visiting, sooner or later they would have said something to my parents, or done something that could change the path I was on. If what they did would keep me from eventually leaving?" He shrugged. "I was a dead man, no matter what. Either I died as the Emperor, having cared for them and loved them as my own, or I died without them knowing me, when the meteor hit." He considered it for a moment and added, "If they changed anything, it also meant growing up without my father. He would have been stuck in twenty-four-fifteen with no memory and no way home."

"He would have eventually remembered, don't you think?"

"Possibly, but it was getting him home on time that was important."

We crossed the Square; he and Aisha slipped into chairs at a table close to the building and in the dimming light watched an older Oz and Drew several tables away, cuddling with a toddler, planting kisses on his forehead and his cheeks. We listened to his squeaky laughter as Drew told him over and over what a good boy he was, and how much he loved him. Aisha sucked in a deep breath when Oz told him that he was her special little man, and always would be.

A few minutes later the little boy waved to them as his father carried him off. Oz slumped against Drew and he held her, whispering to her things I couldn't quite hear.

After a long minute, before Oz could work up a cry from which she couldn't easily stop, Will stood up and took a few steps, cleared his throat, and said their names.

Other than having streaks of gray in their hair, there was no mistaking who they were. Drew slumped at the shoulders a tiny bit and he'd gotten a bit soft in the belly, and Oz looked as regal as Aubrey did, wrapped in quiet dignity, but I would have known them even if I had come alone.

Neither was surprised at his sudden presence—the Emperor could travel through time. He stepped closer, and through her tears Oz said she had to ask him the thing she always did. "How old are you?" Before he could answer, though, she said, "No, wait. Let me guess. You always looked young. I'm thinking thirty-eight, maybe thirty-nine?"

"Close. Forty-three."

The tears Oz had fought against while saying goodbye to three-year-old William spilled over her cheeks and she gulped in air, trying hard to not break down. Drew sucked in a ragged breath, and said, "You did it, then. You and Finn, you saved the world."

"Truthfully, you did," Will said. "You had an idea that Finn was able to work with, a critical detail that made all the difference. I very nearly died anyway, but you—" he looked at Oz "—you saved my life."

It means I lived, too, you know.

"Wick!" Oz rushed to the table but stopped short. "Mrs. Okuda?"

She stood up. "Aisha, please. But, yes. I'm honestly surprised you remember me. It's been thirty-five years for you, hasn't it?"

"Are you kidding? I still have nightmares where you make me come back to re-take my algebra final, only the test looks like it was written with hieroglyphs and there's no keyboard to type in the answers."

"Hey, don't give her any ideas," Will said. "She might do that to her summer term students."

"She can think about it in our own When," Drew said. "We need to get through the portal before someone comes along. If Eli—"

Oz agreed. "He'll recognize you, Emperor. He won't be able

to stop himself from going back inside and getting Finn. It could all become very complicated."

So, routine.

Will reached for Aisha's hand, causing both Oz and Drew to raise an eyebrow. "Do you mind? They still don't know why we came, and—"

"Sweetheart, you know it's all right."

Oh, Oz wants to ask you so many things right now and she just checked your hand to see if you're wearing a ring.

"Eli won't be on the other side," Drew said as they headed for the portal. "You don't have to see anyone else unless you want to."

I want to see Jax and Aubrey. Are they still alive?

"Yes, Wick," Will whispered to me. "But no promises, all right?"

When we were through the portal, before I was even oriented, Oz threw her arms around Will, apologizing as she did. "I haven't hugged you since I was eleven years old, and I'm sorry, but I just have to."

"It's all right," he said, pulling her tight. "Living gave me this. *You* gave me this."

When they parted, Oz let out a chuckle and nodded toward Aisha. "I hoped when you reached for her hand that meant it was okay. I've never been so happy to see people holding hands."

You should have seen what they were doing last night.

The royal apartment looked much the same—the furniture was newer and the walls had been repainted—but it smelled different. There was a sweaty, little-boy aroma in the air, and scattered across the floor were toys and an odd trail of socks. Drew apologized for the mess; they'd had most of the grandkids for several days, and this was the inevitable result.

"You're a grandmother," Aisha said. "Why does that surprise me so much?"

"Because twenty minutes ago she was eighteen and arguing with him about their wedding," Will said.

"Did we argue?" Oz asked Drew.

Drew nodded. "That would be an understatement. Yet, I imagine we argued less around him, maybe barely at all."

Oz and Aisha went into the kitchen to get drinks and Drew gestured to a chair, inviting Will to sit. "I know why *we* fought. We were both angry that you weren't going to be there and angrier still that we didn't do it while you were still alive. What could your Oz and Drew possibly be fighting about?"

"Where and when," Will said. "Oz doesn't seem to care about the particulars, Andrew wants her to have an opinion."

That made him smile. "She was a stubborn girl, wasn't she?"

"And now?"

Drew glanced over his shoulder, making sure she wasn't sneaking up on him. "She's made it an art form. It's served her well."

When Oz returned with drink glasses—Scotch for everyone but Drew, tea for him—Will apologized for intruding on their grief after saying goodbye to their great grandson. "I perhaps could have chosen a better time, but I wanted you to know that you hadn't seen the last of that little boy, and his ending will be different than your Emperor's. Before the pain built up."

They wanted them to know.

"Indeed, Wick. The catalyst for this visit was a drunk Andrew begging me to let you know that I didn't die after all. He knew it wouldn't change the years I've been absent from your life, but he felt that it might ease any lingering grief. He also felt you might want the hope that comes with knowing the world will be there for your descendants."

Drew nodded, but Oz laughed. "Drew? Drunk?"

"It may be a singular occurrence," Will allowed. "Five tall shots of cinnamon whiskey. I last saw him standing on Union Square, swearing he didn't have a hangover. He did."

"I appreciate that you took his request seriously," Drew said. "I'm not quite sure what I'm feeling, but the idea that the next version of us will still have you in our lives?" He looked at Oz. "Imagine."

"I know. We can walk Eli downstairs at three in the morning, and when the Emperor opens the door, shove him in and say, 'Tag, you're it,' and then run."

"Your grandfather was a handful," Drew explained. "But seriously, I am happy the next us will have you."

Will was honest; he had no idea how many years he would live, but he hoped they would have him in their lives for a long time.

"And that includes my math teacher?" Oz teased.

"Oh, honey, if this man runs again, I'm going after him," Aisha said. "Your parents will help me, too."

"You ran?" Drew asked Will.

"When I was young and stupid. It won't happen again."

"Everything changes, doesn't it?" Oz mused.

Will nodded. "The war ended in months, not years," he said. "Drew will never take Midlam's throne because there is no Midlam monarchy. Your father acquired all of it within a month of the first Florida bombing. The First Minister of Florida was removed from power. I am assuming that life after this will bear little resemblance to the lives you knew."

"But we'll be together?" Drew asked. "Oz and me."

"I don't think anything can stop that, Andrew. Regardless of the amount of arguing you'll endure getting to the actual wedding date, you'll get there."

Soul mates.

"Perhaps, Wick," he said. "If there is such a thing, I would easily believe that they're soul mates."

"As long as we're together," Drew said. "No matter the When. Or universe."

"Universe?" Aisha asked.

"Finn is playing with the multiple, parallel universes idea," Drew said. "His current theory is that not only can someone bounce off null space to travel through time, it's possible to break through null space to another universe. He's less sure of how one would then return."

"Unless he has a deadline, he'll get distracted by something else eventually," Will said. "His current projects may endure that fate. He suffers from an abundance of ideas and not enough of himself to complete them all."

"Did Finn finish the transporter early?" Oz asked. "It was years before he was confident enough to use it to push the bomb through to Florida."

When he told her it was unnecessary, that the war ended without the bomb and that Florida was still part of the continental geography, she and Drew were both visibly relieved.

"That might be one of the few things I ever disagreed with my father over," Oz said. "All those people…but he couldn't see another way out. He knew if he had taken action early in the war he could have stopped it, but he wanted to avoid mass destruction."

"And then Russia began providing them with weapons," Drew said. "It went from skirmishes to all-out war in nothing flat. My brother—"

"Right now, Carter is helping rebuild Chicago," Will told him. "He never saw the front lines in Kansas, Andrew. He didn't die in a burn run. Chances are very good that he will live long enough to find the one girl out there who will tolerate him, grow old with her, and possibly even procreate."

Happy and relieved, Drew asked, "Is he still an asshole?"

"Indeed. But he recognizes that within himself, and is working on it. Truly."

"And my parents? My mother was nearly destroyed by the war and losing him. It broke her heart to abdicate at the end of it, but she knew she was losing the confidence of the people—"

Will cut him off. "Shazia is Midlam's Prime Minister, and she's a formidable one. She may be the single reason why your people have so easily accepted becoming part of Pacifica. Her willingness to give up the throne for their good did not go unnoticed. They trust that she will fight for them and make sure that Pacifica never takes them for granted."

"You're not white-washing things a bit, are you?" Oz asked.

"No." He thought about it and added, "It hasn't been long since the end of the war, though. Seven months. But I have faith things will go smoothly until after you have the throne, and begin making changes to the government."

"Biggest mistake of my life, Emperor," Oz said. "We were so caught up in the ideals we had when we were kids that we didn't study our history well enough to understand what might happen."

Will leaned back, studying her face to see if she was serious or not. "What happened? As I recall from my childhood history lessons, it was a success."

"By the narrowest of definitions," Drew said. "We brought back the United States, but along with it returned every ill intention of those who seek politics as a way of life."

Dude, old Drew talks like you.

"We wanted a solid socialist democracy," Oz said. "Will of the people, freedom of choice, with a collective of social care policies… what we got was a congress filled with rich people bent on taking care of their own without even thinking about how they they things they did affected those who don't have as much. We're teetering on an oligarchy, and the only thing stopping it is a President who actually gives a damn. But she won't be there forever, and the next likely candidates are positioned to strip away every decent social program we have left."

"The Emperor's Paradigm," Drew lamented. "Your programs brought our homelessness down to under one per cent. Now? One in twenty-five adults are either homeless or teetering on it. There is no more fundamental right to work, nor rights to housing and medical care. It all comes down to money—the money is there, but they refuse to spend it on those who need it the most. And it all happened so fast."

Will crossed his arms. "It gets better. I know it does."

"But will we live to see it?" Drew offered.

Will said he didn't know, but he did. He just didn't want to give them an answer that would make them sad.

I don't suppose they have a litter box.

"The cat flaps are still in place, Wick," Will said. "Run downstairs, pee on the sidewalk, and then come right back."

"Oh! Wick!" Oz got up. "There's a litter box."

"You have a cat?" Will asked.

"The grandkids have two," Drew answered. "We keep a box for when they're here."

He pointed me to the guest bathroom, and when I was done, Oz and Aisha were in the kitchen and Will was out on the balcony with Drew. I wanted to be with all of them, but Will was the only one who could talk to me, so I opted for the balcony and hoped that it was too late in the day for the pigeons to notice I was there.

Drew poured more scotch into Will's glass and then poured one for himself.

"The Drew I know took his first drink last night," Will mused. "He enjoyed it, but I don't think he'll ever be much of a drinker."

"I didn't, not until you died. My first taste of alcohol was raised in tribute to you, and since then, I've limited myself to twice a year. The day of your birth, and the day of your death. Which, to be honest, pisses my kids off like you wouldn't believe."

"I would think their birthdays would be the more appropriate occasion. Celebrate their milestones, not the dates I came into this world and then left. Drink to their wonders."

"If I drank every time they did something wonderful?" He snorted and then took a sip of his drink. "There's not enough alcohol in the world, Emperor. Not to mention what it would do to my liver."

"Will," he said. "And I always had the feeling you'd be a very good father."

"I hope I have been. And now I'm wondering how different raising those kids would have been if you'd been here to scare the hell out of them on a regular basis."

"Ah, I reserved that for you," Will said. "Still, that is part of why I'm here. You didn't understand—he doesn't understand—and in the last several months we've become quite close. He wanted closure for you."

"I had closure," old Drew said. "In those last months, Oz and I spent a considerable amount of time with you, especially when you reached the point where you needed someone on hand all the time."

If he'd been a little bit drunk, that idea would have sobered him up. "How bad was it?"

"You couldn't sleep," Drew said. "The longer it went on, the worse you felt, and even though you would zone out, you just couldn't quite fall asleep. Your body began breaking down—you barely ate, until you completely stopped, and then getting water into you was an event. Oz rushed to change your sheets before you could see how your hair was falling out in clumps—you lost so much weight that I was often afraid of breaking your bones moving you from the bed to a chair."

"You cared for me?"

"Oz and I were your primary caregivers, Emperor. Your mother wanted to, but was so broken with grief…Emperor, she tried, she honestly did, but her being with you was such a stress that we were afraid she was doing more harm than good. And Finn? He was torn between being here with you and getting the damned work done on the transporter. I don't think Jo ever forgave him for putting that ahead of you."

"He knew I was going to die no matter what he did, but he had a chance to end the war. Surely I understood."

"You did. Your mother, not so much. Neither did Aubrey. She spent as much time with you as she could, and I think it was harder on her than anyone. She knew who you were, Will. She couldn't tell Jax, but she knew. Both of their hearts broke, but it nearly destroyed her. It took a long time before she was truly happy again."

"What brought her around?"

"Eli." Drew smiled and sipped his drink to the memory. "When Oz realized she was pregnant, Aubrey was more excited about that than she'd been about our wedding. When he was born? Jax cried, but it was more because he took one look at her holding him, and realized he finally had her back."

"He abdicated not long after that," Will mused. "Oz became Queen when Eli was only a year old."

"He apologized to her for it, too. But he knew he was distracted as King, and given a choice between the two, he chose Aubrey. The war had ended, and he thought it was a good time. Oz became Queen, and within days of that my mother abdicated...we had two countries battered by war, and neither one of us felt ready to face it."

"You never wanted to be King."

"And yet, there I was. We were new parents, new heads of our countries. I don't think we slept more than four hours at a time for the next ten years."

"Ah, now that's your own fault for having more kids."

"You sound like Oz," Drew snorted.

"Worth it?"

"Worth every frustrating second."

"I remember a moment when you weren't sure you wanted kids at all. You had just kissed Oz for the first time and knew you wanted to be with her, but the concept of children frightened you a bit."

Drew remembered that, laying on the roof late at night, staring up at the partially constructed Elysium. He was still afraid of Will, but he needed a sounding board and Will provided one.

"I asked you if you'd ever been in love, and you said no."

"I lied," Will said.

"Aisha?"

"I broke her heart when we were kids. I'm damned lucky she's giving me another chance."

"Oz was looking for a wedding ring," Drew said.

"It's only been a couple of weeks."

"But?"

Will chuckled. "I have hopes."

They were quiet for a while. Drew poured more scotch, and they stared down at Union Square, the same way Will frequently did with Jax.

"The other me," Drew said softly, "he was worried because you and I never had the chance to be as close as you've become to him?"

"The notion upsets him."

He swirled the ice in his glass. "You can honestly tell him that we did get that close, Will. Oz and I spent long nights with you, and when she fell asleep, we talked, about anything and everything. I think I knew more about you than even Jax did, and you learned every hope and every fear I had. I was terrified of marrying Oz and ruining her life...you promised me it would be amazing. And you were right."

Will waited, sensing he wasn't done.

"About a month before you died, you had a surge of energy and for a few days had an appetite, and hoped you were rebounding." He chuckled, but it was sad. "You wanted scrambled eggs. That's it. Scrambled eggs. So while Oz made them for you, I carried you from the bedroom into the living room to the sofa, and while I propped you up on the pillows, you made me promise that when you were better, we'd go for a drink. You wanted to be the first to corrupt me, and you wanted us to make it a regular thing. Once a month, no matter what, we planned on going to a bar down the street, no girlfriends, no wives. You were going to teach me to drink fine scotch. And I started to believe it would happen."

He looked up, and his eyes had rimmed with red. "Tell your Andrew that. I only drink to remember the brother I had for such a few short months, and that I loved him as much as I possibly could. And I swear, he didn't die without hearing that. I made sure. If I knew I was going to be gone longer than an hour, I told him. I cracked when you died, Will. The only reason I didn't break apart was because Oz needed me not to."

Will nodded.

Tell him you love him, too.

"If it helps," Will finally said, "he loved you from the moment he first held you. Even when he was tormenting you, he loved you."

"Even when I peed in his hair?"

"I have always loved you, Andrew. No matter the When. And now I look forward to being there when Eli is born, and to three in the morning when you knock on my door and shove him at me. It changes nothing for you now, but I hope you understand how important it is to me that I'll be there."

"I hope you understand how important it is to Oz, my Oz, that you keep coming back."

"For Oz, sure."

"All right, maybe for me. A bit. Just promise me that when you go home, you'll tell your Andrew that no matter what happened, he was close to you."

Will gave him his word. They were about to go back inside when Oz and Aisha came out; Oz chided them for turning into her father, standing on the balcony drinking, ignoring the fact that there were people inside waiting. She wasn't too upset, though, because she pulled chairs together so that they could stay outside.

They were on their third drink when Oz asked us to stay the night. "It would break my parents' hearts if you didn't see them," she said. "I'd take you to them now, but they're probably already asleep."

"Ah, using guilt on me," Will chuckled. He looked at Aisha, eyebrows raised, asking, well?

"You know the rules, sweetie. Just get me home on time, and we can do anything you want."

"I have rules now."

"Very flexible rules."

"What about your mother?" Drew asked. "If anyone needs closure, she does. And it would have to be soon."

"She's ill?"

"She's given up," Oz said gently. "And she's also not here. It would mean going forward quite a bit."

Will crossed his arms, and scowled. "My parents went home? I didn't think that would ever happen, not knowing what was coming."

There was an uncomfortable beat of silence until Drew sighed and said, "Finn is still here. Jo fell apart, Will. She got to a point where staying here was killing her, so Eli took her to a time where she could be a little more comfortable and live out her life. Finn visits, but…"

"They're not together," Oz said gently.

"Because I died?" Will asked.

She felt buried by guilt, because she'd withheld truths from him, thinking she was being kind, but she realized in the end, when he died with Oz and Drew by his side and not his own wife and children—something she suspected he wanted—that what she'd done had been particularly cruel. She hadn't saved him from heartache but instead left him to a crushing loneliness. "She knew you could learn to control your gifts, Emperor," Drew said. "She'd known since you were four or five years old. When you were gone? She hated herself for it. I don't think Finn was any too happy to hear it, either."

He thought that if Will saw his mother, if she had the chance to tell him while he was still relatively young, she could die happy. It didn't matter if he was already aware of what she'd done and why. "Let her tell you. Give her that."

"I can do that much," he said thickly. "I often wondered why Eli left and why you allowed him. I never would have guessed—"

"He only intended to stay long enough to get her settled and make sure she was all right. But she never got better, and then he met Harper—the pieces fell into place. We knew he couldn't come home to stay. And Jo does need him."

Aisha reached over the arm of the chair to hold his hand. "You weren't kidding when you said your family ties became complicated."

"I didn't know the story," Will said. "Only that Eli had a reason to live his life in more than one When. How far forward will we go?"

"To a few years after Finn is born. We try to keep our visits chronological," Oz said. "The last time we were there, she was not well."

"She's in palliative care," Drew added. "And you should know, she has a Nightwatch switch."

"But you don't know the date of her death," he guessed.

Oz shook her head. "We've intentionally not checked. We've gone forward far enough that we could, but when we take that leap it's to see you. I don't want it in my head, and I especially don't want to find out and then be the one to tell Finn."

"I wouldn't be surprised if he doesn't regularly go home," Will said. "Right up to the last minute, looking for clues that he can leave in the Old Mint. If they split up, he's probably looked up her date of death."

Unless he doesn't want to know.

If he doesn't know, he can pretend she's all right forever.

Drew patted his lap, inviting me over. "I have missed you, Mister Wick. We even had a cat who looked quite a bit like you for a while, but he was three times your size and kind of an asshole."

Oz reached over to pet me. "We've had a string of cats," she said. "All wonderful, but none as smart as you." She looked up, as the notion hit her. "You know when we die, don't you?"

"Who says you die?" Will said lightly. "You may be standing on Ocean Beach when the meteor hits, waiting for the massive wave that swallows the city."

"Ew, is that what happens?" Oz asked.

He shrugged. "I honestly have no idea. I died long before then, remember? But I will tell you this much—you have many years left."

"I sure as hell hope so," Drew said. "I'm not even old yet."

"That's not what your daughter says," Oz snickered.

"She's why my hair is prematurely gray. I'm not old."

"Keep telling yourself that." To Will and Aisha, she said, "He's old."

"Fifty is not old!"

"Sweet stuff…you're fifty-five. Let it go."

"I'm not old," he grumbled.

"Your daughter," Will said, "she's fourteen or fifteen now?"

"Fifteen going on thirty," Oz answered. "She knows everything, she's stubborn, and her brothers have spoiled her like you wouldn't believe."

"Not too spoiled," Drew added. "She's working with Zed this summer, covering memorial services on Elysium. She might be as gifted as he is."

"And yet, I hope she doesn't follow in his footsteps," Oz said.

"How is he?" Will asked.

"Lonely, I think," Oz replied. "He lives for his kids and grandkids. If he's not with them, he's working."

"He never recovered after—" Drew sighed "—he just didn't recover."

What happened to Zed?

I stood on Drew's lap and sniffed his chin. *Is Zed okay?*

"You're hungry, aren't you?" Drew said. "You're always hungry." He looked to Oz. "The kids left cat food here, didn't they? If not, I'll cut up some chicken for him."

"Cat food on top of the fridge, chicken in the top drawer. You'll have to give him both now. He's not like Jumbo and Fred, he knows what you said and will bother Will all night long if he knows there's chicken to be had."

I'm sorry I died and missed watching you guys get old. I think I would have liked it. Drew would have fed me everything.

Drew set me on Oz's lap and told me to stay put; he would bring food to me.

Yeah, I would have been really happy with you.

The plate he brought back had enough food for three meals, but he said I didn't have to finish it. He would also make sure there was a plate on the kitchen floor if I got hungry at three in the morning.

"Sure, spoil him," Will grumbled. "You don't have to go back and live with him."

"Do you ever do that?" Aisha asked them. "Go back?"

Drew laughed and pointed out that teenaged Oz had a bad habit of going back and spying on Will. So yes, they did. Then he wondered, if they went back now, would they see themselves in their own timeline, or would they see the Oz and Drew of Will's new When?

Will wasn't sure. "Pick a date, if you wind up in the new When I'll meet you at the portal."

"You went back a few times and literally changed things. You always made it home."

He nodded. "I did, but I can also no longer get to those timelines, the one where you died as a child, nor the one when Drew was killed at twelve. I remember them, but if I went back, it would be to the timeline I altered."

Aisha was stunned. "You did what?"

"I have gone back and changed a few things that I knew were not supposed to happen. One time, to keep Jax from killing himself by riding into the path of a delivery van on California Street. Once to keep Oz from drowning. And twice, attempts were made on Drew's life." He explained that he only changed things he knew were not supposed to happen, based on the history he knew and the information he regularly accessed at the Old Mint. He wouldn't change something if it were supposed to happen, no matter how badly he wanted to.

Oz snorted. "Liar."

Sheepishly, Will asked if she could see his lie color; the other Oz didn't see it until three months after he should have died.

"I saw it frequently in your last few months, every time you swore you were all right. It's a very pretty orange, and for years after you were gone, I couldn't go near anything that color."

"I ruined orange for you," he mused, not at all sad. "Your favorite fruit."

"And I'm still upset about that."

"My apologies to the Queen."

"Just Oz. I haven't been Queen for several years now."

"Ah, then. I'm not sorry."

5

We stayed in Oz's old bedroom, which had become Eli's bedroom, and when he left home, a guest room. Drew said that they left it for him with all his things in place, until he met a girl named Harper and it was clear that he wasn't coming back. They'd offered it to their other sons, who shared Zed's old room, but neither of them was interested in changing and they liked being together.

"I had visions of them living together until they were old, old men," Drew said. "For some reason, their wives wouldn't have it."

I was just glad the window seat was still there. I curled up on one side of it while Will and Aisha cuddled together on the other side. They sat sideways, the way Oz and Drew often did. Will's back was to the window frame and she snuggled up to him, pulling his arms around her. They had turned the bedroom lights off, and the city lights washed over them, spilling across the floor and the bed. She asked him about Oz and Drew's kids—she wasn't sure she should ask them directly—and he thought it was fine if she knew because she wouldn't say anything to them and even if she did, their Oz and Drew might have a very different future.

"They broke the two-royal-offspring standard and spurred the end of the one-child norm for Pacifica," he told her. "They had four kids. Eli, Liam, Ben, and Sam. Eli is my grandfather, Liam and Ben are Irish twins, fewer than ten months apart. Sam is the youngest and only girl. The first three were close together, and Sam came along ten or eleven years later. From what I know, she was the light of Drew's life and her brothers adored her."

"Does she follow in Zed's footsteps?"

"No but she'll follow in Aubrey and Jax's. Working with Zed taught her to deal with people at their most vulnerable, and she used that skill as a teacher for children with critical needs. The homeless problem Drew mentioned? It will get worse. Sam will become one of their fiercest educators, and her efforts will spur others to follow her lead. She becomes a driving force in teaching people to lift themselves from dire circumstances and a light that wakes up Congress to the epidemic they created through oligarchical policies."

"I'm not sure how you keep it all straight in your head. Or how you managed to sit there with them all evening and not say a word about where they're headed."

"I'm not a fan of robbing people of the experience of meeting the new things in their lives," he said. "Even more so now. I'm not sure anyone should ever know the detritus they leave behind."

"Your mother?"

It hurt to know that his death broke his mother and nearly did Aubrey in. "And yet, it also makes me happy to know that Oz and Drew were there for me in the end, especially knowing that Drew and I became close after all. I hope Zed gave me a stellar eulogy."

"You think he handled your service? He was just a boy."

"Zed has already served some difficult memorials and cared for several bodies that met heartbreaking ends. He wouldn't have allowed anyone else to speak for me."

He would never forget bathing the Miller twins, and the song the Emperor sang to them just before sending them off to be with their parents. I would never forget any of it, the moment the Emperor placed their tiny hands together, the sound of breath not taken and suckling that would have told me they were merely sleeping. Their deaths were the first salvo fired before the war, and we didn't even know it.

"How does it feel knowing how badly they all missed you? Aside from what it did to Aubrey and your mother."

He nuzzled his face to her neck. "I feel loved. I wish they hadn't been in such pain, but I feel loved."

They fell quiet; she leaned her head back against his shoulder and stared out into the night, smiling softly when he planted a kiss at the spot where her neck and shoulder met. I waited for hands to start moving, doing groping things that I didn't really care to see, but for a long time they were content to be quiet and look out the window.

It was summer in San Francisco, and night time at that; I didn't think there was a lot to see.

"We're both forty-three," Aisha said, breaking the silence. "If we're lucky, we have another fifty years left."

"It could be more than sixty. Practically another lifetime."

"I feel like we wasted twenty years that we could have been together. Don't get me wrong, I don't regret a damn thing that got me Jimmy, but I'd be lying if I didn't admit that I'm starting to feel some anger toward your mother for keeping the truth from you."

He was right there with her. All the information he took from the lab simmered in the back of his brain, and he wrestled with how to approach her about it. "She owes me answers for not only that but how she's been reacting to us as a couple. I want an explanation, yet I also just want to be angry about it for a while."

"So, the Emperor is human," she said lightly.

"Well, there is an ongoing debate regarding that."

"I am just so stuck on the idea that we could have been together and had a family, Will. All I wanted then was to be the other half of you, and now that I know all of this, I'm afraid I'll boil over."

"I know. And yet, I'm not sure it's something I would go back to change."

That made her pull away and turn around. He explained that if he went back and told his younger self—showed his younger self—how to control the way he listens to peoples' thoughts and opens his mind to them, they might have been together, but for how long? They were kids. The odds were not in their favor. And what if he'd learned control before they met, and was tangled up in some other relationship when she came along? "This is the timeline that puts us together, Aisha. We're mature enough to not do anything too stupid, I think, and I know my heart better than I did twenty-five years ago. That arrogant kid would have done *something*, I know he would have. But I won't. I know what it's like to lose you and to miss you, and I won't put myself through that again. I won't put you through it again."

"Those are pretty strong words for a guy who's been in a relationship for all of about three weeks," she mused.

"I know. I also know that I'm basically a walking hormone right now, but it doesn't change the fundamental fact that I've loved you for my entire adult life." He reached up to push a strand of hair from her forehead, just to touch her. "I'm not asking yet because I know it's too soon…but I *will* ask, Aisha."

Softly, she countered, "Unless I ask first."

That made him laugh; if she thought the time was right, if they reached a point where she was confident that her son was all right with them being together in more than an abstract sense, and she had him trained well enough that sex wasn't a crushing disappointment to her time after time, by all means, be the one to ask. "But I want it to be special. I'm only doing this once in my life, and I want to feel like a princess."

"Sweetie," she said lightly, "the odds are that if I ask, it'll be when we're in bed and you'll say yes just to make sure I don't stop what I'm doing."

"I'm okay with that."

You could just skip all that and just do it.

"No, Wick, we can't jump right into it. We still need time. Jimmy needs time to get used to the idea of us."

He said he was all right with it.

"He said he was all right with us dating. That's not the equivalent of seeing us together as a couple."

That surprised her. "You and Jimmy talked about this?"

"He says he's fine with us dating, with the caveat that I'm not stringing you along with a dozen other women. And if I hurt you, he gets to punch me in the groin."

"Then don't hurt me." She leaned in and kissed him, then gestured to the bed. "How awkward will you feel making love here, with Oz and Drew right down the hall?"

"I'll feel awkward because this is still new to me. I don't care if they're down the hall."

I care.

"Wick, there are cat flaps. If this bothers you, go sleep with Oz and Drew."

I don't want to watch old people go at it and I bet they still do it every night.

"We're not exactly young," Will said, "but it's going to happen, so either close your eyes and pretend it's not, or accept it."

Someone needs to tell you what you're doing wrong. Aisha's too nice to.

"Come on. I'm not doing it *wrong*. I'm just not very good yet."

"Stop it," she said, getting up. As she crossed the room, she started pulling her clothes off, and said, "Strip," without looking to see if he was following. He stayed on the window seat, slow smile forming, and watched as she tossed her clothes on the floor. When she realized what he was doing, she put her hands on her hips and pretended to be annoyed, but her eyes were twinkling and she stood there completely, unselfconsciously naked.

"You have no idea what you're doing to me," he said thickly.

"Take your pants off, give me an idea."

He finally got up, and slowly—purposely slowly—began undressing. She watched without any degree of embarrassment, her head cocked a little to the left as he let his jeans slide down his legs, and then when he hooked his fingers into the waistband of his underwear.

"All right, then," she said after he pulled them off. "I have a very good idea."

"Sorry if I'm pointing. I know it's rude."

"Pointing at the ceiling light isn't rude, sweetie," she said. "Now the view you're giving Union Square…"

"One-way polymer acrylic. No one can see in."

"Unless the windows have been changed in the last thirty years."

He shrugged lightly. "Then I hope they enjoy the view of my ass."

"Hon, you've got a *great* ass. I would be happier if it were over here."

That's pretty much all I could see of him and I wasn't nearly as impressed, so I jumped down and headed for the headboard. It was six inches wide, plenty of space for me to stretch out and pretend my sensibilities weren't being offended. That was easy, initially, because they stood next to the bed for a long time and fished for each other's tonsils. By the time she pushed him onto the bed and sat on him, I was bored.

One hand on each boob, and slap 'em together a little.

He ignored me.

Not hard. Just enough to make them go 'boing.' She'll like that.

"Hush, Wick."

Or push 'em up and let 'em fall. They jiggle. It's kind of cool, actually. Like Jello.

Boing.

Boing.

Boing.

I peeked over the headboard; he was biting his bottom lip, trying to not laugh. "I'm sorry," he said to Aisha, "but apparently he's significantly more experienced than I am."

"Wick's a voyeur."

"I can make him leave."

She leaned over his face, bracing her hands against his pillow. "Since you can talk to him and he obviously grasps what's going on, it should bother me to have him stay, but it doesn't. I wish I understood him, though."

"No, really, you don't."

She doesn't need my help.

She apparently didn't need any foreplay, either. While she was kissing him she slipped her hand between them and held him steady while she settled on him, and then whispered to him to sit up. He had to brace his hands against the bed and his face wound up between her breasts. He would have happily suffocated there, but before he could they rolled together and he was on top of her, kissing her deeply.

Where are your handcuffs? Handcuffs are important. And the chocolate pudding. You need handcuffs and chocolate pudding, and a can of—

"Wick, what the hell kind of weird sex are Jax and Aubrey having that you think that's normal?"

"Do I want to know?"

"Handcuffs and chocolate pudding."

"Ah." She wrapped her legs around his waist. "I'll show you sometime. I promise."

"How—?"

"Sweetie." She moaned a bit and started breathing harder. "I'll tie you to the headboard, cover you with pudding or syrup, and slowly, and I mean *very* slowly, lick every bit of it off your body. I'll start at your neck—" she inhaled sharply "—and work my way down. All across your chest. Every divot in that glorious six pack. And when I'm done with that I'll clean up all the little drips that work down your groin, and then—"

She wasn't done telling him, but he was done hearing it. He uttered a surprised "Oh" and sucked in a hard breath through gritted teeth, thrusting in hard.

Dude. If you finish first, you're not finished.

When he could breathe, he kissed her again.

Come on. One time I heard you say you would eat anything. Prove it.

I know he was listening, because his lips worked their way down her body, until she grabbed him by the hair and tugged him back up.

"I'm not done kissing you, mister."

"But you're not there yet—"

"You have hands."

"I have hands."

"Play. Explore." She took his hand and guided it where she wanted it, whispering what she wanted him to do. "God, yes."

Pudding would have been more fun.

You're gonna like the pudding.

He laughed through his nose. "There's a very good chance that I will never again be able to look at a bowl of pudding without getting an erection."

"That'll be awkward when Oz and Drew have kids that you're babysitting, and they all want pudding for a snack. But at least I know now you're really looking forward to something."

"What's that?"

She snuggled up to him. "Let's talk about blowjobs."

"Oh. I've never given one."

6

"He could be your twin," Aisha whispered to Will. "If his eyes were a brighter shade of green—hell, at a glance I could easily think he was you."

Eli Blackshear the third, named for Oz's grandfather, who was named for his grandfather, was thirty years old and stood between his parents and the room where Jo was resting. He knew without asking who Will was, and his first impulse was to refuse to let him past the living room. It was a bad idea; she would only grieve him more when he left, and she didn't have it in her to survive that.

"He's forty-three," Drew said simply.

It took a second for that to sink in and when it did, Eli twitched in Will's direction. "Go in first and prepare her," he told Oz. "Don't tell her who, just tell her she has a visitor that you want her to see. She'll tell you no, just promise her she would regret it if she didn't. She can't bear the idea of new regrets."

That sounds kinda mean. Just tell her that her son is here and he's old.

"Wick, the talking cat?" Eli asked. "Can you really understand him?"

"I told you, we weren't making that up," Drew said as he opened the door. "Jaded young man, all the time."

How did you know? No one else knew until after we didn't die.

"My parents, Wick," Will whispered to me.

Eli shrugged and pulled the door closed behind his parents. "I honestly thought he was just a story. I mean, I was sure there was a Wick, but never quite believed you could communicate with him."

"You're capable of time travel, you know who Jo will become to your son, you exist in multiple Whens, and someone understanding a cat is a stretch?"

"Well, when you put it like that."

"How difficult has it been?" Will asked. "Seeing them here and at home, stretching yourself through time?"

Eli asked them to sit, and they took the sofa in the small, bright living room. "We're careful," he said as he sat in a comfy chair where he could still see Jo's bedroom door. "We keep track of our ages and the time between visits on either side, and we're careful to not tell each other anything that happens out of sequence."

"Then you've seen them older?"

He nodded. "Curiosity. They can't get too upset. I know they've done the same thing more than once. They spy on their younger selves, too."

"Going back in their own timeline—" He grinned. "Of course. Their future is your history."

"I knew life would become complicated when I brought Jo here. We cope. The difficult part is being here with her and then going home to my wife and the little boy who will grow up and fall in love with her. I wish I had no idea what's coming."

"Has he met her?"

"No. We're careful to never mention her name. All he knows is that Daddy has a patient he needs to spend a lot of time with. And the few times we've taken him to see his grandparents, Finn—your Finn—stays away."

"They could see each other," Will said. "I've interacted with myself. It's odd and disconcerting, but as long as the elder Finn was careful, it would be all right."

"He's a sensitive little boy and hyper-focuses on details others might not even see. It's better not to."

"Still—"

"Listen to your grandfather, Will," Aisha said. "Let it go."

Eli grinned. "That's right, you're my grandson. My brain wasn't moving in that direction. Now I wish my wife was here to meet you."

The bedroom door cracked open, and Eli stood. "Emperor. Will. Before you go in, I need to warn you. She's been on the precipice of ending her life for some time now. She's hooked up to a Nightwatch—it's an IV that will deliver drugs to stop her heart, if she chooses to activate it. I've promised her that when she asks, I'll do it, and my gut says that once she makes her peace with you, she'll ask. All you need to do is come get me."

Will took a deep breath before he went in. Jo was lying under a single baby-blue sheet that was tucked around her up to her waist, and Oz was helping her sit up against a pillow. She kissed Jo's forehead and told her they would be just outside if she needed anything, and then closed the door as she slipped out.

Jo was somewhere around one hundred years old but looked older. Ideally, she should have another seventy to eighty years left. Her jet-black hair was now thin and silvery white; her pale skin wrapped tightly around bones that could break with a single sneeze. She looked confused at first, and a look of panic glittered in her eyes.

"Eli? Oz said I had a visitor." The panic softened as quickly as it had come. "No, you're William. I know my William. I am so sorry."

His voice cracked when he spoke. "Mom." He sat carefully on the edge of the bed, and I jumped up to sit by her knees. "I came as soon as I could."

Slowly, painfully, she reached for his hand, not taking her eyes off his face. "I know who you are. You're the William who lives."

"They weren't supposed to tell you."

"Oh, sweetheart, they didn't have to. Only the William who lived would have come this far forward. But you're still my William. The timeline doesn't matter. You're still my baby."

"Always." He carefully lifted her hand and pressed a kiss against her fingers. "I'm sorry I was gone for so long. I'm sorry you had to watch me die."

"No, no, no." She struggled to sit a bit more upright, and he scooted closer to her, easing her back onto the pillow. "You're here, which means it's not too late."

"What for?"

She coughed; there was a rattle in her chest, one I didn't think he could hear. "Oh, no, you'll hate me. I am so sorry."

"I promise, I could never hate you. Even when I threatened to run away to Elysium and then Mars, I loved you."

Her eyes moistened, and she smiled wanly. "I wish you had gone when you threatened to. You could have lived an adventure. If I had known…"

"I've had a good life, Mom."

"But it was *less*, and that was my fault. I have so many things to tell you." Her fingers tapped against the back of his hand. "But you survived, so maybe I told you after all. Surely I would tell you, once I knew you would live."

"That I can touch people?" he asked. And then he lied through his teeth. "Of course, you told me. And once I knew, Oz helped me to learn to control it."

"Oz?"

"She began the process of it, setting a hand on my arm for a few minutes at a time, until I was sure that I could keep my thoughts to myself. She allowed me to invade her privacy until I learned to not listen. Then Aubrey forced me to allow her to kiss me on my cheek. Jax is still threatening to plant one right on my lips. I might even let him."

"Did I tell you why I did it?"

He couldn't bullshit his way through that one, and shook his head.

She'd come to realize that he had a sense of control when he was in preschool. He'd learned to touch the lab techs without listening to them, and they never heard any child-like whispering when he sat on their laps or gave them sloppy kisses. But she was afraid, because when he was upset, he lost all sense of control, and she knew that the man he would become would be lonely and angry. She couldn't bear the thought of his heart breaking over and over because his brain could betray him at any turn. With one moment that was too angry, or too excited, he could destroy a relationship. She decided to not tell him, to let him—and his father—think he had to be alone.

She knew who you were even then?

All the information they gleaned from the Old Mint pointed to that: The Emperor was alone throughout his adult life and died young. She thought she was sparing not only him but anyone who would love him. "But I was wrong. I was wrong and I'm so, so sorry."

But she didn't know you were the Emperor until you were a teenager.

"Perhaps you did spare someone the pain of losing me," he said, ignoring me. "There was a girl when I was young. I think losing me would have destroyed her, if we'd taken the chance."

Her eyes filled with tears again. "No. It was wrong. If she was strong enough to love you, she would have been strong enough to survive. You'd never settle for less. You would have been with a woman who could stand up to the awful little details of your life."

Tell her. She needs to know.

She reached toward me with her other hand. "Wick. Are you still telling him what to do?"

"At the most inappropriate times, even," Will said. "But he's right, he wants me to tell you about her. She found her way back to me, and she's in the other room, waiting with Eli. You could meet her, if you'd like."

Her hand went to her mouth, both surprised and hopeful. "Oh, no. She shouldn't have this awful picture of me in her head. But tell me about her. Is she the one? She loves you?"

"She loved me then, and she loves me now," he said. He opened his mouth to say more, but then realized he could show her. He touched his fingers to her cheek and showed her all the highlights of his life, the moments that made him happiest, from the moment he came to stay, until the moment Aisha told him that the truths of his life were not something to deter her.

Don't give her the horny details, dude.

She saw as Jax and Aubrey pulled him closer, making him a part of their new love, and as he stood beside Jax when they married. She watched as his heart broke on Union Square. He gave her the magic of playing with Oz and Zed when they were little, and the loud, wonderful moments filled with laughter. All of the important moments of his life, when he lived instead of dying, and when Aisha kissed him at his birthday party.

"It's been a wonderful life," he said quietly as he pulled his hand away. "The good has far outweighed the bad, and the pain of my childhood was erased with every moment I spent taking care of Oz and Zed when they were small."

"And you're in love," she whispered.

"So much."

She smiled impishly. "You could make me a grandmother," she said. "The mother who waits at home, I know she wants that."

"I probably shouldn't." He laughed lightly. "Dad has made a point of reminding me, reproducing would not be my brightest idea."

"But he doesn't know!" She sat up sharply and reached for him. "*You* don't know! Andrew knows but he might not think to tell you."

After he was gone, while she tried and failed to heal her own heart, she decided that she had to know—what had happened to him, what made her son so different? She melted into research, looking for answers, testing every half-baked notion she could think of, until Drew postulated that perhaps he had been exposed to something early in life, or even in utero.

The lightbulb went off, and she turned to the days between the moment she knew she was pregnant and the moment she returned from twenty-sixteen to her own When. She and Drew built a set of small time machines, scaled-down versions of the egg-shaped ship that Finn used to move through time before he created the portals, and she sent tiny living things into null space, collecting data. Everything she sent that was in some state of reproduction came back whole, but the offspring had unique abilities. Their gifts were not identical, but it happened enough to affirm the hypothesis.

"They didn't pass it on. None of them did. After noticing a pattern, we took a chance and sent slightly larger animals—cats and small dogs—and then allowed their offspring to breed—there wasn't a single instance of their mutations being passed on."

You're a mutant, Emperor.

I think she means that in a nice way.

He didn't lean in the direction she was pulling him. "Is that why you finally broke, Mom? Knowing I could have had a family and didn't?"

Her hands were on his face, eyes darting back and forth as she tried to take in everything about him. "The guilt, William. But hear me. It's not too late for you now. You could still have children. You could have the family I robbed you of."

"I had Oz and Zed," he told her. "I didn't miss out on that. I don't feel cheated."

"But you were."

"So were you." He wanted to know what happened, why she and Finn parted. How awful was it that she felt like she had to not only leave him, but move to a completely different When?

Finn had never gotten over being angry with her, not once he found out the extent of the things she'd hidden from him. "He still loves me, but he doesn't like me. We had to learn to live apart. And then I started feeling—" She sighed. "My anchor was gone. We both knew it. He plotted out where I could likely live without being a wound on time, and I left. He visits now and then, but we were damaged and there was no way to fix it."

"Eli came with you."

"He wasn't supposed to stay. He was only supposed to make sure that I didn't need an anchor."

He glanced at the machines near the head of the bed, and the tubes that ran into ports at her neck and arms. "But you did, didn't you?"

"His presence slowed down how quickly I failed, but he couldn't stop it. He's given me a decade instead of the short months I would have had. But I think I could have gone home, just before the end of everything, and still would have died from a broken heart." The tears finally spilled over. "I know what's coming for me, William. I saw how awful it was for you in the last weeks. Eli promised I wouldn't have to live through that."

Sooner rather than later, she would stop sleeping, and not even the heaviest of medications would change that. Her already frail body would wither, and one by one her organs would shut down, slowly and painfully, until her heart stopped beating. She knew she was nearly to that point, and couldn't bear to face it.

"You won't have to," he whispered.

I crept up to her pillow and curled up, paw resting gently against her head, half listening as they continued to talk. She peppered him with questions about his life and about Aisha and her son, and I concentrated on the feel of her skin, the tiny beads of sweat that broke free, and how quickly her heart was beating. There wasn't much oxygen leeching from her skin, and there was that small, subtle gurgle in her lungs.

She was tired, and her voice was fading. He was reluctant to leave, but told her he could see she needed rest, and promised to sit with her until she had fallen asleep.

She was silent for a long minute, and then opened her eyes. "Would it break your heart if this was my last sleep?" She glanced toward the machine just a few feet away. "I am so tired. I've been ready for so long, and I didn't know what I was waiting for until I saw you again."

If not today, she'll die tomorrow. I can feel it.

She's barely breathing, Will. Her heart only half beats and it sounds wet. She's in pain. Something besides time is killing her.

"My heart won't break," he said softly. "But are you sure? I could come back to see you again."

Her voice was thin and filled with sadness. "I don't want you to see me like that, William. I saw you when…please, don't make me go through that."

"I could take you home," he offered. "I can take you to the timeline where home goes on, and you'll be all right there."

"A home without my family," she said thinly. "I'd rather die than be alone, William. No matter how often you came to see me, I would still be alone. I can't bear that. I would always know that you're leaving your true mother to come see me—"

"You *are* my mother, no matter the When."

Jo's eyes filled with tears. "I am so tired and ready to go. Please, don't make me live through this."

Eli promised.

"I won't. And you know, in a little while I'll go back through the portal, and you'll be there, at home, probably yelling at Dad for missing lunch with you again."

"You'll go find me, won't you?"

"I swear. And I will tell you I love you, because I do. It was all right, Mom, you did what you thought you needed to do when I was a boy, and now I've got the girl, and she loves me more than you could ever imagine."

She closed her eyes and asked him to flip the switch, and to stay with her until she had taken her last breath. She wanted him to be the last thing she ever saw, and his voice to be the last she ever heard.

I was careful to not make a sound. I could feel her slipping away, and couldn't take those wishes from her. I breathed quietly and didn't move, but kept a paw on her skin so that she would feel me there and know that I would miss her, too.

After he flipped the switch and made sure that the pump activated and was sending the drugs into her body, Will stretched out on the bed and held her close, whispering *I love you* over and over, until her breathing became ragged, and then stopped.

He stayed curled up with her for another five minutes, making sure she was gone before he let go.

Are you okay?

He sat up, one hand lingering on her arm. "I'm fine."

Your heart hurts but remember what you told her, you get to go home and she'll be there and you can tell her you love her and you know about the papers in the lab, and it's ok.

"It's not okay, Wick. She not only withheld all of that from me, she's still holding it back. She doesn't think enough of me for the truth—and why not? What could she possibly gain from any of this?"

She's your mom, dude. She wouldn't hurt you on purpose.

He kissed her one last time and got up. He had no answer for that.

He knew I was right, though, which made him even more upset. The woman laying lifelessly in that bed loved him enough to have shattered over the truth. It would be so much easier if she would just tell him, and save them all the heartache.

$$= = =$$

We were through the portal and in old Oz and Drew's When before the weight of it hit him. He stepped out, still holding Aisha's hand, and stumbled to the closest bench, closing his eyes as he tilted his head back.

"Just give me a minute," he said. "I need time to process."

Aisha kissed him on his cheek and told him to take all the time he needed. I slid from his shoulder to his lap, and then stretched up to sniff him, and carefully stuck out my tongue and touched it to his chin.

He smiled then. "That's the first time you've done that, Wick. Thank you."

"I'm sorry, Emperor," Oz said. "We knew how close she was. We should have thought it through."

He took a deep breath and then opened his eyes. "I could step into that portal and be home within seconds, walk five minutes to her apartment, and she'd be there. I haven't lost her yet."

"Still."

"What you did was generous," Drew said. "And thank you. Eli promised he would help her at the end, but I know the idea was killing him. She's half of why he went into medicine. I think he believed he could save her."

Hard to save someone who doesn't think they deserve saving.

With a heavy sigh, he picked me up and then stood. "I should be the one to tell Finn."

"Not how you wanted to see him," Aisha guessed.

"Whatever went wrong between them, he'll care. Did he know how close to the end she was?"

Oz nodded. "He visited her from time to time, and Eli has kept us all updated."

"In the lab?" Will guessed. "Does he still take root there?"

"I honestly don't think he has an apartment anymore," Drew said. "At least I don't think he's been to it in years."

"I hope he didn't have any pets."

Oz scrunched her nose up at the idea. "Ugh. Really."

"Finn is in great shape," Drew told Will. "Don't base your expectations of him on your mother. He barely looks older than I am."

"You look pretty wrecked," Will said.

"I think I hate you a little bit."

Oz was amused. "I think I know where Eli gets his sense of humor and why Jo constantly mistook him for you. He hated it when he was little, but by the time he was a teenager, I think he appreciated it."

"A lot of love between those two," Drew said.

Aisha asked Will if he wanted her to go with him, if being there would make it easier. He considered it, and then decided that if nothing else, Finn would want to meet her and perhaps warn her about what she was getting into.

"If he tells you to run, please don't."

Finn was hunched over his desk in the first-level lab office, lost to whatever he was reading. Will waited for a few seconds and then knocked on the open door. "If it's an equation tripping you up, I brought a math teacher with me."

Finn looked up and broke into a wide grin. "Dash. I never thought you'd jump forward," he said as he got up. "I hoped, but—" He stopped, searching Will's face for the reason he looked sad. "What happened?"

He couldn't bring himself to tell Finn that Jo was gone. Instead, he reached for his father and placed a long kiss on his forehead, and let the thought move freely. He let his father see Jo's last moments, and hear her last words.

He and Jo might have fallen apart, but Finn still fell against Will. He buried his face against his son's shoulder and allowed himself a minute of wrenching sorrow, until the realization hit him that along with the news of Jo's death was Will's age.

"Tell me everything," he said, pulling away from Will.

It amazed him, how Finn clicked from sorrow to curiosity in a blink, but he also understood his father had always been like that. He knew that the grief would drop him to his knees soon enough and that Oz and Drew and their kids would be there to help him through it.

Will pulled two chairs from the far wall near the desk and offered one to Aisha. Finn watched her, a curious grin playing on his face. He also played through some of the things Will had let him see and knew who she was. "I am thrilled to meet you," he said as he sat back down. "It doesn't matter what happened in the life I'm going through now. As long as I know that in the next loop of time that William not only lives but has love, I'll die happy. And how could I not? The next me doesn't lose you. He gets to watch you be in love and I hope it sticks." To Aisha, "No pressure."

Will reminded him that the Finn he would return home to also wouldn't have to lose Jo, and he understood that's exactly what happened even if he did visit her often. "She and I are about to have a frank discussion about the things she withheld from me, but you have to know—fundamentally, I understand why she did it. I don't like it, and I wish she would be more forthcoming about the things she knows, but I appreciate her reasons for letting us believe I had no control. I absolutely will not hold it against her as long as she accepts Aisha into my life."

"She's a stubborn woman, you know that. She can dig her heels in harder than seems possible."

"I know. But she also raised a stubborn son. I am owed answers, and I will get them."

"Will," Aisha breathed. "Don't charge after her like an angry bull. She'll run."

"She'll charge right back."

"No." Finn shook his head. "She's right, Dash. Look at what happened to us. I was angry, and she scampered away from it. I was furious, and it frightened her so badly that I was no longer her anchor. She can be a formidable, tough woman, but where *you* are concerned, she will wither, and she will run."

"She's strong—"

"I have loved that woman for most of my one hundred plus years, William. I *know* her. If I had paid closer attention instead of spending every waking hour on those goddamned transporters…I had her heart in my hand. After losing you it was barely beating, and instead of caring for it I set it down and went back to work."

"But *my* Jo, my mother, didn't lose me."

"But she knows how close she came," Aisha said. "Will, I resent the hell out of the years we lost, too, but what good will it do to punish her for it?"

"That's not what I mean to do," he sighed.

"You want the truth from her. But sweetheart, sometimes the truth comes with a price, and she may not be ready to pay it."

"Then I extend her credit?"

"Oh, I like her," Finn said. "Promise me you'll visit now and then, and bring her with you."

"Ah, you don't want to see me, do you? Just her."

"Well, grandbabies, too. I get grandchildren, don't I?"

= = =

Aubrey wasn't three feet out of the elevator when she spotted Aisha and squealed "You came back!"

At nearly eighty-five years old, she still carried herself with a quiet dignity that belied her excitement over seeing the friend she'd lost to Will's heartbreak fifty years earlier. Decades hadn't diminished her memories of Aisha; she hadn't been relegated to storage in the recesses of Aubrey's mind, not like an acquaintance she might recall with some effort. It took only a fleeting glimpse for her to remember, and for her to run straight to Aisha for a hug that went on for a long time.

Jax—his jet-black hair now snow-white, though he didn't seem like he was nearing his eightieth birthday—looked at Will and shrugged, as if they were still in each other's lives, as if no time had passed since he'd cried over his best friend's body.

While Aisha and Aubrey hugged, they stared at each other. When Aubrey finally let go of Aisha, Jax broke, and blurted, "You son of a bitch, you went and died without me telling you I loved you."

"I always knew it, Jax. It never had to be said."

Defiantly, Jax spat, "Yes, it did! You tell the people you love that you love them. I needed to say it and I never did. And you never told me who you were. Never!"

Will was a bit taken aback and not sure what to say.

Jax balled his hands into fists. "I'm mad at you, Emperor!"

"Oh, stop it," Aubrey said as she hugged Will. "You're just upset because he's still young, and you're an angry old man." She kissed Will's cheek and said, "Oz filled us in, Emperor. You have no idea how relieved we are."

Jax wasn't as willing to be nice. "He's a little shit," he grumbled. "All those years and you never told me who you were."

"I promise," Will said, trying to be serious but failing hard, "When I go home I'll tell you."

"And these two?" Jax asked, pointing at Oz and Drew. "Do they get to know?"

"They already do."

"Oh, *they* get to find out!" He stomped toward the sofa and sat down hard, folding his arms over his chest. "Fine. I put up with your sorry ass for *years* and you tell my daughter before you tell me. I see how you are."

He's not really mad. Look at his eyes. He's happy to see you.

"I know, Wick."

"You!" Jax pointed at me. "Get your furry ass over here and sit on my lap."

Will plucked me off his shoulder and set me on the floor. I ran to Jax and leaped onto his lap, standing on my back legs so that I could rub against his face.

"I missed you, Mister Wick," he said without any of the pretended anger he'd flung at Will. "When you went into the portal… that was one of the worst moments of my life. I'd thought you would live forever. Now maybe you will."

I'm not sure I want that.

"How old is he?" Jax asked Will. "Did you ever figure it out?"

"Dad brought him home when I was two or three, and we've learned that he was in San Francisco for roughly three years before that. He's at least forty-five."

Jax tucked a finger under my chin and looked into my eyes. "He forgets the years you lived with me, doesn't he? Emperor, I was a baby when Finn brought him here and almost eighteen when you decided to stay. Those years happened to him even if they didn't happen to you."

"Huh. Indeed. He's in his sixties, then."

Aubrey sat next to Jax. "Our best friend has come back from the dead, and you're talking about how old Wick is."

"I'm still mad at him," Jax insisted.

"Stop being mad and I'll crack open the bottle of sixty-year-old scotch I was going to give you for your birthday," Drew said. "Keep being mad and I'll send it home with him."

"You're a bastard," Jax growled.

"We established that years ago." He was already reaching into the cabinet near the fireplace. "Still mad?"

"He thinks I'm a five-year-old," Jax said to me.

"Jax, I swear, I have never offered alcohol to a five-year-old."

"I hope not, at least not without feeding them first. We were promised dinner. What are we having?"

"Aubrey," Will said, still amused, "did he not get his nap today?"

"I put him down for one, but he was too excited to sleep."

Oz looked at Aisha and sighed. "Are you sure you want to sign on for this? They're never going to grow up."

Aisha grinned, but before she could answer, Jax set me on the coffee table and pushed up from the sofa. "I hope not. Growing up is overrated. It stinks. Come here, you glorious bastard. I want a hug. And then dinner. I'm hungry."

Will let Jax hug him hard, and he didn't flinch when Jax put his hands on his cheeks and told him he missed him, but when Jax kissed him full on the mouth, Will's eyes went wide and Drew nearly dropped the bottle of scotch.

"Jesus, Dad," Oz laughed.

"I'm making up for decades," he told Will. "Get over it."

They bickered through dinner; Jax sat at the head of the table and Will was at the corner near him, letting him pick at every quirk of Will's personality that he could. They were still picking on each other when Drew suggested we all go to the balcony to enjoy the night air and the scotch, but once they were settled in chairs opposite each other, both softened.

"I am happy tonight, Emperor," Jax said. "I hope my younger self appreciates that you're still there."

"I believe he does."

"You'll really tell him who you are? Because he wonders, you know. He spent a lot of time looking at you and then his father, trying to figure out the connection."

"He didn't cheat on your mother, Jax," Aubrey said.

"No, of course not. But I did fixate on what time period he came from. And I couldn't ask. I knew I couldn't ask."

"You could have," Will said. "I wouldn't have told you, but you could have asked."

"Fucker."

Aubrey slapped at his arm. "Jax!"

Does she still have the bad word list? Because that was number one.

"Yes, I do," she said when Will asked her for me. "Polite conversation is not too much to ask for."

"Eh, the kids are grown and none of the great grandkids are here right now, who cares?" He took a sip of his drink, laughing into the glass. "My father taught little Eli to swear in Scottish Gaelic. He called Drew a—" he fished for the words in his memory "—*bod ceann*, at least a dozen times before anyone else knew what he was saying."

Will snorted. He turned to Aisha and said, "Dickhead. Jax's father is a classy guy."

"You should have heard what he called you after your memorial service," Drew said. "The Queen was not amused."

"Hell," Oz said, "you should have heard what he called Finn. Oh my god, I thought they would come to blows."

That surprised Will. "Why?"

"Wick, at first," Jax said. "He blamed Finn for sending him into the portal. He was furious. We'd barely interred your stone, and he was shouting at Finn that he could have found another way to test whether he'd pushed the meteor away from the planet. Finn shouted right back, until my father screamed that he had the goddamned Old Mint. He could have used it."

"It was brutal," Drew said. "He hit the one nerve Finn hadn't protected, and he didn't realize it."

"Grandad reminded him that his grandfather had allowed Finn ongoing access to the Old Mint just for that, to protect the future and the people in it," Oz said softly. "And he railed at losing his son. He didn't care if Finn was your actual father, you were his second son."

Aisha reached for Will's arm, and her eyes were suddenly red.

"Finn," Jax said, "tried to explain that he was protecting the timeline as much as possible and that every piece of research they'd read that came out of the mint indicated that Wick was the one who would test their success. And Dad would have none of it. 'You could have changed the goddamned timeline for that boy,' he said. And he wasn't shouting anymore, he was crying."

"Eli turned around and walked out, and they never spoke again." Aubrey shook her head sadly. "They were friends, Will. But neither one could bear losing you."

"The Old Mint wouldn't have worked," Will said. "You leave in the same time frame you enter. It's not a portal. There's no magic door to open to look out to the other side."

Not everyone left San Francisco. People stayed behind.

"What's that, Wick?"

Someone who stayed behind could have gone into the Old Mint and told Finn that it worked. If they didn't show up then he would know it didn't.

"Surely Finn thought of that," Aubrey said. "There must have been a reason he didn't do it."

But Drew figured out the gates and Finn didn't. No one else did.

"People make mistakes," Will said, voice soft. "And we will never tell him this." He looked at Jax. "Neither version of him. Don't break his heart, please."

"Of course not," Jax said. "You're the bastard, not me."

"Aye, ya bod ceann," Will snorted.

"Fucker."

= = =

They stayed on the balcony until it was too cold for Aubrey and Jax was slowing down, taking long pauses when he spoke. Instead of going home, they decided to stay the night in the other guest room so that they could say goodbye to us in the morning.

To Will it felt like the nights they'd sat on the roof with the fire pit going, drinking cheap beer and expensive scotch, when the kids were old enough to put themselves to bed and they could stay up late into the night, ignoring how hard morning would be.

Before they went to bed, Will promised them he would come back; he'd already promised Finn and if they thought they were up to it, he wanted to see them again, too, and often. Aubrey asked him to examine the dates carefully; she wanted him to visit, but under no circumstances was he to come back when they die. "You're likely going to bury us one day as it is, and I know how hard it is to let go of your best friend. I don't want you to do that twice."

She made him promise. One memorial only, when their younger counterparts went. She made Aisha promise to hold him to it because he was the type to suck it up and say goodbye as many times as he could.

I didn't think he would break his promise.

He had already learned how hard it was to say goodbye to his mother and knew that he would do it again one day.

That was enough.

$$= = =$$

They sat on the window seat in Oz's room again, bathed in streetlight. They'd started to climb into bed, but Will decided to sit there for just a moment, which turned into an hour because he knew he wasn't going to be able to sleep. He urged her to go ahead and go to bed, but she wanted him to hold her, so they snuggled together and talked in hushed tones.

"After a little while, I think I forgot they were older," she said. "But sitting out on the balcony with them makes me miss all the time we should have had together. I hate it, but I'm really starting to resent those nights on the roof you had together, laughing until almost dawn. I miss something I never had."

"Those days aren't over. Hell, I suspect the best of them are yet to come. The kids are adults now, they'll probably join us. I have a feeling in a year or two, Oz and Drew will be a hell of a lot of fun and Zed and Jimmy won't be far behind."

"You already have a hell of a lot of fun with Drew," she chided lightly.

"Indeed." He let out a small sigh. "I think I'm going to convince Oz to move in with him so that I can move into her room. This view is magnificent."

She tilted her head back to kiss him. "I feel kind of bad that I'm not missing my son as much this time."

"You know he's safe with his father," Will said. "And you might have come to terms with how much time doesn't pass on the other side."

"Or maybe I'm finally doing nasty things with you, and for once I'm putting myself on the list ahead of everyone else. I refuse to feel bad about taking time to spend with you."

"Any time you want a night or two with me, but the timing is off, we can do this. We can pick another When, spend a day or two together, and then go home a minute after we left."

You could turn a nooner into a week long sweat-fest.

"As tempting as that is, I want to spend time in real life with you. We need to learn to navigate being together with jobs and families and figure out how to make time with each other a priority. Make plans. You're not a flight risk. I think I can talk about next year, or the year after that, without you freaking out that I'm suffocating you."

"I think I might be breathing easy for the first time in my life. Why would I give that up?"

"I worry. The more we learn about each other, the more secrets we share, those might become roadblocks."

"You know my biggest secrets," he said. "Any others I can readily think of happen to be state matters, and I won't ever be able to discuss them with you. I don't think I was ever a bedwetter, so that's not a secret. I don't have any embarrassing hobbies…unless you count the bedroom jammed full of books. Fair warning, that room has a particular and peculiar odor. Oh. I may or may not have an embarrassing reason about why I'm circumcised. That one may remain a secret."

"I wondered," she said, snickering. "I just assumed your parents were Jewish or something."

"Definitely 'or something.' They're atheists, but that's not a secret."

"I may have one or two," she said quietly, hesitating as if she wanted to tell him.

"You'll tell me when the time is right. And unless the secret is a husband you keep hidden in a closet at home, I don't see an issue." When she didn't answer right away, he said, "That's it, isn't it? You have a husband named Troy living in the basement, and he's six-foot-seven with muscles that have their own postal code. In order to win your heart forever, I have to engage in a ritual battle requiring oil and wrestling."

She laughed lightly. "You know me so well."

"I'll do it, you know."

She reached a hand over her shoulder to touch his face. "So would I."

I thought they were going to fall asleep sitting up, stuck to the window. She closed her eyes and pulled his arms around her a little tighter, and her breathing slowed almost to the point where I was going to tell Will he needed to carry her to the bed. He took a deep breath then, and her eyes opened.

"I learned something in talking to my mother today," he said. "Something that might matter to you."

"*She* has a husband named Troy hidden in a basement? I get to wrestle him?"

"You would enjoy that perhaps a bit too much. But, no. And I ask you for honesty, because no answer you give will be wrong." When she turned toward him, he asked, "Had I not told you that I should never reproduce, would you want another child?"

The question gave her pause; she had never seriously considered having more kids because Jimmy was enough, but being with Will changed everything. "I would have another if you wanted one. If we're together in six months and still planning a future…ask me again. If you think you want a child of your own, my god, Will, ask me."

"If we're not still together in six months, I'll be heartbroken."

"No more broken hearts. You're stuck with me, for no reason other than I want to sit on the roof with you and Jax and Aubrey when we're ninety, and laugh about all the stupid things we've done."

"Jax's list alone could take until then."

"Sweetie, if we do decide to have a child together, don't be surprised if I ask you to curb the time travel. I get that you might have to do it for work, if there's a life to be saved or a blip in time to be fixed, but random trips for no reason other than to go? I'm not sure it's worth the risk."

"I could be convinced to stay put."

"Do you ever just go somewhere for the hell of it?"

He told her about taking me to sit on a bench near the Ferry Building, where we watched the crowds while he complained about wasted resources. "I don't do it often, but it's a way I can center himself, and a way I can remember why I appreciate my adopted When. I don't, however, ache for it. It's something I can do or not."

That you know of.

She surmised that she could become comfortable with it, but she wanted to put it out there. "Having a child changes everything, and if I'm going to do it, I want a present and engaged partner."

"I don't want you to feel pressured. I had all of the benefits and few of the drawbacks when Oz and Zed were younger. Don't think that if you don't want another child you're keeping me from experiencing fatherhood. Being an uncle was enough. And those kids would warn you, I can be somewhat stern."

"Will, I'm a teacher. Those kids would warn you that I'm *very* stern. We could warp a kid."

You would be a pushover. You're only stern when you're the Emperor. Daddy would melt at the first tear.

"You may be right, Wick. Oz certainly got out of a lot of trouble by batting those eyelashes at me and Zed's ability to cry on command worked quite well. But otherwise, yes, I am…mean."

"You are not."

"I'm mean enough to tell you that you need to get some sleep. It's late, and we'll be expected for breakfast. Aubrey will have no problem throwing the door open and hauling us out of bed."

I'd like to see that.

She grabbed his hand and pulled him off the window seat. "You're not sitting here all night. At least crawl into bed with me for a while."

"I would, but you might take advantage of me. And then what would people say?"

Forget people. Think about me.

"Emperor, I am definitely taking advantage of you."

He stopped just short of the bed. "You truly do need to sleep. And we'll return home just a minute after we left—we have the rest of the day together. We can hide in my apartment if you want. You can teach me nasty things."

She liked the idea, but thought that if Jax and Aubrey weren't busy, perhaps they might be up for an evening on the roof. "Just a couple of hours with friends. I've missed you all for so long—"

Before she could get choked up, he said he would call Aubrey.

"And your mother," she reminded him. "You promised."

"I did. I know. And I will eventually, but I need to compose my thoughts before approaching her." He didn't think he could tell her he was with her when she died in another When, nor that he knew everything. She needed to be honest with him first, but he didn't know if that was being overly passive aggressive or not, and he didn't know how to bring it up without saying more than he should. "I am fairly skilled at manipulation, and I could force her to admit her deliberate withholding of that information, but…"

"Sweetie, at the risk of comparing you to a sixteen-year-old— if Jimmy were coming to me, I would want him to trust in the truth enough to lead with it." He didn't have to tell her that he knew everything, but he could tell her about finding the paperwork in the lab, all the data she'd collected running scans on his brain, and some of the conclusions she came to. Then give her the chance to open up.

"And if she doesn't come forth with the truth? I can forgive her for what she did when I was a boy because I somewhat understand it, but if she continues to hold that line and uses it to attempt to pull me away from you? It would destroy my relationship with her."

"You have the ace up your sleeve, Will. If it comes down to it, tell her about this visit. Let her know her anguish in the end. I swear to you, if I thought I was hurting my son and pushing him away, I'd do anything to fix it. There's nothing more important to her than you and your father."

He knew that but wasn't sure she could let go enough to welcome the idea that he was about to choose another woman over her. Until a couple of weeks ago, she was the number one woman in his life, a step or two ahead of Oz and Aubrey. She could see the shadow forming; if she made him choose, she would lose.

Aisha reminded him about the picture on Jo's desk, the rocket ship he drew; Jo knew she would lose him a long time ago, and was probably just grateful to have him back no matter what. "I know that one day Jimmy will bring someone home, and it will be *the* person, and I'll have to step aside. I'll be happy for him, Will. That's all a mother wants."

"You're a mother who has had her son all along," he pointed out. "And until it happens, how can you know for sure? Jimmy might bring home this tall, beautiful blonde with giant breasts and sharp fingernails, and you'll hate her on sight. You certainly won't want to know what they're doing together."

"Not likely," she snorted. "Zed is more his type."

"Does Zed know that?"

"I think he does, but Jimmy has never felt like that about Zed. Zed is to Jimmy what Aubrey is to you. There's a lot of love, but no attraction."

"I promise you," Will said, "Zed is not secretly Jimmy's great, great grandmother. I've met that woman, and she had considerably more facial hair."

That made her laugh, and she kissed him, long enough that I felt like I needed to attack whatever was twitching under the sheet.

"What the hell, Wick?"

Someone had to kill it.

"Wick, sweetie," Aisha said, "you might want to go curl up on the window seat. I'm going to do things to him now."

"I will survive an unintended erection. You need to go to sleep."

"Ten minutes won't make a difference."

"I think ten minutes is unrealistic, even for someone as inexperienced as I am."

Her hand slipped under the sheet. "Trust me."

Great. He's learned to grope.

7

Oz and Drew—the younger—were sitting on the bench near the portal when we came back. Drew was hunched over with his head in his hands and Oz was rubbing his back, oblivious to our arrival. Will stepped over and grunted, "Scoot," and then he sat down, hard.

He'd been fine all morning; it wasn't even all that difficult to say goodbye because he promised to return soon and old Oz and Drew had picked a date and time when they would attempt to go through the portal, hopefully landing in this When.

Will was sure they would wind up here; he thought that their timeline erased as ours progressed, but he couldn't promise them. They picked a date to meet on Union Square, Will let them hug everyone and kiss him, and we left.

There was no real fuss.

Once we were home, though, he turned to Aisha, his face pale, and said, "I have to sit down."

Oz had barely made space for him when he sat. Aisha crouched in front of him, her hands on his thighs, and whispered that it was all right. He closed his eyes and leaned back, breathing with deliberation, trying not to cry.

She's still here, dude. You can go see her.

"I did see you," he said without opening his eyes. "Jax and Aubrey, as well. My father. They all know that I lived."

"What about your mom?" Drew asked. He'd barely looked up and didn't notice the pain Will was in.

I stretched to see his face; his eyelashes were moist, and a tear was trying to squeeze its way out. Aisha rubbed his leg gently, and said, "He spent an afternoon with her, but it was right at the end. She went in his arms."

"Jesus, Will," Drew said. "I'm sorry. I didn't even think—"

"It's all right," Will managed to say. He took a deep breath and then opened his eyes. "I needed to be there for her. And other than that, it was a fairly nice couple of days."

"You were gone two days?" Drew sputtered. "Damn, time really is kind of trippy."

"Indeed." He took another deep breath and got up, indicating for them to stand up as well. "You already know this, but I'm saying it anyway. I love you. Both of you." Before they could say anything, he looked at Drew and added, "I hated that the Andrew I just left never truly knew how much I loved him. And yet, when I was dying, he took care of me. You both did, without knowing who I was." He hugged and kissed them both, Oz first and then Drew, and held Drew especially hard. "For all the times I terrified you when you were a boy…well, I'm not sorry, not really. But I do wish we'd spent better time together when you were younger, and I wish I had let you know I loved you."

"It's okay, we'll make up for it," Drew said.

"I know. And I also know that there are things that aren't worth fighting about." He looked right at Oz. "Grace Cathedral. You won't be able to get married as soon as you'd like, but it will be as private as you choose, as small as you want, and isn't out in the open which will ease your parents' worries. It doesn't have to be a religious ceremony, but it's an appropriate venue for a princess and will satisfy your worry about the peoples' expectations. They don't anticipate an open, public wedding, but it can still be broadcast and will be beautiful. You both *deserve* that. Spend the money, and celebrate."

They both looked dumbfounded.

"Yes, it's a lot of money," Will said. "But it's not an unreasonable expense. You are worth it, I promise you."

"Grace Cathedral would definitely make Mom happy," Oz said.

"It will make them both happy. Now go tell them, and also tell your father to fuel the fire pit, because we're all having drinks on the roof tonight." Before they could turn around, he added, "And ask your mother to please not invite my parents. I'll explain later."

As they walked away, Aisha slid as close to Will as she could get; I jumped to the ground where I could see them both, and watched how Will practically melted into her; he didn't flinch when she set her hand on his leg and rubbed his thigh, when a week ago it would have made him twitch. She kissed his shoulder even though he probably wouldn't feel it through his shirt. Then she slid her arm behind him, onto his shoulders and kissed his cheek, and rested her forehead against his head. This felt like the quiet sadness between Jax and Aubrey, before the First Minister of Florida came to Pacifica to pee on everyone's happiness. She was trying to heal him and to make him feel better.

It caught me by surprise. Will was comfortable and the moment felt intimate, something I'd never thought he could handle, not even when he learned to touch without listening. This was more than bouncy things.

I jumped back onto Will's lap and stood on my back legs to sniff at their faces. I had just finished sniffing Aisha's chin when I heard the first click.

I hear an old camera. Click, click, click. Like that.

"We're being photographed," he told Aisha. "Wick can hear the camera. I should have warned you about this—people used to be quite a bit more considerate about the privacy of the royal family, but lately…"

Now they're clicky little douchebags.

"I saw the pictures of Jax and Aubrey on the balcony last year. It surprised me. The gossip sites are one thing, but that was intrusive."

"Very," Will agreed. "It was the norm until the old king mandated privacy for his wife and son. Apparently, the so-called journalists have decided that the mandate is over. Anything taking place where the public can see is evidently fair game."

She didn't think she'd mind having pictures taken with him. "I'll caution Jimmy, though. And hey, what a way to get him to behave in public."

"You'd think. But last September, right there on the steps—" he pointed across the Square "—I found Oz peeking into Drew's pants. Granted, he only had the waistband rolled down a couple of inches, but from the right angle?"

She laughed. "Why was she looking into his pants?"

"He'd gotten a contraceptive implant before he left Chicago and had just told her. At the time, she was trying to wrestle him into bed and oddly, he was resisting. But he was certainly prepared for the inevitable."

"And he convinced you to be proactive."

"I'm not sure it would have occurred to me. No matter how badly I wanted to be with you, I wasn't sure it would ever happen."

"No regrets?"

He laughed softly. "My only regret would be if you decided this wasn't working. At least before I didn't really know what I was missing."

"There are other women in the world, Emperor, and I know personally of a dozen who would do anything you wanted."

He set me on the bench and got up, reaching for her hand. "I can't imagine wanting to be with anyone else."

"Well, no pressure there." She looped her arms around his neck, pulled him closer, and told him if whoever was out there wanted a picture, then they were getting a picture, and kissed him.

Keep that up and they're going to get way more in the picture than they thought.

Will pulled away a little, and said that I was right. "Tight pants, hot you…I'd rather that not make it into tonight's entertainment news."

I'll distract you. We're hungry, right? Can we go to the place with the lady who gives me meaty bites, even if I have to sit in a high chair?

"I could eat. Wick's taking us out for lunch. He's even paying."

Sure. Take it out of my allowance.

As he took her hand, he mused it might be the closest thing to a normal date that they'd had. No portals, no other people.

I could go home and let you be alone. It's not too far for me to walk by myself.

"You're coming with us," Will said. "We'll be in public, and might need adult supervision."

8

The fire pit was already going when we got to the roof. Jax had fired up the grill and had a cooler filled with dead delicious things he was going to cook, and another cooler filled with drinks. He and Aubrey sat in chairs next to each other with their bare feet on the lip of the fire pit; they were tapping each other's toes, laughing at how stupid it was.

I bolted across the grass and leaped into Jax's lap so that I could give him a good head bonk, and then went to Aubrey to do the same thing.

"He's just seen you thirty years older," Will said, "and he's happy to see you young again."

"I don't feel young," Jax snorted. "And what the hell did you say to my daughter? We've gone from arguing over where the wedding would be to knowing for sure and OH MY GOD we have to make a list of guests and what are our colors going to be and OH MY GOD do we do a formal reception or just have a party and OH MY GOD is it too tacky if we serve pizza?"

"Don't make fun of them," Aubrey said, though she was as amused as he was.

"I hope I didn't overstep," Will said. "They weren't making any progress on their own and were getting terribly irritated with one another."

"We're grateful," Aubrey said. "The cathedral wasn't something I wanted to push Oz toward, but I'm thrilled she's excited about it."

"Will gets to pay for it," Jax grunted.

Aubrey tapped his foot with hers. "Hush. You're not paying for it either. And even if you were, they're not going to be able to get the cathedral as soon as they like, so you'd have time to save for it."

"You can't play the royalty card?" Aisha asked.

"We could, but they won't," Jax answered. "Doing that might push someone else's wedding off the calendar."

"And we need time to plan. A roof-top wedding we could have thrown together in a week, but if they're marrying in the cathedral, then we're doing it right."

They still wanted a small wedding with no dignitaries beyond those who had kids they were close to—meaning the Governor of Texas and the daughter of Japan's Prime Minister—and the reception could be held in one of the nearby hotel conference rooms. They didn't want stuffy and traditional, they wanted fun and a party, and that's what Aubrey wanted to give them.

Jax decided he was a little jealous. "We were kind of forced into doing what my mother wanted and invited the people she thought were appropriate. I don't remember being asked my opinion."

"You didn't care," Will said. "You just wanted to get to the wedding night."

He grinned.

"Sweetheart, it was wonderful, and no matter what you think, your mother went out of her way to make sure it was special," Aubrey said. "She knew who my father was even if I didn't admit it outright. She might not have liked me at first, but once she accepted that we were getting married? She worked hard to give me the fairy tale wedding, Jackson. She included all the things I didn't even know I wanted."

"Even the horse-drawn carriages? That was just odd."

She thought it was touching, even if impractical. "But when we plan Oz's, she'll make her own decisions. I'm not going to force her into the whole princess theme. That's just not her."

"Our daughter will walk down the aisle in that neon red tuxedo, won't she? With matching sneakers. There won't be a wedding march. There will be early twenty-first-century rock music, and she's going to dance down the aisle and make me dance with her."

The idea made them all laugh, and Will surmised that would be like Oz, and it would be right.

"What about your wedding?" Aubrey asked Aisha. "Big or small?"

"Tiny. James and I got married at three in the morning by a drunken drag queen in a chapel just off the Strip in Las Vegas. It was fun and surreal and spur of the moment. No regrets about doing it that way, but oh my god, the hangover."

"Royal regret," Jax mused. "Not being able to go to Vegas and really enjoy it. A couple of really weird nights without having to be me would be fun."

"I know the city," Aisha said. "Say the word, and I'll make sure you have the time of your life."

"I'd still be me. I wouldn't be able to do a damned thing without drawing a crowd or making the news. I could spend five minutes in a casino, and the next newscast would speculate about a gambling problem. If Aubrey wasn't there and I so much as glanced at a woman walking by, the gossip sites would tell the world I'd hired a stable of hookers. One for each guard and five for myself."

"What the hell would you do with five women?" Will asked.

"Curl up in a ball and whimper a lot, I imagine."

"It would be fun," Aubrey said. "But no, we wouldn't be able to get away with it."

Will had a notion. "You can, if you're willing to use a portal again, Aubrey. We go back to its heyday, somewhere in the early twenty-first century when it was loud and insane, and no one will look at you twice. And I swear, we'll keep him off you. No coming back knocked up again."

"Oh, god, if I got pregnant now. Shoot me. I turn fifty years old this year, I am not having more children." She play-glared at Jax. "I am at least five years past the age I would have even considered it. If you want to go…you're getting fixed first." To Will, "Unless you plan on sleeping with us, you're not keeping him off me. I swear, he goes through a portal and it's like this horny little switch gets flipped."

Jax grinned. "Hey, new place, new atmosphere, new fun. Yeah, don't ever ask what happens when I go through portals alone with Will."

"You wish," Will grunted.

Aisha patted Will's arm and said, "Well, that certainly explains a few things."

Jax nearly choked on his beer. "Wait, what?"

"She went with me, and we spent a couple of nights away. What more do you need to know?"

"I need to know if you finally pulled the stick out of your ass and got yourself laid."

Instead of tapping his foot with hers, Aubrey kicked him. "Jax!"

"Oh, like you didn't want to ask the same thing."

Aisha raised an eyebrow and looked at them over the rim of her cup. Will sighed and said, "This is going to sound like I'm fourteen years old, but…please don't tell my parents. I'm not willing to get into it with them right now. My mother—"

"It's about fucking time," Jax said.

He swung his legs out of the way before Aubrey could kick him again.

"What? I'm not telling his parents." He pointed at Will. "But only because you didn't tell mine. I owe you."

"If we go by that, you owe me two years' worth of excuses and alibis."

"Eh, fourteen, maybe fifteen months," Jax countered. "We weren't actually sleeping together the whole time."

"I'm sure there was very little sleeping going on, regardless." Will looked at Aisha. "Remember lying to the King? He stomped into the Ferry building and you swore that Jax had left us just two or three minutes earlier, while I texted him to get his ass home. You were very convincing."

She laughed. "Except I don't think he believed me."

"My dad only went looking for me to appease my mother," Jax said. "As long as Will could contact me and get me home in time, he didn't care. Hell, I think he half approved."

"Only because you were finally settled with one woman," Aubrey said. "He was tired of keeping track of your string of little sluts."

"Ouch."

"Oh, stop. You were a little man whore and you know it."

"Hey. I never once got paid."

"And that makes it so much better."

Oz and Drew are coming out. I hear them on the stairs.

"Offspring in ten seconds," Will said. "You can chide him for his whorish ways later."

"And don't think she won't," Jax chuckled. He reached into the cooler and pulled out two bottles, a root beer for Drew and a beer for Oz. "If you're old enough to get married, you're old enough for a beer."

"My dad, bad ass law breaker," Oz said as she took the bottle.

"Only one, and only when you're with me, your mother, or Will. You can have the beer, or if you prefer, I have a bottle of forty-year-old scotch, and we're opening it tonight."

She handed the bottle back. "I'm not stupid. I'll hold out for the scotch."

"It won't go down as easy as the cinnamon whiskey," Will warned. "I may have gotten them a little bit drunk last night, Jax."

"Drew was drunk," Oz said. "I was just warm and happy."

"You had a nice buzz going," Aisha snorted.

Before Jax could get mad, Aubrey told him she was consulted before the first drink was poured. "I consented to a couple of drinks and he held her to that."

"Well, I held Oz to it. I kept pouring for Drew when he wasn't looking."

"Did you tell him about your trip?" Drew asked, deflecting. "I mean, we kinda told them but we didn't have the details."

"Only in vague terms," Will answered. "And perhaps tonight is not the time."

Jax wanted more. "Do I ever learn who the hell you really are?"

Oh, he's asking and you promised to tell him. Old Jax made you promise.

"Come on, Will. Do you know how many times my father was asked if you were actually his son? You look more like him than I do. And Oz…she looks like her mother but she damn well has your eyes. I'm just hoping that you tell me how we're related before I die."

Oz and Drew looked away, and Aubrey reached for Jax's hand. "You don't need to keep secrets anymore, William."

Jax was a mix of surprised and upset. "What, he's already told you?"

She reminded him that she accidentally touched his face when he was young and startled. "I learned more than he realized, I'm afraid." She looked to Will. "The details didn't matter. It broke my heart that you were so lonely all the time, and filled with so much anger. But I don't feel that in you anymore."

He held his hand out to her. "Set your hand on mine."

They sat like that for a moment, until she slowly pulled her hand away. "I'm sorry. I thought the anger was gone. And you need to deal with your mother before it destroys your relationship. You know why she did it, William. Give her the chance to explain why she didn't tell you later."

He explained to Jax, "My mother was fully aware when I was very young that I could learn to control what happens when I touch people. She knew and deliberately withheld that from me. Worse, she's been feeding the lie. If I'd never given Oz my memories—" He looked at Oz. "I am still sorry I placed that burden on you, but truthfully, had I not, I would still be recoiling from even the chance that I might touch someone."

Aubrey said gently, "William, your mother can see that you're in control. Why rock the boat?"

"Because I'm owed the truth. And it goes beyond that. When we were shooting pool last night? She specifically warned me that this—" he gestured to Aisha and then himself "—should never happen. She has my father believing she wants this for me, but to my face?"

Drew, quietly, "Better to ask forgiveness than permission. Don't let her get in your way, Will. It's like Carter and the army—he joined up, got in too deep for my parents to interfere, and once they knew, they accepted it. He did it because he knew it was the best thing for him, and they can't argue with the results. She won't either, once she sees how happy you are together."

Will didn't think it was that simple, nor should she be let off the hook. Aisha didn't think he should burn that particular bridge. Aubrey added, "Listen to the mothers here. If my kids held my feet to the fire for every horrible decision I made for them, I'd never walk again."

Oz protested that. "Stop. You're a damned good mother."

"And regretfully," Will said, "As much as I love her, my mother often was not."

"The world was about to end," Jax reminded him. "She was trying to save it."

He sighed and asked both Aubrey and Aisha, "If the world was about to end, where would you be? In a lab compiling data and teaching young scientists, or with your children?" He pointed out that his father did ninety percent of the work, and she kept Will isolated on a level of the lab while she bounced between her work and teaching him, and often his only time out was for karate. From birth to pre-school, he was in the lab or at home and didn't think he saw another child until he began training in karate. "I spent my life with adults, learning from them, studying with them, fighting with them. But from age six or seven, I don't feel like I was parented much, and perhaps it's wrong, but—"

"You resent it," Aubrey said. "And you resent her attempts to pick up where she left off."

Will nodded. "She's not trying to pick up with the seventeen-year-old who left home. She's trying to pick up with the seven-year-old who was suddenly in the way because he couldn't handle being around other children. But she knew by then, she *knew* she could teach me to control the things they were afraid of. You never would have kept that from Oz or Zed. Hell, you helped them deal with their own differences when they became apparent. You taught them to treasure those things."

"Differences," Oz snorted. "That's a nice way to say it."

"All right. Zed calls them gifts, and he's right. I would love to see the world through your eyes, Oz. And you have to admit that your parents made sure you were comfortable with it, and how normal you really are."

Jax, amused, "I'm not sure I'd call either of them normal. I mean, you did have a large role in raising them." Then he realized Will never said who he was. "You distracted me, dammit. Who the hell are you?"

Will leaned forward, elbows on his knees. "Be very sure you want to know. Be very sure you *can* know, and not change how you see me or how you treat me."

"No matter what, you're still my brother, and I will still give you all kinds of hell anytime I can."

Will looked at Drew. "You tell him."

Drew hesitated and glanced at Oz first. "Will is our great grandson. Oz's and mine, I mean. Not, like, yours and mine or… anything."

Jax sat stunned for a moment, then sputtered, "Are you fucking kidding me? You're my great, great grandson? How? You won't be born for nearly two hundred years. There has to be more than a couple of generations between us."

Oz reminded him of time travel, and Drew chimed in, "It gets complicated."

Jax pointed at Drew with his beer bottle. "I swear to God, if you're not married before she's pregnant and this whole weird family dynamic starts, I will string you up by your balls."

Drew crossed his legs. "Ow. That's mean."

"These two are still together thirty years from now," Jax sighed. "You're not violating some huge temporal law by telling me that?"

"Their history is not necessarily our future," Will explained. "I changed it first by creating the gate that sent my father home, and then by living. Anything I know is no longer valid."

"But I'll still be with Oz, right?" Drew asked.

"That's up to the two of you. But I have no doubt."

"Neither do I," Jax admitted. "And to that…stop pretending. No more sneaking around. I know you spend most nights in his apartment, Oz. Stop trying to hide it from me."

"Mr. B, I promised to not shove it in your face," Drew said.

"And I appreciate that. That said, I also don't want you two formally living together. Spend a night in your own bed every now and then," he said to Oz. "But I'm all right with your relationship as it is now."

"Because you can't stop it," Oz snorted.

"Well, there's that." He took a deep breath. "But I swear to God, Drew, if you don't finish school and if she gets pregnant before the wedding—"

"You'll love that baby no matter what," Aubrey said, touching her foot to his. "You're a softy, Jax. You might as well get used to the idea."

"I am not soft," he protested. "My daughter just proclaimed me to be a bad ass law breaker. We'll go with that."

"Of course we will," Aubrey said. "Now go be a bad ass grill master and throw the burgers on. Will will help."

Jax got up and grunted, "You can hold my meat for me."

"I will not."

Aubrey sighed. "The one thing I could count on was Will's maturity overriding Jax's," she said to Aisha. "Now you've taken it away from me."

"Sorry," Aisha laughed. "Not sorry."

= = =

Later, after everyone had eaten and I'd scored bites from each burger he'd grilled, Jax pulled his phone out, glanced at it, and told Will he needed to speak with him. They went over to the bench where the wall dipped a few inches for a view of Union Square, and as he sat, Will said, "They think you had something official to discuss, but you really just want to grill me about Aisha, don't you?"

Don't grill her. She might be delicious but she's not food, you know.

"Hell, yes. I'm nosy and it's not often someone my age gets laid for the first time. So, when, after we shot pool and you fought with your mother?"

"Before. We almost didn't come."

"Well, yeah, seeing as how it was with you, I'm sure she didn't."

Someone go tell her to stay away from the grill. You know she's not meat, right?

"Very funny. What I meant was that had I not been so hungry, we would not have shown up. And yes, she damn well did."

"You fucking have food in your apartment, Will. One text message telling me you were busy would have been enough."

"She insisted. I was in no frame of mind to tell her no. To anything."

"Worth the two-decade wait?"

"Considering I never expected..." He swallowed hard. "We should have had that time together, Jax. We could have. It was worth it, but goddammit. I could have been with her twenty-five years ago."

"It was a shitty thing for Jo to do," Jax said.

Will didn't know what he was going to do, other than avoid her for a while. "If I confront her now?" He shook his head. "I'm typically far better with conflict, but I honestly don't know what to do."

"Aisha knows all?"

Will told him they talked about it, and she thought she understood why Jo did it in the first place, but there was no excuse, not really. "Even knowing how little time I had, we could have had a life, Jax. Everything that she wanted? It was possible. I wouldn't have been willing to father a child, but we could have used a donor. We could have adopted. We could have had a family."

"Look at the bigger picture," Jax said. "You were a bit of an asshole back then. Full of yourself and never wrong. You were also too busy parenting me and keeping me out of trouble, I realize that now. But honestly? If you two had hooked up back then, I don't think you'd still be together. There's no way that woman would have tolerated your arrogant bullshit. Same way she won't tolerate it now, so don't fuck it up."

He's right. You were a tool sometimes.

"Allow me to indulge my anger." He told Jax about being with the future Jo as she died, what she said about why he was the way he was. "Two weeks ago, a child of my own was off the table. Now?"

"That's big. Have you talked to Aisha about it?"

"She told me to bring it up again in six months. I like the idea, but her son is almost seventeen and that much time between kids?"

"You could raise yours along with the grandkids I am apparently getting."

"Don't ask me when or how many," Will said. "I was serious when I said nothing I know of your future applies now. I'm about to throw an even bigger wrench into it soon. Drew and I are going into business, and that was never a remote possibility for the man I saw just a few hours ago."

"Business," Jax grunted. "I want that boy to finish school and get his degree, Will."

"He will. A degree is an implicit condition of this venture. He understands that. Having this also fulfills his wish for employment. You both win."

"You're paying him?"

"This isn't busywork, Jax. We'll secure the necessary licenses, lease appropriate workspace, purchase the equipment, and apply for grants under the business name so that we don't incur accusations of favoritism."

"This business won't interfere with your current duties?"

"I am first and foremost at your beck and call. This will be no different than the hours I spent tinkering in my workshop."

Tinkering. Is that what we're calling it now?

Someone warn Finn to never shine a black light down there.

"All right. Anything you need from me?"

"For now, refrain from mentioning it to my father. We'll essentially be competitors. I'm not sure how well he'd take that, especially if he knew that I think he's on the wrong track, and that I'll beat him to it."

"You have the answer to the transporter?"

"I know where he's going wrong," Will said. "He tends to focus on the end game and often fails to see the bigger picture. The gates he built, for instance. He knew how they would work, but he counted on them to contain a mass large enough to destroy the planet. He failed to account for failure. Andrew, on the other hand, when presented with even a notion of how they functioned, saw the bigger picture. He accounted for the possibility of failure, and visualized the gates pushing the meteor away from earth."

"So you send him to school to learn physics, and take over?"

"I understand the physics," Will said. "He's changing his major to computer science. We're building the system that—in his words—could change the world. Along the way, we'll work on the transporter issue and half a dozen other things."

"I still don't understand why Finn is having trouble with it. He can move from where he's at to his ship. Those gates transported the meteor, didn't they? Why isn't it that simple?" When he realized

Will was fighting a grin, he said, "That's basically it, isn't it? He's trying to complicate something he already made simple."

"Essentially."

"And you can't just tell him that?"

"I could. I could spoon feed him every step of the way, and he would resent it. He'll eventually get there, Jax. He'll come up with a way to transport large items across long distances without the use of transponders. Drew and I will focus on personal transporters. Moving people. And I'll get there first."

"How long will it take him?" Jax asked. "You already know."

"I know that in another timeline, it took several years, and he used it to transport a bomb to Florida that ended the war. Since he's not under the same pressure to deliver, I would expect it to take him even longer."

"You're going to piss him off, Will."

"Perhaps. Initially, all he needs to know is that Drew is focusing on building a holographic computer system. He knows Drew is interested in that, and won't think twice. He doesn't need to know that we'll have more than one iron in the fire."

"Boy, you're just itching to have it out with both of your parents."

"I didn't get to rebel much when I was a teenager. It's about time."

I hear people on the stairs. Boys. They're laughing.

Will got up to meet them at the door—no one else was expected, and he wanted to get between them and the family—but it slammed open before he could get to it and Zed ran out with Jimmy on his heels. They were out of breath and sweaty, and Zed started jumping up and down with his fists raised, claiming victory.

"That's a fucking lot of stairs," Jimmy huffed.

"You're just out of shape, loser," Zed said.

"You smelled the burgers, didn't you?" Jax said as he took his chair again. "I thought you two were staying at his Dad's until late."

"My dad sent me over to talk to my mom." Jimmy shrugged. "I wasn't allowed to call her because texting is for cowards and calling would be rude or something."

"Your dad said that?" Aisha asked, confused.

"George came home." He rolled his eyes. "Usual stuff."

She got up and guided him away from everyone else to talk to him. Zed watched them, and then said, "It's not secret stuff. His dad's boss offered him her Tahoe condo for the weekend and he wants to take us. And he knows a couple of guards would have to tag along. So, if it's okay with you…?"

Jax looked right at Will. "If I tell him yes, it counts against what I owe you."

"This is her weekend, Zed," Will said. "Don't get your hopes up that she'll be on board with it. She already gave up last night so that you two could play video games."

"God, you're an idiot," Jax muttered.

When Aisha came back, she asked if Zed had told them where they wanted to go. "It will just be James with the boys. His husband has other plans."

Jimmy muttered, "Thank God" under his breath.

"They plan on hiking and boating, and James understands about the guards."

"I'm fine if he goes if you are," Aubrey said to Jax.

Jax got up. "I'll go inform the guard. Someone is going to be very happy about his assignment this weekend."

Zed kissed Aubrey. "And I'm gonna pack a few things."

Jimmy hugged Aisha, but before he followed Zed, he bent over and whispered to Will, "I'll be back late Monday. Don't wear her out, all right?"

Will ignored Drew's laughter. He reached out for Aisha's hand as she sat back down. "You gave up your weekend."

"I did. And for more than you think. He gets three days with James that don't include George but do include Zed. He needs that more than I need to have him home where I can nag him about finding whatever it is in his room that smells like it died."

When Jax came back—he was sending two guards, Zed's favorites—he pulled the bottle of scotch out and filled several glasses with short shots. "You like it, you get more. You grimace, you don't."

"I'm going to grimace," Drew guessed.

Jax toasted Oz and Drew and Will and Aisha with, "To beginnings and reboots. I look forward to seeing what both will bring."

= = =

We stayed on the roof until it was too cold for the fire pit to be of any good, when Oz stood up and said she was freezing and she was dragging Drew downstairs to do things to her. Jax watched her drag Drew by the hand, until the door closed behind them, his mouth half open.

"You did tell her you were all right with this," Will reminded him.

"She's also toasted," Jax said. "Poor Drew."

"He owes her. Last night, that was him."

"She's not wrong," Aubrey said. "It is cold now. Smarter people would follow their lead."

"We be smart." Aisha got up and reached for Will's hand. "Come on. You can warm me up in front of your fireplace."

He didn't even wait for me. I had to chase after them, yelling as I ran that they better not mess up my rug again.

They did.

An hour later I was curled up on the hearth while he and Aisha sat on the floor. He leaned against the sofa and she was propped up against him, her back to his chest, head resting on his shoulder. Both were covered in sweat that was definitely dripping onto my rug.

Still, I didn't note him doing anything obviously stupid, unless you count all the noises people make when they bounce around. While they caught their breath and indulged in the afterglow, it occurred to me that pretty soon I wouldn't need to stick around to tell Will what to do. Aisha had no problem giving him directions and he was eager to do whatever she wanted.

But, I also thought I would miss this, after, when Will was more content than I'd ever seen him.

It wasn't even the bouncing parts that were making him so happy. They could not do those things at all; they could sit on the sofa with all their clothes on, snuggled up together, and he would still be calm and content. When Will nuzzled her neck, it occurred to me that for all his life, he'd been like a pond that someone tossed a pebble into, and it had been one ripple after another. Now suddenly the water was still, and he could just…be.

Aisha realized I was watching them and asked if they were bothering me.

No, I was just thinking. You're good for him.

"Indeed, Wick," Will said. "She is very good for me."

Also, I want a new rug. You've ruined it for me.

"The rug isn't ruined. I can wash it."

Fine. Tell her I think she has nice boobs.

"I will not."

No, say 'magnificent.'

"I will not."

"Are you arguing with him?" Aisha asked.

"It's been a daily occurrence lately. He keeps telling me things I know better than to translate."

"Ah. Like calling me hot chocolate?"

Everyone likes hot chocolate, don't they?

"He means well. That was a compliment. He finds you quite attractive."

Her boobs, too.

I think her boobs are magnificent.

"Seriously, Wick, what is your fascination with boobs?"

She laughed and moved his hands from her waist to her chest. "Really now. You don't know?"

"If you're trying to turn me on, I need about twenty minutes."

That's because you're old.

"Thanks to my ex, we have all night."

"Hm." He pushed her hair out of the way and kissed her right under her ear. "I'm only a tiny bit sorry that he asked you to give up your weekend with your son."

"I wouldn't be the least bit surprised if he decided to take the boys because of you." She turned her head to look at him. "If Jimmy told him about us, that would be very much like James. He gets absurdly excited at any chance I have to be happy. I honestly do think you'll like him."

"Then I look forward to meeting him. Perhaps when he brings the boys back. I'm fairly certain you and I will be required to pass muster with Jimmy."

"Oh?"

"He told me not to wear you out. I think he approves."

"I hope so, though I think we need to give him time, just to see how well he really takes this. His life is complicated as it is and I've always made an effort to keep my social life in the background, but I don't think I can do that anymore. I don't want to."

"I will do whatever is needed to make him comfortable."

She'd never intentionally tried to hide her social life from him, but it also never felt like a great idea to expose him to someone who wasn't likely to stick around. "It's not fair to let him get attached. But you? He can get attached. He's already attached, in a way. You've been on the periphery of his life for a while now."

"Regardless, I will protect his feelings as much as I can. If that means standing five feet away from you when he's near, so be it."

"You don't have to go that far. I just want to be careful with him. He has a lot to deal with, and I don't want this to be something that hurts him."

"And you don't want this to be something that ruins his friendship with Zed."

"Sweetie, you have no idea."

She wanted to tell him the things she hadn't been able to. Will gave her an out; if it was Jimmy's secret, then Jimmy needed to have a say in when or if he was told. "He hinted that there was something, and I promised him that whatever it was, it would not come between us."

"It shouldn't be a secret, but his stepfather is an ass and it's just been easier…"

She trailed off, and he reminded her, he wasn't entitled to Jimmy's secrets, not yet.

It was more than that. "At some point, you're going to meet his stepfather, and a little forewarning is probably in order."

"I am fairly adept at dealing with people of every temperament," he told her. "I can deal with an ass."

"That's just it. He can be very charming when he wants to be. Most of the time he's easy to be around, and he can make people laugh without much effort. Sometimes I can see how James fell for him, and I almost understand why he stays. But when George digs his heels in about something? No matter how wrong he is, he won't let go. He can be a bully and he has a temper, which is a horrible combination when there's a child involved."

"That's a horrible combination for anyone. It's abusive."

"Toss in a layer of overt bigotry, and you have the man who thinks he should shape my son's life into something he doesn't want and shouldn't have to deal with."

"Noted," Will said. "I will not allow any initial charm to fool me."

"Sweetheart, somehow I don't think many people fool you. I just wanted you to know, he's a major part of the problem, and as soon as I talk to Jimmy, I'll color between the lines. And yes, I am horrible with mixing metaphors."

"You teach math, not English."

"Numbers turn me on," she said. "Geometry, calculus…there's my porn, right there."

"I am quite adept at both," he said.

"Really." She put a hand on his chest and pushed him to the floor, and then sat on him. "Talk nerdy to me, Emperor."

My poor, abused rug.

Much more of that, and there would be no saving it.

PART 2

BECOMING DAEDALUS

9

Aisha's fourth-floor apartment was a spacious corner unit with giant windows that had wide, Wick-sized window sills and nice views from every spot in the living room. She had a clear view down the street, and at the end of it, if she squished her cheek against the window, she could see a few inches of the Bay Bridge. She preferred looking at the small park on the other side of the street, which required no contortions to see. There was a small playground with swings and slides and a large sandbox, and a walking path that wound through a splash of trees, up one small hill and down another, splitting the grass into four separate lawns.

During the day, the playground was filled with kids laughing and yelling at each other loud enough that she could hear, and in the evening couples strolled the border walkway, holding hands. In the six years she'd lived there, she'd seen three marriage proposals, including an unfortunate one from which the prospective bride ran, crying.

She always wondered what happened to that couple. Was it the place where he proposed? The way he asked? Had they only been seeing each other for five days and she realized he was a little bit creepy?

"I decided it was that last one. Crazy stalker date with attachment issues."

We were there so that she could get clean clothes for the rest of the weekend and not to stay. For that, I was grateful, because my food and litter boxes were back at the royal house and I didn't want to have to pee in the bathtub.

"Living here wasn't my first choice," she told Will, "but once I saw the big windows and the park, I decided James had chosen well.

Even if it did include George in the package."

He'd bought the apartment before she decided to move back to San Francisco to keep their son close to him. It was technically hers in lieu of child support, but he maintained the taxes and utilities, and all he asked in return was easy access to Jimmy.

"That's why this monstrosity is here," she said, gesturing to the odd wrought iron spiral staircase that took up the far end of her kitchen. "I keep the lock flipped and neither James nor George has the pass code, but it does mean Jimmy can see his father on a whim. We have our scheduled days and weekends, but it's not unusual for him to bounce between the apartments half a dozen times a day no matter whose weekend it is."

"Whatever works," Will said, though it was clear he found it odd.

"It works for Jimmy," she said. "I didn't say it works for me. Honestly, if James hadn't bought the apartment before we got here, we'd be living halfway across the city. I wanted James and Jimmy to be close, but not this close."

"I understand James' thinking. But this had to be hell on your social life."

"Not really. I don't bring men home, Will. That's a hard and fast rule. No men in the apartment, not if it gives him the impression that they might stay the night. Whatever James and George do is none of my business, but this is Jimmy's safe place. God knows he needs one."

"And I will endeavor to respect that," Will said.

"God, you're sexy when you get all stuffy on me," she teased. "Go on, either sit down or enjoy the view while I grab some clean clothes."

He was drawn to the wall that divided the living room from the dining room; it was waist high topped with frosted glass and had slick black shelves that went to the ceiling. At Will's eye level, there were a dozen framed pictures; almost all of them were of Jimmy at various ages, and Zed was in two of them, taken on the beach and at the park across the street. In the first, Jimmy and Zed were eleven or twelve and close to the same height; in the next, they were fifteen, and Zed was head and shoulders taller and looked like an adult in comparison.

The first photo in the lineup was a picture of a little boy in bright red shorts, a sliver of bare tummy sticking out from a yellow shirt that was splattered with drips of ice cream; one hand clutched a blue stuffed bear, the other had a death grip on a toy car. Will picked it up to look at it—the disheveled little boy with spiky hair made him grin—and from the back dropped several pictures of a smiling baby girl, and then an unhappy little girl in a purple dress with ribbons in her hair. Will was still looking at the photos when Aisha came back. I thought she was a little upset, but she covered it up quickly.

Will looked up and asked who the little girl was.

Dude, it's the same kid. The little girl, the little boy.

Will set the pictures down and looked again at the first one he was sure was Jimmy. "Ah. You did tell me his life was complicated."

She took one uncertain step toward him. "This doesn't bother you?"

"Why would it? Jimmy is Jimmy. This doesn't change anything."

"Not everyone understands."

"I'm not sure what requires understanding beyond the facts. I will admit, I'm curious about the particulars. Given his seemingly late adolescence, I'm guessing he hasn't fully transitioned?"

Her eyes moistened and tinged red. She plucked a picture off the shelf and then led him to the sofa, and when he sat next to her, she handed him the photo. "His birth name was Jaime. I don't think there was ever a time he didn't realize who he was. This—" she gestured to the picture of the girl in the purple dress "—was George's doing. He wanted a picture of 'our little girl' and took him out, alone, to have this taken. Poor Jimmy was traumatized. And after that? Temper tantrum after temper tantrum anytime he was presented with something even remotely considered to be for girls. Even toy soldiers. Those were dolls and George had told him dolls were for girls, and he wasn't having any of it. By the time he was four, James and I were talking with doctors, and when he was five—"

She took a deep breath, and Will waited. "There were signs and hints from the moment he could crawl, but the light bulb moment came when he was three. He and his friends discovered the bulb end of a turkey baster and did what kids do…they gave each other hickeys with it. It was funny, but I told him not to do that again because they were bruising each other. I took the bulb and put it away, and didn't think anything about it until a couple of days later, when James found him in the bathroom with it." She smiled wanly. "He was trying to use it—and I quote—to 'suck my penis out a-cause it hidin' in there.' He thought he was in trouble for playing with the turkey baster bulb again, which started a flood of tears that James had no idea how to handle. He dragged Jimmy out of the bathroom to tell me what was going on, and George had an absolute, insanely angry meltdown. He got down at Jimmy's level and told him it was time to stop the nonsense because he was a little girl and he needed to learn to act like it. Pretending to be a boy was just stupid, and it was ending right then and there."

"How hard did you hit George?" Will asked.

Tears slipped over her cheeks. "Oh, I wanted to. Jimmy's little fists were balled up and he *wailed* 'I'm a boy, I'm a boy, I'm a boy.' He was heartbroken and terrified and didn't understand why his stepfather was being so mean to him. But before George could get another word out, James picked Jimmy up, put him on his lap and promised everything was all right, of course he was a little boy, and asked him if he could take him for his very first big boy haircut. And then told him that afterward we'd both take him shopping for big boy clothes, just the three of us. George stomped out, and we didn't see him for three or four days."

"George was not on board?"

"Oh, that asshole *broke* the board. And because James and I were stupid beyond belief, George has third-parent rights, which means we *all* have to give written consent for major, non-emergency medical treatment. He'd die before he'd sign the papers. Which I am actually in favor of, even if it makes me a horrible person."

Will wanted to know how that had happened.

"Ignorance of the law," she said. "We were stupid. Did you know that Pacifica's third-parent charter states that if you present your spouse as your child's parent enough times, it becomes a legal issue? We didn't, and allowed George to deal with school matters as Jimmy's parent for too many years. We didn't object when he took

Jimmy to the ER for a broken finger when he was three and gave his consent for treatment, as Jimmy's parent. We let him enroll Jimmy in extracurricular programs at school, thinking it was a way they could get closer. Apparently, six times is the legal threshold. And we didn't know."

"George did, I presume?"

She nodded. "Oh, he knew. And when it came time to start planning a treatment protocol for Jimmy, he swore it would take the mother of all lawsuits to get him to agree to anything."

A lawsuit would drag through the courts for years. And without George's consent, the best options for Jimmy would never be available, because the closer to puberty he got, the less effective they would become. The easiest form of transitioning—essentially flipping his genetic code, leaving him with only one major surgical procedure—would likely never be available to him.

"So, we go about it old school. He started medications to delay puberty and prevent feminization early on, then began a very low dose of testosterone at fourteen. And, really, that was just to give him a sense of normalcy and a budding libido. Anything else will have to be done in multiple surgical procedures after he turns eighteen and doesn't need anyone's permission."

"That's insane," Will said. "Surely, George understands that Jimmy will transition later regardless of his wishes and that it will be far more painful if he waits."

"He doesn't care. And I know James loves him, but this?"

Will wanted to know how late into life the gene therapy would work.

"He has until he's all the way through puberty…which is why he's been on very low dose T. We're trying to buy him some time, but he's practically seventeen. By the time he's eighteen, it might be too late. Nineteen at the latest. And god, Will, if he has to wait for all the surgeries? The results aren't perfect, they're prohibitively expensive, and he would have to have artificial implants if he ever wanted a decent sex life. Donor transplants are iffy and generally only available to cancer and trauma patients. It's all hard enough that he's left the option open to not have surgery at all. He'd go on full doses of hormones, but he would still be biologically female.

He'd be miserable, but he grasps that someday he'll have to make that choice."

"That's hardly a choice," Will said thickly.

"I know. And yet, here we are. I don't know what to do, not without destroying his dad's life. I could sue, but George would drag it out in court until it's too late. In the end, Jimmy still has to wait, James loses his husband, and there's no telling what it would do to his relationship with his son."

"James is fully on board?" Will asked.

She sighed and scooted closer to him, wrapping her hand around his arm. "Sweetie, I know what you're thinking. That James wants to avoid the idea of Jimmy doing this, too. But he doesn't. He's just caught in the middle."

Lube him up and squeeze him out.

"You understand, I wield a bit of power in this kingdom?"

Aisha let go of his arm. "Will, I didn't tell you any of that to get you to interfere. I just wanted you to understand."

"I do understand. But if I can help Jimmy get what he clearly needs? Withholding treatment from him is cruel, and I can't for one moment understand why his stepfather is stonewalling."

"George can be very backward in some things, Will. If it doesn't fit his idea of normal, then it's wrong. He'll rally against it— no, he'll bully his way—until people just give up. I haven't given up, but I don't see a way around this and time is running out."

Bully him back.

"Then please, at least give me permission to speak with Jax. His word is law and so is his signature. If he signs a proxy allowing Jimmy to receive treatment, there's nothing George can do, other than bitch about it."

She was conflicted. Jimmy never wanted the King and Queen to know. Zed knew, but understood why Jimmy didn't want it to be public knowledge.

"Jax and Aubrey aren't the public. They've known him for years, and they care about him. It won't change how they see him, if that's what you're worried about."

"Of course, I worry about it. I *always* worry about it. It's a non-issue for people who don't have to deal with it, and most people don't seem to care when it doesn't touch their lives, but there are always those who think like George, and some of them are dangerous. My god, Will, school? He's always on edge, worried someone will find out, and kids can be total assholes about anyone even a little bit different. He's already picked on and teased for being small and for how high his voice is. Zed has been the only thing between him and getting beat up for being different. When Zed was with you last year? Jimmy's life was hell."

He acknowledged that kids could be cruel, but that didn't extend to Aubrey and Jax. "Jimmy is not unusual in their world, Aisha. And Jax is, arguably, responsible for the budget that keeps the treatment programs funded. His decision to do so is intentional, and by his own law, this is considered medically necessary treatment."

"Think it through, Will. Our sons have been best friends since sixth grade, and I not only hid from them all these years, I hid *this* from them. Zed is spending the weekend with someone who has, in spite of himself, a biologically female body. Zed is very much a hetero, curious male, and Jimmy just might be outright curious. How pissed could that make them?"

"They won't see him like that. And you may have hidden from them, but Jax has met James. Zed never would have stepped foot in this apartment if he hadn't."

He was trying to reassure her, but now she was crying and couldn't stop.

"This isn't even a progressive issue. I would expect George's reaction from someone raised in Florida, perhaps, where the masses still cling to misguided interpretations of the Bible and are only now coming to grips with the idea that men and women should be on equal footing. If Jax hears from you and from James that this is what your son needs, he'll sign as proxy and cut George out of it entirely. Neither he nor Aubrey will judge you for how you handled this. It's Jimmy's *life*. They'll understand."

She was crying hard enough that he sat back and put his arms around her, and waited until she was done.

She's been scared about this forever.
Half the reason she's crying is relief that you're not mad.
I don't know why you would be mad but she was afraid of it.

When he was sure she was done crying, he tilted her chin up and kissed her lips, and then her forehead. She still couldn't talk, so they sat quietly for a long time. When Will broke the silence, his voice as soft.

"When Zed was fourteen, he applied for a volunteer position at Alcatraz. He didn't ask for permission before he submitted the application. He wanted to know if he could get a foot in the door first, and decided the fallout would be worth it if he were accepted. It was, without a doubt, a major, life-changing position that he was pursuing. When Jax and Aubrey were notified—there wasn't a single person on that island willing to offer it to him without their consent—they discussed the enormity of what he would be doing and how it would affect him. Neither wanted to consent. He would be exposed to so much of the saddest parts of life and would have to deal with people on the cusp of the worst moments they would ever endure. But, it was his life, and for whatever reason, he was drawn to it. So they gave their permission. Zed never knew. He still doesn't. And he will never guess, not unless they one day choose for him to know."

"I'm not sure I understand the point, Will."

"As his parents, they made the decision, right or wrong, to allow him to set foot onto a path that would forever change his life and could fundamentally change *him*. Because they are his parents, they had the right to interfere. For the good of their son, they made the decision. You know Jimmy better than anyone and know he needs this. Nothing else matters. James can protect his marriage or not, but it's unfair for him to expect you and Jimmy to help him hold it together. Do whatever you need to do for your son, and risk being wrong. He never needs to know that you told me, or that I spoke with Jax. Not unless you want him to."

Her arms tightened around him.

"Give me permission to talk to Jax. If he doesn't feel comfortable signing the paperwork, he'll surely allow me to act as an official proxy."

She hesitated. "And if Jax refuses? What will that do to your relationship?"

"Nothing long term. We've disagreed over fundamentals before and gotten over it. We will again. I have to keep in mind that if he refuses, there's a legitimate reason I haven't considered. It won't be personal."

"Remind me of that. He's the King, it's not personal."

He also wanted to talk to Jimmy's doctor. The more information he had to give to Jax, the better. He wanted as many details as he could to justify the end result, which would probably be quite a bit more than Jimmy getting his surgery.

= = =

Three hours later, Will and Aisha were sitting in uncomfortable chairs near an overly-large mahogany desk that was cluttered with electronic tablets and synthetic, extremely personal body parts made from squishy stuff. The office was decorated in early funeral director, which felt like an odd choice for a doctor specializing in helping people sculpt their new bodies and new lives.

I alternated between Will's lap and Aisha's as I tried to get a better view of the entire space because something felt off and I couldn't put my paw on it. They weren't bothered by my rapid changing of seats because they were busy trying to distract themselves with small talk while they waited for Jimmy's doctor to arrive. Will tried to get her to think about going out to dinner; Aisha wanted to ponder whether the squishy things on the desk were molded from one of his patients.

Aisha left him a message shortly after Will convinced her there was nothing wrong with going behind George's back, and two minutes after that the doctor called her back. He was seeing patients and would be available after lunch; if this was the first move in getting on with Jimmy's treatment, he wanted to see her as soon as possible.

When I was done changing laps for the fifth time—right when Will caved into Aisha's idea of small talk and mused that if the squishy things were molded, then it was cold the day they had it done—I realized what felt odd. Every office I had been in, there were personal pictures all over the place. Kid's pictures, parents, vacation things, even pets. This doctor had only two, and they were cropped oddly, as if he'd tried to remove the background from each of them while leaving all the people.

There were few personal items in his office and little in the way of intentional decoration.

There are only two pictures in here.

"So?" Will said. "He's a minimalist."

They look weird.

He picked me up and went over to the shelf where the frames were. "Nothing odd about these, Wick, it's just—" He leaned closer, squinting. "He looks very familiar. Is this Jimmy's doctor?"

Aisha glanced up. "The man in the middle of both pictures. But he's not nearly so young anymore. Those photos have to have been taken thirty or forty years ago."

The door clicked behind her, and the doctor came in, chuckling. "Are you insinuating that I'm old?"

"I'm not insinuating anything." She got up and gestured to Will. "I hope you don't mind, but I brought someone along."

The doctor tilted his head a little to the left and grinned a bit, and Will just looked downright puzzled.

"I know you," Will said after a moment.

"It's been a very long time." He went over to the picture Will was looking at, at pointed at a spot near the top. "Splash Zone, just before they tore the sign down. Your father took this picture. You were maybe ten years old? I tried to throw you into a wave pool but you somehow hip-checked me and I wound up going in instead."

"Goddamn," Will breathed. "Mass. How long have you been here?"

The doctor—Brian Massimo—carefully skirted around Will, and dropped into the chair behind his desk with an *oof*. "Finn dropped me off here about a month before you popped up. Though technically you'd left home five or six years before that."

Will sat back down. "I had no idea."

"Well, that was the plan. Finn agreed to drop me here as long as I promised I wouldn't try to contact you. There are at least twenty others that I know of. All we had to agree to was to stay out of your way unless you found us first. No idea what he was worried about, but here we are." He looked at Aisha. "And you don't seem the least bit surprised."

"Nothing surprises me anymore. What, were you friends before?"

"I worked with his parents for a while, before Jo pushed me out of the lab to go to medical school. When was the last time I saw you?" he asked Will. "I know that when I heard you'd left I was kicking myself because it had been a long time. Years."

Will stiffened a bit. "I'm not entirely sure."

"Ah, yeah." He laughed and then said, "Shampoo bottle incident."

"Do I want to know?" Aisha asked.

Will said "no" at the same time the doctor said "hell, yes."

"All right, we'll leave it at that. But we're ready to begin Jimmy's treatment plan? His stepfather finally consented?"

Aisha shook her head. "He'll never budge."

"But King Jackson might," Will said. "I need as much information as you can give me, enough to convince him that signing his proxy for this surgery is a good idea. If he agrees, there's nothing George can do."

He agreed to give the King anything he needed, including presenting a personal assessment if Jax wanted him to. He didn't mind being grilled for all the little details. He welcomed it. "But damn, this would all be so much easier back home."

"How so?" Will asked.

"It's like night and day. A case like this, before I relocated? Instead of invasive surgery that requires several weeks of recovery, I'd tank him for a few days, there would be three injections and one small incision to clip a ligament, and we'd just wait. Once out of the tank, he'd need roughly one more week of only moderately painful recovery. Honestly, it's more dangerous to take out an appendix here than a complete physical reassignment is there. And an appendix is a cakewalk."

Aisha reached for Will's arm and squeezed.

"End results are better, too," he went on. "The surgery I can do for him here…the results will be damn near perfect visually, but someone digging deep into his genetic code would find telltale signs. If he wants kids, he'll need donor sperm or he'll have to adopt. At home? What he would end up with would have him one hundred percent biologically male. His DNA, his physical structure, everything. He'd even be fertile."

Aisha's fingertips created dents in Will's arm.

"Would you be willing to do that?" Will asked him. "Take Jimmy back home long enough to do the surgery?"

The notion surprised him. "I suppose it would depend on the risks. The idea of going home just as the meteor hits isn't exactly appealing. I may be old, but I'm not done yet."

"It won't hit. That issue has been dealt with. Truly, if you wanted to go home permanently, you could, whether you agree to do this or not. I'll personally escort you back. I simply ask you to consider that if not for Jimmy, you wouldn't know the possibility exists."

"Meh." Mass shook his head. "My life is here and it's a pretty good one. But if you can get me home and I can get set back up at the hospital, I'd be happy to go. I still want the King's permission for all of this, just to cover my own ass if George tries to sue. But yeah. Going home for a bit would be nice."

"Aisha?" Will turned to her. "Is this what you want?"

Her voice was shaky. "We'd have to tell him about you."

"He'll find out eventually," Will said. "If it's prefaced with the knowledge that he gets his surgery now rather than later, and that it will be perfect and less painful, perhaps he won't care."

Mass didn't think it mattered if he cared or not. He needed to get it done sooner rather than later, and even if he knew, who was he going to tell? Who would believe him? He started compiling the information Will needed for the King, and handed it over stored in a tablet.

"It's nice to see that the bastard won't win this one," he told Aisha as we were headed out the door. "I relish seeing the look on his face when he finds out."

"I don't," she said to Will when we were partway down the hall. "This could get ugly."

He didn't care.

= = =

He had his phone in hand, ready to call the King. He wanted to meet with Jax and his legal advisor and had started punching the numbers in when Aisha covered his hand with hers and asked him to stop.

"I need some time to breathe," she said. "I'm not changing my mind, but I'm not quite ready to run head first into this wall."

She wanted to walk. They headed for the Embarcadero and then toward Pier 39, where Will stopped to get drinks for them and fish bites for me, and she still wasn't ready to have him call Jax. We went on to Ghirardelli Square, where he bought her a small carton of chocolate pieces and bottles of water, and then they wandered down to the aquatic park to watch swimmers fight the current as they swam laps around the park.

When she had to force him to take a bite of the chocolate, she laughed and started to relax. It was like trying to get broccoli into a toddler's mouth; he grimaced and turned his head away, until she grabbed him by the chin and told him to open his mouth, or there would be no dessert later.

She doesn't mean food stuff, you know.

"What's your beef with sweet things?" she asked after he finally consented to two small pieces of chocolate. "I remember a time when you could wolf down half a cake and chase it with a liter of soda."

He patted at his stomach. "This doesn't happen by itself. And truly, I've lost the taste for junk food."

You like the Queen's cookies.

"All right, that's true, Wick. I do enjoy Aubrey's chocolate chip cookies, but only right out of the oven, and only two or three."

"This—" she rattled the box at him "—once a week wouldn't kill the six pack."

"I know. Truthfully? When I realized I wasn't going to die and that we were headed into Midlam's war, the thought came to me that I needed to pay better attention to the shape I was in. Oz and Zed…" He sighed. "I had a gut feeling I needed to be able to protect them. So I got back into shape, and cut out the little junk that I allowed myself."

Food is fuel.

"Exactly, Wick. Food is fuel. And now I have an even better reason to stay in shape. I have to if I'm going to keep up with Aisha."

"Sweetie, you didn't get this body in just a few months. This is years of work."

"I had the foundation, but I'd gotten a little lazy. I cut my body fat in half last fall and started running and swimming again, and hit the gym. Until I retire, I think I need to keep it up, like it or not."

"For Oz's sake."

He nodded. "Jax is counting on me to be there for her if something happens to him."

You haven't gone to the gym in a couple of weeks. I'm gonna start calling you lard ass.

"I've been distracted, Wick. I'll go this week. You can come with me and I'll find a little kitty treadmill for you."

I'm busy that day.

"You're lazy, cat."

"Maybe I'll let you drag me to the gym," she said. "Or swimming. Something to get me in better shape."

"Not a thing wrong with your shape. I quite enjoy it."

She set her hand on his thigh and rubbed it, but it didn't make him jump and he didn't suck in a sharp breath. He was getting used to it. "I don't mean to lose weight. Just to get into better shape. Oz told me that you and Drew can run from home to the Golden Gate and back with no trouble. I'd like to be able to do that and keep up with you."

"I would like that, too." He lifted her hand, kissed it, and then purposely did not set it back on his leg. "I enjoy that a little too much and there are kids running around."

"Then pull your shirt off and let me enjoy the six pack," she said, tugging at the hem.

He pretended to consider it, and when she lifted an eyebrow as if to say, "Well?" he reached behind his neck and pulled the shirt over his head.

"Now there's something I never thought I'd get you to do."

"Only you could," he said. He wiggled his eyebrows at her and said, "You could return the favor."

"No one else wants to see stretch marked, middle-aged-Mom flab."

"You're not flabby."

"Hey." She poked at his ribs. "Let me have my excuses."

She has nice boobs. A lot of people would want to see that.

"Indeed, Wick."

There was a little boy running on the sidewalk between the stadium bleachers and the water, barefoot and squealing as he chased a seagull that waddled quickly, half a bagel in its mouth. They watched him toddle after the bird and laughed when he stopped in his tracks because the gull turned and bellowed.

I expected tears, but once he was sure he wasn't going to get eaten, he jumped up and down, giggling.

"They grow up too damned fast," Aisha sighed. "Today he's chasing seagulls and before his parents know it, he'll be chasing some girl across the beach."

"Or some boy. Who knows?"

"Who knows," she repeated. "How creepy is it that I look at that little boy and then look at you, and wonder what Jimmy will look like in six months? Will he be all soft and adorably squishy like my baby was, or will he suddenly be this…man? And will he be happy with what he ends up with? I mean—" She laughed at herself. "I should not be wondering how well his genitals will turn out."

"Ask Mass when it's over," Will said. "Unless he's changed a lot, he'll be happy to tell you."

"The whole thing is unreal. Of all the specialists we could have picked. We chose him when we were still in Las Vegas, Will. James and I were willing to travel as often as we could to have him treat Jay."

"Kismet. I remember when he left the lab to go to school. He'd been focused on applied physics, but after indulging my mother and her interest in neuroscience, he realized medicine was more his forte. And she forced him out. He could do far more good in the world if he followed his passion and then left home."

"I wonder how he went from neuroscience to gender medicine."

Will shrugged. "I was not present for that decision. But he was available when I needed medical care later, and I remember him being quite gentle."

"What's with the shampoo bottle?"

His face flushed. "There was an incident," he said reluctantly. "I don't suppose we can leave it at that?"

"What the hell did you do, Will?"

I know. Tell her. If you don't, I'll tell Drew and he can tell her.

Will bent his head back and stared at the sky, willing it to open up and swallow him. "I was twelve," he finally said. "I saw the bottle when I was showering at the lab, and somewhere in my brain was the notion that I would…fit."

She was already laughing.

"I also had the notion that the texture of the shampoo would feel good. What I failed to account for was that because it *would* feel nice, I would get hard—and once that happened, there was no getting the bottle off. I panicked and tugged it down to the tip and then made a huge mistake. I tried to twist it off."

"Oh my god, Will."

She was still laughing.

"The bottle's neck had a jagged little piece and when I turned it, it sliced right through my skin. Then I seriously panicked, because it was agonizing and the bottle was filling with blood. I had no choice but to yell for help. Fortunately, my dad had come upstairs and my mother was three levels down."

Finn didn't lose his cool; he cut the bottom of the shampoo bottle off to ease the suction, taped it to Will's stomach, wrapped him in a towel, and rushed him to see Mass.

"By then I'd definitely lost the erection, and he was able to slide the bottle off, but there was no saving my foreskin. So, there you have it. The reason I'm circumcised. And I essentially did it to myself. All Mass did was cut it the rest of the way off and made it pretty."

"I am so sorry for laughing," she said, even though she was still laughing.

"To their credit, my parents never made me feel bad about it. My father's only real comment was, 'Dash, I understand why you did it, but next time you're tempted, think it through.' And trust me, the next time I had an impulse to stick my penis in anything, I considered the end result."

"All right, you have to tell me. What was the next thing, and did you do it?"

"Oh, it was more than one thing. There was a tube of butter. That proved to be messier than it was worth. I once hollowed out a loaf of bologna. And when I was fourteen I created this odd contraption with balloons. Yes, I tried them all. And my mother found the balloons and knew damn well what I was doing with them."

"Oh my god. Poor Will."

He sighed. "That was the day she set a bottle of lube on my nightstand and said, 'You have two good hands, William. Use one of them, and stop screwing things around the house.'"

She was laughing so hard that she buried her face against his legs.

"I stopped screwing things around the house."

"God, I love you." She left her head in his lap, and stretched out, laying on the cement bench. "Thank you for making me laugh. I needed that."

"Just remember it if Jimmy ever gets stuck in something. We all try it sooner or later."

She started tracing over the lines of his tattoo with her fingertips. "I'll try to keep it in mind. I wonder what else he'll do to himself."

He watched her for a while. She brushed over all the fine lines that made up one the wings on his chest, tracing over a nipple. "You really don't like the tattoos, do you?"

"I don't have to." She stopped tracing and set her hand on his stomach. "You got these for a reason."

He nodded. "I thought they would help me hear my mother's voice when I began to forget what she sounded like. I rarely notice them anymore, though. It would be simple enough to have them removed. An afternoon with a removal specialist, the ink is essentially pulled out of the skin."

"No." She sat up. "I won't ask you to change yourself, and you got them for your mother. I'll get used to them."

"My mother doesn't know about them," he said. "And if she did, she'd be horrified."

"Because you did something to honor her?"

"Because I did something relatively permanent to the perfect body she and my father created for me. She's actually quite spiritual in that regard."

Aisha laughed again. "Well, here's your leverage. When you finally talk to her, if she's still dead set against you and I being together, let her see the tattoos. She'll forget all about us and fixate on that."

"She can multitask, Aisha."

"I know." She leaned in and kissed him. "All right. I can breathe. Call Jax and see if we can get the ball rolling."

= = =

Jax was at his desk, feet up, with the giant monitor on, tuned to an old broadcast entertainment video. Will noted what he was watching and sat down to wait, because Jax didn't often watch things for fun, and this was one of his guilty pleasures. "The guy with the pointy ears," he once told Will, "that's you."

There are newer things to watch, you know.

Old entertainment was more fun to watch when they were drunk.

When they were drunk, they talked back to the people on the shows they watched.

The lawyer got there right at the end, right when the pointy-eared guy raised an eyebrow and said, "Indeed," and Jax clicked the monitor off. Will didn't bother with any pleasantries; he waited for the lawyer to open his computer, and then began explaining what he needed.

Without identifying the boy, he outlined the issue and stressed that time was running out. The transition would happen either way but noted if he had to wait until age eighteen, it would be far more painful, require multiple surgeries, and in the end, it would cost five to ten times as much.

"I'm asking now so that all the bases can be covered. There may be another way around this hurdle, but something needs to be in place in case the best option fails."

"And if your best option fails?"

"That's why I'm asking for your proxy. This needs to be done now, while he would be covered under the state genetics program. If he has to wait, he shifts from the fully funded genetics program to the elective surgical program. The surgical program is funded on a month to month basis and has a triage-based scheduling system, so he could potentially go years between surgeries. He would also be at the mercy of the state to pay for this because neither he nor his biological parents would be able to fund it all."

Jax glanced at the lawyer, who was listening and tapping away on his computer but remained silent. "You're asking me to set a precedent. If I usurp the rights of a parent in this matter and it becomes known, the requests to do the same for children in custody disputes across the country will skyrocket. Follow the breadcrumbs, Will. This could very well open up the need for formal applications to royal intercession, and an agency to handle them."

"Would it set the same precedent if you named me as the boy's proxy instead?"

Jax looked to the lawyer, who said it was a gray area. By signing the proxy or permission for an assigned proxy, depending on the minor's age, Jax was stripping the third parent of his parental rights for the duration. "However, this could also be considered a case of medical neglect, as transitions are, arguably, a medical necessity under the law and by withholding treatment, the parent has set himself up for this very scenario. Given that he is not a biological parent, the court would likely issue a decision based on what both biological parents want."

"Am I setting this up as precedent?" he asked. "Am I essentially giving myself the legal right to act as a parent by proxy for any given minor in the kingdom?"

"Technically, you already have that right. But this would test the limits regarding what the people consider to be a boundary. It would also provide a test for the rights of declared third parents. Do they, even when given full parental rights, actually have that?"

"The third parent in this situation," Jax said to Will. "Will he fight this?"

"Without a doubt, yes. But by the time he can get a lawyer and file, it will be too late to stop the procedure. I'll be honest, some of the pressure to get this done now is to prevent him from having the time to file an injunction."

Jax leaned back in his chair, considering it. Then, "I know this boy, don't I?"

Will nodded.

"Jimmy?"

"I realize this is not the ideal circumstance under which you would choose to be told."

Jax turned to the lawyer. "How soon can you draw up the paperwork?"

"I've been putting the pieces together. I only need his legal name, the names of his biological parents, and his physician. You sign, and I'll forward it to the boy's physician, and then file with the court."

"James Jordan Okuda, Junior," Will answered. "His birth name was Jaime, but I don't know if there was a middle name. Father is James Jordan Okuda. Mother is Aisha Salazar Okuda."

"Legal name is all I need." He typed it in and then handed the King a digital pen to sign the screen.

After he signed, Jax said, "I hope this doesn't bite us in the ass, Will. If it were anyone else, I would take more time to let the legal team examine every possible outcome."

The lawyer closed his computer and left without saying anything else.

"Tell Aisha I won't say anything to Aubrey without her permission, but I also don't like keeping secrets from her. This isn't a state matter."

"I understand."

"But?"

"She's worried, Jax."

"What, because her son needs surgery? The nature of it was none of our business."

"Because of Zed. He's known for years and has spent dozens of nights with Jimmy. She feels as if you had a right to know. She's equally uncomfortable with the idea that Zed kept Jimmy's secret from you for so long."

"What the hell was he supposed to say?" Jax asked as he got up. "'Oh, yeah, my best friend? He's a guy, but, hey, funny enough, he has a vagina.' It was none of our business, Will. If the kid doesn't identify as female, then it's a moot point. I doubt Zed has ever looked at Jimmy as anything other than another male, and it's not like he hasn't whored himself around town anyway."

"Aubrey may see it differently."

"Aubrey will see it more clearly than any of us, Will. She won't understand why it was a secret, but she'll damn well see the bigger picture, and Aisha better be prepared for the breath-sucking hug she'll probably get."

"I'll warn her."

"Brace yourself, too. Once she gets going, everyone gets squeezed."

= = =

They curled up together on Will's sofa through two crying jags and a panic attack. He gave up trying to tell her that everything was going to be fine, and if Jax was any indication, Aubrey was a non-issue, and just held her. I sat on the sofa next to Aisha and draped my chest over her legs so that she would feel me purr, and we waited.

This isn't because she's scared to face Aubrey.

Will rubbed between my ears to tell me he'd heard me.

This is years of not being able to share with anyone.

Her eyes were still a little puffy and her nose gurgled a bit when they got into the elevator to head up to the balcony—normally Will took the stairs but didn't even suggest it—and he kept kissing her head, right at her temple, until the car settled and the doors slid open. Aubrey was right there, and without saying a word she held her arms out to Aisha.

Jax was right. There was a lot of hugging going on. Aubrey didn't let Aisha go until she wasn't sniffing anymore, and the edge of panic had softened.

Does Aisha know what Aubrey can do? Have you told her how Aubrey heals?

"No," he whispered. "Do me a favor. If you think she's going to start crying again, jump in her lap."

Got it. I'm in charge of purr therapy.

They had beer and soft drinks on the balcony. It was still light out and the damned pigeons were making obnoxious cooing sounds all around us, so I stayed at Will's feet where it was safe and listened to see if Aisha needed me. I didn't think she would, because Jax and Aubrey weren't bothered at all that they'd never been told. Jimmy's junk was not an issue; Zed thought of him in no terms other than his best friend, and they didn't think they would have, either.

Her grip on Will's hand eased up as she calmed down. They were interested in the particulars, how she came to know that Jimmy was Jimmy and not that it was a phase. "Oz?" Aubrey said. "Ultimate tomboy, and she still is. But we never questioned her gender. I don't think she did, either."

"Jimmy insisted he was a boy from the time he could speak. I'm not even sure how I can explain it. There was never anything about him that told me he was in any way female, except for the obvious. And when we finally took him to see someone? We had the first scan of his brain done at age four, and several times since. Every marker has been the same. His brain in nearly every way presents as male, always more than ninety percent. He just got stuck with the wrong plumbing."

"The scans don't really matter, do they?" Aubrey said. "He knows who he is."

Jax nodded. "Oz presented as sixty per cent male. It didn't matter. She knew."

Aisha was surprised by that and wanted to know why they had her tested in the first place.

"Royal offspring," Will answered. "Tested for everything you can imagine."

Aubrey added, "The results are interesting but nothing we paid a lot of attention to. It certainly didn't change how we raised them."

Will grunted, amused, and wondered if Drew was ever tested. Jax raised an eyebrow and took a sip of his beer. "Come on, spill it," Will pressed. "I know he's biologically male and obviously hetero, but what's brewing inside his head?"

"Don't you dare poke at him for his sensitivities," Aubrey chided. "He and Oz are well matched."

"Eh, I suppose," Jax said. "Drew and Zed both hover at the eighty per cent mark of male attributes. As do I."

Aubrey was unimpressed. "Don't ask me, that wasn't anything I went through. And given that I don't need confirmation, I'm not inclined to find out. Do we really need a test for this? Why does anyone have to legitimize what they already know about themselves?"

"Originally," Will said. "It was to get insurance companies to pay for surgery. Later it was to convince those who didn't believe it was possible to be stuck in the wrong body—which is clearly still an issue, hundreds of years later."

Aisha finally let go of Will's hand. "I wonder if they can scan for asshole tendencies. George would score off the charts."

Will reminded her that she initially told him she was happy for James and George, and she sighed. "Most of the time I *am* happy for James, really. I don't know what attracted him to George, because the man is a mess of contradictions, and he's a bully to boot. I imagine he was a horrible little boy who got away with far too much and is just used to it."

"James can deal with it all he wants. What about how he treats Jimmy?"

"When he doesn't have to think about it, he's actually good with Jimmy. But he sees the daughter he thought he was getting, and he can't wrap his head around the idea that he's wrong."

"Good Lord," Aubrey said. "Did he escape from Florida?"

"Oddly enough, that was my thought," Will told her. "I expect those views from a Floridian who was raised with centuries-old standards and I wouldn't necessarily hold it against them."

Aisha shook her head. "He was born in San Francisco and moved to Vegas when he was in his early twenties. I can't explain him. But I do know that his anger will be explosive, and when he finds out?"

"He wouldn't go after you," Aubrey said, worried.

"I doubt it. But he'll never forgive James."

"Not your problem," Jax said.

Will touched his beer bottle to her soft drink bottle. "And if he is inclined to take anything out on you, he has to go through me."

The idea made Jax grin. "God, I want to see it if he does. Please let me be there."

You, Jax, Drew, Zed, and Oz, all in a nice line behind the Queen and Aisha. He'll pee his pants.

Will translated, and Jax added, "If it didn't lend an additional layer of officialness to it, I'd have a few of the royal guard standing by."

"Well, someone has to be there to protect you if you intend on waiting while he has surgery. There's a possible threat to your safety."

"That's what you're for," Jax said. "We'll put you up front, let him swing at you first."

"Indeed. Let him try."

Testosterone, dude. Puff your chest out when you say that.

"I don't need to puff my chest out when I say things like that, Wick. Flexing would get the point across far better."

Laughing, Jax reached over to pet me. "He's a hell of a lot more verbal now, isn't he?"

"He's always been mouthy. But yes, he seems more willing to speak to me now that I don't feel pressed to ignore the things he says."

"The other day he sat on my lap while I read," Aubrey told them. "I swear, it was like he was reading along with me, and then asking questions I couldn't answer."

"He can read."

"No fucking way," Jax sputtered. "Prove it."

Will pulled out his phone and opened the Internet on it, and told Jax to pull something up, randomly, and then show it to me. After he found something he was sure Will wouldn't have read before, he invited me onto his lap and held the phone so I could easily see it, and after a few seconds I read out loud, "The Emperor's cat is off the market, ladies."

Will repeated it, laughing, and then asked for context. Jax handed him the phone; it was a picture of Will, Aisha, and me. I was on his shoulder, stretching out to nose-kiss her. Aisha thought it was terribly sweet, but presumed they did that to deflect from Pacifica's Most Mysterious Bachelor inching his way off the playing field.

"They don't want to shut the rumor mill down," Will speculated. "Though I cannot understand why anyone cares about my love life."

Aisha leaned away from him. "Have you *seen* you?"

"I have, and I am not impressed."

Liar.

"I am not lying, Wick."

"We need Oz," Jax said. "She would know."

"So would you, if you looked close enough."

"My daughter's ability is far more nuanced. I think you're a bit embarrassed, but there might be some ego flaring up in there."

Will explained to Aisha, "Jax can see colors in sound almost as well as Oz. And yes, it's a state secret, because he can use it in negotiations and summit meetings. No one can lie to him about their intentions."

"No worries."

"You'd think it would have helped with Florida," Jax said with a sigh. "But damn, Munson believed every morsel of bullshit he tried to feed us."

"Try growing up on that diet," Aubrey groaned.

"Speaking of diet." Jax patted his stomach. "I'm starving, and there are chicken wings dripping with barbeque sauce and pitchers of beer just down the street."

"Wonderful," Aubrey said. "From talking about bullshit to you wanting to eat—"

"Oh, look at you," he said cheerfully. "We got a swear word out of you."

She rolled her eyes. "I meant that I would cook. There's perfectly good chicken right in your own kitchen."

"Come on. There are pool tables at Fuzzy's and I'd like to destroy Drew in a game or two. Please?"

"You can't say no, Aubrey," Will said as he got up. "He said please. We'll go get Oz and Drew and meet you downstairs."

She grumbled as she got up. "It's Sunday. We should be sitting down to dinner as a family, but no. We're going to a bar. The boys will get drunk, and we'll have to drag them home."

"You say that like it's a bad thing," Jax said. He kissed her and grinned stupidly. "We'll still be together as a family."

"In a *bar*, Jackson." She reached down to pick me up. "Wick, are we the only two adults in this house now?"

Drew might be one. Can I have meaty bites at the bar? I think they have meaty bites.

"He agrees with me, Jax. The rest of you are hopeless."

= = =

"See?" Jax said when they entered Fuzzy's. "Nearly empty. Perfect time to come here."

Unimpressed, Aubrey said, "That's because all the decent people are at home with their families, Jackson."

"And we're here with ours. Except for the wayward son who is off ogling half-dressed girls at Lake Tahoe, and who can blame him for that?" He grabbed her hand and pulled her toward the back of the bar where the pool tables were and where there was a five-foot square of empty floor space. "Come on. There's even music playing."

When he pulled her inappropriately close, she grabbed his face between her hands. "What has gotten into you tonight?"

"He's horny," Will said as he brushed past. "Try to contain him."

"You know, we can leave," Oz said to Drew. "No one said we'd have to watch the old people groping each other."

"To be fair, they kind of put up with us a lot," Drew pointed out.

"Indeed." Will grabbed a stick and ordered Drew to rack up the balls. "I'll humiliate Andrew while Jax orders food." He looked to Aisha. "No helping him tonight. He wins or loses on his own merit."

"That's not fair," Drew mumbled.

"Yes, it is, sweetheart," Aubrey said. "Will can't play, either."

"I'm told I play quite well," Will said.

Aisha walked behind him and brushed her hand across his back. "Very well."

"Seriously," Oz said to Drew, "we don't have to stay. You pour beer into this mix, and it's just going to get…hornier."

"We'll rein it in a bit," Will said.

No one's getting naked, right?

"That depends on how drunk we can get Jax," he said, smashing his stick into the little white ball. "You never know."

He didn't take anything off at the pizza place.

"So tonight might be the night."

Get Drew drunk.

"I'm not drinking, Wick," Drew said. "I came for the free food and the inevitable lecture about my school plans."

"No lectures." Will missed his shot and sighed. "You've made an appointment to discuss changing your major?"

"Yeah, tomorrow. I looked over the courses, and it might not add any time if I take an extra class each semester. But I won't overpack my schedule. I'll leave work time."

"School is your primary work. I'll be spending most of your first semester securing grants and licenses."

"You're going to be very busy," Aubrey guessed. "That won't excuse you from dinner. I still expect you to be there."

Drew glanced up from the table. "As often as possible, Mrs. B."

"Both of you can study at the kitchen table, you know," she said. "Or take over the living room every afternoon. Just be home more, all right?"

They were home, technically. Oz spent more time in Drew's apartment than she did upstairs, but it was still home. They'd missed a lot of dinners, even before they started spending nights together and Aubrey understood why, but she still wanted them to make an effort.

She had another suggestion, but Jax was back with beer bottles; he handed her one and said, "No. He's not moving back upstairs. It's already too easy for them, they don't need us to make it any easier."

"My dad, the walking contradiction," Oz muttered.

"I can be fine with your relationship but not be willing to throw you into the same damned bed together, Ozzie."

Drew lined up for his next shot, warning me that my spot on the edge of the table was risky. He didn't let them pull him into it; instead, he started telling Will about a book on old heads-up computer displays he was reading; it employed hundreds of tiny holographic displays that could be manipulated by touch. It was old tech that never really made it to the public sector because of the expense, but he'd been picking apart the schematics and thought it could be scaled down and done cheaply enough that it could at least be offered on high-end private systems.

"It's not even a quarter as sophisticated as the one you showed me," he said, watching his ball bounce two inches away from where he wanted it, "and it has major heat issues, but changing the materials used could fix that. Spread out some of the processing power, too. I'm thinking nanobots."

Under her breath, Oz said, "And yes, let's talk about *that* at three in the morning."

"Hey, no one said you had to answer the texts."

"Like you weren't in the same room," Will said.

Drew grimaced as Will sunk his shot. "We weren't. But it's seriously cool stuff. The military abandoned it because parts kept melting and it was too expensive to maintain, but when it worked it was a fairly valuable tool."

"Parts didn't just melt," Jax told him. "An entire building burned down because they caught fire."

"It was a building without sufficient cooling, and they had fifty machines in use at the same time. It was like they wanted each unit as compact as possible, without accounting for operating temperature. Increase the size of the system, change the materials and how the data exchanges, keep the building at near-freezing temperatures, and it will work."

Jax folded his arms, regarding Drew seriously. "You bring people into the equation, and the room temperatures go up."

"Dual-location operation," Drew said. "The computers can be in one place, and the projections in another. We can send data points wirelessly."

"Is this part of what you planned on working on?" Jax asked Will.

"I told you, he can visualize what others don't. If we can build the system he has in his head, we can then use it to build the system I have in mine. And the future applications are numerous. It's more than a sophisticated hologram. What he has in mind could solve long term and long-range applications that stalled because of those heat issues."

Jax took a beat and then breathed, "Elysium."

The game stopped. Will set the end of his stick on the floor and leaned on it. "Remove the holographic projectors from the system he envisions, and you have something that can handle both life support and artificial gravity demands on a significant scale. Mars colony twenty times over."

"You'll get your grants," Jax said. And to everyone else, "This goes no further. Not to siblings, not to parents, not to children."

"I'm sorry," Drew sputtered. "I didn't think that mentioning it—"

"You're fine," Will said. "But once Jax realized the implications, it became a state matter."

"No worries about me saying anything," Aisha said. "I have no idea what you three are even talking about."

"Boring boy things," Oz said. She pulled a stick out of the rack on the wall and gestured to another table. "And before you start lecturing me on girls in science, I know. But you guys are really boring when you get going."

Will didn't look up from the shot he was setting up for. "Sure, play Aisha, and ask her about the geometry of the game."

At the same time, Oz and Aisha said, "No one said there would be math involved."

"She can insinuate math into everything," Will said as he scratched his shot.

"Everything?" Drew snorted.

Will raised an eyebrow and was probably going to say something that would get him into trouble, but when he looked up he saw the front door open and his parents walking in.

It took a couple of minutes for them to notice him at the back of the bar, and when Aubrey realized they were there, she waved them over. Will might not have wanted to invite them, but they were there, so she was going to be polite and invite them to play.

"Moms," Drew grunted, soft enough that only Will heard.

Aisha abandoned her game with Oz and whispered to Drew to go play with her, and she sat against the edge of the pool table while Will pretended to set up his next shot. "Take a deep breath," she told him. "This has already been a hard day."

"This cannot end well." He missed and told her to take Drew's place. "How the hell did they end up here?"

Without thinking about it, she rubbed his back, trying to reassure him. "They live up the street, sweetie."

"My favorite bar is ruined."

"Stop it," she chortled. "You hit a speed bump with her, not a wall."

"It could become a wall."

"Only if you let it." She kissed him and then pushed the cue ball into a pocket with her hand. "Come on, let's start over."

Jo was talking to Aubrey but noticed them at the table together, and when Aisha kissed him she ground her teeth together a little.

You're going to give her a stroke.

"Promise?"

You should go say hello or else she's going to know you're not happy and then she'll want to talk to you right here in front of everyone.

He sighed. I was right, and he knew it. He told Aisha he would be back in a minute and went to kiss his parents hello.

"You're a wise man, Mister Wick," she told me.

I've had practice.

"I'm glad he listens to you."

You should be. My directions are why he hasn't fallen off you yet.

"Jesus, Wick," Drew sputtered from the other table. When Oz asked him what I'd said, he quietly said he'd tell her later, and yeah, she wanted to know.

I walked to the end of the pool table closest to him and reached out with my paw to touch him.

I can tell Will things about you, too.

"Wick, you never stick around."

Yes I do. I could give you great advice.

He turned around. "All right. What's your advice?"

Pudding.

"Pudding?"

Aisha laughed, tossed her stick on the table, and picked me up. "Wick, stop teasing him. And save that nugget for when you're alone with them."

"You know what he's talking about?"

"Yes, and you don't want him to tell you right now."

I think he does. And Oz is sure interested.

I would have told him anyway, but the food was ready and there was even some chicken without sauce all over it for me. Will wound up sitting between his parents and Aisha was at another table, but she still managed to flirt with him. I was on a stool pushed up the edge of the table Will was at—no high chair this time, because it was a bar and they didn't have any—and watched them grin at each other and suggestively raise eyebrows. If Jo thought that by grabbing Will and making him sit with her was going to stop anything, she learned the hard way it wouldn't. She glanced at Will and then at Aisha—right when she was suggestively licking the barbeque sauce from her fingers—and was not any sort of happy about it.

Even when everyone was done eating, she didn't get the time with Will she wanted. As soon as they got up, Will told Finn he needed to speak with him, and they moved to another table while the rest of them went back to play pool.

Jo sat on a stool against the back wall and pretended to watch Jax and Aisha play, but she was paying more attention to Will and Finn. They were sitting with their heads close so that they could talk without anyone overhearing, and neither one looked up at all.

"Frost warning," Oz whispered to Drew.

He looked up from the shot he was taking. "Yeah, whatever they're talking about she wants to be a part of."

Oz slid her hand across his back and leaned in like she was going to kiss him. "I don't think it has anything to do with Finn. But I think if Jo had the power, Aisha would go up in flames."

"Seriously?"

"Don't turn and look at her. Wick, is Jo mad at them for something?"

That would be telling.

"You don't have to get specific," Drew said. "Just give us a hint. What's going on?"

Will is mad at her. She doesn't want him to touch anyone.

"Kinda late for that," Drew snickered.

She doesn't know that.

"What, really? Doesn't she know they're dating?"

Oz had to actually kiss him to make it look good. "Maybe she thinks he's just getting started and the only thing he's done is kiss her."

Well, they've seen each other naked and done a whole lot about it. He's braver than you are.

"The cat thinks Will is braver than I am," Drew muttered. "How?"

He'll eat anything.

"Oh my god, Wick." He rested his elbows on the table to that so he could get closer to me. "It took me a while to work up the nerve. I'm sorry it took any time at all, but I *did* do it. Maybe not well, but it takes practice."

Oz leaned her face next to his. "What did we work up the nerve for?"

"This cat gets *really* personal," Drew said.

"And?" she pressed.

Drew glanced over to the other table to make sure no one else was listening. "It took me a while to, you know. Taste…things."

"Oh." She laughed and ruffled his hair. "It's all right, Wick, it took me a while to work up the nerve, too. You—" she made Drew stand up straight so she could really kiss him "—are doing just fine."

"I probably suck at all of it," he said quietly.

"So do I. Who knows? We're having fun, aren't we?"

"We are."

"Hey," Jax barked, tapping the edge of the table with his stick, "if I can't dance in the corner with my wife, you two can't play tonsil hockey."

"It's Wick's fault," Oz said.

"Wick," Aisha said, "I told you, save the advice for later."

"Do I want to know?" Jax asked.

"God, no," Oz said. "It would be seriously creepy if you did."

Will and Finn came back, and Will wanted to know what was creepy. Jax shrugged said they wouldn't tell him, but he suspected it wasn't nearly as titillating as they wanted him to think. "Wick started it," he said. "How bad could it be?"

"Wick sees more than you'd like. Come on, rack the balls. It's my turn to humiliate you."

They rotated players through both tables, everyone except Jo, who said she preferred to just watch. She bristled every time Aisha touched Will, even though she carefully avoided anything more than brushing her fingers across his back; and when he tried to sneak a kiss, she waggled her finger at him and told him he wasn't going to distract her from winning.

The next time they played, he stood exactly opposite her, pressing his legs against the table. No one else noticed, but she glanced up from the shot she was taking and knew what he was doing, and barely touched the cue ball. "Fluffy wants to play," he growled.

I jumped onto his shoulder.

I miss Fluffy.

She set her stick on the table. "All right," she said. "I have a ton of things to do before the boys get home. I should probably take off before I really do lose a game to you."

He was confused, even moreso when she kissed him quickly and started for the door. He went after her, reaching for her arm to stop her.

"I'm giving you an out with your mother, to make things a little more comfortable. If I leave now, there won't be any weird awkwardness later when it's clear I'm going home with you."

"You're going back to my apartment, then?"

"Of course I am. I'm going to put some music on, stretch out on your bed, and read. Text me before you leave here. I'll fill that oversized bathtub of yours with hot water and wait for you."

"Hell, I'll leave with you right now. I don't care if it bothers her."

"Spend some time with your parents, sweetie. Your mother has wanted time alone with you since she got here. It won't hurt to sit there and talk to her."

"It might."

"Will." She kissed him again and said she'd see him in a bit.

Go tell your mom you need to leave so that you can practice not falling off Aisha.

"Very helpful, Wick."

I do what I can.

When he turned around, Jo was the only one looking. He took a deep breath and went to sit on the stool next to her, and before he was settled she said, "Will, what are you doing? You know you're playing with fire."

"Maybe I just want to light the match."

"William… I don't want to see you get burned. Blow the match out before it's too late."

Will waited a beat, grinding his teeth together. "We can stretch metaphors to the breaking point all you want, but it doesn't change anything. This is my risk to take. And until you're willing to trust me with the truth, you don't get a vote."

She argued that the truth was that she didn't want him to get hurt.

"But by whom? You don't want me hurt, yet here you are, inexplicably opposing what is very likely my future."

"I'm not—"

Will reached up to make sure I was balanced, because he stood up and didn't want me to fall. "Unless you can give me concrete proof that my brain will defy me if I allow myself the luxury of intimacy, then stop. Goddammit, Mom, you know more than you're willing to admit, and it's pissing me off. I love her. Not just a little bit. This isn't a crush. So you either start talking, or just stop."

He gave her a moment, and when she didn't say anything, he headed for the door. I looked over his head; she stood there, looking a bit shocked, and guilty as hell.

= = =

All but the bedroom lights were off when we got back to Will's apartment. He closed the door behind him and leaned against it, listening to the roar of water coming from the bathroom, and he muttered to himself that he needed to be in the moment and not thinking about his mother.

I've seen your mother naked. She's never looked that good.

"Damn, Wick." He sighed hard and pushed away from the door. "I'm sure she did when she was younger. And either way, she's a beautiful woman."

So is Aisha.

"Indeed. Inside and out."

He didn't seem to want to move, so I headed down the hall and called out for her.

Will is here and he wants to see your insides.

He might need a flashlight.

Aisha was coming out of the bathroom, wearing one of Will's

t-shirts and nothing else. He stopped and leaned against the door frame. "You wear that far better than I do."

"It was on the bed and smelled like you. I couldn't resist. But if you want it back..."

"Maybe I do."

"Well?" She held her hands out, beckoning him closer. He took it off her slowly, keeping his eyes on hers, and when he pulled it over her head he was even slower in running his fingers back to her waist. He trailed over her shoulders and down her ribs, and then kissed her as he maneuvered her onto the bed.

"You could take your clothes off," she said breathily, trying to grab for his zipper.

"I might." He began trailing kisses up her leg. "I might not."

I decided to sit at the bathroom door and didn't watch because what he was doing didn't require any input and he wasn't going to fall off. I heard her gasp and then moan, and figured the begging of God was about to start. After a couple of "oh my gods" and then "Jesus, Will," I turned back around and jumped on the bed, and told Will to go look in the bathroom.

His face was buried between her boobs, so he either didn't hear me or was ignoring me, so I did what I had to do.

I bit his ear.

"What the hell, Wick?"

The bathtub is almost full so unless you want to mop the whole floor you better take a break and turn the water off.

Aisha laughed as he jumped up, and yelled after him to take his clothes off already. He lingered at the door and nodded toward the tub.

"I've never shared a tub with someone before. I think I'd like to."

"Sweetie, the water needs to cool. I had the heat turned up."

"I noticed."

"But?" She scooted on the bed until she was sitting up, and patted the mattress so that he would come sit by her. He pulled his shirt and jeans off and then crawled onto the bed with her, but he didn't try to kiss her again. "Come on. I fully expected the little emperor would want to play right about now. What's wrong?"

"Nothing. Right up until Wick bit me, trust me, the little emperor was raring to go. But for some odd reason when I was shutting the water off I thought about talking to my dad tonight, and that pretty much ended it for the moment."

"You talked to him about your mother?"

"Your son, actually. It would have gone a lot quicker, but he fixated on Mass and what he's been doing with his life. I couldn't answer any of his questions."

"I'm glad he's focusing on the important things."

"He gets distracted, Aisha. But he's excited about helping Jimmy get this done. He'll call Mass in the morning and arrange to take him home to get his credentials reestablished at the hospital and to set a surgical date. And he also thinks it can all be done without exposing James to anything."

Finn had a smaller version of his ship, the one he used to create the portals that ran along part of the transit system tube. He'd created a few in varying sizes as test modules, including one that opened a me-sized portal in the back of Oz's closet. He had one that would easily ride up the hospital elevator and could be used in the OR corridor to open a portal that he and Mass could use to take Jimmy and Aisha forward.

James could stay in the waiting room in this When.

"We'd be there about a week, but as far as James is concerned, you'd go back to the OR with Jimmy for a minute or two."

"And how do we explain you going back with me?"

"We don't. You'll go first with my dad, and Mass will find an excuse to call me back. James will have to believe that we're old friends. Or we find an excuse to leave the waiting room and approach the portal from another door."

"I hate lying to him."

"The only other option is to tell him."

"If I tell him you can time travel, and then don't prove it? Will, the man is open minded, but that might push him to go for sole custody. As it is, I'll have to really press home with Jimmy that he can't ever tell a soul."

"He won't. Can we make James a bridge we'll cross when we get to it?"

She sat up and patted him on the leg. "We can. Come on. Let's see if the water has cooled down enough." She started to scoot off the bed, but when he didn't move fast enough, she snagged the waistband of his underwear. "Or not. I was pretty sure that you'd never taken a bath with anyone, but I guarantee no one's ever done to you what I'm about to."

She was right, too.

10

The door to Aisha's apartment slammed open at five-thirty the next afternoon; Jimmy and Zed were laughing loudly and talking over each other, too wound up to notice that Aisha was anxious and that Will's presence in the kitchen was its own oddity. She hadn't been able to sit still all afternoon. She flittered around cleaning things that were already clean, doing laundry, and she started making stew, which she forgot about until she realized Will was in the kitchen chopping carrots and potatoes to finish it for her.

When the door flew open, she stopped. She left the pile of towels she was folding on the sofa, and while the boys went into Jimmy's room to drop off his backpack, she went into the kitchen and pulled Will into a tight hug.

"He'll be fine," Will said. "Zed is here and can vouch for all the weirdness."

"Then you admit, it's all a little weird."

"My end of it? Yes, it falls directly into the category of weird."

"I don't want to know what weird things you two are doing," Zed called out from the hall, "but stop because we're coming out."

"We were discussing the two of you," Will said dryly.

"When did you get a sense of humor?" Zed snorted. He picked his backpack up from the floor and told Jimmy he'd see him later, when Will asked him to wait. Puzzled, Zed set it back down. "What's up? Mom and Dad expect me home soon."

"They know you're here and presume you're staying for dinner," Will told him.

Jimmy pulled a stool out from the breakfast bar and sat down. "What did we do? I swear, we did everything Dad said to this weekend. The only trouble we got into was because he started it when this girl walked past and he said she was cute, and then she thought Zed had said it—"

"She was totally into me," Zed said. "Your dad, on the other hand? She thought he was creepy old."

"That's not what this is about," Aisha said. She started to say something else, but then looked to Will for help.

"Zed, what have you told Jimmy about your abilities?" Will asked, sniffing lightly so that he would know what he meant.

Zed sniffed hard in return. "He knows I can smell feelings. And I can tell you right now, one of you smells anxious, and the other is worried."

"Those don't smell the same?" Jimmy asked.

"Close. Like the difference between potato chips and French fries."

"Well now I want French fries," Jimmy said.

"What else does he know?" Will pressed. "And yes, I need an honest answer. You're not in trouble if you've told him anything."

Zed shrugged. "He knows about Oz and Dad being able to see sound. I mean, it's not a common thing, but it's not unheard of."

"It's also a state secret," Will reminded him.

Zed's mouth formed the word "Oh."

"As is everything different about me," Will said.

"I'm not sure what to say to that. I haven't said anything to anybody about you. What happened?"

Jimmy looked at Aisha, confused.

"Nothing happened," Will assured him. "But something will, and we need to fill Jimmy in on some of the particulars and I need your help for that. He needs to understand the truth, and I think we all know he won't believe it."

Zed pulled out the stool next to Jimmy's. "You're serious. You want to tell him."

"Tell me what?" Jimmy asked. "Mom, what's going on?"

"About the portals, yes," Will said.

Zed squinted as he looked at Will, trying to decide if he was serious or not, and Will stared right back. After a moment, Will reached over and tapped the back of Zed's hand, giving him in one quick thought all he needed to know: he needs to know about time travel, but not what can happen when I touch someone; he needs to know because we're taking him to get his surgery.

"Will's a time traveler," Zed said, as if it were an everyday thing. "And I'm not bullshitting you. He's even taken me through a portal, to twenty-sixteen. I don't recommend it. Way too many people back then and the city stinks."

Jimmy sighed and started to get up. "I thought this was something serious."

"Sweetie, it is," Aisha said. "It's also important for you to know."

"And fucking keep it a secret," Zed said. "People would kill Will if they knew. And I mean, like, beheading or cutting him in half with a laser gun, not like every time I say I'm gonna kill you for the stupid shit you say."

"Fine." Jimmy sat back down, but he didn't believe a word of it. "The Emperor is a time traveler. So, you're here for what? Harvesting body parts because the future ran out of brains and little toes?"

"Yes," Will said, matching Jimmy's sarcastic tone. "I came here over two decades ago and have waited patiently for the one brain that will rule the world."

"Mine, right?" Jimmy grunted and looked at Zed. "Come on, what the hell?"

You could touch him and make him see it in his own head.

"You were much easier to convince," Will said to Aisha. "Jimmy, it's important that you know, and important that you believe it."

"Why? So you can take me on a field trip to the Civil War or something? I have a melanin thing going on. Wouldn't be a great idea."

"Opposite direction. We need to take you roughly two hundred years into the future."

Zed's eyes went wide. "You're going forward? Seriously? Can I go?"

"Yes, yes, and don't hold your breath," Will said.

"You believe this, Mom?" Jimmy asked. "How?"

"Jim," she sighed. "I get it. It's just so far out there. But if you can just try to accept it…"

"Man, just tell him *why*," Zed said. "Give him a reason to want to believe you. Feed him the whole truth and he'll swallow it without chewing."

"Puppy," she breathed. "This isn't some stupid joke. I know it sounds insane."

That caught his attention. "All right. You called me 'puppy.' You haven't called me that since I was maybe eight. What's really going on?"

"Your surgery," she finally said. "Will can take us to a time when you can have it done, and there's not a damned thing George can do to stop it."

Every morsel of doubt withered from Jimmy's face. If he didn't believe in time travel, he trusted she wouldn't lie about that.

"I wouldn't mention it to George," Will said. He was looking at Jimmy carefully, trying to gauge how close to believing everything he really was, and he nudged Aisha gently to get her to go around the counter, because Jimmy was about to fly off his seat toward her.

Will leaned over the counter and whispered to Zed, "You will no' tease him for crying."

"Are you kidding me? Will, I'm a hiccup away from it myself. You have no idea how badly—" Zed swallowed hard, and then laughed at himself. "I'm glad she told you. I swear, if I'd known you could take him to the future for this, I'd have told you myself."

"I didn't realize I could until I met his doctor."

Aisha explained it to them as Will finished making dinner. Whether Jimmy believed he was taking a trip through time barely mattered; he grabbed hold of the truths he needed. He would get everything done at once, and his recovery would be far quicker than he had expected.

"We say nothing to George," Aisha pressed. "Not a word. He'll just have to accept it when it's done."

"He'll explode. What about him and Dad?"

"Not your fucking problem, Jay," Zed said.

Will and Aisha both looked confused, and Zed thought it was his use of the number one thing on the Queen's bad word list, and he started to apologize for it.

"No, sweetie," Aisha said. "Jay?"

"You hate it?" he asked. "I was thinking like, James Jorden Junior which was Trey-Jay and then JJ for a while and then Zed shortened it to Jay, and I kind of like it."

"I don't hate it," she said gently. "It suits you. But I'll need time to get used to it."

"Jimmy's a little boy's name," Zed said. "Time for your grown up one."

Jay. Jay. Jay. Jay.

I wasn't sure I could get used to it, either.

Jay. Jay. Jay. Jay.

Jay. Jay. Jay.

"What's he going on about?" Zed asked.

Trying to etch the new name into my head. Jay.

"He's repeating 'Jay' so that he remembers it."

"Oh, yeah," Zed said to Jay. "Will can understand Wick, too. And I'm not joking about that, either."

"Any other surprises I should know about?" he asked.

"That's enough for one night," Aisha said.

"So there is something."

Tell him it involves handcuffs and pudding.

"No surprises," Will said. "Now you two—" he pointed at them "—you get to clean up, and then I'll take Zed home."

"I don't need an escort," Zed said as he started clearing the table. "I'm actually allowed to be out past seven o'clock. All by myself, even."

"It's a school night," Will said.

"And it's summer. Two more weeks before the summer term."

"Fine. Do you work tomorrow?"

"Hell, I work tonight. Are you escorting me to Alcatraz, too? I'd like to go home and shower first, but if it means that much to you, I'll let you take me there. You can stand on the beach and wave to me as I ride my skiff into the sunset."

"Just do the dishes."

He went into the living room with Aisha, and they sat together on the sofa. She glanced back at the kitchen, and with it let go of half of her in-home rules. She sat sideways and put her legs across Will's lap, and pulled his arm around her.

"He knows already," she said. "It might do him some good to see it."

"Good." He kissed her. "I will still respect your rule of not staying the night. Don't give him more than he's ready for."

"Thank you. Now how do we tell James any of this? And when?"

"Wait for Mass to tell us he's ready," Will said. "My dad can have a portal open with little notice, and he can do it from either side."

"Tell James at the last minute?"

"To avoid complications with his husband? Yes."

She leaned her head back to look at the boys in the kitchen. They were laughing, but they were working. "I hate having him lie to his dad."

"He's not lying. He's simply waiting for the right time for the truth to come out."

"It feels like lying." She set her head on his shoulder and her hand on his chest. "I am really sorry we're not going to spend the night together."

"It was an amazing weekend, but you haven't had any real time with your son since Drew dropped us into the simulator. Even if you thought he was ready for this, I don't think I'd stay."

"He doesn't know how long I've been gone," she mused.

"But you do, and you missed him."

"You damn well better call me tonight."

"I will. Or you call me." He started to kiss her, when Zed yelled from the kitchen, "Ugh, Jay, they're making out RIGHT IN THE LIVING ROOM!"

They both came out, declaring the dishes done.

"I told you," Zed said. "He's doing things to your mom."

Not very well, he's not.

"Seriously? He's figured out a way to get all my man parts. He can do anything to her that she wants him to do."

"He'll have to come back after he escorts me home. Apparently, I'm still too little to be outside by myself."

Will sighed. "Was I this obnoxious when I was a teenager?"

"When you were with Jax? Hell, yes."

He got one more kiss before he got up, and as we were heading out the door, Jay yelled out, "I wouldn't mind a little brother or sister, you know."

11

Will's job during council meetings was to pay attention. It was rare that he was questioned directly, requiring a reply, but when he was asked for his opinion or input, he was invariably quick with his answer and concise in his response. No one at the table presumed his silence equaled inattention. On the contrary, everyone presumed his silence meant he was soaking in every word said and every word left unspoken. And without question, if he felt someone was holding back information, the King would know before the post-meeting vacated seats were cold.

If anyone else at the Tuesday security council meeting had zoned out, unable to relate the necessary information or answer questions posed to them by the King, they would have incurred more than a tiny bit of his irritation, and faced ejection if they were habitually unfocused. Will stared at the tablet in front of him on the table, barely registering it was there, when the head of the royal guard asked him about his preferred location of a new safe house. He repeated the question, which Will finally heard, but he hadn't paid attention to everything leading up to it, and couldn't offer an opinion.

The fifteen participants of the meeting all looked to the King, waiting for his reaction. Jax raised an eyebrow, sighed, and called for a break.

"Half an hour," he said as everyone stood. When a few seemed as if they would wait it out at the table, he added sternly, "Clear the room."

Will got up with the others, but instead of leaving, he went over to the window and leaned against the wall. It looked out over Union Square, where dozens of people were taking their lunch and breaks from shopping. I jumped onto the sill to watch with him; we weren't as high up as we were when looking out Oz's window or from the balcony, and the people didn't look so small.

"Where the hell are you?" Jax asked. He leaned against the wall on the other side of the window. "You zoned out forty-five minutes ago."

"My apologies."

"My patience is a little thin, Will. Don't make me try to figure it out."

"I am truly not aware of what I was thinking, Jax. I suspect it has something do to with them." He gestured to the Square. Aubrey and Aisha were near the steps that faced the door of the royal house, and they were talking to Finn. From our spot in the conference room across the hall from Jax's office, they were just to the left. "I would be lying if I said I would rather be here than out there. I am far more interested in what my father has to say than whatever the head guard is blathering about."

Everyone is more interested in that, even the guard.

"Has he taken Jimmy's doctor to set things up yet?"

"Jay," Will said. "He wants to be called Jay. And I don't know. But I presume that's what they're discussing."

"And you want to go outside and play."

He nodded. "How much longer do you intend for this meeting to go on?"

Jax hadn't wanted it in the first place. "How bad would it be if I blew it off? Call General Myers, tell him to either declare it over or carry on. We could take them out to lunch, you'd find out what you need to know, and we score points with them."

"Points implies it's a game to win or lose."

"No losing. Everyone wins." He dug his phone out of his pocket. "You text Aisha, I'll text Aubrey. If they're up for it, we leave the meeting to Myers. If not, I get your full attention until it's over."

Do I get lunch?

"Depends on where we go, Wick."

"You really think I'd be turned away if I brought Wick with me?" Jax said. "I'm not proud of it, but I'm not above using The Look to get away with him joining us."

"Let's see you try that at Kaluto's," Will said.

At the same time, Aubrey and Aisha looked up and waved. A second or two later, Finn grinned and waved, as well. "I'm asking them to invite my dad, too," Will said. "Hold your breath that he doesn't call my mother."

He sent the text, and Finn looked up again, shaking his head. "He promised her he would go home this afternoon."

"A nooner?"

"He tends to stay in the lab for days on end," Will said. "She probably wants him home for the day."

"Night, too."

Will grimaced. "Ugh."

"For someone who's finally having sex, I wouldn't be making that face."

"Fine. But I now understand Oz's aversion to even a hint of what you and Aubrey do."

"She doesn't need a hint of what we do. I don't care what she and Drew are doing, but she's too innocent for that."

Will raised an eyebrow.

"The Queen can get a little nasty," Jax said.

"I don't need to know that, either."

"You're a big boy now, Will. It's fine if you know that your great, great grandmother occasionally pins the King to floor and growls 'fuck me.'"

"All right, that's rather tame. I thought you were heading in another direction."

"It involves any direction you can think of."

"I presumed it involved pudding and handcuffs."

Jax popped me on the head with his pointy finger. "You lousy little shit."

"He never exactly said that's something you've done. He suggested it as a possibility, and I inferred."

"You're supposed to be sleeping, Wick."

Sometimes you're really loud and I can't.

"He thinks he's helping," Will told him.

"Well, he's not wrong. But I recommend using neck ties instead of handcuffs. They don't dig in as much."

"That may be a bit beyond my current skill set."

Jax chuckled and pushed away from the wall. "You don't need the skillset, and I'm willing to bet it's well within hers."

"I think I liked it better when we didn't discuss these things."

"Bullshit. We discussed this a lot before I married Aubrey. After that, you seriously backed away out of respect for her."

"And I still respect her. But that's not entirely why."

"Why?" Jax asked as we got onto the elevator. "It's not like I ever got too graphic. Or did I?"

"Aisha had left, Jax. I was miserable. I didn't want to hear about your married love life. And later it was habit. I do hold your wife in high regard, and I still don't want to do or hear anything that would embarrass her."

"She probably knows that you're aware we have sex, Will."

"Yes, and given how often Wick complains about it, I'm aware that it's frequent and often loud. I don't need to know if it's kinky."

Jax was quiet the rest of the way down, but when the elevator pinged just before the doors opened, he said, "You don't *need* to know, but now you're thinking about it and I bet you're curious."

He got Will to chuckle.

"Fine. The truth. I'm not even sure what kinky *is*. But I'm putting the handcuffs in the definitely weird column."

Jax nodded to the guard on duty. "Yeah, you heard him right. Carry on."

Just outside the door, Will said, "You know he'll repeat that."

"And no one will believe him." He poked at me and said, "You. When we get to the restaurant, don't move. If you fall off, they'll make a fuss and won't let you in."

I never fall off. Will does.

"I didn't fall off, Wick." He sucked in a deep breath. "It's his latest thing to goad me with. No, I did not fall off. Not yet, anyway."

"Give it time," Jax said. "Sometimes you get going and wind up on the floor. Either get back up or ask her to jump on you."

"I'm quite content to just not be horrible at the basics for now."

You guys should cross the street. They're waiting.

"I envy you a little, you know. I regret not finding new things with someone who truly cares about me. By the time Aubrey came along, I knew a little too much."

"She needed you to have experience, Jax. It's the only reason you were able to be as patient as you were."

"I know. But still."

They know you're talking about them. Even Finn is giggling.

"Wick thinks we're amusing them."

"We are."

They're pretty. You're allowed to look.

"Indeed, they are, Wick. The most beautiful women in the world."

What about Oz?

"I include Oz in that."

You think all women are beautiful.

"Truly, I don't, Wick. I have met some exceptionally unattractive women. It has nothing to do with how they look."

But you think Aisha is hot.

"Yes, I do. Incredibly hot."

"Your dad is over there, you know."

"He's not hot," Will said, stepping out into the street. Even though there hadn't been traffic downtown for at least two decades, he still looked both ways. That was how much faith he had in humanity. Delivery vans are piloted by people, he pointed out. Air bikes are ridden by people. Both were quiet, and he didn't trust them to stop.

Will kissed his dad before he kissed Aisha, which surprised me but didn't seem to surprise her. Finn beamed, but not because Will went to him first; Jo might not be happy about Will and Aisha, but he was and he did nothing to hide it.

"Sure you don't want to join us?" he asked Finn.

"I promised your mother my undivided attention for the rest of the day. But there's news, and Aisha can fill you in. I may need your help late tonight to open the portal."

"That quickly?"

"Dash, I've been gone for four weeks," Finn said as he walked away. "Nothing quick about it."

The infrastructure for the new portal was ready on the other side. What Finn needed was clearance when he shot his ship through the spot in the hospital corridor he wanted to use. He wanted Will, and possibly Drew, to be there when he did it, to make sure there wasn't a human standing anywhere in the ten-foot area he needed to be clear.

"I didn't understand any of what he was saying," Aisha said. They'd ordered their lunch—shrimp bites for me—and she was trying to remember exactly what Finn had told her. "He mentioned a gate and a flap of paper? I have no idea. Something about the flap of paper holding time in place?"

"He was offering a visualization of how he creates the portals," Will said. "He uses his ship to punch a hole through time, much like punching a hole through a piece of paper. The little flap that often remains when you punch a hole through paper is symbolic of the flap of which he speaks. It's the portal. He's using a gate on the other side because this portal won't run along the loop of the underground tunnel he used to create most of the others."

"How's that work for this specific thing?" Jax asked. "Is the hospital in the same place?"

Will nodded. "Newer building, same location. I presume he made sure the hallway aligned before building the gate."

"You better hope so," Jax snorted.

"He says the portal is permanent," Aubrey said. "And the doctor now has a transponder. Finn thought it would make things easier."

"Did he give you an idea when Mass wants to do this?" Will asked Aisha.

"Mass wants to talk to us first, including James, but it sounds soon. Will, we can't let him give James too many details."

"Cut James out of it until the day of," Aubrey said.

They all turned to her, surprised.

"There's too much at stake," she said. "This isn't just Jimmy's surgery we're talking about. It's Will and Jax and Oz and Drew. They've all used the portals and the more people who know, the greater the odds are that at the very least, rumors will start."

"Jay had to be told," Will said.

"I'm sorry. Jay. And yes, he needs to know, but his father does not."

"I agree with that," Aisha said, "but I'm not sure what to do about it."

"We talk to Mass," Will said. "And we'll take it from there. James will be able to be in the waiting room, and we'll even be able to make him believe we're waiting with him, but at no time will he be exposed to Jay's location. And to that…you need a transponder. You need to be able to go through that portal without assistance, just in case."

12

Aisha's learning curve wasn't nearly as steep as Drew's. Will took her through two different portals a total of six times, quick trips that assured him she had control over her thought processes and that she could go through the portal unassisted if she needed to. She went through once on her own and met Finn near the lab in his own When and then came back with him, and when she was all the way through she grabbed Will's shirt and fell against him, muttering, "This is really going to happen."

"Exciting, isn't it?" Finn said.

"Terrifying, too." She let go of Will's shirt. "But so exciting."

"And I got to be part of it!" Finn kissed her on the cheek and practically skipped toward the lab, calling back, "Thank you!"

"He'll be available on the other side the morning of the surgery," Will said as he reached for her hand. "Depending on how we decide to do this, he wants to wait on the other side, in case something holds me back here."

"By something, you mean James."

He allowed for the possibility that he might need to stay in the waiting room with James for a bit. "I'll be there with you while Jay has his surgery, I promise. But I may also need to go after you do. I would only be a minute behind."

He could wait with James for hours, if necessary, but he wasn't abandoning her to the future for more than a few heartbeats.

We headed for the big coffee shop near the hospital. It was loud and always crowded, and an ideal place to meet with Mass. They could talk, and their conversation would be lost in the din, and even if James walked in—which wasn't likely—there was nothing suspicious about it. They were simply out for a walk, stopped for a cup, and ran into him.

People noticed me, though. Every few minutes someone passed the table and wiggled their fingers at me, squealing, "kitty!" or "furball!" and I spoke back, calling out *meat bag!* or *biped!*

"Everything is ready to go," Mass told them. "The room is reserved, and I was able to hand pick my team. Will, almost everyone is there, all the old techs from your dad's lab and most of the people I worked with in the hospital."

"Tempted to go back to stay?"

Mass tapped on his neck, just behind his ear. "Finn's made it possible to have the best of both. I didn't think I wanted to give up my life here, but after going back? I'll feel like a butcher every time I operate here."

"And you felt reset after a few nights there," Will guessed.

"I slept for two days," Mass said. "I feel about fifteen years younger right now."

"Yeah, you're going home. Did you take your anchor with you?"

He nodded. "And she stayed. I have obligations here, though. I'll see them through."

"My father manages. He keeps a foot in both Whens."

"And not why we're here. Pick a day, Aisha. We're ready to go and all you need is to tell James."

"And do it without telling George," she sighed. "I don't think James would say anything, but I'm not sure we can count on him not leaving hints."

Mass shrugged. "You'll be far from his reach."

"There will be guards," Will said. "Several, in fact."

Puzzled, she asked why.

"Because Zed will want to be there in the waiting room, and Jax and Aubrey are likely to stop by. Where they go, the guard goes. It'll be fine."

She wanted to believe him, but the butterflies in her stomach were stopping her.

= = =

Aisha dropped heavily onto the sofa and groaned, "I am really sort of loathsome. I can't believe I just did that with a phone call. He's right upstairs."

"So is George," Jay said. "If you go up to talk to him in person, George will be right there sticking his nose in it, and if you ask Dad to come down here, George will pester him all night, wanting to know what was so important."

Will agreed with Jay. "He brushed it off as a work issue. It'll be fine."

"And you can tell Dad more tomorrow at the hospital."

Will reminded him again that he couldn't give his father the finer details, no matter how tempting it was. Aisha jumped on the thought. "Their lives could be at stake if you slip up, Jimmy. Jay. God, I'm sorry."

"My new name is JimmyJay, isn't it? It's all right. And I get it. Foreign spies and blowing shit up and stuff no one wants them to know. I'm not saying anything to anyone, but Dad might get curious when I'm not still in a metric shit-ton of pain three weeks from now."

"It will be the miracle of youth giving you the ability to bounce back quickly," she said. "And it's almost nine o'clock. You have one hour until you can't eat or drink anything. Make the best of it."

"Not really hungry," he said with a shrug.

"There's a white cake with chocolate frosting on top of the fridge," she said.

He still maintained he wasn't hungry.

Aisha feigned offense and sighed, "Aubrey made it."

"Okay, I'm hungry. You guys want some?"

"Will breaks out in hives if he even thinks of junk food," she teased. "She sent it because she feels bad that you're missing out on your birthday. So eat the whole damned thing if you want."

He blinked a few times, thinking. "Wow. I honestly forgot that tomorrow is my birthday."

"We'll celebrate when you've healed up, I promise."

Jay blew air out, making a *phfft* sound. "I'm getting *me* for my birthday, Mom. That's it for this year. No presents or anything else later, okay? Promise me. This is it."

"We'll talk about it in a few weeks, sweetheart. I can't promise you that right now."

"You may feel like celebrating later," Will said. "Aubrey would even be willing to bake another cake."

Aisha laughed. "He'll be happy as long as I'm not the one making it."

He cut into the cake and pulled a massive slice out. "Sure you don't want some?" he asked. "It's not like I can actually eat the whole thing myself."

"Small piece," she said. "Will?"

"I should get going," Will said. "I'll meet you there at six-thirty."

She frowned as he got up, and Jay leaned over the counter and asked, "Why the hell don't you just stay? It's not like she's going to get any sleep anyway and you'd just be going back out in a few hours."

Aisha got up and followed Will to the counter. "It's not necessarily so simple," she said.

He stuck his tongue out a little and blew a tiny raspberry. "Stop pretending. You're dating. We all know it."

Will couldn't help grinning a little bit. "Propriety aside," he said, "I have Wick's needs to consider. And your mother wants time alone with you. It's *that* simple."

I could have peed in the tub, I told him on the elevator ride down. *And I bet she has chicken or something else dead for me to eat.*

"I appreciate that, but she truly does want to spend some time alone with him. Tomorrow morning she's going to let go of the son she knows and all she wants is to hold onto him for a bit."

But she wants him to do this.

"I know. Do you remember how much Zed changed between twelve and fifteen? Jay is going to do that in about a week. He'll go from looking like a boy to a young man pretty much before her eyes. It won't be easy for her."

Won't be easy for you, either.

"How so?"

She'll be distracted. You won't get much attention.

"And that's fine. I'm a big boy, Wick. I don't need constant affection."

I'll sit on your face and purr if you get lonely.

"You're a big help. But I won't be lonely. I'll be with her while he's undergoing the procedure."

Fine. She can sit on your face.

= = =

Will and I arrived at the hospital first, a few minutes ahead of the guards who came dressed in blue medical pajamas. The waiting room was within sight line of the nurses' station and when the guards arrived, the on-duty employees were dismissed and replaced with Mass's crew and several of the royal guard. One guard in a tactical uniform was posted outside the OR doors—he was for show, the visible just-in-case-of-George threat—and the others waited at the station.

None of them, Will assured Aisha, were aware of the portal; they were there to protect the King, and to protect everyone else if anything went wrong.

She arrived right at six-thirty, with Jay and James right behind her. James was nothing like I expected; he was pasty white with not a lot of pink, and he was skinny but not frail. He was also much shorter than Aisha, barely reaching her nose. Still, standing together they looked like they had once been a cute couple, and there was something about him that I instantly liked.

I felt Will relax; whatever it was, he liked James, too.

James offered Will his hand, but didn't look confused when Aisha set her hand on his arm and said, "The Emperor doesn't shake hands."

He didn't pull it back. "I knew that, but I thought your boyfriend might."

Will shook his hand. "It's a quirk. I'm working on it."

"Yeah, with my mom," Jay snorted. James' eyes widened a touch and his mouth opened to say something, but Jay grinned and said, "You'll like him, Dad. I promise."

"After this, I think I'm required to. Seriously, Emperor, thank you. If I'd had any inkling this was possible I'd have picked Aisha up and tossed her at you years ago."

Do it. Do it now. I want to see that.

"Totally," Jay said. "I owe you."

"And yet, I owe you an apology," Will said to Jay. "I only know because of my intrusive curiosity when I picked up your baby picture. I am sorry, I know you weren't ready to disclose this. And truthfully, your mother didn't violate your privacy. I deduced."

"Zed said I should tell you guys. I dunno. Not saying anything was just easier."

"I understand. It's incredibly personal."

"Is Zed in trouble for keeping it from his parents?"

"No. It was none of their business. It would still be none of their business, had I not needed the King's help. And know that they will never bring it up directly. They may inquire about how you're doing from time to time, but that only means they want to know how you're healing. They aren't asking for particulars."

Jay snorted. "Seriously? I'm going to be so happy when this is all done that I'll show anyone who asks."

Will was amused but told him he might wish to refrain from exposing himself to the Queen. "Protocol and all that."

"Yeah, but if she *asks*…" he started to laugh, but it faded quickly, and he sucked in a deep, nervous breath. The OR doors opened and Mass came out, tablet in hand, to get both Aisha's and James' signatures.

"You about ready?" he asked Jay.

He nodded.

"He'll be under for about seven hours," Mass told James and Aisha. "Expect another half hour after that for him to be awake enough to talk, and then I'll come out and get you."

"Wait." James' hand went to Jay's shoulder. "Can't we go back with him? Until he's under?"

Jay sighed hard. "Dad, come on. Let me do this on my own. Someone will come get you if I need you."

He hugged his dad and didn't protest when Aisha grabbed him and placed a really long kiss on his forehead. "I love you, puppy."

"Mom, we have to talk about that name. And what it implies."

He kissed her back, and as Mass led him away, he said, "Love you, too."

Aisha fought against tears as the doors swung shut. James twitched in her direction, but she laughed, thinly, and said, "I think he just insinuated that I'm a bitch."

Dude, she's gonna blow.

He barely lifted his arm when she tumbled against him. "I don't care. He's still my puppy."

"Remind me of that when he's more comfortable with me," Will whispered to her. "Somewhere in that name there's a paper training joke."

King coming. The guard outside just snapped to attention.

Zed popped through the door first, and he didn't note how uncomfortable James suddenly became when he realized Jax and Aubrey were with him, with Oz and Drew right behind them. "Did I make it in time to see him beforehand?"

"Just missed him," Will answered. "He'll be out of it for the rest of the day, Zed. You might as well go home and be comfortable. We'll call you when he's out."

"Screw that. I'm waiting until he's done."

"It will be several hours."

"And?"

"We'll see," Jax said. He turned to James and held out his hand. "Nice to see you again. It's been a while."

Great. He can't tell if Jax is being sarcastic or not.

James shook it anyway and simply nodded.

They wound up in small talk hell, sitting in uncomfortable chairs while searching for safe things to discuss. I jumped from lap to lap giving head bonks, because it was all I could do, until I reached James and didn't know what he might need. I sat on the floor and stared at him. At some point, he would notice and would either invite me up or ask me what the hell I wanted, and then I would know what to do.

Aisha noticed before he did. "Wick, he likes cats. You can jump on him."

He patted his lap. "You're a friendly guy, aren't you?" he said as he rubbed my head. "I had cats when I was a boy. I miss them."

"You could get a cat, James."

He tucked a finger under my chin. "George hates pets, so it's probably not a great idea." Then a few seconds later, "That probably doesn't matter anymore, so maybe I will think about one. Maybe two. Littermates. Or an older, bonded pair. What do you think, Wick?"

Six. You need six kitties.

Aisha wanted to know if he honestly thought this would break them, and James said it would. "My marriage is over." He stroked my chin, deliberately looking into my eyes. "It's been over, I just didn't realize it until this weekend. Jay overheard him on the phone with his boss last week. He asked for a transfer back to Vegas and said that 'freak kid' would not be making the move with us. Even if this hadn't happened, I would have ended it over that alone." He finally looked up. "I'm glad I took the boys to Tahoe. I'm not sure Jay would have told me at home."

She tried to tell him she was truly sorry, but he waved it off, and then looked to Jax. "Did the proxy really strip George of his parental rights?"

"It does, until Jay's treatments are complete. Given his age, it's essentially for the duration."

"That helps. One less thing to fight over."

"When are you telling him?" Aisha asked.

"Tonight. Maybe." He smiled wanly. "I am not a brave man."

He and Aisha fell into a quiet conversation. Will sat next to Drew and leaned over to ask him what happened after he left the bar. How angry was his mother?

"Not angry, exactly. She looked shocked, though. You know, mouth open, eyebrows knotted together. No one wanted to ask her what had happened."

Oz said that she ran into Jo earlier, and she was a little snippier than usual. "The odd thing about that, though, is that every time I see her, it's like she's a tiny bit more irritated than she was the last time. If that makes sense."

He thought it did; she'd been irritated for weeks, but lately it was aimed right at him. He knew why, but he wasn't inclined to deal with it yet.

Oz muttered, "Menopause" which made Will snort and admit it was possible. In her own When it wouldn't likely begin until late 60s to early 70s. Jo was in her early 70s.

"I am not going to inquire."

"Be a man, Will," Drew said. "March up to your mom and ask her about hot flashes."

Aubrey heard that. "William, she will find a way to ground you."

"Does that mean we can't ask about yours?" Jax asked.

She elbowed him.

Hard.

James' phone pinged and he frowned when he looked at it. "Dammit. Text from George. He wants to know where I am. My boss called the house phone wanting to know how I was feeling." He glanced up from the phone. "I called in sick. Son of a bitch, the first time I've called off work in years, and she calls to see how I am."

Well, yeah, maybe that's why. If you never call in, you're probably really sick.

"Ignore it," Aisha suggested.

"George is a worrier." He held his phone up, turning it over in his hand. "He'll track my location."

"That's not concern," Aisha said. "That's control."

"That's my life," he said quietly. "And he is worried. He panics easily."

"No shit," she mumbled under her breath.

I jumped onto Will's lap and reached up to his face with a paw. *I have to pee.* When he didn't react—and I expected that—I pulled my paw back and slapped at his chin. *I have to pee.*

He sighed and got up. "I need to take him outside."

I like this. I should hit you more often.

Aisha stood, too. "I'll go with you. I need coffee. Anyone else?"

They committed to coffee and tea for all. Will put me on his shoulder and we headed toward the elevator, but just before we reached the door, he turned right down into another corridor, and we slipped into the hallway where the portal was, from the other side.

"I feel a little bad for this," Aisha said. "I know we'll be back in a few minutes, but my brain keeps telling me we're leaving James sitting in the waiting room while he waits for days on end."

"He has company. No one else is going anywhere until we get back, and he's comfortable with Zed."

She reached for his hand. "I know I don't need to do this to get through the portal anymore, but I'm damn well not letting go until I have to."

= = =

Mass and Finn waited for us on the other side of the portal; Finn only stayed long enough to make sure Aisha was fine and to see if she needed anything. He planned on staying in this When until early afternoon and then was going home, but he could still be contacted; one of the lab techs would not mind popping through a portal to get him.

Jay was already in a room changing from his street clothes to thin, paper surgical shorts. We waited, silently, until he came out, shirtless and barefoot, and then Mass led the way to the OR.

Once through the portal, the pale-yellow corridor we'd left behind became a blueish, polished metal hallway, and the walls were pocked with oddly shaped doorways that had windows near the top.

This looks like those space shows Jax likes. If there's a pointy-eared guy, I'm going to wet myself.

The OR door opened with a *swoosh*; Jax would definitely like it. It felt like being on a space ship, but without the nausea he'd probably get from launching.

The room was cold; Jay's skin prickled with goosebumps and my nose stung, but I skipped over being annoyed at the cold when I saw everything waiting for him. Near the back wall, there was a waist-high tank filled with thick orange goo, and it rested on a metal base that had hoses leading to out to smaller tanks filled with tiny metal things, and there were wires leading to several computers. There was a padded table in front of the tank, and next to it was a metal stand that had large syringes and a mask that looked like it was made for deep sea diving, and under the table was a metal cylinder.

Everything looked shiny and new, and the room smelled like Aubrey had just cleaned the kitchen. Jay took it all in; machines beeped and hummed, half a dozen computers that were connected to the tank with thin, plastic-covered wires. In the small tanks near the metal base the tiny metal flakes looked like they were swimming, and as Jay turned from one side of the room to the other, a technician tapped a switch with his foot, and the flakes were sucked away, into the big, goo-filled tank.

Mass patted the padded table and told Jay to hop on up, and then he held up each piece to explain what it was for. The mask was a respirator to keep him breathing during the procedure. There was a clear tube that ran through the center of it, one that would be threaded down to his stomach so that he could be fed. After it was inserted, the tube would be sealed around his mouth, to prevent anything else from sliding down the outside of the tube.

"Nothing in that tank would hurt you, though," he explained. "It's all digestible."

"If you're feeding me, why did I have to show up with an empty stomach?" Jay asked.

"In case the initial anesthesia makes you nauseated. Don't want you throwing up in there."

He picked up the syringes one by one. The first one contained a long-acting analgesic and anti-inflammatory medication. The second was a timed-release hormone pack. The last was a green liquid that would go in just before he was lowered into the tank; it contained approximately 200,000 nanobots that would work on him from the inside, as well as carrying material that would change his genetic code. "They're programmed for specific tasks," Mass said. "Some will essentially consume and digest what's left of the uterus, while others move and transform the ovaries, lengthen and relocate your urethra, and both fuse the labia to create a scrotum as well as remove the vaginal canal. If there's any tissue that could later form breast buds, they'll remove it. They'll begin enlarging your larynx as well."

"Damn," Jay breathed.

"Once you're under the anesthesia, I'll make a small incision just above the pubic bone, and cut the suspensory ligament to release the internal parts of the clitoris. Those will come together, lengthen, and extrude to form the penis."

"And the tank?" Aisha asked. "What's its function?"

"The tank is filled with a gelatinous substance that contains over a million nanobots. They'll surround him and heal any exterior wounds and will begin sculpting his body from the outside. The internal nanobots are the workhorses, the external are the artists. They make sure that where the labia fuse, there are no small tears or holes, and they expedite the process of lengthening tissue for the penis and thickening it a bit to reduce sensitivity."

"Don't I want sensitivity?"

"Not that much. You want to be able to wear pants, I assume."

Jay laughed nervously. "I suppose I need to."

"You'll be in the tank for five days, and you'll be kept sedated until you're cleaned up and back through the portal." He looked to Aisha. "I assumed you want him still at least loopy when I bring you and James back to see him."

"How risky is that?" Will asked.

"I would prefer to wake him up here, but the risks are minimal."

"Then wake him up here."

Jay shrugged. "I don't care. Just make sure I wake up."

"You'll wake up, I promise," Mass said. "Now give your mom a kiss, and she'll see you in a few minutes."

"Do I really have to be awake when you jab me with those needles? Those are…big."

Aisha leaned in and kissed him and told him it would be fine and only hurt a little bit, but his eyes were wide, and for the first time, he was scared.

"Wait," he said before she could step back, "you'll be here when they pull me out of that tank, right?"

"Sweetheart…I'm not sure you want me to."

He sighed. "You were there the day I was born the first time, Mom. Like, exactly seventeen years ago. You should be here this time, too." He looked over her shoulder. "You, too. I want you to be here. I don't care what you see. I just don't want to wake up alone, you know?"

"We'll be here," Aisha promised.

"Still have to be awake for the needles?" he asked Mass. "I'd really rather not."

"Happy birthday, kiddo." Will reached past Aisha and put his pointy finger against Jay's forehead, and he went out like a light. "It's a helpful skill to have when it's nap time for a small, stubborn child. If you want to assure he has pleasant dreams, I can arrange that, as well."

Mass nodded toward the door. "He'll sleep, but he won't really dream. Unless you want to watch the first part where I cut him open, you can wait in the hall. Someone will get you when it's time to put him in the tank."

Even though it was a very small incision, she didn't want to watch as he was cut open, and she didn't want to see the injections or as the tube was put down his throat. She wanted to wait outside with her face buried against Will's shoulder, and she wanted the five days to be over with already.

Go back to the portal and come forward five days. Then it'll be over.

"He'll be fine," Will said. "There's not one thing in his body that won't be monitored. His breathing, his heartbeat, how much oxygen he's taking in, everything. If he urinates, they'll know. A hiccup, a muscle cramp, hunger, they'll know."

"He didn't mention any monitors," she said.

"The nanobots. They'll report everything. As he cycles through slumber, the duration and intensity of his REM cycles will be recorded. If he's hungry, the nanobots will send a signal ordering nutrition. Pain of any sort will trigger delivery of an analgesic. It's an elegant system, and essentially fool proof."

"Essentially."

"There was one time," he started. She pulled away from his shoulder. "When I was young, six or seven, there was a neighborhood boy who'd lost a foot to an accident. Someone misprogrammed the system and he came out of the tank with an extra hand and four thumbs. But that's rare."

"Dammit." She poked him in the stomach. "I need you to be serious."

"No, you don't. You need to be reminded that Mass is damn

good at what he does, and you sought him out as Jay's specialist for a reason."

She nodded. "Hearing everything that will happen, though... I'm not sure what I expected, but it's more than that. I don't know why it didn't occur to me that his existing organs needed to be removed."

Eaten. They'll be eaten. Jay is lunch.

I wonder what people innards taste like. Probably not like chicken.

"I'm curious how the repurposing of his ovaries works. Mass did say he would be fertile after this."

"You're going to spend time studying, aren't you?"

"It sounds like we'll have a lot of time on our hands."

The door opened, and one of Mass's aides beckoned them inside. Jay had been stripped of his shorts and the respirator was firmly in place, and there were four people moving him from the table into the tank, gingerly lifting him over the side. When they set him on top of the goo, he slowly sunk in, until he was covered and suspended halfway between the bottom and the top of the tank.

Aisha crossed her arms as she watched, like she was trying to hold her insides from coming out.

"And we're off," Mass chirped. "Give us about two hours to watch the initial processes, and then you can come back and spend the rest of the day with him if you want." He gestured to a pair of recliners in the corner. "You can move those, just not past the blue line on the floor."

Five feet out from the tank was a thick line, and it was well scuffed up on the safe side.

"You can be here all day, every day, but I ask that you not sleep here. Mostly because I will, and I'm not an entertaining sort of person after nine o'clock."

She didn't want to move. She was locked onto Jay floating in the tank, and she didn't want to leave him.

"We'll go to the cafeteria," Will said, gently pulling her away. "It's only a floor up, and he can get you if you're needed."

She relented, but backed out of the room slowly, and watched him through the window of the closed door for a minute before inhaling deeply, and agreeing to go.

Five feet into the cafeteria, she stopped and clutched at Will's arm. The far wall was a giant window with an unobstructed view of a commuter launch pad, and there were dozens of people suiting up and taking off. Will nudged her forward and went with her to watch as people slipped into flight jackets, securing straps around their legs and waists, and then as they ran to get momentum before jumping up. She was glued to the sight of people taking flight without cars, and he watched her, amused.

"Will, what the hell?" she said after a few minutes.

"I showed something similar to Drew with a holograph. His reaction was, 'are those freaking jetpacks?' And yes, they freaking are."

A bike shot past the window and she startled.

"The future of air bikes," he said. "Faster, lighter, considerably more nimble, and a hell of a lot more fun. And that rider was an idiot. He was far too close to the building."

She craned her neck to look up at the line of cars zipping overhead. "And those. The flying…breath mints."

"Just cars."

"Either the window is thick or they're all incredibly quiet."

"Both. These windows are meant to withstand the impact of an out of control flyer." He pointed to the launch pad on the neighboring rooftop. "It's not unheard of for new pack pilots to throttle harder than necessary. Once or twice a week someone winds up sliding down the front of the building. The emergency entrance is right there." He pointed downward.

She finally looked away. "Come on."

"This time I'm serious. People are rarely hurt, but if they are, help is just a few floors down." He pointed to a series of small nubs just outside the window. "There's a safety net, much like the ones we have on the bridges at home. It cushions the impact somewhat."

"Just somewhat."

"A lesson to be learned," he said. "You'll only do it once."

Did you do it?

"No, Wick. I've never flown into the side of a building."

Just crashed a shuttle into the forest.

"The shuttle was damaged," he said. "And shut up."

After she'd watched for a few minutes, Will led her to a nearby table. She could still see from there, but he knew she hadn't eaten anything and was intent on feeding her. The cafeteria was massive, with more than a hundred tables, but there were only a dozen people scattered throughout, and it was relatively quiet.

Where's the food?

There were no machines to buy food and drinks from and no counter with someone wearing a net hat and sweating while making unhealthy things for people who should eat better.

Will tapped on the table top, and a thin heads-up display lifted, hovering an inch above it. He scrolled through the menu and found grilled chicken for me, and then eggs, fruit, and coffee for them. When he was done ordering, he tapped again, and the monitor disappeared.

That still doesn't tell me where the food is.

A minute later a flap in the wall lifted, and a hover cart floated out and brought everything to the table. The cart was thinner than the one Zed had modified for me at the reception for Florida's First Minister, and it had a lip all the way around to keep things from sliding off. It settled on the table top and Will pulled everything off, and with a nudge sent it on its way.

Aisha was impressed. "I suppose serving isn't much of a job here."

"On the contrary, it's a career. Quick-stop eateries utilize robotic units for everything from food preparation to delivery, but middle and high-end dining establishments have professional wait and cooking staff."

You're my wait staff. Wait to eat your eggs, and tear up that chicken for me.

"Professional," she repeated. "As in, there's a school for that?"

"Apprenticeships," he said as he cut the chicken into small bites. "It's a skill and it pays well. At least two of my cousins went into food service. I assume that if they returned to this When, they're still working."

I bet they're better at it than you are. You cut with the speed of a two-hundred-year-old woman who's been drinking all day.

"Hey. I don't have to give this to you, Wick."

"I've never heard you mention family other than your parents and grandparents," she said.

"I never knew them well. My uncle had two daughters and a son, but they were born when I was almost in my teens. I admittedly had little interest in engaging with them at the time."

"Regrets?"

"They were too young to have clear memories of me. If they know of me at all, it's as a story."

"I hope they have stories about you. Someone mythical to look up to. I hate that Jay has no one. No cousins, no aunts or uncles."

"But one day he may have children. He won't be forgotten."

That made her smile. "I hope so. And I hope he doesn't stick to this one-child mythos. I'd like him to have two or three little monsters running around."

"Kids you can send home at the end of the day." He grinned. "That was a perk to watching Oz and Zed, and I admit, I hope that the future hasn't changed too much. I'd like to be there to see Oz and Drew wrangle the first three. And then to watch them all melt over the last. Drew especially."

"As long as they have Eli," she said.

"I don't think it will matter. Even if I'm not born the next time around, I'm here now and I'm not going anywhere."

"My heart needs to think that you will be, and maybe next time, you won't have to run."

He scattered the chicken on the plate for me, and then leaned back in his chair with a heavy sigh. "I have to run, Aisha. I have to break your heart over and over, in every timeline, forever. And I've made my peace with that."

"Just like that."

"An hour ago, when your son asked for me to be there at what is essentially his rebirth, I understood that fundamentally, it doesn't matter how badly either of us was hurt. He needs to be born, and he needs to be yours, because no one will ever love him and fight for him the way you do."

She burst into tears again.

It was a theme now.

He needed to get used to it.

They went back to the OR ninety minutes later and stood outside, waiting for someone to tell them it was all right to go in. When the surgical tech waved them in, the recliners had already been moved to near the blue line and were pushed close together. Mass told me not to put my feet on the floor—I could stay as long as I was on a lap or shoulder—and then he went to take a break.

There were five other people in the room keeping an eye on Jay, but they were quiet and after a while faded into the background.

He floated in the tank, his arms out to his sides, legs bent at the knees, dangling a few degrees. After a while, tiny little bubbles surrounded him, and then the little bubbles began to look like shiny crystals, which worried Aisha.

"The nanobots," Will reminded her. "They're repairing tissue, and you might see them more concentrated in one spot, then realize they've moved to another an hour later. It's normal."

They sat like that the rest of the day, only getting up to take care of personal business—Will made me hover on the edge of a toilet to pee, which left him with a mess to clean up but he didn't complain about it—and when it was getting late, he reminded her that Mass wanted them out so that he could get some sleep.

We were in the elevator before she realized they hadn't made plans for a place to stay, and asked if Finn would mind if we camped out in the lab.

"He wouldn't mind, but we don't need to. My parents still maintain the family apartment, and we can stay there."

She let him lead the way; he held her hand not just because he wanted to, but because she was easily distracted by the air traffic and people zooming just overhead, and there was the real chance that she would wander into the street without looking. He hailed a cab at the corner, even though it was only a mile and a half away, because she was tired. We rode in the back and she put her head on his shoulder, not paying attention to where we were headed.

She was confused when we got out at Union Square. "What? Tell me you didn't actually live in the lab."

"No," he said with a chuckle. He gestured to the royal house.

"The apartments stayed in the family. It was sort of a parting gift to Oz when she abdicated."

"Your family kept it all this time?"

He nodded. "It's been renovated a few times, and the occupants change from time to time, but my grandfather handed over the main apartment to my dad. He offered its use for as long as we need it."

The royal house we knew had been torn down over a century earlier; this building was glass and metal, the windows smoky colored. The balcony was where it belonged, but it was longer and jutted out farther than I remembered.

It looked nothing like home on the inside, but I remembered this place with its mismatched furniture and worn ceramic floor. I ran into the kitchen to see if my bowl was still there, even though Will called after me, reminding me that it had been too many years since I lived there, and my bowl was long since gone.

He was wrong.

Right by the refrigerator was the crystal bowl Jo bought for me the day after Finn brought me home, and there was an identical one next to it filled with water. Will was as surprised as I was, until he spotted the note on the cupboard.

"Dad was here," Will said. "He stocked it with cat food and there are steak bites in the fridge."

What about food for you?

He opened the refrigerator door. "Eggs, milk, cheese, fruit, sliced meat for sandwiches, and beer." He pulled two bottles out and offered a one to Aisha. "Raspberry wheat. His own brew, which means he hauled it from home."

They drank the beer on the balcony and watched people zip by, though there were fewer out than there were earlier, and most of the people out and about were walking around the Square. As the light dimmed, all but one lone flyer was gone, and he was practicing taking off while in mid stride, trying to gain height quickly. He speed-walked, hit the throttle and hopped up, but kept falling within a few seconds, landing on his backside.

"Jog a few steps and then chamber your leg," he said, as if the man four stories down could hear him. "You need some speed and to get that knee up."

"Can't resist those teaching moments?"

He leaned back in his chair and looked at her. "Is that a nice way of saying I'm a know-it-all?"

"Of course not, sweetie." She rubbed his arm and was grinning, so I don't think she meant it.

"The kids would love to play with one of those packs," he mused. "Part of me wants to bring them here and let them. The other part thinks it would be mean since they wouldn't be able to take one home."

Let Drew take one home so he can take it apart and see how it works. Then he can invent it.

"That's cheating, Wick."

So? Isn't that exactly what you're going to do anyway?

After a long stretch of quiet, she wanted to go inside and go to bed, and then worried about how the hospital could contact her if something happened. Her phone didn't work here, and she suspected his was just as useless.

"There's a house phone," he told her. "Mass has the number, but he won't need it."

"You can tell me that until you're hoarse, sweetheart."

"I know." He went into the first bedroom and flipped the light on. "I will undoubtedly say it often enough that you get angry with me. But truly—"

"It's all right. This is Oz's room, isn't it?"

"She has the better view, I think, but yes. It's similarly located."

I raced to the window seat. He was right. The Square was nice but not as brightly lit and not as much fun to look at as it was when it was Oz's space.

I can sleep here. It's still comfy.

"You can sleep with us if you want," Will said. He started to kick off his shoes and spotted the clothes laid out at the foot of the bed. "T-shirts and shorts to sleep in. And I'll bet there are toothbrush heads and toothpaste on the bathroom counter."

She peeked in. "Yep. A stack of clean towels, too. Your dad has a sweet streak."

Will picked up a shirt and held it out to her.

"Unless you object," she said, "I'm sleeping in the buff. And I wouldn't mind one bit if you did, too."

"No objection, but—"

"I know. I'm exhausted. I don't have the energy. But I really want to be skin to skin with you tonight. That's enough."

When the light was out and they were snuggled together, she sniffed a few times like she was trying to not cry again.

"He's fine, you know he's fine."

Her nose gurgled. "He's not the only one I'm worried about. I'm terrified that you're going to sleep so well that it will be hard to wake you in the morning. And every morning coming."

"Sleep is not what I do best," he reminded her.

"But you're *home*, Will. You heard Mass. He got here and slept for two days. He initially wanted to go back when this was done, and now he wants to stay."

"I won't."

She took a deep breath. "You might."

"Aisha. I swear. I won't. My sleep issues didn't start when I left here. I haven't slept well since I was a toddler. It gets worse if I'm apart from Wick for too long, but I promise, it's nothing new and won't change here."

You'll sleep better.

"Not likely, Wick."

You've slept well every night you've been with her. At least five hours, usually a little more.

"Huh." He told her what I said. "Don't worry if I do sleep, then."

"Wonderful. I'm so exciting I put you to sleep."

You're just wearing him out.

They drifted off after that, and Will slept for eight hours, but he refused to believe it had anything to do with being in this When.

13

When they weren't glued to Jay's tank, watching bubbles pop and the thin layer of crust move around, they were in the cafeteria. Will kept his nose buried in books on a tablet Finn left in the apartment for him—by the third day he could have performed Jay's procedures himself—and Aisha entertained herself with watching people flying outside and the sporadic crowds in the cafeteria. She learned how to order food and drinks from the table, although she wasn't as clear about how to input quantities and wound up with three sandwiches for lunch, and she learned a huge difference between our own When and this one.

On the fourth day, when she was overly tired and coffee wasn't enough to lift the fog, she turned to Will with a worried sigh, and said, "I can't pay for all this, Will. And how the hell will they even bill me? There's no way my insurance will work here."

"Coffee's free," he said, wiggling his cup. "You can drink until your kidneys float out your nose. Not a problem."

"Everything," she stressed. "I didn't stop to think of the bigger picture because all I wanted was for Jay to get this done now. How massive a hole am I in?"

"Massive," he said. "Grand Canyon three times over."

She closed her eyes and groaned.

"Or perhaps it's more like a tiny divot in the sand." When she opened her eyes, he said, "You're not in debt, Aisha. Mass might have a bill waiting for you back home, but given Jay's age, it's covered under Pacifica's genetic medicine program. Submit it to the agency, and he'll be reimbursed by the state."

"How?"

"Medical care is a basic human right, Aisha. Here, if you need care, you get care, regardless of its nature. There is no insurance, and there aren't as many hoops to go through. Once Mass signs him out, that's it."

"That's it."

"You might want to get my dad a bottle of booze. He did help a bit. And he's kept us fed at night. Plus, the beer. Remind me to tell him this batch is excellent."

"Oh my god, anything."

"He'd settle for a hug. The man is both cheap and easy."

She was about to lean across the table and kiss him, but a woman in the same kind of surgical pajamas Mass wore came up to the table, smiling curiously. "William?" she asked, unsure. "Is that seriously you?"

Her name was Kathleen Rosy; she'd gone to school with him in preschool and first grade and later took karate lessons with him. He remembered her, and he didn't bristle when she approached so I guessed that she wasn't one of the people who had delighted in tormenting him, which meant I didn't have to worry about finding the right moment to spray or bite her. Will was polite but reserved, and I think she was about to beg off when someone else joined her, a man around Will's age with a badge that said he was a pediatric operating room nurse.

"Bilbo!" he said gleefully. "Man, I never thought I'd see you again. Where the hell you been? Or when the hell, I suppose. I know you left and I think later we all assumed it was somewhen else." When Will clearly had no idea who he was, he said, "Peter Lucas. You regularly kicked my ass in karate. Skinny little weirdo with the starter mustache that made him look like a ten-year-old with cat fur stuck to his lip? Yeah, me. That's the kid whose ass you kicked."

Then Will remembered him. "I recall being quite easy on you."

"Your ass kicking *was* a lot easier than you were capable of. But it was still an ass kicking."

"He kicked everyone's ass," Kathleen said. "Even the sensei's. *That* was a ton of fun to watch. It gave us all goals."

Aisha invited them to sit with us, and Will introduced her as his girlfriend.

"Finally, someone who can kick *your* ass, eh?" Peter said.

The notion amused Will—he knew it was true—and he nodded, but Aisha skipped right over that and asked, "Bilbo?"

Peter and Kathleen looked at each other. "That goes back to, what, preschool? We always called him that."

"Good or bad?" Aisha asked Will.

"These two were not part of those who took joy in torturing me," he said. "It started after we read *The Hobbit* as a class. I didn't mind."

"You read that in preschool," she said, disbelieving.

"Different times," he said. "Most children here enter preschool already able to read."

Kathleen had a different take. "Sort of. There's a divide. Half the kids can read at an advanced level. The other half, usually the jerks and kids full of shit, ride on their coattails. I know you could read far beyond everyone else, and a couple others were right behind you, but some of those were jerks. I still have nightmares about the things they did to you. I still can't swim."

"Jesus, the assholes you had to put up with," Peter said. "You know, a bunch of us tried to find you partway through eleventh grade, to see if you would come back to school. We figured by then you could take care of the fucking idiots who were afraid for no good reason."

Kathleen nodded. "You'd already left. I don't think any of us realized why until years later, when your dad was shuffling people through portals."

Neither of them had been willing to leave. They knew the odds were against them, but, Peter said, if the meteor hit and there were survivors, someone needed to care for the wounded. "Pipe dream, but still. If we made it, we had the skills to help."

"Luckily, we didn't get to be the heroes," Kathleen said. "Now our lives have no meaning, beyond early morning shifts and surprisingly tasty cafeteria food."

"The whole saving lives every day thing, that's just the boring part?" Aisha asked.

"It's a whole lot of staring at machines and watching people float," Peter said. "But I wouldn't do anything else."

"Same," Kathleen said. "It looks boring from the outside but knowing what all the data points mean and knowing what to do? And then when the patient recovers? Ah, man."

"Especially kids," Peter said. "Every day I take a kid out of the tank, and I'm the first person they see. First friendly face. Most of them feel well for the first time in weeks, and damn, the smiles. I live for that."

"I can imagine," Will said.

"What are you doing these days?" Peter asked.

"I serve at the leisure of the King," Will said. "I guard his children and sometimes serve as an advisor. I side with the Queen when she's picking on him and remind him that he is not worthy of her affections."

"How far back? I figured you went a ways but your parents wouldn't say."

"A couple hundred years."

Kathleen cocked her head to the side a bit. "That's right. You're a descendant of the old royal family. You'd be King if we'd kept the monarchy."

That made Aisha's eyes go wide. "Really, Will?"

"Probably not. The gymnastics my grandfather did through time would have put a choke hold on that. Since he left his own When, Oz and Drew would have chosen another heir. And even if they hadn't, my father is still alive. He would be King."

King Finn. Bast, no.

"Oz and Drew," Kathleen repeated.

"Queen Australia was better known as Oz to her friends and family. Drew is Prince Andrew, her husband. My great, great grandparents."

"And you know them in person now?" Kathleen asked. "How weird is that?"

"Surprisingly, not very."

Aisha laughed. "Admit it, Will, it's a little weird. This is *all* weird. Being here…so weird."

"Ah, not from here?" Peter asked.

Her "no" was soft. Will reached for her hand and squeezed gently. "Just another day, then we take Jay home."

"You brought someone from a different time for treatment?" Kathleen asked. "Very cheeky. I approve."

"I was worried about that," Will said dryly. "But yes. Brian Massimo relocated to the same When as I, and he was willing to do this for us."

Kathleen perked up. "Mass is back? Please tell me he's not all old and wrinkly. Or married. I had such a crush on him."

"He's old," Will said. "And married."

"Wrinkly, too," Aisha said. "But he's still hot."

"Well, married won't keep me from flirting. Good."

Peter's badge beeped, and he got up. "Duty calls. Nice to see you, Bilbo. And I'm really sorry we couldn't catch up before you left. I hated that you were still pretty much hiding from all of us, but I'm glad you're doing well."

Kathleen started to get up, too. "File this away just for the info, but all those assholes who picked on you when we were little kids bolted the first chance they got, and now they're all dead. The few who stayed turned out all right, and if they saw you, they'd apologize. Not that it helps, but there it is. We were *all* sorry, once we grew the hell up."

"Thank you."

She stood up and laughed. "Hell, they might even be whenever it is you settled. I hope to god you're famous or something and it's really pissing them off."

Aisha snorted. "Famous or something. He's well known."

She started to walk off, but then came back. "Son of a bitch. You're the Emperor of San Francisco. I remember the pictures from history class. You had a beard, but it's you, isn't it?"

He shrugged lightly. "Guilty."

"What do you know. Out of everyone we started school with, you may be the only one who actually did something big."

"I babysit the King," he said. "You save lives."

"The way I hear it, you saved us all." She looked at Aisha. "Seriously, keep him away from the public. If word gets out that the Emperor jumped forward and is here, you'll have hundreds, maybe thousands, trying to get to him."

"Slight exaggeration, I'm sure," Will said.

She pointed to his tablet. "Look up the Cult of the Emperor. Seriously. They're messed up."

You have a fan club.

"Not a fan club, Wick," he said. "Just—I don't know what the hell it means."

"I'm assuming the Emperor's life was taught as part of history in school," Aisha said. "All those kids who knew you, why wouldn't they recognize your picture?"

"Probably assumed he was an ancestor, if they thought about it at all. If you read about Michelle Obama and her picture resembled your neighbor, you wouldn't assume they were the same person."

"Who's Michelle Obama?"

"Wife of the forty-fourth president—" He stopped himself from launching into a lecture and exposing his history teacher side. "Never mind. They simply had no reason to suspect."

She reached for his tablet. "All right, tell me how to research this cult. I want to read up on my competition."

When we were back in the OR, watching Jay float, Will showed her how to access the Internet. He leaned back and read a book on his phone while she jumped from site to site, soaking up as much as she could, occasionally snorting or giggling.

"They want to find your burial site," she said a couple of hours later. "They think if they can find your remains, they'll be able to extract your DNA and clone you. And there's an entire lot of them who think that you're immortal, still alive and well and living somewhere in the northwest."

She showed him the page she was looking at. "This one wants to figure out how time travel works, so she can go back and have your babies."

He glanced at the tablet. "I don't think so."

"They want an army of little Emperors." She went back to the tablet and swiped to the next site, mumbling, "Sorry ladies, but that's my job."

He raised an eyebrow but didn't say anything.

"What's the Emperor's Paradigm?" she asked after a while. "This group wants to revive it."

"The shelter, housing, and employment program," he answered, not looking up from his phone. "It fell into disrepair after the Emperor's death. Oz and Drew tried to maintain it, but lost its main infrastructure and funding when she gave up the country to democracy."

"Damn. I'm sorry."

"It was a little too socialist for the more conservative citizens. If someone can reinvent it, more power to them."

"You seem remarkably calm for someone whose major life work ended."

"That Emperor's did," he pointed out. "I have hopes I can hold onto it." He finally turned his phone off. "It helps to think of the man you're reading about and of me as two different people."

"Even so, let's not let these groupies find you here, all right?"

"They're looking for remains or a portal. Neither of which they have access to."

"Your DNA can't be extracted from your remains, can it?"

He shook his head. "I was probably pressed into stone and laid to rest in the royal home." He thought about it and then said, "Huh. We could go look. It's just downstairs a few floors. It'd be nice to know what color my stone is. I've always assumed it would be black."

"No. Absolutely not."

"I'm sure it's nicely displayed."

"No," she insisted, voice cracking. "I don't want to have to face your death no matter when it happens. And I don't want to see what's left of Jax and Aubrey, or even Oz and Drew. They would be there, too."

"Indeed." He reached over and took the tablet from her. "And to that end, don't look up your own name, or Jay's. Your history from this point in time is not the same as what your future will be, but if you find it, you'll have expectations."

"I just wanted to find out about your groupies. I don't need to know what sad little life I lived without you."

"It might have been wonderful."

She gazed at the tank. "If he was happy, I'm sure it was."

"He was certainly less crusty."

"He'll be upset he missed this part," she mused. "This is the kind of thing that fascinates him. He would have tried scooping out the goo and smearing it on something to check it out, though."

Will held up his phone. "There are pictures. I presumed he would eventually want to see what he went through."

"Sneaky son of a bitch. I should be irritated."

"The pictures are not revealing."

"Well, of course not. He's covered in…stuff."

"Less so than he was a few hours ago," Will said. "Considerably less."

"That's normal, isn't it? He comes out tomorrow."

Will got out of the recliner and walked to the far side of the room, where he had a better look at the monitors displaying Jay's vital signs and progress stats. The technician monitoring him glanced up but didn't say anything, until Will asked, "He's coming out tonight, isn't he?"

"Not allowed to say," the tech said. "But I am about to alert Dr. Massimo if that means anything to you. It's going to get busy in here."

Will turned and pointed at me. "You don't move from that chair, no matter how loud it gets or how many people are in here."

"Will?" She was out of her chair and looked terrified. "What's wrong?"

"You're about to watch your son's second birth," he said, grinning. He started pushing the chairs out of the way, reminding me again to not move. "He's fine, Aisha. He's just ready to come out a little early."

"He's not done cooking!"

The tech laughed but didn't try to assure her. Will put his arms around her and promised that he wouldn't be taken out before it was time, and by then Mass had come in, already pulling gloves on. Four of his aides followed and surrounded the tank, ready to fish Jay out.

"Let's see what we've got here," Mass said, mostly for Aisha. He went to the tank first and walked the length of it on all sides, and then went to the monitor Will had looked at. "The internal nanobots have disengaged and have worked their way into his colon. Another three to four minutes for the exterior 'bots to finish sloughing off, and we can bring him out."

"But you said five days," Aisha sputtered.

"I did say that, didn't I?"

"I suspect Mass is the man who pads his estimates," Will said. "If it's six days, he says a week. Five hours, he says seven."

"Some patients take the full five," he said. "But yeah. I tend to do that." He started flipping switches on the side of the tank. "If I'd told you four and it took five, you'd panic."

"But what if you're wrong? What if he's not finished?"

"Then we'll put him back," Mass said simply. "We can reboot the nanobots. Once we get him out and cleaned up, we'll scan him before we wake him up. But he's done."

"But—"

"He had a head start. We kept him on the fringe of puberty, and that's generally where the first day goes, undoing all the damage of adolescence. He'd barely begun, so less to repair."

Bubbles formed at the bottom of the tank and the stream increased rapidly, lifting him to the top of the tank, where the techs slid a board under him and then moved him to the exam table. Orange goo dripped from him onto the table, and they worked fast to suction and then scrub it off him.

"All right, Mom," Mass said as he moved to grab equipment from behind the tank. "It's time for you to step outside for a few minutes. He's about to expel a couple hundred thousand nanobots along with the liquid nutrients we've been giving him, and it won't be pretty."

She wanted to stand her ground; it didn't matter, she could stand the sight of that.

"Remember his first dirty diaper? Multiply that horror by a few hundred. This is meconium on steroids. You really don't want to be in here."

Will gently pulled on her arm, until she was backing out of the room with him. I stayed in the chair, out of the way like he'd told me, and watched what Mass didn't want her to see. As soon as the door closed, he rolled a glass canister from behind the tank, attached a hose to it, and wedged it where Jay surely didn't want anything wedged.

There was a quiet hum, and the canister filled with green and orange liquid that had tiny metallic flecks in it. It wasn't as disturbing as I'd thought it would be but I wasn't his mother. She'd probably care that his colon had been invaded and was being vacuumed out.

Still, it was the removing of the respirator he truly hadn't wanted her to see. It made a horrible sucking sound as it was pulled away from his face, and when the gastric tube was pulled out with it, Jay's back arched from the table and he let go a rattled, painful groan. Mass waited a few seconds for Jay to take a breath on his own, and when he did, he gestured for the aides to finish cleaning him off.

It was a detailed bath, something else he probably didn't want her to see. They rolled Jay from side to side to clean every inch of him, even the parts that no one else would ever see. When he was clean, his hair washed and body dried off and thoroughly inspected, Mass opened the door and let them back in.

Aisha went straight for him, placing a hand on his chest while she kissed his forehead. She stood quietly while she stared at his face and felt his heartbeat, her hand riding on the rise and fall of his chest. "I'm here, puppy," she whispered.

Mass was on the other side of the table. "Healthy, bouncing adolescent boy. All ten fingers and toes. His vitals are right where I want them to be. He came through it just fine."

They let her watch him quietly for a long stretch. When she exhaled and placed another kiss on his forehead, Will asked what they should expect after this.

"Well, he's about to go through the last part of puberty in a major way. His voice will be a bit squeaky when he wakes up, but it will be a little deeper. His body hair will be more noticeable over the next couple of weeks, and his facial hair will thicken. He'll start growing taller soon, and within three months he should be within an inch or two of his full adult height. Genital growth will also occur at a fairly rapid rate. Less than a month."

She finally looked at the rest of his body. "I think he'd be happy with what he's already got."

"Most patients are," Mass said. "They're happier later. Right now he has the body he would have had at about thirteen. The average thirteen-year-old boy is thrilled with what he has and can do with it, but I've never heard one complain down the road when they have significantly more girth and a few more inches."

"I still can't believe he was all right with us seeing him like this."

"Not uncommon in younger patients," Mass said. "Somewhere in the back of their heads they know it may be the only time their parents see what they fought so hard for. My adult patients are far less open."

"They had to self-advocate," Will guessed.

"After years of fighting family most of the time. Their journey was and remains private. Give Jay time, and he'll recoup any lost body shyness. Probably around the first time he realizes that you realize he masturbates like a little fiend."

As one of the aides covered Jay with a table-width tiny tent from his waist to his knees, Aisha asked if things were different here. "Do people here, now, have to fight so hard for this? To be themselves?"

"There's not nearly the stigma," Mass said. "There are always people like James' husband who believe you are what you are were born as and you leave it alone no matter how miserable you are, but for the most part no one cares. I'm not required to do multiple brain scans to confirm gender. I only need to know a person's personal history and their own account of whatever level of dysphoria they've been living with. If they decide later it was a mistake—which, to be honest, I've never had happen, either here or there—I could reverse it."

"I wish it had been that easy for him." Her hand went from his chest to his face, rubbing a thumb over his chin. "You always knew who you were."

"Could have been much worse," Mass said. "There was a time when he would have been forced to wait until well into adulthood, then live as a man for a year before even getting hormones. And surgery wasn't an option beyond mastectomy and hysterectomy."

"Far worse," Will said. "He could have been killed for who he is."

Mass snorted. "So could his stepfather. You'd think he'd see the irony."

She didn't understand.

"He's gay," Will pointed out. "Take him back a few hundred years, and he'd be just as much at risk as Jay would be. Historically, the world has not been kind to those who fall outside the mainstream."

"Can we send George back a few hundred years?"

Jay took a deep breath. The tech sitting near the monitor said he was coming around, and another placed a small bucket near his head.

"In case he throws up," Mass explained. "Happens once in a while. If we suddenly roll him onto his side, don't panic."

He didn't vomit. His breathing became less shallow and his eyes fluttered a few times, and he moaned softly.

"We have liftoff," the monitor tech said. "Heart rate is good, blood flow is good. Respiration increased by twenty."

Aisha's brow furled. "What's happening?"

Mass was matter-of-fact. "You got to see his first moments as a biological male. You don't get to see his first erection."

She took a startled step back, and then laughed at herself.

"He's awake," the tech said.

Jay opened his eyes, looked at Aisha, and then closed them again. It took an hour before he was awake enough to speak, and when he did, he asked for water.

Mass wet a sponge on a stick and swabbed his mouth.

A few more minutes later he moaned, "Mom?"

Her hand went to his chest again, and she leaned over so that he could see her. "Hey, puppy."

"Hurts," he said thickly.

Mass patted his shoulder. "We'll give you something for that, hold on." He nodded to a tech who held a bottle to Jay's nose and then sprayed. "Less than a minute and you won't hurt as much."

"I'm okay?"

"You did fine," Aisha said.

"All the right parts in all the right places," Mass told him. "Once you're fully awake, we'll sit you up and you can see."

That could take place back home; Mass suggested they head back and he would follow. He planned on timing it so that he came out into the waiting room six hours post-op, long enough for James to hope it would be over soon but not so quick that he would worry corners had been cut.

Jay would be waiting in the recovery room, and they could both go back to see him. He would still be a little bit groggy, but able to carry on a conversation.

She kissed Jay half a dozen more times and then reluctantly left with Will. They were both quiet until we were on the other side of the portal.

"Coffee," he reminded her. "We left to get coffee for everyone."

And for me to pee.

She went into the cafeteria while he took me into the men's room. Like it or not, I was using a toilet, and like it or not he was cleaning up after me.

"You could aim better," he grumbled.

I could, but why?

He was too tired to argue, and still had several hours to kill in the waiting room.

= = =

"That was fast," James said when we came back with the coffee and juice. "No line in the cafeteria?"

Aisha handed him a cup of coffee. "Will made Wick use the men's room instead of taking him outside. Wick's not happy, but it was a time saver."

"That's an option?" Drew sputtered. "Cat, how many times have I scooped the freaking litter box for you, and you know how to use a toilet?"

It's not pleasant. I might fall in. Plus, I can't flush.

"How many times have I picked up your dishes off the counter? And out of the sink?" Oz said. "And you know how to use a dishwasher."

"Don't help him."

But she's right and you know it. Besides, my aim is bad and you'd have to clean it up.

James' phone pinged, but he set it on a little table near his chair and then ignored it. "At what point can we expect someone to come out and give us an update?" he asked.

In a couple of centuries.

"They might not," Aisha said. "No news is good news."

He got up and went to the double doors to peek through the window, and then began pacing nervously. Every ten minutes his phone pinged, and he twitched toward it but didn't pick it up.

He stayed on his feet for over an hour, until Aisha told him he was making her nervous. "When did you last eat something?" she asked. "You're getting twitchy."

"No idea," he said. "Yesterday, probably."

"Killer burgers in the cafeteria," Zed said. "Jay and I have come here just for those a few times."

Will handed his bank card to Zed and asked him to go get food. As the door swung closed, James' phone rang, and he ignored it the same as he did the texts.

"You have to answer sooner or later," Aisha told him.

"Maybe once we know something."

There were still two hours to get through before Mass would open those double doors to tell them everything went well. Even knowing that, Aisha was nervous, and she reached for Will's hand, looking for comfort.

Five minutes later, the door slammed open. I expected Zed, loaded down with burgers and fries and soft drinks, but it was a broad, angry looking older man with one hand wrapped around a phone and his other balled into a fist. He went straight for James, who stood up but flinched and wilted against the anger.

"I've been texting and calling you all damned day," he barked. "Answer your damned phone when I call. I've been worried sick. Why didn't you pick up?"

James reached for his phone but didn't make any excuses.

"Answer me!" he bellowed.

Aisha was the one who finally said something. She got up and stepped toward them, more resigned to his outburst than angry. "Stop it, George. Just…stop."

He didn't look at her. "Where's Jaime?" He waved the phone at James' face. "Do you know how much I panicked when I tracked you to the hospital? Then I got here and discovered you were on *this* floor? What do you think you're doing? I won't allow it, James."

"Kind of late," Aisha said.

He spun on his heel. "What the hell did you do? How—" He stopped when he saw Will, who had gotten up and was stepping toward Aisha. They stared at each other, clearly uncomfortable. George didn't even seem to register that the King and Queen were there; he just stared at Will, mouth half open, until Aisha asked what the problem was.

"I wasn't expecting him," George sputtered.

Will's voice was nearly a growl. "Neither was I."

"I didn't realize you knew each other."

"I had no idea that this is who George was," Will said.

George grumbled, "We knew each other as kids, that's all."

Dude, he's like a hundred years older than you.

Jax looked at Oz and Drew, subtly shaking his head: say nothing.

"Indeed, we did," Will said. "And it was not pleasant."

Aisha reached for Will's arm but didn't ask him to explain.

"Don't touch him!" George screeched.

"And why not?"

"He's a—just don't."

Will deliberately slipped his fingers between Aisha's as he held her hand. "I'm what, George? A freak? Is that still the word you fling at people you don't understand? Or are you still holding to the notion that I exist to suck the souls out of small children? That *is* what the playground threat was, wasn't it? Stay away from William Blackshear. He'll eat your soul."

George's chest heaved; fast breath in, fast breath out. "You know what you are."

"So does she," Will said evenly.

He's a pleasant fellow. I'm not sure he's human, though.

Drew's fingers tapped on my back. Be quiet.

Well, I'm not. I think he's probably from the species Assholus Rectus. You can tell because his head is so small. That's so it will fit—.

Drew thumped the top of my head with his middle finger.

George snapped back to James. "Where the hell is Jaime?"

James, quietly, "You know where he is."

"You damn well better not go through with it." His face was red, nostrils flared, and he stabbed his pointy finger at James. "I'll *never* give my permission."

"It's done, George," Aisha said. "Not a damned thing you can do about it now."

George grabbed James by the arm and yanked him close, hard. "What the hell did you do?"

James did nothing to break George's grip. Their noses were less than an inch apart, and his muscles strained against George's fingers—even as skinny as he was, he was the stronger of the two, physically, and I thought if he wanted to he could lay George out flat—but he refused to give him the fight he was itching for.

Will said evenly, "He didn't do anything. I did."

Jax got up and stood next to Will. "To be clear, it was mutual effort resulting in a state declaration. In light of your refusal to agree to the appropriate medical care for your son, I agreed to be his proxy."

"You can't do that."

"Actually, I can. You can pursue the matter with a lawyer, but legal gray areas always end up on my desk. If I don't rule in your favor, you can file an appeal with the Supreme Court, but that will take years." He glanced at his watch. "The surgery will be over with in an hour or two, so I suggest you hurry."

George let go of James and stepped close to Jax; two guards at the nurse's station as well as the one guarding the OR doors started to come toward him but held back when the Queen gestured for them to wait.

"Even the King has no right to get between a father and daughter. You can't just decide for me."

Jax put a finger on George's chest and pushed him back a step. "I believe that you'll find I can do exactly that. You'll also find that in doing so, I have stripped you of all parental rights. Jay's medical treatment will continue without interference."

George shot an angry look at James, and then—presumably without thinking—he took a swing at Jax.

Will was on him instantly. He blocked the punch from connecting and put George in an arm lock, pulling his arm tight to his shoulder blades. At first George was just angry, but after a moment, he looked terrified.

A fraction more of pressure and his arm would break.

A little more pressure around his neck and he wouldn't be able to breathe.

A step to either side and Will could break his neck.

Will asked Jax if he wanted to have him arrested.

Jax waved the guards off. "Understand, the Emperor could have easily killed you for that. Because of the circumstances, I'll let it go, but it will be reported throughout the guard and if you raise your voice again today, argue over Jay's treatment, or cause any other issue that I *personally* find unsettling, I will have you arrested."

Will let him go, shoving him away from Jax.

George turned to James, quietly, "Why?"

"Because Jay needs this."

"Jaime—"

Calmly, Aisha said, "Jaime never existed, George. You know that. Let it go."

His eyes flicked toward Will. "I don't have a choice, do I? We're Jaime's *parents*, and you go running to the King?" To James, "You know what this means."

"I know."

George waited, as if he hoped James would bend or tell him it wasn't too late to stop the train he saw coming right at him. It wasn't going to slow down; it was only going to speed up. When James said nothing, he murmured, "I'll come for my things later."

As the door closed, Aisha softly said, "James, I'm sorry."

He shook his head. "I'm not."

When she looked surprised, he said, "He didn't ask if Jay was all right. You told him the procedure was done, and he didn't ask if the child he claims to love is all right."

= = =

The quiet that fell after George stormed out was heavy and reverberated off the walls hard enough that when Zed came back, he stopped three steps into the waiting room. "What happened? What's wrong? Jay?"

"George," Aisha said.

"Ah. Good." He gestured to Drew to pull two short tables from the corners and set them together, and he put the food there. "As long as it isn't something about Jay."

"No news yet," James grumbled. He slumped in his chair, embarrassed and uncomfortable, unwilling to meet anyone else's gaze. I crossed the waiting room and stretched up on my back legs to pat at his arm, and then rubbed my face against his leg.

It wasn't his fault.

You're a dude. You don't need a douchebag.

"Eat," Aisha ordered him. "I'm sorry George showed up and made such a fuss, but you won't do Jay any good if you pass out in front of him."

"Still, I—"

Softly, "I know, James. Your stomach is tied up in knots. But you need food, and I will sit here and bitch at you until you eat something. I still know what buttons to push. Don't make me do that in front of everyone."

Reluctantly, he accepted the burger Zed held out to him. Jax and Aubrey took this as a moment when they could leave; she asked Will to call her when Jay was out of surgery and to make Zed come home with Oz and Drew. He would want to hang on until the very last minute, not realizing he might be intruding. Let him see Jay for a minute or two, then send them home.

Right at the six-hour mark, Mass pushed the OR door open. He greeted them with a smile, and even though she knew Jay was all right, Aisha popped up, concern painted on her face.

"He did just fine," Mass said. "No hiccups along the way and everything looks great. He's still groggy, but he wants to see you. And in a little bit, we'll sit him up so he can get a good look at himself."

He was in a recovery room just past the doors. Will watched as Aisha and James walked down the hall together, and as she reached for his hand.

"How much does that bother you?" Drew asked when the doors swung closed.

"They're both still worried. It doesn't bother me at all."

"You're allowed to be like a real live boy and get jealous sometimes, you know."

"I have no reason for jealousy," Will said. He had no doubt that others would flirt with and pursue her, but he had nothing to worry about. And regardless, she would always have a connection with James. If she reached for his hand in times like these, he understood.

"Yeah, but if he starts to hump her leg like a horny little dog, you'll care."

He raised an eyebrow. "That might be worth seeing."

"So, what?" Oz asked. "You watch him get off and then kick his ass?"

Will shook his head. "Oh, she'd do that long before I could."

"You people are gross," Zed grumbled.

"Says another horny little dog," Oz said. "How's Sophia? Have you gotten her to flash you on a video chat yet?"

"What the hell is wrong with you?" He wasn't upset; he just didn't want to answer that in front of Will.

Twenty minutes later, the OR door opened again, and Aisha came out. "You can go back and see him, Zed," she said. "First door on the right. But keep in mind, he's still loopy from the drugs and is in some pain."

He nodded and jumped up.

"Five minutes," Will called after him. "Everything all right?"

"Mass sat him up and offered him a chance to look. He refused. I couldn't even tell him I knew everything was all right and looked good, because James was right there. Mass offered three times, and he absolutely refuses."

"He'll look when he's ready. It might be overwhelming right now."

"Still." She let out an exasperated, but amused, breath. "All this, all the years of fighting with George to get this done, and he's afraid to look down and see for himself that yes, he finally has a penis."

"He's afraid he won't," Drew speculated.

"His journey," she said, mostly to herself. "He's allowed baby steps."

"His journey, his pace." Will held his arms out for her. "We'll be here to help, no matter how long it takes him to get there."

14

An hour after Jay was home and settled into bed, Will kissed Aisha and reminded her he was just a phone call away and left James with her. No matter what she needed—someone to run errands, fetch food, an ear to simply listen—call. It didn't matter what time it was; if she realized at four in the morning she was out of milk and wanted some, call. If Jay woke up wanting pizza or burgers or even donuts, call. He didn't mind, and she wouldn't be waking him up, so call.

When I asked why we weren't staying to help and be right there if she needed something, he said that Jay needed his family without intrusion and that he would see her in the morning. His presence might make them feel awkward, and Jay was in too much pain to deal with that.

But you want to be there.

"I do. But what I want is irrelevant right now."

She called him at seven the next morning; James had to work, and she wanted company while Jay slept. He made lunch, which Jay groggily proclaimed to be healthier than any human needed, when the truth was that he didn't have much of an appetite, and later on he washed the dinner dishes while Aisha helped Jay clean up. When James came home from work, Will scooped me up, kissed her long enough to make James squirm, and left.

Dude, that was like a dog peeing on everything in the yard. She's not your territory.

"Was it? She didn't seem to mind."

Maybe next time save everyone the time it takes to think about it and just pee on her leg.

On the third day, she needed to spend a few hours at school to prepare for the summer term and James had meetings he couldn't miss, so Will stayed with Jay while he slept the afternoon away. He was there in case he needed help getting out of bed for anything. He only rolled over a few times, and when Will heard a soft moan, he crept into Jay's room and sprayed his pain medication into his nostril without waking him.

You should have been a nurse. You're not half bad at it.

"It's easier when the patient is out of it," he said as we rode the elevator down. "And I'm not sure I would have been a decent nurse. They work far harder than I do, and I'm just a tiny bit lazy sometimes."

No, you're not, but okay.

By Jay's fourth night home, Aisha was exhausted, but he was feeling better, more awake, and he claimed to have less pain. James spent an hour with him after he got home from work, and when he left Jay was sitting up in bed, reading. Aisha puttered around in the kitchen, trying to come up with something to make for dinner.

Will watched as she slammed the pantry door closed for the third time. He didn't say anything, but slipped in behind her and put his arms around her. She stiffened at first, but then the tension rolled away and she turned, burying her face against his shoulder.

"I'll call for delivery," he said. "You go lie down for a while. Or soak in a hot bath."

She didn't argue against the idea of ordering dinner in but balked at the idea of not being available if Jay needed her. "He still needs help getting up, Will. He doesn't have full bladder control yet, and he still won't…look."

After Mass brought him back through the portal and had him sitting up in bed, he refused to look. His entire body hurt, and he was sure the pain meant that everything was a jumbled mess of blood and bruises, and he didn't want to see himself like that. He wanted to wait, even though he'd been promised there was nothing externally obvious. He hadn't showered and made a conscious effort to not see himself in a mirror.

"I am fully capable of helping him get out of bed and headed for the bathroom."

"But if he's not comfortable—"

"Then he'll tell me. And if he won't get up, I'll hand him a trash can and tell him to pee into it, and then he'll have to look."

She laughed in spite of herself. "I'll order food, but I can't lie down, Will. If I do, I'll fall asleep, and it's so early."

He didn't argue. She didn't want to risk falling asleep that early and knew he wouldn't wake her if she did. Instead, he asked her to bend her rule about men spending the night. "You need to sleep uninterrupted, and I have no problem staying awake all night. I have work I can catch up on, and if he needs anything, I'll see to it."

She worried that Jay would be uncomfortable; being tired was something she could handle, but this wasn't the time to stress him.

"I'll consult with him while you call for food."

He didn't give her a chance to argue because she was cranky and anything misunderstood would have to be smoothed over later. He was out of the kitchen and down the hall before she could think of a reason why he shouldn't.

I'll snoopervise him.

As I jumped onto the bed, Will dragged a chair away from Jay's desk, and he turned it backward before he sat down. It was the way he sat when he was younger, with his folded arms across the chair back, and it used to make the old Queen three kinds of twitchy and upset. It was rude and undignified, and worse, Jax often copied him. Jay scooted up on the bed and put an extra pillow behind his back, and asked what was up.

Will went right to it. "Your mother needs an uninterrupted night's sleep. You're increasingly ambulatory and don't need her hovering. Would you be comfortable if I stayed tonight, and helped you get out of bed if you need assistance?"

He shrugged. It didn't matter to him but he'd be surprised if she would be all right with it. "I'm pretty sure she thinks if she doesn't get up five times a night to check on me, everything will suddenly reverse and boom, she has a daughter."

If it all falls off, I bet Mass can glue it back on.

"You may be right."

"I don't think I'll need much help tonight. I know she keeps coming in here to check on me, but the pain meds work pretty well. And I'm not always as asleep as she thinks I am. I just don't want her to worry."

"You don't have to pretend. If you're awake and want to talk or sit up, anything, just tell me. I'll be staying up all night, so you don't need to worry about keeping me awake."

"You're kidding. Man, if you're sleeping with my mom, at least sleep some, you know?"

"I truly don't sleep much. If I doze, it will be on the sofa in the living room. Wick will wake me if you need something."

He swung his legs over the side of the bed. "You don't have to pretend, Emperor. Will. I won't be shocked or need therapy or anything if you're sleeping with her." He winced. "Screw it. I hope you are."

"Really now."

He closed his eyes and arched his back, trying to stretch. "I'm not the kid that hopes his parents will get back together so he automatically hates anyone they're interested in. And I'm not stupid either. She always puts me first, and she ignores the men who are obviously flirting with her. If she's finally dating openly and wants to sleep with you, I'm all for it. Just be nice to her, that's all I want."

"I fully intend to be."

"It's kinda serious, isn't it? You're not going anywhere for a long time."

Will nodded.

"All right," Jay grunted as he slid off the bed. "Then you get to help me hobble my way to the bathroom, and no saying anything when I wind up dribbling pee down my leg halfway there. Apparently, bladder control is a learned skill that I lost in the last week."

"Kegels," Will said as he helped Jay to his feet. "And stand when you urinate."

Jay hesitated at the door. "How'd you know I wasn't?"

"Old habits die hard, I imagine. But if you want to gain control, stand and take aim. Stop and start the flow, the same way you would have two weeks ago. You may dribble less afterward as well, since sitting may be preventing you from fully emptying your bladder."

"Two weeks ago I wasn't standing."

"You know what I mean." He patted Jay on the shoulder to get him moving. "It might hurt a bit, but you'll manage."

He's gonna pee all over the place.

"That's fine," he whispered. "As long as he makes an effort."

When he was still in there several minutes later, Will knocked on the door and asked if he was all right. Aisha stood at the head of the hall, worried, and she was about to march down the hallway to throw the door open when Jay answered.

"Yeah, fine. I just—" He opened the door. "I didn't realize it would be this squishy."

Aisha had to put her hand over her mouth to keep from laughing, but Will kept a straight face. "All right, I suppose squishy is one way to put it. Now, back to bed or do you want to sit in the living room for a while?"

"What if I dribble?"

"I'll throw a towel down first."

Will made him walk by himself, though he was ready to grab him if he started to fall. He took smalls steps and only reached out for help when he was trying to sit, and then said he felt a whole lot better than he had even a few hours ago. "I'm still super sore but I don't feel like a bus ran over me anymore."

"You look better, too," Aisha said.

"Don't smell better." He looked up at Will. "I need to take a shower. Any chance that after dinner you can sit in there and make sure I can get in and out?"

"I can. Would you prefer your father? I'm sure he would come downstairs to help."

"Yeah, he would, but if I hit the floor, he'll never be able to get me up."

"Sweetheart, you don't weigh more than he can lift," Aisha said.

He leaned his head over the back of the sofa to look at her. "And you know this, how?"

"None of your business." She bent over to kiss his forehead. "He'll come down if you want him to."

"He'd also worry if I need more help than he thinks I should need. And I just want to get clean, you know?"

"All right."

"Hey, will I lose my new man card if I take a bath instead of a shower? Maybe soaking in hot water will help with the soreness."

Will assured him it was still manly to take baths—he refrained from mentioning the only bath he'd taken in over twenty years was with Aisha—and even bubbles didn't mean an automatic revocation.

Jay made it to the table on his own and chatted throughout dinner—Chinese food for them, which made Jay ask if Will overdid the vegetables in everything edible and if the chow mein was made from something weird like zucchini because that seemed like something Will would ask for, and there were chicken chunks for me—but he was starting to fade as the table was cleared. Aisha suggested that if he wanted the bath he'd better do it before he fell asleep sitting up, and told Will to fill the tub in her bathroom. "He can run the jets in there and it'll be easier to get him out after."

He got in on his own and sunk down until the water was up to his chin. Will offered to wait in the bedroom, but Jay shook his head and told him it was all right. "I've lost all sense of modesty for now, I think. I lost count of how many people scoped out my junk before I left the hospital. It's still not quite real to me, you know?"

He didn't, but he nodded anyway.

"I can't even remember most of it. I know Dr. Massimo had a list of things I was supposed to do, but I can't remember anything except him saying I needed a good nutrition plan and he'd be pissed off if I let myself get out of shape."

"He was mostly joking. He said he wanted you fit so that you didn't undo all the hard work he did, sitting for hours at a time, watching you float. But there is some truth to what he asks. You're now at higher risk for heart disease. Staying in shape and watching your nutrition is easier than getting a new heart."

"You eat clean, right?"

"For the most part. I could do with some changes. I could cut the amount of alcohol I consume."

"You could, but why?"

"Indeed."

"I could work out, I suppose."

"After Mass gives you clearance."

"Yeah." He dipped a washcloth into the water, and then pressed it against his face. "I'm normal, right? I look normal?"

"You are definitely normal, Jay."

"I think I finally feel like me," he said softly. He left the washrag on his face, and he leaned his head against the back of the tub. Will was about to peel it away to see if he'd fallen asleep, when he spoke again. "The whole time traveling thing. My mom knew about that before you found out who my doctor was."

"She did," he answered carefully.

"Did you ever take her anywhere? Like, lunch with King Norval back in the day, when Pacifica was new?"

"I have never met King Norval," Will said with a chuckle. "But yes, I have taken her through a portal or two."

"Damn. That's a hell of a date. You're kind of stuck with her now, then. No one else will ever be able to top that."

"It's less impressive than one might imagine," Will said.

Yeah sure. Tell him how his mom fought in a war.

Tell him about Fluffy and Jeff.

Dude, your mom rode on a dragon.

"You better hope so. Otherwise a year from now when you take her on a picnic she'll remind you about how you used to make an effort. You *used* to take her to America where you had dinner and drinks with the Colonials." He peeled the washcloth off. "That was a thing, right?"

"Possibly. I honestly haven't gone back that far."

"My dad would know. He loves American history." A deep breath, and then, "His feelings would be hurt if he knew I asked you for help with this, wouldn't they? I didn't want to bug him or worry him, but thinking about it, he'd be hurt."

"He would certainly come and he would be happy to know he was helping." Will picked me up. "I'll have your mother call him. You can honestly tell him you were able to get in on your own, but you're tired enough that you wanted him to be here when you got out. Just in case."

"How weird will it be for you when he's here?"

"Not at all. I'm comfortable with your father, Jay."

"I dunno. Thought it might be awkward."

"He's a part of your mother's life. If I weren't already comfortable, I would need to get so very quickly."

"He's a nice guy. I mean—"

"He's your dad. I get it."

"No. It's just that he's a *really* nice guy. Like, he and George were one person, but he's the good half? I think. Maybe that's not it. George can be nice but when he gets upset…yeah, George is like this douchey winter cloud where my dad is springtime sunshine. Does that make sense?"

Will thought it did.

Jay went on, "George cares about me, but I scare him, I dunno why. Dad gets between us and makes him shut up when he goes on a you're-a-girl roll, but we've had fun together. I didn't mean to be why George is leaving."

"You're not the reason. In leaving now, he's using all of this as an excuse, but it has nothing to do with you."

"You wouldn't leave, would you? When things were happening, even if you didn't like them?"

Will thought about it carefully, and then told Jay about leaving home when he was seventeen, and most of it was because he couldn't handle the life he had. He was different than everyone else and he couldn't cope anymore. He wasn't entirely sure he would be able to stay in a situation that wore him down. But if Jay worried that he'd leave his mother behind if life threw a curve ball at them, he would fight like crazy to keep that from happening.

"I'll be honest with you. I walked away from her when I was the most scared I had ever been. I loved her and knew I couldn't be the man she needed, so I walked away and I hurt her terribly. I'm not proud of it, but I know I have that in me."

"Yeah, but you grew up, right?"

"I certainly hope so, but I reserve the right to my moments of stupidity."

Jay laughed. "Yeah, girls will do that to you."

"Are you dating anyone?" Will asked.

He shook his head. He'd never been sure what to tell someone he liked about himself. And then confessed he was pretty sure his mom thought he was gay, but he wasn't. "I'm just more comfortable around my guy friends. If I ever get the nerve to ask someone out, it'll be a girl."

"You mother doesn't care one way or the other. She just wants you to be happy."

"After this week? That's pretty obvious. Best birthday ever."

"Indeed. And I'll go have her call your father now."

Aisha was sitting on the bed, her eyes wet and red. He followed her into the hallway and apologized if he overstepped.

She put her hand on his chest. "Mister, I love you, and right now a lot more than you realize. You're not sleeping on the sofa. If you get sleepy, you're sleeping in my bed. Wick can find you there just as easily."

"You have rules for a reason."

"I made the rules. I can break them. All I ever wanted was to protect him from becoming attached to the wrong person. Well, he's attached. We're all attached, Will. The rule is now null and void."

He kissed her, and then pulled away. "I'm still staying on the sofa. You need sleep, and I have work to do."

"I'll win this one."

"I know you will," he said, amused. "But not tonight."

= = =

Will helped with the dishes while James was with Jay. I lounged on the counter and watched him slide into domestic bliss, which involved a lot of bubbles and getting pinned against the stove so she could torment him with wet hands, threatening to rub them across his face. When the last dish was dried and put away, she pushed him up against the fridge and kissed him, until he eased her back half a step and said, "I'm still staying on the sofa."

"You're no fun."

"So I've been told. By the King, no less, so it's official."

She let out a frustrated breath. "Will, I'm not asking you to get naked and grind me into the mattress. Just sleep in the same bed."

"If we sleep in the same bed, eventually we'll wind up doing just that."

"Hey, we've slept together and just slept."

"And you're tired enough right now that good judgment might fly out the window. I'm not tired, and if you got your hands in the right places—?"

"Have a little faith in me, Will. I may joke about keeping you around for your massive dick, but I can keep my hands off it for one night."

"Aisha."

"Really, what the hell? And so what if I did jump on you? Stress release, Emperor. Sex is good for that, too, you know."

James is in the hall with Jay.

He lowered his voice. "Are we going to fight about this? Because this seems like a non-issue to me. You need sleep, Aisha. I would be a distraction."

She patted his chest and stepped away. "Not a fight."

You're an idiot.

She started a pot of tea—herbal, she assured him, nothing that would keep her awake—and when James came out—sheepishly, because he'd overheard at least a little bit—they sat together at the table. Will talked to him like he was an old friend and their being together was a common thing. They told Will stories about Jay when he was younger, and they told James about some of the things they did when they were not-dating as teenagers. It was like watching him with Jax, but without the insults and jabs.

Mostly, though, they talked about Jay and how quickly everything came together.

"If you hadn't seen those pictures," Aisha mused.

Will thought it would have all come together at some point. "Sooner or later you would have told me, or Jay would have. I could have approached Jax at any point."

"But the timing," James said. "Another year and it might have been too late, at least for it to be this easy on him. He's healing remarkably well."

Dude, it's a shame you can't tell him.

"I don't think it would have been another year," Aisha told him. "The minute George met Will?"

"He never spoke much of his childhood," James said. "I knew he was born here, but he never mentioned knowing you."

"We were not friends," Will said simply.

James let out a sad chuckle. "I figured that out. He admits he was a bully when he was little. I take it he tormented you?"

"Horribly."

"James, he and his friends went after Will so badly that his parents yanked him out of school in second grade."

"I'm sorry," James said. He sounded sincere. "Not that it helps, but he's afraid of you now."

"That came later, in our teens. We trained in the same dojo for a few years."

"Karate," James sighed. "His glory days. Honestly, if I have to hear one more time about his domination in tournaments and his undefeated status."

Will tried to not smile. "He told you he was undefeated?"

"Third-degree black belt, Pacific Rim Nationals champion several years running."

"Interesting."

"Come on, Will," Aisha prodded. "Spill it."

Will explained that when they were in preschool, George was bigger and even at four and five, he was a bully. He led the masses in tormenting him. But when they were twelve, George began taking karate lessons at the same dojo Will had trained in starting at age four. He had no idea. Will noticed him once during warm-up exercises, and after that he made an effort to not be there while the beginner's classes were in session. Then somewhere at around the one-year mark, when George was preparing to test for an intermediate rank, Will had no choice. He was selected to be part of the examination process, to spar with those who were eager to move into the next class. He waited in the lobby while the students went through the initial part of their test, and watched through a window in the door as George sparred students his own skill level. He was clearly talented and was much bigger than most of the other kids, so he had intimidation on his side.

His instructor did not require his students to wear formal uniforms or their rank belts; Will took his belt off and placed it in his gear bag, so when he was called onto the floor there was no indication of his capabilities. He watched George bounce on his feet eagerly as he slipped on socks and gloves—he always trained and fought while fully clothed—and was astonished at how much George was looking forward to beating him to a pulp. He was certain that was what George thought he was going to do: beat the snot out of the skinny, weird kid that no one wanted to talk to. He was bubbling over with joy and couldn't wait.

"We stood at the center of the room with thirty people looking on, and after we bowed to our instructor he began hopping around, bobbing back and forth as if I would somehow be intimidated by a moving target. I simply stood there, waiting for him to come to me. The longer I waited, the more confused and angrier he became, because I wasn't allowing him his quick and easy victory. Then he finally moved in and punched...I ducked. He kicked, I stepped out of the way. I let him wear himself out, and when he became especially sloppy, I kicked him in the chest and knocked him out of the ring. He was furious."

Aisha asked how that made him afraid of Will. Anger she understood, but if he wasn't hurt, how did that turn the tide and make him fear Will?

"That was the beginning. A year later, during one of my own pre-test sparring classes, I was required to engage in a three-on-one match, and he was one of my opponents. The end result did nothing to endear me to him. They lost, and then had to watch while I sparred the instructor."

"Who also lost?"

Will nodded. "It was less impressive than it might have appeared to other students. I'd fought him often enough that I knew his weaknesses and his tells. Even then...I avoided George, but he had witnessed me fighting fairly often. He had considerable talent of his own, but as time went on I think he knew he no longer wanted to make me angry. And when we were seventeen, he was scheduled to test for his black belt. He easily handled the kata and sparring against students his own skill level, but in the end, in order to advance, he was required to fight with me."

"How badly did you beat him?"

Will shrugged lightly. "Just prior to his match, I sparred with a student who was testing for his fourth degree, and George was at the edge of the carpet, watching. It was a bloody, brutal fight with an opponent who had specifically asked me to not hold back. He wanted to earn his victory, if he could, and wanted equally to earn his defeat. I think George assumed that because I had already engaged in an exhaustive match, he would be paired with someone else, but when he was called to the ring, I didn't leave. The instructor called for us to bow, and he didn't. He couldn't. He was frozen in place for several seconds…and then ran from the room. As far as I know, he never returned."

"Then he was never a black belt at all." James sighed unhappily. "All those stories."

"He may have returned after I stopped training, or moved onto another dojo," Will said. "But he did, indeed, lose several fights. He never had the nerve to face me again."

Aisha shook her head. "And yet, he had the nerve to take a swing at Jax."

"He has no idea how fortunate he is in how that turned out. Any other time—"

"You would have knocked him on his ass," she guessed

Will looked right at James. "I would have killed him. You don't attack the King and expect to survive. The only reason he's alive is because of the two of you and Jay."

"Thank you, then," James said quietly. "He's an idiot, but…"

"You still love him," Aisha said, irritated.

"He's not always like that. He has it in him to be gentle and sweet." Before Aisha could say anything, and her mouth was open, probably to list all of George's faults, he added, "I know. He didn't treat our son fairly, and I screwed up when I let him stomp all over me and allowed him to snare third parent rights. The odd thing is, he really does love Jay."

"He loved Jaime," Aisha snapped.

"He loves *Jay*," James insisted. "In quiet moments, when it was just the two of them sitting on the couch watching some video that I didn't understand, or when they played games and shared books—I could see it, so clearly. They laughed together more often than you realize. They share secrets you and I will never know. He *loves* Jay. He just doesn't understand."

"You don't get in the way of someone you love," she contended. "You think I was thrilled when you started seeing him? And when you said you were marrying him? I was happy for *you* because you were getting what you wanted, but don't think for one minute I thought it was a good idea. George? If he truly loved Jay, he would have signed the goddamned papers years ago, even if he didn't understand any of it. He wouldn't have done backflips to wedge himself into our *rights*, James. And I know you had doubts. You were ready to leave him—"

His head snapped up, eyes wide, and she stopped.

"Whatever this is," Will said evenly, "don't let him overhear it."

"I didn't fight for him," James said. "I know why she's angry."

"Fight for him? James, you never fought for *us*."

"You were relieved when I left, Aisha."

"Because I was *tired*. We didn't work, but at least I tried. If we'd *both* tried—"

Will very carefully scooted his chair away from the table, and said he would give them some privacy. I wanted to follow him into the bedroom because he looked like she'd just pulled one of his nose hairs, but I also wanted to see what was going to happen. James was a little dude but he wasn't delicate; even so, I was sure she could snap him in half.

Neither watched him leave. James had both hands flat on the table and his temple was twitching. Then, "That was not fair."

"I'm right, and you know it."

"Not to me. I'll take every angry word you have and I'll shoulder the blame for our marriage falling apart. But insinuating we would have eventually worked? That wasn't fair to *Will*."

She flinched.

"It's also not true, and you know that. It's why I didn't leave him, Aisha. Whether you like it or not, he loved me, and he loved Jay."

"I meant—"

"I know what you meant. I could have tried harder early on. I could have not cheated on you. I could have done a dozen things, but the end would have been the same. And that's not George's fault."

She took in a deep, ragged breath, and then nodded.

"You know how I know he loves Jay? When we moved here and you were still in Vegas, he begged me to buy this apartment, just in case. You hadn't said a word yet about following us, but he wanted you to have a place to live, close enough that we could see Jay daily.

He designed that staircase you loathe so that Jay could come and go as he wanted, and it was his idea to put in the dual locking system so that *you* would have privacy. And he did it because he wanted Jay close. All of us knew by then that Jay would transition someday. He knew it even if he fought against it. But he wanted to be in Jay's life, as often as possible."

"I'm still not sure I'd call that love."

"Because you don't want to see it."

There was a soft knock on the door. They tried to ignore it, but another knock came, and then another. Aisha got up with a huff and yanked the door open, and then groaned.

"Really. What the hell do you want?"

George stayed in the hallway outside. "To see Jaime. Jay. To talk to…him."

"He's asleep, and so help me god if you wake him up, I'll turn the Emperor on you."

"Indeed," Will said from the inside hall. "We will be civil for no reason other than Jay needs his rest."

George looked past Aisha, and when he saw James, his gaze dropped to the floor. James stood up and crossed his arms, glaring.

Why not be grownups and, you know, talk?

Will heard me, and asked George to come in, because if nothing else he had a few questions and surely Aisha did. It was time to talk—but keep the volume down, and don't drag Jay into it.

James was not ready to talk; he headed up the stairs, adding that if Jay needed him again, call. They watched him go and when the door closed, Aisha turned sharply. "How the *hell* could the two of you know each other when you were kids?"

"She knows?"

Will nodded.

"And you believed him?" George asked her.

"The man touched my arm and spoke inside my head. It wasn't a stretch after that. But goddammit, you're at least twenty years older than Will. Start explaining."

It was Will he started with. He admitted that he was terrified of Will when they were kids. "I still am. What you can do isn't natural, and I still don't understand it."

"I don't either, but I live with it."

"He never hurt you when you were kids, did he?" Aisha challenged. "So you went after him anyway? What the hell? You kept it up until you weren't the stronger one anymore?"

"I wasn't alone," George said. "He was an anomaly and we couldn't make sense of him. But I never laid a hand on him, not exactly."

"My god, you're an ass. You don't have to hit someone to damage them. Now really, what the hell? Will's forty-three and you're over sixty."

"We were the same age, once. When I was twenty, his father was publicly moving people, and I'm sure you know why. He brought me to twenty-three-seventy and left me with a job that eventually took me to Las Vegas. Then a decade and a half later, I watched as Will became a public presence. I'd been here for twenty years, yet seeing him on the news, close to the Prince and then the King, scared the hell out of me. You were a goddamned teenager, Emperor, and it still scared the hell out of me."

"Then you had to return to San Francisco," Will said.

"I did everything I could to stay off your radar. Several years ago I changed jobs within my company to assure I wouldn't draw a government contract that would risk putting us in the same room."

"And just your luck, I started seeing him," Aisha said, a bit amused.

He nodded. "When Jay told me, I asked to transfer back to Vegas. I don't understand you at all, Emperor. Nor do I care to."

Will skipped over the insult. "Who's your anchor? How are you managing?"

His anchor had been his brother, who died fifteen years back. By then, he was more attached to James. He had no idea what would happen to him without James, but he didn't imagine it would be pretty.

Aisha started to tell him it was his own damn fault, but Will touched her hand, stopping her.

"You can go home, to your own When."

"And then what?" he spat. "Sit on the beach with a beer in hand as the world explodes? I might as well stay here and die."

Will explained that he would have to be taken to a date at least two decades from when he left, but home was still there. "The meteor was dealt with. Life will go on. So can you."

George's eyes narrowed a tiny bit. "Then why haven't you gone home?"

"For the same reasons that I left. There's nothing for me there. I was miserable there, here I am not. Everyone I love is here."

"And if I go back, everyone I love will be dead."

Aisha had no sympathy for him. "You'll be just as dead if you stay."

Will told him to think about it; he could tell Finn that he'd located someone who wanted to return home and arrange for transport through a portal.

"What happens to my life here if I go back?" George asked. "Am I officially dead? Missing?"

"What do you care?" Aisha asked.

"I own property and have life insurance. There's a trust for Jay. I'm a bastard but if I'm going home, I want James to have everything I'd be leaving behind. It might be better if the world thinks I'm dead. I would prefer that I was declared dead."

"I would need to consult with my father about that," Will said.

Aisha thought George owed it to James to give him some sort of explanation. Whatever he told him about his boyhood home, he needed to find a way to tell him he was going back, and that they would never see each other again—yet he couldn't tell him the whole truth. "Be very sure, George. You'll never see James, never speak to him again. You'll never see Jay again. Everything you built here will be lost to you."

"He has no choice," Will said. "He either goes home and starts over, or stays here and dies." To George, "But you need to see Jay, and leave him with some peace. Don't make him carry the burden of being abandoned. I don't care what you really think or feel, but you'll tell him you love him and will miss him. Wish him well."

"That wouldn't be a lie," George said.

He headed up the stairs with a promise to see Jay the next day, and we watched until the door closed behind him. When it clicked shut, Will said gruffly, "You should get some sleep."

He picked his tablet off the table and went over the sofa, and didn't look at her.

"Will."

"It's late, Aisha. I had hoped you would have been in bed much earlier."

"Will."

"I'm still staying on the sofa."

"But I think the reason has changed."

"No, it hasn't."

"Dammit, Will." She dropped onto the sofa next to him. "When I poked at James for not fighting for our marriage, I didn't mean that I wished we were still together."

"I know."

She pulled the tablet out of his hand and tossed it onto the end of the sofa where he couldn't easily reach it. "Why did you get up and leave, then? You heard something that bothered you."

"You were arguing. I was not a part of that."

"You were hurt."

Be honest, dude. Even I saw it.

"For a fleeting moment, yes. The notion that there was ever a possibility you would have stayed with him, and that I wouldn't be sitting here right now bothered me. But I was past that by the time I was in the bedroom. I don't regret leaving, however. I did sense you needed privacy."

"What else?" she prodded. "Something else raised your antenna."

Right from the back of your head. Like a Martian.

"You mentioned that he'd almost left George before. Whatever else you were about to say, he undoubtedly did not want you to and you looked shocked that you nearly said it."

She didn't want to tell him. Her eyes closed and she took a deep breath, delaying.

"Their marriage survived, Aisha. Whatever it is, it can't be that bad."

"It is if it changes how you see me."

He stretched his arm along the back of the sofa, trailing his fingers over the back. He tapped lightly, something she wouldn't notice but I would. I ran to her and jumped in her lap to give her a head bonk, and then to purr while I rested against her legs.

"I told you about the turkey baster," she started. "George was mad enough to leave, and neither of us was terribly upset about it." Jay was excited; they were going out together, first to get all the curls cut from his hair, and then to buy him clothes he'd get to choose for himself. They turned an afternoon meant to soothe Jay into a family outing, the first they'd had without George since they'd divorced. After the haircut and complete wardrobe purchase, they took Jay to an indoor playground where he could run around and they could sit and watch, and they both realized it was the most stress-free afternoon together that they could remember.

While Jay ran around the playground with a group of little boys, James confessed that he thought he'd made a mistake. He loved George but he wasn't sure it was enough, and he still loved her. He missed his family. He hated that he'd let a few weeks of doubt be the catalyst that tore them apart.

"I was lonely, Will. I hadn't really started dating, and my life was nothing but work and Jay. I was drowning in it. He went home with us so that he could give Jay his bath and to tuck him in, and after he was asleep we opened a bottle of wine and kept on talking. I admitted that I missed him, too."

Will knew what she was going to say, but he waited.

"I don't even know what I was thinking. When we divorced, I honestly was relieved because we were crumbling and it felt like too much work to fix things. But that night, I missed my husband. And I slept with him."

"That's not awful."

"But that's not it. It didn't end there, Will. I basically had an affair with a married man, and it went on for *months*. He started talking about leaving George, hinting that he wanted us back. He wanted his family."

"And you?"

"I didn't know what I wanted. I just didn't want to be by myself. And I won't lie, I'd been alone long enough that I was seriously horny and James knows what he's doing."

"Kudos?" he asked lightly.

"I know I don't have a right to be the least bit irritated that he stayed in his marriage because in the end I was glad that I didn't have to make the decision to give him another chance or not. But when he sat here tonight and tried to tell me George loves Jay, it all came back and I just wanted to smack the hell out of him."

"All right."

"Stop being so goddamned reasonable!" she said, slapping at his chest. "Be mad. I should have told you this already."

"Had I indulged your wish to discuss former partners, perhaps. But I did tell you that your social life was none of my business, and I meant it."

"Anyone else would be upset."

"I never was a real boy," he said lightly. "Aisha, you were with someone you cared about. You took care of all the 'what-ifs.' I understand sleeping with James more than I would if it had been some other married man. Right or wrong, you trusted him, and it's probably what allowed you to finally let go."

"You know, I don't think I want you to be reasonable right now."

"I know that. You've been spoiling for a fight all evening."

"Then give me what I want. Just argue for once."

"The only thing I'll argue about is sleep. Go to bed. If you still want to pick a fight with me in the morning, then I'll fight."

"If you want me to sleep, come to bed with me."

"No."

They went back and forth several times, until a tired sigh came from Jay's room. "Just go to bed with her already. Damn. You've got to be the only straight guy in Pacifica who wouldn't jump at the chance."

"How much did he hear?" she whispered.

Will shrugged, but then got up. He told me to stay in Jay's room, and to come get him if Jay needed to get up. "You win," he told her. "I feel like I was ganged up on, but you win."

One, two, three…

"I don't want to win," she cried, falling against him.

"I know."

Her forehead was pressed against his shoulder, and she grabbed fistfuls of his shirt. "I don't know what I want right now."

"I do. Come on." He pulled his shirt out of her grasp and then led her down the hall, ignoring her protests that it felt a lot like being put to bed by Dad. When he realized I'd followed them, he pointed toward Jay's bedroom and told me I was sleeping in there.

I'll go in later. I'll hear if he stirs.

There was no light coming in through the window, so when Will turned the light out, it was dark. I stayed in the doorway, where I could hear everything around me. If Jay sat up, I would know. If Aisha pushed Will out of bed, I would see it and would be able to tell Drew all about it.

Nothing bouncy was going to happen. They weren't even going to grope. I started to relax and was going to catnap, when Will's phone buzzed. He fished it out of his pants on the floor and looked, the light from the screen bathing his face in blue.

"Just my mother," he whispered. "I'll call her in the morning. Go to sleep."

She went quiet, long enough that I thought she'd finally fallen asleep. Then, in a soft voice, "You have to talk to your mother, Will. She needs to hear from you that no matter what you and I are doing, she won't lose you."

"She should already know that."

"Knowing it and *knowing* it aren't the same. She lost you once and came here expecting that she would lose you again, and deep down she's probably terrified that the third time's the charm. Fight it out if you have to but don't leave her thinking she'll lose you to me because she won't."

"If she makes me choose—"

"No. Don't allow that. Tell her you love her as many times as she needs to hear it, and promise her that you're not choosing another family, but adding to your own."

"If I say that, she'll ask if we're getting married."

"I don't need to be married again, Will, but you can honestly tell her we have every intention of staying together until one of us dies. That's my goal, at least."

"What if I truly want to get married? I know we can make the commitment without a legal ceremony, but if I want that?"

"Then when you're ready, ask. Or I might still be the one to ask you. But be honest with her. That a life-long commitment to each other is our goal, and we want her to be a part of it."

"Be careful what you ask for."

"Will, please."

He promised her he would talk to her, and then they were quiet. I listened as her breathing slowed, and then went into Jay's room until he woke up just before one o'clock. Will slipped out of bed to help him get up, although he barely needed it, and after Jay was back in bed, he went out into the living room and stood by the big window, looking down at the park.

I jumped onto the window sill and looked down; there was no one in the park and nothing to see.

What are you thinking about so hard?

"Icarus and Daedalus. I thought I had taken flight already, but really, I've just been running, trying to pick up enough speed to get airborne. I know I have you and Aisha and Jax and Aubrey, and the kids, to catch me if I fall…what about my own mother?"

You won't go =splat= on the ground.

"I wonder." He sat on the sofa and patted it, inviting me to sit with him. He didn't make a lap and instead of looking at me he looked at his bare chest, bathed in streetlight, and then set his hand on the center part of his tattoo. "I'm getting this removed, Wick. I don't think I need it anymore."

All of the tattoos?

"I'll keep the crowns and feet."

But your parents' faces?

"They would hate it if they saw I had them. And now that they're here, I don't feel as pressed to have something to remember them by."

He could tell himself that was the reason why all he wanted. The real reasons were asleep in the next room, and trying to get him to answer his phone.

= = =

At three in the morning I heard Jay stir, and ran down the hall to see if he needed help. He inched his way out of bed and stood up slowly, wincing, but he walked to the bathroom on his own and didn't ask me to get Will. Still, I waited right by the door, ready to bolt for the living room. I listened for moans and groans, and little noises that suggested he was struggling, but all I heard was him peeing and then the whoosh as he flushed.

I was prepared to watch until he was all the way back in bed, under the sheet, and asleep. He took a right turn out of the bathroom, though, and went into the living room where Will was reading work things on his tablet. All the lights were off and his face glowed in the light from the tablet, making him look stern and upset.

Jay either didn't notice or didn't care. He sat on the far end of the sofa, stretching his legs out as far as he could.

"Can't sleep?" Will asked.

"I feel like I've been sleeping for about a month. I just wanted out of the room for a while. And why are you up? I thought she won the argument."

"She did." He held the tablet up. "I had some work to do. I got up once she was asleep."

"I won't interrupt."

Will set the tablet aside, and reached for the bottle of Jay's pain medication that was waiting on the end table. "You're not interrupting. This is tedious material and I welcome the diversion." He handed Jay the bottle and told him to snort. No argument.

Jay snorted. "Oz is right. Sometimes you do sound like a history teacher. Maybe you missed your calling."

"Had I been able to finish my education, perhaps," Will told him.

"You dropped out?"

"In second grade, no less."

"Come on. Zed said you were home schooled. That counts. Didn't you finish all the requirements for high school?"

"My mother made sure I was well educated," he said, skirting around the question. "That did not, however, lend itself to having higher education available as an option. I was on my own quite young, and without the paperwork proving my education, nor the financial resources? I would have continued if I could have."

"Sucks. You were seventeen when you moved out?"

"I did it in increments. But I left for good at seventeen."

"Damn. You were my age. There's no way in hell my parents would let me move out now."

"Different circumstances," Will said, "as well as living in a completely different time. My independence was cultivated from a very early age. I don't recommend it."

"Yeah, I'm not in a hurry. I'd like to get the hell out of high school, but I'm not ready to leave home. Free rent, free food, what's not to like here?"

"Not enjoying your time in school?"

"It's fucking hell," he said. He was beginning to sound sleepy again, but most of that was from the medication. "I'm surrounded by teenaged versions of George. I mean, they don't *know*, but they know there's something different about me, and I'm supposed to pay some kind of price for it. It was fine until everyone around me started getting taller and the guys' voices started changing, and then it was like, what the hell's wrong with Okuda? He's still a fucking twelve-year-old. And when everyone realized I had permanently gotten out of taking phys ed? Then they were positive something was wrong with me. Ninth grade, holy hell.

"Like, by the third or fourth week, it was like I was their personal kickball. Literally shoved back and forth, calling me 'chica' and fucking checking me for breasts."

That made Will sit up. "What?"

"Like, grabbing my chest from behind and pretending to fuck me in the ass. If Zed hadn't stopped them…" He swallowed hard. "Zed has been the only thing between the fucking idiots who think it's funny to pick on someone smaller and me. Calling me things like chica, like somehow it would be wrong if I *were* a girl. I mean, these assholes would never do that to an actual female, but it was all right because I'm not? And if they'd known what the deal was, who knows what the hell would have happened."

"Does your mother know any of this?"

Don't freak out. He needs you to not freak out.

He shook his head. "She knows I get picked on. I'm not telling her how bad it gets. I mean, when Zed is around, it's not horrible. No one has the guts to piss him off. But last year when you guys were gone? Every damned day, something happened. I either got shoved around or things thrown at me, and the name calling was like…it just kept going on. I didn't even realize what a buffer Zed was until he wasn't there.

"He used to tell me that if I were honest with people, they'd understand and let up, but fuck, Will, I'm not the only trans kid in school and it doesn't go half as well as he thinks. The kids that are out? It's like people think they'll catch some kind of disease and their own gender will flip. You can't reason with anyone, tell them it doesn't work like that because this is just the fucking card we drew at birth because they don't want to listen. We're freaks to them. And maybe I'm a coward, but I don't want to tell anyone else a damned thing and face any more than I'm already getting. I just want out."

"Of school," Will said, wanting clarity.

"Yeah, just school. Not, like, *everything*. Zed thinks it'll all ease up when the next school year starts because I'm taller and my voice is changing and they'll have fewer things to pick on me about, but fuck them, you know? Why would I give any one of them another chance? Fine, they don't make my life hell for a few months. I still know what kind of people they are, and I don't want to have anything to do with them. I just want to, you know, start over with people who see *me* and not some little kid. I'm not a goddamned freak."

"No, you're not. Not in any manner."

"Yeah, well, you're not a backward fifteen-year-old bent on using someone smaller than you to make yourself feel bigger. And I'm not even sure things will change. People are so used to the way they treat me that I don't think it will make a difference. And Zed won't be there this year. I have to find some way to suck it up and deal." He took a deep breath. "Can I tell you something? And you have to swear to not tell my mom?"

"I'm not comfortable with keeping secrets from her, Jay."

"But it'll be for a good reason if it pans out. She won't be mad."

"All right."

"Zed's helping me study for the exit exam. I was going to take the prep class this summer, but since I can't, he said he would help me figure out the things I need to focus on. I can take it next month, and if I pass? I'm out. I graduate. I won't have to go back."

"Why not tell her? She could also help you."

"I'm not a great student, Will. She knows that. I think she might try to talk me out of it to spare my feelings if I can't pass all three parts of the test. And then I would have to explain why I want out so much."

"I think you should explain that, regardless."

"No. You know how bad that would make her feel? She knows I get picked on but not how much, and she would hate herself for not seeing it. I've gotten really fucking good at hiding the worst of it, and it's not like she could do anything about it."

"There's actually quite a bit—"

"I don't want her to know, okay? She has to teach at that school, and how fucking awful would it be for her to have to stand in front of the kids she knows treated me like crap for years, and then if she *did* try to stop it and it blew up in her face? She fights for me every goddamn day, like half of everything she thinks about is how to keep me sane and feeling like I'm normal, and not letting George trample over every shred of self-worth that I have. If she thought there was even one thing she missed…I'm not breaking my mom's heart, Will. I know her, she would probably quit her job and yank me out of school, and then what? We hide in here until I'm done growing so no one will look at me twice? Become hermits until I'm an adult? Because she would do that for me."

You know how he feels. He doesn't want to be isolated. Like you were.

"All right," Will agreed. "At least until you've taken the exam. And after that—"

"I suck it up and deal with it. It's one more year. Nine months. I can do that."

"And after that," he pressed, "if needed, I can pull some strings and get you into another school. Are you planning on college after this?"

"Hoping to."

"Jax spent his last two years at Pasteur Preparatory Academy. The classes are very small and the curriculum is concentrated on the fundamentals, with the goal of getting every student accepted into a university after graduation. It would be intensive study, but I can promise you, your experience would be far less stressful than in your current school."

"I'll pass the test," Jay said. "And that sounds expensive."

"It's a public school. Not expensive."

Liar. You'd pay for it, wouldn't you?

"I'll pass the test," Jay repeated. "I have to. It's like, hell, I'm a different person now, and I need to reboot everything. If I pass, I can go on to UCSF, and just…start over. No one there will see me as Jimmy Okuda, no one will care that three months ago I looked like a twelve-year-old. I'll just be Jay. To them, I'll never have been Jaime, and Jimmy will be the name I used as a kid. I can just be Jay."

"All right. I understand that."

Is that why you don't want to be called Emperor anymore?

"Indeed, Wick," he said. "It's not exactly the same thing, but given that I prefer to be called by my name and not 'Emperor,' I can empathize a bit."

"You've never screwed up once," Jay said, softly. "Once you knew, never Jimmy or JimmyJay. I mean, I'm okay when it happens, but I noticed that you get it right all the time. Even if I don't get yours right. I almost called you Emperwill the other day."

He's kinda high, isn't he? Drugs make him gabby.

They fell quiet, and Jay's eyes were only half open. I sniffed at him, checking, because maybe he'd fallen asleep that way, but he reached out to pet me.

"George hates himself," he said after a while. "He loves my dad, he loves me, but he really hates himself. And I kind of get it, why he didn't want me to change. He had this picture in his head of the way his life was supposed to go, him and my dad and their daughter, and he loved that little girl. He really did. When my mom and dad agreed that I wasn't just playing make believe, he felt like they were ganging up on him and trying to take away his little girl. He was scared. He's still scared. I think he's been scared his whole life, and it turned him into a raging asshole."

Will could have told him about five-year-old George and the hell he unleashed—the name calling and throwing things, and bullying other kids into tormenting him as well—but Jay was speaking softly, almost to himself, and he was only half awake.

"I know he's thinking about leaving for good. I mean, they haven't said anything to me but I know they split up. And he's torn between leaving forever and trying to get over this. I mean, really, we talk shit about him a lot but he's put up with an awful lot from my dad, too. I love my dad but, damn, he can't keep his pants on. And he's not good at hiding it, or maybe that's intentional, I don't know. Like, fuck you, George, you can't accept my kid being different, well then accept the fact that every now and then I like to go out and fuck women, and there's not a damned thing you can do about it except leave. But he doesn't leave because he loves my dad and he loves me and keeps hoping that I'll change my mind. And I think he puts up with a lot of the cheating because he doesn't think he deserves anything better.

"Man, in school, I'm always worried, but George? I think he's scared *all the time*. Like, from the time he wakes up until he goes to sleep. It's really hard to stay pissed off at someone who just can't get past being afraid all the time. Now his worst fear is coming true. He's losing my dad, he'll lose me, and he has no one else. Everyone else he's ever loved is long gone, and I think if my dad divorces him...yeah, he'll be dead soon. And I don't want that, I really don't. I don't hate the guy, Will. I hate what he says and does sometimes, but I want him to be all right. And I wish he could figure out how to not be scared of everything because he's going to be miserable until he gets it.

"Mom won't ever forgive him. I don't think my dad will, either. But fuck, Will, I have to. I know what being scared is like and I know it makes you do really stupid shit. Someone has to forgive him, you know? Someone has to be the bigger person, and it might as well be me."

"You're a better man than I am," Will said quietly. "I cannot fathom forgiving him."

"The alternative is hating him, and I can't do that." He set his head on the back of the sofa and closed his eyes. "This stuff. Please don't tell my mom. I know, you don't want to keep secrets, but please."

"I'll cut you a deal."

Jay opened one eye.

"I'll keep all of this between us if you work on cleaning up your language a bit. I expect that you'll be spending more time with the royal family, and the Queen has her issues."

"The list," Jay laughed. He closed his eye again. "Deal. I'll work on it. I love a good f-bomb, though, so I might need reminders."

Get a squirt bottle. Every time he says it, spray him.

At seven in the morning, Will was still sitting on the sofa, reading, and Jay was stretched out with one foot pressed up against Will's hip and the other across his lap, sound asleep and drooling, and even though she'd gotten enough sleep, Aisha took one look at them and almost started crying again.

= = =

The next night, there was no argument about where Will would sleep. He was drained and thought he would be able to slip into at least a glimmer of slumber. He opposed the idea of bouncy things with Jay in the next room with both bedroom doors open— she didn't fight him on it, she was just as tired—and he fell asleep within a minute of setting his head on the pillow.

There was no plush window seat in Aisha's bedroom, nor a wide, comfortable headboard, so I curled up at the foot of the bed between them. I could still hear Jay from there, and Will wasn't a sleep-kicker, so it felt like a safe place to be. I dozed off until one-thirty, when something pulled me from my catnap.

Will was flat on his back, his hands on his stomach, fingers twitching. His breathing rate had increased, and his eyebrows knotted together. I crept up between them, careful to not step on Aisha's arm. Her hand was on his chest, rising and falling with each breath he took, and that hand was moving faster than it would have if he were awake.

It was rare that I noticed when he was actively dreaming; with his limited sleep patterns it was hard to catch him dreaming, so I decided to be rude and took the opportunity to peek inside his head. I curled up on his pillow and set my front paws on his head and closed my eyes, hoping I could slip into the dream unnoticed.

He was too tense to feel me there, and I bathed in the fear swirling around him, not knowing how to brush it away.

Seven-year-old Will stood next to a long, eight-lane swimming pool near the deep end, his back to the water. He didn't want to be there; he wanted to bolt through the door in front of him, and then grab his clothes before running home. If anything were fair, he would be sitting somewhere with a book, away from the classmates who hated him, and away from the few who were terrified of him.

He glanced over his shoulder to the fifteen other boys and girls clustered near the shallow end. They were all dressed in the same swimsuits, bright red jammers and skin-tight white shirts; there was a high-pitched buzz of young voices, a dozen kids complaining about being cold and having to stand outside while they waited for the teacher to come out of the locker room.

He turned to stare at the door. The tone of the voices behind him tinged with something other than impatience; it was of uselessness. They were about to be tested on their swimming abilities, and several whined about having to prove that they could make it from one end of the pool to the other. One girl pointed out that they all lived close to the ocean, so swimming was a necessary skill. One boy countered that—this was nothing more than fulfilling an activity credit they all needed before they could move onto third grade. Another voice proclaimed it all stupid and worthless, because it was January and there were still four months to find other credits to advance with, and whoever decided this was a good idea was an idiot in need of a hard kick to the nuts.

Will cringed when he heard the boy speak. I could feel his stomach churn; he wanted to turn around but strained against his own impulses. He didn't want any of them to see that he was afraid. He didn't want to face *him*, and risk giving him an excuse to invent another reason to pick on him.

He decided to mind his own business and wait for the teacher so that he could get this over with. He was a fast swimmer and could be across the pool and done well before anyone else in the water with him. If he hit the water first, he could be out of the pool and dressed before the last group dove in.

"Who wants to swim with *him*?" It was the voice that made him cringe, the *him* that made his stomach flop over. "Hey, Blackshear, go fucking swim in the toilet where you belong."

Will stiffened. He heard kids moving closer to him, and he only wanted to be left alone. That was the truce; he'd stay far away if they would stop throwing things and shouting at him. He'd begged them to leave him alone, and most of them did, after some time. He held up his end of it; he stayed as far away as he could when it was possible, and made himself as small as he could when it wasn't.

There were the unruly few, though, the boys who couldn't resist the small, skinny kid who was the easiest target they knew of.

He crossed his arms, hugging them to his stomach, which now felt like it was on fire. He started to shiver even though he didn't feel cold, and he struggled to breathe normally. If they saw his fear, it would only get worse, but he could feel himself beginning to gasp for air.

The teacher had to come out soon. He willed it; he stared at the door and pleaded silently for it to pop open and for her to come skipping out with her grading tablet in hand, ordering the first group to line up at the deep end of the pool. He had already picked the lane he would start from, one over from the wall closest to the locker room. From there he would have no splash back from the side of the pool to slow him down, and he would still be able to scramble out of the water and get inside before anyone else.

The crinkling of plastic startled him, and he twitched to turn but before he could, everything went dark and his feet were pulled from underneath him. There was sharp pain as his back slammed onto the pool deck, and muffled voices puffed around him. Someone shouted to tape the bag closed, someone else shouted to let him go.

He lashed out, slapping his hands against the wet plastic bag. He kicked, but the bag had been taped closed and he couldn't get enough leverage to break through it. It was heavy plastic; his fingers slid down the bag near his face and he realized it was a bio-bag, meant to contain decaying, dead things. There was no punching through it; he would need a knife.

Suddenly, he felt enveloped in cold, and he was sinking. The sound of water was far away, yet he felt it swirling across his body, through the plastic, pushing against his back. Pain exploded through his shoulders as he hit the bottom of the pool.

He didn't know what to do. It wasn't a fight he could reason his way through, and he was struggling to breathe. He thought he needed to stand—if he could get to his feet, he could use sheer force to stretch the bag and break the tape it had been shut with—but he couldn't make sense of up or down. He felt the bottom of the pool under his back, but every time he moved he lost track of where he was, and he couldn't get a foothold.

The air around his face was an odd mix of hot and cold, and he couldn't get enough of it into his lungs. He wanted to scream; in his head he did, yelling for someone to let him out, but he couldn't draw in enough breath to get a sound out. He tried three times and then realized there was no more air in the bag. He was eight feet under water with no air, and none of the kids waiting around the pool were going to help him.

He knew where they were: every one of them stood at the edge of the pool, watching as he struggled to break free. They watched as his movement slowed and then stopped, because he had nothing left to fight with.

He tried to open his eyes but wasn't sure if he had or not because there was no light in the bag. He knew he was out of time. There was no air.

Mom.

I could hear him crying inside my own head. First a whisper, then sobbing.

Mom. Mom. Please, Mom.

I want my mom.

I want…

There was jerking and a sudden rush of cold, and then a hand clamped over his mouth. He couldn't fight against it, he couldn't move. He thought he should bite down, but even that little bit seemed like too much effort. But, he was moving up, the cool water wrapping around him until the hand suddenly left his face and he heard a woman's voice yelling *Breathe, William. Breathe!*

She dragged him from the water onto the deck. Her hand went to his chest, and he heard his classmates screaming, *let him go, don't touch him.* She ignored them, and her hand went to his chin, then there were warm lips on his, blowing air into his mouth. *Breathe,*

William, please. Oh my god, breathe. Warm lips again, another rush of air.

His chest heaved and he began sucking in one deep breath after another. She set her forehead on his chest, and cried *thank you thank you thank you,* and all he could do was turn his head and open his eyes. Everyone was on the far side of the pool, staring, all except for George Denton, who thrust his middle finger toward Will and then stomped into the locker room.

I twitched away from his head; he was still asleep, but Aisha was awake and on her knees on the bed next to him, one hand on his chest and the other on his cheek, trying to wake him up.

"Will," she hissed. "Wake up." She shook him gently and said his name again.

That won't work.

I pulled my paw back and smacked him right between the eyes.

He inhaled sharply, his chest heaving the way it had in his dream. He fought for breath, until he realized where he was, and then he let it out slowly, relieved.

"Will." Her voice broke, and she was crying. "Sweetheart."

"What what what," he said thickly, still not quite awake. "What. Just a bad dream."

"That wasn't a dream."

He sat up against his pillows, blinking against interrupted sleep. "Pretty sure it was."

She reached for his face again, hand on his cheek. Her fingers trembled and her breath hitched. "That was a memory, Will."

That woke him up. "You heard something?"

"I *saw* it," she sniffed. "Every horrible second of it. He tried to kill you. You were just a little boy and he tried to kill you."

"To be fair, he was also a little boy."

"He was a goddamned sociopath!" she cried. "Will, what did he do to you?"

"You saw my dream," he said. "Were you already awake, or did it wake you? Did you know—"

"Will, what did he do to you?" she insisted. "Tell me."

He decided to ignore the thing he saw as the bigger problem: she'd seen inside his head when he hadn't intended her to. Worse, it was more than hearing a stray thought or two; she'd seen the dream as if she'd been there.

"He threw a bag over me," Will said. "You know the extra thick bio-bags? I think he'd worked out that I could be touched if there was a layer between us. When my back was turned, he threw the bag over me, knocked me onto my ass, and taped it shut. And then rolled me into the pool."

While the class watched him sink, while George and his friends howled with laughter, one girl broke from the others and ran to get the teacher.

"I never found out who it was. But if not for her?"

"George was more than a bully, then."

He nodded. "No one would speak up when asked who'd done it. I had no proof. I still have no proof. But the last time I saw him that day, before my father could get there, he found me in the teacher's office in the locker room. Her back was turned away from the door and he whispered, 'next time, Blackshear.' But that was it, my mother pulled me out of school the next morning."

I thought she didn't know the worst of it.

"She doesn't know the worst of it, Wick. That was the closest he came to killing me, but he'd hurt me far more before."

Aisha's gonna lose it.

"I'm fine, Aisha."

"I'm not." She crawled over him and slid out of bed. "I have to get up. I can't breathe right now."

He followed her to the living room, whispering that they didn't want to wake Jay. "What's bothering you more?" he asked. "The dream, or that you saw it?"

"The dream," she hissed. "The *memory*. Oh my god, Will, you were so young, and you were terrified." Her breath hitched again. "You thought you were going to die, and all you wanted was your mother. And if the teacher had been even a minute later—"

"I know. But she got there in time, and it was years before I had to deal with him again." He managed to steer her to the sofa, and she sat with her legs over his lap so that he could pull her close. "Are you all right?"

"I've had that man in my home, Will. He's been alone with my son. All I ever thought was that he was a bit of a bully, but I had no clue how truly evil he is."

"Should I have told you earlier?"

"How would you even lead up to that? 'Oh, by the way, James' husband is a sociopath with homicidal tendencies that go back to *preschool*, but hey, maybe he's changed.' You were clear he was the one who fueled your worst nightmares. It's not like you tried to hide that from me."

Softly, Will said, "But I never wanted you to witness it."

"I needed to," she whispered. "He and James are splitting. I don't want him getting even a tiny sliver of hope that he'll ever have a right to see Jay again."

"Jay might want—"

"Never again, Will. And I swear to god, if he hurts you, or hurts Jay, or even James, I'll kill him with my bare hands."

"He's out of their lives, for the most part," Will reminded her. "Sooner or later Finn will take him home, and that will be the end of it."

As far as she was concerned, that was too easy and too fair. He'd gotten away with every horrible thing he'd ever done; George didn't deserve to have Finn escort him home, where he could live out a nice, comfortable life. She was fine with the idea that he could stay here and die slowly and horribly.

Will didn't argue with her. "I admit, that thought has occurred to me, as well. I'm not sure I want to lower myself to his level, though."

Jay wants to forgive him.

Jay had no idea, though.

Does Finn know George is the one who did that to you?

"No, Wick, I don't think so. I never gave my parents the names of the children who joined him in his efforts in anything he did to me. I didn't want them to worry."

Like Jay doesn't want Aisha to worry.

"Kids are blind to the bigger picture. Sometimes they don't grasp that parental worry is necessary."

"You wanted your mother," Aisha said, the words catching in her throat. "You couldn't breathe and knew that was it, and all you wanted was your mother."

"I know."

"You're calling her tomorrow, Will. This has to end. I don't care if she doesn't want us together and if she hates me for loving you, but you are damn well calling her in the morning. And you are going to forgive her because she's your goddamned mother and you need her in your life as much as she needs you."

"I don't know if I can get past what she refuses to tell me, Aisha."

She jabbed him in the chest with her pointy finger. "That little boy is still in here. He wants his mother. Don't you dare take that away from him."

15

Two days later Will waited on a bench on Union Square. He sat in the center, his arms stretched across the backrest, a clear message to anyone tempted: mine, don't sit here. He was there reluctantly, because Aisha wanted him to be. I sat on the ground at his feet, keeping an eye on the Square, because he'd closed his eyes and was soaking in the sunshine instead of paying attention.

He stopped ignoring his mother's texts once Aisha found the right button to push. He resisted a bit even after he promised Aisha he would make an effort, because he was still upset and thought that if Jo phrased something even a little bit wrong, he'd go off on her.

"You mean like I did with you a few nights ago?" she asked.

"You didn't go off on me. You just made me sleep with you. Horrible, you are."

He slept through the next night—he wanted me to wake him if Jay needed help, but he got himself up and stumbled to the bathroom on his own—and the next morning Aisha handed Will his phone and told him to call Jo. "Don't text her. Call her. And don't hash it out on the phone. Make a lunch date with her."

He argued that she was headed for work, and he should stay to be available to Jay, but James had taken off work to spend the day with his son. Unless Will wanted to supervise them, he had no reason to not make a date with his mother.

"The longer you wait, the harder it will be. Pick up the phone, Will."

"And if it explodes in my face?"

"Then you'll know."

Mom at twelve o'clock. Wakey wakey.

It was easy to forget that Jo was in her seventies; she walked with the gracefulness of someone decades younger, and even Will had to admit there was nothing elderly about her. "She's in her prime, Wick," he said as he watched her cross the Square. "This Jo could easily live another hundred years."

Aisha realized that, too. No matter how many years she had left, Will would outlive her. Jo and Finn would outlive her. They would probably outlive Jay. Will might not be willing to think about it, but she was, and she wanted someone to be there for him when she was gone.

When Jo was close, he got up, the same way he did when the Queen entered the room. He kissed her on the cheek and gave her a quick, tight hug, which delighted her since he no longer had the beard and wasn't so itchy.

The first thing she said was, "How's Jay?"

Peeing by himself and not even dribbling now. He's also looking and touching...a lot.

He didn't relate that piece of information.

"Up and about. Still in a bit of discomfort but well enough to go to lunch with his dad today."

"Finn didn't tell me what the problem was," she said as she sat on the bench. "I hope it wasn't too serious."

She knew what Mass's specialty was; Will wasn't sure if she was fishing or making small talk, so all he said was, "He's fine, Mom. That's all that matters."

Tone, dude.

She caught the edge of irritation in his voice, too, and patted him on the leg. "All right, William. You didn't ask me to lunch just to have lunch. Something is on your mind and you might as well tell me now."

Lead with the truth. Isn't that what you say?

Or maybe Aisha said it.

Someone said it once. But do that.

He slid his arm onto the bench behind her. "I know you don't want me to get involved with anyone."

"It's not a good—"

"Like or not, I *am* involved with Aisha, and I honestly can't think of a single reason why it would be anything other than wonderful."

Her list of reasons why unfurled in her brain, a parchment of pretexts that once let free would get away from her, unrolling until it hit the ground, hard. In milliseconds, she scanned them and went with the one that seemed most pressing. She told him it would be wonderful until they became intimate, when he probably wouldn't be able to stop himself from invading the privacy of her thoughts, nor from imposing his on her. "That wouldn't be fair to either one of you."

He sighed hard and then told her that when we were in the simulator, he realized that the lab was partly time locked and not part of the simulation. That the things that were there—the clothing and food and the computer—were real. So he explored. "I went downstairs, to your desk, and was humored by all the typical clutter. It was a bit touching to see that you'd never broken that habit. I was surprised that you kept the rocket ship drawing for so long."

"Really? I still have it."

"You also had a tablet loaded with all the data from the brain scans done on me as a child. I was amused at first because I remembered what a game it had been. You were teaching the lab techs to use old equipment, and because I wanted to play with them, you were able to get a dozen years' worth of scans of me. When I was going through the tablet, I realized there had been a greater purpose to it. It wasn't that you indulged my wish to play games— you were trying to figure out what was wrong with me."

She bristled at that. "No. There was never anything wrong with you. I wanted to know where your abilities came from."

"Still. You were looking. What was a series of games to me was actual research to you. I had fun answering all the questions and watching the colors on the screen flicker and pulse, and you kept all the data."

His irritation confused her. "It started as a game for you and it was beneficial to the students who were just learning. But of *course* I kept all the data. You don't destroy data. I realized I might be able to pinpoint the region of your brain most responsible for your abilities, and since your father was functioning in his own research just fine without me, I had time."

He wanted to know what she learned.

"There were no clear answers, not in the tests. Your brain was normal, although your synapsis fired faster than average for your age, and you responded to certain emotional stimuli in a way I would only expect to see in an adult. There was significant early prefrontal cortex development. But bear in mind, I was not a neuroscientist. It became a hobby of sorts, and if I'd been able to dedicate myself to it, I would have."

She was not heading in the direction he hoped. She thought she knew what he was after, and admitted to him that she knew she didn't have enough time when he was young. It always felt unfair, keeping him in the lab so much of the time, isolating him from the world while she bounced between teaching him, helping Finn, and juggling her own research. If she had to do it all again, she wasn't sure she would focus so much on what Finn was doing, because in the end, nothing she did mattered. "Your dad made his breakthrough because of you, because of the gate. And then it worked because of Drew. My only solid contribution was that I'd taught you well enough that you were able to conceive of the gate and build one in under less than ideal circumstances. The power that needed—"

"What about when I was younger?" he asked, ready to push a bit more. "You pulled me out of school when I was seven because I couldn't cope. I know that."

She nodded. "Those children were horrible."

"I don't argue that. But could I have learned to control myself?"

All right then. No more bush beating.

Good. The bush is tired.

"Of course you could have."

Will scooted a couple of inches away from her, surprised that she came right out with it.

"There was so much more to it, though. Those kids had marked you as odd and an outsider for life. They would have wrecked you more than they did. They never would have believed that you learned to not listen on purpose, they never would have trusted you enough to let you get that close, and it was breaking my heart."

She might as well have slapped him.

"You knew I could control it. That I could learn to touch people and not listen and not be heard."

"I highly suspected it. You didn't listen when you touched your father or me, and we stopped hearing most of your thoughts when you were around five."

"Then why didn't you tell me? Neither you nor Dad, no one told me. Quite the contrary, Dad has always been adamant about keeping the secrets, that once here I could never risk telling anyone my name, or why I was here. He told me over and over that I had to be careful, no matter how difficult it was. If anyone knew, they could destroy his chance of remembering who he was, and getting him home was pinned on getting his memory back. Someone would tell him—"

She acknowledged that and told him that the few times they heard things from him after age five were during emotional outbursts, especially when puberty hit. She wasn't certain that Finn ever really grasped that Will had a sense of control, but she did, and yes, not telling him was intentional.

He pulled his arm from behind her and sat forward, elbows on his knees.

"Sweetheart, it was to protect you. You weren't going to have us here and had nothing to fall back on if you did slip up. But more than that, I wanted to protect anyone you might become involved with."

He gave her a sideways glance.

"We knew you were going to die, Will. *I* knew you were going to die. How could I send you out into another world and let someone fall so deeply in love with you that losing you that young would shatter them? I know, we always take that chance, but this was a certainty. You knew you were going to die…it would have broken your heart, too. I thought I was protecting you and someone you might meet."

She's got a point, dude. You've even thought about that.

"I am sorry. I really am," she said. "But if it got you to this point, alive and well after all, if your pain helped spur you into creating that gate and saving not only your father but all of us, billions of people…then I'm not as sorry as I could be. And don't ask me to apologize for being the reason you couldn't be with Aisha when you were young. You were able to do the things you did because of how you are. Even how lonely you were."

"Were." The little muscle at his temple was twitching. "All right, you know what? I can accept that, I really can. But I didn't die, and you *still* didn't tell me you knew I could control this. You've seen me with her and know how badly I want this relationship, and you keep telling me it's a bad idea. This isn't a little thing. This is *huge*. The moment you realized that the gates worked and I was not going to die, you should have told me. I shouldn't have had to take the word of an eighteen-year-old girl that I could learn to keep my thoughts to myself."

"What?"

"Oz, Mom. *Oz* is the one who insisted I try. *Oz* is the one who sat with me patiently, touching me, risking that I would invade every private thought she's ever had, including her very raw thoughts about Andrew, simply for the possibility that I would learn enough control to have someone else in my life. You saw that happening, too, and said *nothing*."

"There's a world of difference between someone holding your hand or kissing you on the cheek and being intimate. I've been trying to protect you."

"Protect me, or protect yourself? You thought you were losing me before, but now you're trying to hold on? Tell me the truth. Because worrying that I can't hold it together when things get heated is not honest. Admitting you're afraid of losing me is."

She patted his leg again. "I really want to be angry with you right now, William. Accusing me of something like that."

"Then tell me the truth. Why didn't you tell me what you knew before now? And why don't you want me to be with Aisha?"

I jumped into her lap, because she looked like she was about to panic.

Dude, she probably doesn't really know.

She rubbed my head, musing that I was sharing bits of wisdom with Will when she could use some herself. "Sweetheart, telling you didn't really occur to me until your birthday party. And when she kissed you, I thought, well, he'll figure it out."

"But you've actively tried to convince me not to be with her."

He wouldn't look at her. He stared ahead, not seeing all the people passing by, not noticing the pigeons that were twenty feet away yet still uncomfortably close. She couldn't turn away from him, struggling with his anger, looking for a way to not fling it back at him.

She doesn't want to be alone in her loneliness.

His ear twitched, I know he heard me.

Her fingers are trembling against my back, dude.

"Where's Dad?" he asked, cutting through the silence.

"Where else?" she answered softly. "I'm alone, Will. I'm not sure that's why, but I can't bear the idea of losing you at the same time I'm losing your father. I hate that I'm doing it, but every time I see you with her all I can think is that once you've really *been* with her, it's over. I'll hardly ever see you the same way I hardly ever see Finn, and it crushes me."

"What do you mean? What's wrong with you and Dad?"

"On the surface, nothing, really. But he's so caught up in building a new lab and all the work he's doing with Richard, he'll stay there for days at a time, and I rarely hear from him, much less see him. I thought that by staying in this When he'd be done with the marathon work weeks, but he's so happy to be doing things he wants to instead of things he has to. And I can't take that away from him."

"Why the hell not? There's nothing he's working on that's pressing. You have every right to ask him to come home at night."

"Perhaps. That doesn't mean he wouldn't resent it. He just gets so caught up—when he realizes how long he's been in the lab he comes home for a few hours, and then goes right back to it."

"So tell him."

"The man has had this work routine for over forty years. And he's excited about perfecting long-range transporters. I can tell him he needs to spend more time with me, and he will, but all he'll want to do is get back to his lab and he'll wind up resenting me. And then I really will lose him. And I see it now…if I push back at you too hard, I'll lose you, too."

"You're not—" He took a deep breath. "All right, fine. Truth. Aisha pushed me to talk to you because she's afraid that I'll feel like I have to choose between the two of you, and all she wants is for you to be a part of our lives. She knows who and what I am, and none of that scares her. She trusts me to not listen to her thoughts, and she knows I can control mine. In any given moment, Mom. *Any*. I can control it."

Dude, do not mention the dream.

Jo twitched away from him. "Will, you've only been seeing her for a few weeks."

Her surprise made him laugh, and he reminded her they spent two years torturing each other as teenagers. "I never once touched her then. But when she came back into my life? There was no way I was not going to be with her."

"But still, William, it's been only a few weeks."

"Fine. A few weeks. But if you're trying to keep me from sleeping with her out of some notion that I might lose control... you're too late. And I need you to be comfortable with her, because this relationship is going the distance. We're not just casually dating. We both have every intention of making it last."

And babies. You want to have babies.

"Wick, stop it. We agreed to talk about one child. Just one. And I doubt—"

"Will, you can't. What if you pass this on?"

"What if I do? We'll deal with it. If I can learn to control it, I can teach my child to, as well. But that's not the issue. The real issue is if we want to start raising a child together in our forties."

She scoffed, that was still young. "I have friends my own age who only recently had their first."

Oh, she's falling in your direction. She wants babies.

"In this When," he reminded her, "menopause rears its ugly head around sixty years old. Even so, I don't know that we'll want to. She has a nearly grown son, and I've had wonderful moments with Oz and Zed."

Her inner scientist kicked into gear. The idea of losing him melted against the heat of exploring something new. "But if you did, then we would be able to determine if it's a new step forward in genetics or a random quirk. Presuming you would allow me to play the same games with your child as I did with you—"

He stopped her. If he did have a child, as long as they were games, he'd allow it. "But it's not genetic. A couple of weeks ago, I leaped forward—I know, risky—and I spent some time with the version of you that lost me. And that woman spent quite a bit of time after I was gone, trying to fit the pieces of the puzzle together. If you want something to work on, you could still do that."

"Not if you already bloody well know the answer. Tell me!"

"And rob you of a new vocation? You could kick Dad out of an entire level of the lab and take it for yourself."

"Tell me, or so help me I'll tell Aisha about all the perverted things you used to do when you were young. I still can't eat bologna."

She already knows some of them.

He pretended to consider it. "Do you remember the day when you sat on the steps at Herman Plaza with me? You were thirty, I was forty-two, and you had no idea who I was."

"Oh, I knew who you were. You don't think I would have wandered off with some strange man after seeing my own husband vanish, do you? I'd known for some time who you would grow up to be."

He blinked rapidly, trying to take that in. "There's no way Dad knew about me."

She admitted, she withheld it from him. She didn't want it brewing in the back of his brain. He needed to not grieve until there was no option.

Will was all right with that. "You were already pregnant with me then. Only a few days, maybe a week at best. But you still had to get home, and the only way to get there was in your ship. Bouncing through null space."

Horrified, "I did this to you?"

"Fetal exposure to null space did this to me. Your future self wasn't terribly clear on why, but her experiments certainly backed that up. And she wanted me to know that, in case Aisha and I decided we wanted children. She regretted never having grandkids of her own."

Jo realized that if she had been honest when he was young, she would likely have teenaged grandchildren now. He said it was possible. It was also possible that he and Aisha would have burned out young and not had a family. He didn't know, and he could accept that part of his life, but, "This is happening now. Sooner or later I'll ask her to marry me, and I hope you'll be happy for us."

"Well, *if* she says yes," Jo said lightly.

"She's already threatened to beat me to the proposal. But even if we never formally wed, we'll be together. I need you to be all right with that, and Aisha wants you to be all right with it. She doesn't want to take me from you—she wants us to all be a family one day."

"How do her parents feel about you?"

He shook his head. "They died when she was a teenager. Her ex's parents have been gone a long time, too, so there's no one on her side to object."

"Except her ex."

"He's fine with us. And understand, she's still friendly with him. They work hard to parent Jay together. He's a part of the package." Jo worried that there might still be something there; he assured her there wasn't. "James is in no way a threat to my relationship with her. It's fine."

"I can't believe you're already sleeping with her. How immoral."

"You're an atheist without any religious bent," he reminded her. "Not only that, sex has never been a moral issue with you."

"No, but this is different. You're my son. I don't want to think about my son having sex."

Will chuckled, "Then don't think about it."

She was quiet for a moment, then, "Oh my god, you're forty-three and just had sex for the first time. How awful was it for her?"

"Mom, holy hell."

"Well, I can't imagine it was wonderful."

"I had a great time."

"Will, you could stick it in a ham sandwich and have a good time. I'm not certain you haven't done exactly that. That poor woman has to wait until you're not so…new."

He grimaced. "I am never eating ham again. I swear, you're something else."

"I'm a sympathizer. I slept with a virgin once. Ten seconds of flopping around and then, what, already?"

Will closed his eyes and groaned. "I don't need to know that."

"He got better, eventually, but oh my god, the first few weeks. If he would have just listened."

"I listen. I'm a good student. And why would you tolerate bad sex for several weeks?"

She laughed. "I loved him. I still do. But I damn well wouldn't marry him until I could at least count to thirty."

"Now you're just messing with me."

"A little bit. But he was pretty awful at first."

"Well, if I'm equally awful, it's a good thing Aisha loves me. But I think I'm doing all right."

She got up and patted his cheek. "Of course you do, sweetheart. Now take me to lunch, and promise me we'll talk about something that isn't about how horrible a mother I've been, or how fantastic your sex life is."

"Sure about that?" he asked as he stood. "Because it's pretty fucking fantastic."

She slipped her arms around him and hugged. "I promise, I will be a better mother to you. I'll figure it out before it's too late. But you have to promise me, too. I need to hear from you more than once a week, and I need to not be an afterthought."

"Every day. If I don't call, I'll at least text."

"We need to make being a family a habit again. We went so long without seeing each other."

"I know. But Mom—I need my mother. I don't need a parent. All right?"

"Fair enough."

Yeah, let's see how well that works.

As they walked, Jo wanted to talk about him seeing her other self in old age. How old? What happened? He didn't know how to tell her and suggested that she didn't want to know the details of her future. She scoffed at the idea and said all the little details had changed.

When he still couldn't bring himself to tell her, he stopped and put his hand on her cheek and let her see. The hours spent with her in the future popped in her brain like a bubble. She was visibly shaken, and he tried to comfort her by reminding her of what she just said; it wouldn't happen that way. "The future changes. I lived, you and Dad stay together, and without that crushing grief, you won't die."

"But I have to!"

"No, you really don't."

"William, think it through. Before Eli is even twenty, I'm the reason he moves to the future."

"We'll find another way to get him to go."

"And risk that the timing of it all falls apart? Eli has to go, because if he doesn't, there's no Finn and then no you. And without that, everything we've done now just goes away."

"There's the Old Mint. Everything you did is recorded there. That won't just go away."

"The paradox—"

"That's why it's been time-locked for so many centuries, long before it was needed. To prevent a paradox from destroying it."

"But *Finn* invented the time lock."

"I'll find a way, Mom, I swear. Eli will move forward, and Dad will be born."

Jo's eyes filled with tears. "Sweetheart…I am sorry for all the pain I caused you by holding onto the truth. It was selfish, especially after—"

Will leaned over and kissed her forehead.

"Be with her, have babies with her, and I promise, I will be your strongest champion. But I will not be the reason that any of this falls apart. Eli never spoke about why he moved and why he was so willing to exist in so many different times, but it got him his family, which got me Finn. There's too much at stake—"

"Mom, stop. No matter how worthy the reason, we were slaves to Dad's mission to save the world. We get to have happy lives now. You are not going to destroy your marriage to ensure his birth a century and a half from now. I'll find a way to get Eli where he needs to be. Trust me on that." When she didn't seem certain, he pressed on. "What's the real issue? Why would you for even a moment be willing to leave Dad if you don't have to?"

She threw her arms around him and buried her face against his chest.

Maybe it's more than long work nights. Maybe they're already falling apart.

He pulled back from her a little. "Come on, tell me. Are you fighting? What?"

She sucked in a deep breath and took his hand, telling him to walk with her. She needed to move. After a bit, "I never see him, William. He's always been the ultimate absent-minded scientist, so absorbed in his work that he forgets there's life outside the lab."

"But?"

"I thought we were done. I thought that part was over. If anything, it's worse, because he has Richard to play with, and because of Shazia's schedule, Richard has an infuriating amount of available time. If I want time with him, I have to go to the lab, and if I try to get him to leave, I can feel the bitterness roll off him in waves. He'll go, but he resents the hell out of it. I take umbrage… we wind up arguing over the pettiest things."

"Have you tried talking to him? Telling him how you feel?"

"Why should I have to beg him to be present in our marriage?"

"Because he doesn't see it. Be the Scottish woman he's afraid of, Mom. You're allowed to demand his attention."

"And if he chooses to still spend all his time in the lab? My heart would break."

"That's when I kick his scrawny little ass." She leaned into him but didn't say anything else, and they kept walking toward the Ferry Building. They ended up on the plaza, and after he got coffee, they sat on the steps the way they had just a year ago for him and over forty years ago for her.

"How did you know who I was, Mom?"

She took a beat before answering and looked at me as if asking whether she should tell him or not. "I knew you were the Emperor, from pictures in history books and old family photos. But when I saw you in the tent? At first glance, I thought you were Eli. A young Eli, just a bit older than he was when Finn was born. It didn't take much to make the connection. And when I asked you about your burr? I just knew. This was the child I was going to have, and this is who he would become."

"And you sat there with me for hours, knowing you were with me toward the end of my life."

"In one day, I learned I would have a child, I met him, and understood I would lose him. I went back to our apartment to close things up—I curled up on the bed and cried all night. I cried nearly every day after that, until…"

"Until I lived."

"That day—I was thirty years old and pregnant with the only child I would ever have, and I realized that no matter what I did for him, he would die at forty-two. Whether I kept you with me, or sent you off, my baby would never live more than forty-two years. If you stayed and we didn't find a way to push the meteor off, you would die at forty-two. If I sent you to fulfill the Emperor's role, you would die at forty-two. It felt so unfair, yet there was no choice. And I couldn't tell Finn, not until he absolutely had to know. I wanted him to love being a father, not to dread how short a time he would have."

He set his coffee down and leaned over to kiss her cheek. "I get it now, Mom."

"Good, because I still don't."

"You were letting go with one hand and grabbing tight with the other before I was even born. But you can stop. You won't lose me now, and if you're truly all right with it, you'll gain Aisha and Jay."

"And grandbabies?"

Will laughed. "I don't know about that, but if she tells me she wants one, I'm open to the idea."

"What about what you want?"

"Mom, for the first time in my life, I have it. I'll be happy enough to spend the next sixty or seventy years with her, whether we have a child or not."

"You'd have one of the most loved babies in Pacifica," she said.

"Ah, well, so would you. You still have a couple years, you know."

"It would be quite the shock in this When, don't you think? And I'm not exactly opposed to the notion, but Finn would have to change his habits. I'm not doing it alone."

"Alone again," Will said. "While I considered him to be a present father, he truly did leave most of raising me up to you."

That was lack of choice. Finn felt pressed for time, always, but when he could take some time to step back, he was a doting father. "He loved spending time with you," she told him. "Do you remember the summer you spent building that internal combustion engine? I originally thought he wanted to teach you mechanics. Truly, he wanted an excuse to get dirty and greasy with you, and you loved old cars and motorcycles."

"I was nine," Will said. "I loved that summer. After that, I secretly wanted to become an automobile mechanic. Imagine my heartache when I discovered it hadn't been a viable vocation for overly four hundred years."

"Ah, but it gave you the skills to restore things. Your motorcycle. You have no idea how proud your father is about that."

"Really. I should offer him a ride."

"He can scream like a little girl, you know," she said. "Put him on that thing and he will."

"All the more reason."

Asshole at two o'clock. He's been watching you for about five minutes but now he's coming over.

"What asshole, Wick?" he asked, just before he spotted George halfway across the plaza. With a couple of expletives, he got up and brushed the dirt off his jeans, then waited with his arms crossed. Jo glanced at me—what?—and then got up, too.

"Emperor," George said when he was close enough.

Will's teeth were practically grinding together as he said, "George."

George nodded to Jo, but when she started to offer her hand, Will set his hand on her arm to deflect it.

"Don't you dare tell me not to touch her," Will growled. "You do and I swear to god I will finish the fight we should have had at seventeen."

"Oh!" Jo smiled. "You're from home."

Will turned to her. "George Denton. He's the main reason you withdrew me from school."

Her smile withered. "*You're* the little shit." Her hands balled into fists, and she stepped closer to him. "All the mocking and the food thrown at him. The torment on the playground. You cut the rope on the swing when he was on it. You pulled a knife on him when he was only four years old. You threw a plastic bag over him and taped it shut, you bastard! You *pushed him into the pool!* You! You tried to *kill* him."

He didn't deny it. Instead, he shrugged and said, "And that's only what you know about."

"He was terrified for his *life!*"

Will pulled her back just as she tried to slap him. "What the hell do you want, George?"

"To see Jay. James won't answer my calls. I know better than to ask Aisha."

"Why should you ever be allowed near that wonderful young man?" Jo spat. "You're a horrible excuse for a human being."

"Because," George said, voice shaky, "he's my son."

Jo looked up at Will. "Weren't his rights stripped? This is the one Jax stripped of his rights, isn't he?" She snapped back to George. "You're not his father. You're *nothing*."

"Is Jay the only reason you're trying to contact James?" Will asked. He slipped his arm around Jo, trying to calm her down. "I won't tell Jay directly, but if you have a good enough reason, I'll ask James to speak with you."

He hadn't made up his mind yet: stay here and risk dying, or go home and risk crushing loneliness. He wanted a chance to smooth things over with James, even if it meant not seeing Jay again. "At the very least, I need to sign over everything to him before I go. Your father wasn't sure how my property would be dispensed if I just vanished, and I don't want the state to take everything. There's a trust fund for Jay—"

"I'll speak to him," Will said. "Are you feeling the effects of being without an anchor yet?"

"I can't sleep, can't eat. I don't know if it's because I don't have an anchor anymore or just because. And that's part of why I haven't decided what to do. If I can function without one, I may just move to Vegas."

"Has anyone survived without an anchor?" Will asked Jo. "Do you know?"

Jo glared at George. "Mitchell Vardimichio," she answered, unhappy to give George even a slim amount of hope. "Finn brought him here when he was twenty-five, and he's ninety-eight now. His anchor passed on thirty years ago, and he's survived well on his own. Finn theorizes that the longer one remains in an adopted When, the more it becomes their own."

Which means you might be all right in a few more years.

"You may do well, then," Will said to George.

He shrugged. "We'll see. If James is willing to talk, he can call me, anytime, day or night."

"Is it wrong," Jo said as he walked away, "that I hope he gets hit by a bus?"

"No worse than the moment I saw him again and wanted to ask Oz to throat punch him."

"Oh. Let her. Please."

"Dad thinks time will allow someone to settle?" he asked. "I wouldn't mind if this became my When."

"It's only a theory, Will. And you may be resetting the clock every time you go through a portal."

And you went back home, so there's that.

"You'd better plan on living for a very long time then, Wick."

"We all want Wick to live forever. Except perhaps Wick." Jo stretched up on her toes to kiss him. "But I also think new connections can be made. You have an entire family here now, William. And more importantly—and yes, you may mock me for saying this—you have Aisha. She may be able to hold you in this When, and surely if you have a child together, time wouldn't dare take you from him. A child of your own might be anchor enough."

"You're just speeding in all directions, aren't you?"

"Because I hadn't thought it through to the next step. Until that horrible bastard—all this worry about losing you to Aisha or what might happen if she hears your secrets, and I skipped over the idea that she may very well be the thing that keeps you anchored here, and well."

"I hope so."

"I'm a bloody idiot, William. And tell her I said so."

Hug her now. She deserves a hug for that.

"I will tell her that you are in favor of the relationship and that your actions of late had nothing to do with us. And it will be the truth." He pulled her into a hug and added, "I also promise you this: if you keep bugging me about a grandchild, I am going to bug you about a brother or sister. And I'll do it in front of the King and Queen."

She kissed him again and reminded him he was buying her lunch, and as he scooped up their coffee cups and invited me back on his shoulder, she said, "Remember, William, you're a lone voice, and I'll have an entire royal chorus behind me."

PART 3

BILBO IN FLIGHT

16

"Puberty," Will said, lightly. "Take every unpleasant thing Zed said and did from thirteen to sixteen, and cram all of it into a four-week period. Toss in 'you can't tell me what to do, you're not my dad' shouted with a dozen squeaky pops and cracks, with an equally squeaky, 'I hate this fucking place' when the door he tried to slam closed with a quiet click."

We were on our way to check out the new workspace Will had secured a few blocks from home, on the edge of the South of Market neighborhood. It wasn't half as big as the space he had when his workshop was under Union Square, but there were three levels and it was more than they needed to start with. Will thought that they would only use a fraction of the lower level area for the first couple of years, but they eventually would need it all.

Drew laughed—mostly because it was Will dealing with sudden-onset-adolescence while juggling his love life, and not him—and then mused, "Eh, so maybe Oz has hit second puberty."

"She's yelling that you're not her dad while stomping down the hallway?"

"Sure, daily. No, she's just been in a bad mood. Stressed out about wedding plans and having to wait longer than we expected, and hinting we should just run off somewhere and do it. Then she gets unreasonably mad at me when I say no. What'd you tell Jay to do that pissed him off?"

"I suggested that he wash the dishes he'd left in the sink before his mother got home."

"How dare you."

"Three minutes before that, he was happily helping me change all the recessed light bulbs. Still, I find it difficult to get upset with him, no matter how hard he pushes."

He usually says he's sorry afterward.

"Indeed, Wick. He's often quick to apologize."

"Gotta be hard going through all of it so fast. He's grown a hell of a lot, too. How painful has it been?"

"Very," Will said.

"So you give him a pass for a lot of the attitude," Drew guessed. "Though my dad sure as hell didn't when I hit my first major spurt. I think I spent most of my freshman year grounded. The only reason I wasn't during the summer was because he wanted to send me here and make me Mr. B's problem."

"It's the voice," Will said, amused. "In six seconds, he goes from baritone to chipmunk to deflating balloon and back. Keeping a straight face is the real problem."

"Be nice. You went through the same thing." Once inside the building, Drew stopped to look around. "Man, this place is huge. And empty."

Their footsteps echoed off the polished tile floor. I jumped from Will's shoulder and ran to the middle, where I let out a magnificent meow, just to hear it swell and bounce off the walls. While they discussed the renovations that Will envisioned—blocking off space to create offices and storage, and another to store his motorcycle—I ran the length of the floor, first to hear my paws pop on the tile, and then to enjoy the slide when I came to a stop.

The red dot game would be awesome in here.

Will pointed to the windows on the right wall. "The view isn't spectacular, but I thought we could create a space at the window for Wick. Give him a wide, padded seat and a covered tree he could scratch at."

Show me?

Will picked me up and carried me to the window. He was right, the view wasn't special. My entertainment would mostly be people strolling by, a mix of tourists trying to find their way to the modern art museum and business people headed for a break at Yerba Buena Gardens. It wasn't as nice as looking out a window at home, but people outside would enjoy seeing me lounging in the window, talking to them as they passed.

Can I have a bed this high up? So that I can lounge and entertain people?

"I don't see why not," Will said. "You're not required to come to work with us, but if you're here, you might as well be comfortable."

A little sign in the window that says, 'This is Wick, wicked awesome cat dude'?

"Perhaps."

"This is a hell of a lot of space for what we'll be doing, isn't it?" Drew interrupted.

I wasn't done with requests. I would also like a treat dispensing machine.

"Initially," Will answered him. "Once the first prototypes are built, we'll need the entire upper floor to run tests."

"We'll need an entirely separate building at some point," Drew said. "Unless we can figure out a better cooling system from the start, we don't want to host it here. We might want to look at workspace near the Wastelands. If we burn down a building there, no one else is at risk, and we might be able to draw power from the old solar farm."

"Baby steps. That's a significant distance down the road. For now, this is the home base for your future."

He led Drew over to the left wall, where there was something covered with a tarp. Will grabbed one corner and pulled it off, unveiling a mock-up of the sign that would go outside

Ozoo Enterprises.

"Seriously?" Drew asked. "Ozoo? Will, what about—"

"You are co-founder and CEO," Will said. "Ultimately, this will be your endeavor. I'm only along for the ride."

And it keeps Finn out of your hair.

"There's also that. The only thing my father needs to know is that you're trying to create something for yourself, a way to support your family. He won't have a problem with the idea that you want to be the one who invents the first practical holographic computer system."

"Will, he might try to help."

"Indeed. He'll offer advice. I suggest you listen to it. He won't give you the answers, but he'll certainly try to keep you headed in the right direction."

Drew was less comfortable with that than Will. As Will locked up, Drew stared down the street; several blocks away someone was laying on their horn, and in the traffic-free zone of downtown, it was unsettling.

"I'm not sure I like the idea of taking Finn's advice when we're trying to trample over his research."

"We're not negating the work he's doing, Andrew. His focus is long distance, high volume transporters. Ours, aside from the holographic computer system, will be personal transporters. I fully expect to get there first, and when we do, we'll share our data with him and with your father."

"My dad." Drew shoved his hands into his pockets. "What am I screwing him out of?"

"Nothing. Your father takes the information Finn gives him and builds the equipment they need. And while this is my father's singular concentration for now, yours has multiple projects in progress. He already understands that he's a government contractor and won't share in any patents that result from their research."

That's not fair.

"That's part of doing work for the government, Wick. They own the intellectual rights to everything Finn and Richard create."

"My dad will want to help, too."

Will nudged him toward the street to get him walking. "Indeed, but if you tell him this is something you're doing not only to be the first, but also that this phase is largely to help you learn and that you feel you need to begin on your own, he'll respect that. It's not a lie. Your task over the rest of the summer is to study. Become familiar with the concepts you wish to begin with, and allow yourself the luxury of chasing rabbits down holes, so to speak."

I thought he didn't want to kill any bunnies. He wouldn't let you hunt for them in Colorado last year.

"It's a figure of speech, Wick. I meant that he should allow his curiosity to guide his studies."

You could have just said that.

"And while I'm studying, what happens?"

"I'll apply for grants, secure business licensing and incorporation status, and have renovations to our offices begun. And then I'll move my equipment out of storage."

"Equipment. You just want to play with your motorcycle."

"Of course I do. I now have an ongoing source for fuel and someone who will manufacture new tires. I'd like to get it back on the road."

Aside from his books, the motorcycle was Will's prized possession. It was a four-hundred-year-old Triumph that he restored, using parts he had to manufacture himself. It had taken years to complete, and he was only able to run it every now and then because fuel for an internal combustion engine was rare, and the tires he needed even more so.

I never wanted to be on it, but I wanted him to be able to ride it. Riding made him happy, and for him an air bike wasn't the same. He wanted to feel the bike rumble under him, and the grips vibrate against his hands. There was a thrill to leaning into a sharp curve and feeling the tires grip the road, his knee inches from the polymer pavement, knowing that if he made even a tiny mistake, the bike would slide out from under him and he'd find himself tumbling after it.

"I get a ride," Drew said.

I don't.

"Everyone gets a ride. I'm hoping it will interest Jay, as well."

"No brainer. You have to worry about Aisha letting him, though. I can see her putting her foot down over that."

She's gonna want the first ride. And then her own motorcycle.

"Jay is also a project for you," Will said. "Once his physician clears him for physical activity, he'd like to explore the martial arts. He thinks you and Oz will be far less intimidating than any of the instructors I would otherwise recommend."

"Does he know Oz can be a really tough teacher?"

"He does. He's fine with that. His feeling of intimidation stems from the fact that he's never taken so much as a gym class. The idea of suddenly participating with several other students is overwhelming."

"Seriously? He got out of gym? Lucky bastard."

"Medical exemption."

"Ah. Locker rooms. Yeah, not a problem. Oz has toyed with the idea of teaching students aside from Zed and me. Like, to the point where she's seriously considering going back to train at her old dojo to get more experience and a higher rank."

"Is she thinking in terms of having her own school?"

"Small school. If she does it, she wants to drop the whole belt system and concentrate on practical fighting techniques. The only things holding her back are her own rank and who she is. She doesn't want people signing up just because they want to be around the princess. She wants kids who really want to learn."

"She doesn't need rank. She has the proficiency and expertise," Will said. "More so than most instructors. Oz has real-life experience. Her own sensei has experience limited to sport sparring in tournaments. He breaks for points, whereas she will insist the fight continue until she says it's over."

"Rank matters to parents who are looking for a good place for their kids. They want to see a black belt with a lot of stripes on it leading each class, and they want to see trophies displayed in the school."

You have rank, Emperor. Lots of rank. And you can buy trophies.

"That only helps if he wants to teach, Wick," Drew said.

"I would be willing to teach a class here and there," Will offered. "Oz should seriously explore the idea. She can be judicious in the students she admits, and it gives her the same footing you have, employment-wise."

"You think that matters to her? We've always expected that I would draw the bigger paycheck. She's headed for the throne and it pays shit, basically."

"It's not about the money. It's about equitable contribution of effort. That will matter to her."

"Money's a good thing, too," Drew chuckled. "I know we're having at least one kid someday, and I'd like him to have a toy or two."

"Him."

Drew stopped at the corner. "We know we're having a son, Will."

Will waited.

"Tobias, in the simulator. When he was super pissed off, he said that the son of our son caused everything to go wrong with his coding errors. Finn wrote the code. Which means his father is our son."

"All right. I was hoping you missed that."

"It also means we're having more than one kid," Drew said as he resumed walking.

"Sure about that?"

"I want a daughter, Will."

"Says the man who only a year ago wasn't sure about any children at all."

"I had *just* kissed Oz for the first time. I wasn't sure about anything."

We were at the corner of the royal house. "I imagine the year you've had gifted you with some perspective," Will said.

"I suppose. I mean, I didn't know what I wanted to *do* until I saw that computer in the simulator's lab, but yeah, more than ever I know I want to have a family with Oz, and I really want a little girl. I want that relationship Oz has with Mr. B."

"Ah, you want someone rolling their eyes half the time and making fun of you the rest."

Drew laughed. "Hell, yeah. But you've seen it. Oz is the toughest person I know, and yet she's still daddy's little girl."

"Well, get the computer built before you spawn. I suspect that if you get what you want, you'll turn into marshmallow fluff and will then be useless."

"And you won't tell me when we have kids, will you?"

"All bets are off now," Will said. "Whatever path you followed in my history might not happen now. You might have a daughter. You might have ten sons. Hell, you might have a puppy. I don't know."

If you have a puppy, you're moving out.

I would tolerate a sticky person or two. A dog? No, they would have to find another building to live in.

"Wick, even if I wanted to move out, Mrs. B wouldn't let me. I'm ninety percent sure she would barricade the door."

"I would have to move before she would let that happen," Will said.

"Yeah, she's not letting you move, either."

We were at the door. Will pulled it open and let Drew in first, and we headed up the short staircase to their apartments. "It may have to happen, Andrew. Once you and Oz start a family, the space in which you currently reside will not be enough."

"No one's asking you to move."

"My apartment will become yours eventually," he said, punching in the pass code for his door. He opened it and invited Drew inside. "Living here prior to taking the throne is practically tradition. Jax and Aubrey lived here, his parents lived here, and his grandparents lived here. It's more or less expected that you and Oz will live here as well. I knew that when I moved in."

"What if we don't want to? I mean, seriously, we can make do with my place for a long time. It's not like a baby takes up much space."

"Babies need room, too," Will pointed out. "You'd be fine as a little family there until crawling became an issue, but after that?" He went to the fridge and pulled out cold drink bottles, and handed one to Drew. "I will happily vacate the premises when the time comes."

"Yeah, well, no one else will be happy if you move out," Drew grumbled. "Wait. Unless you're thinking of moving in with Aisha. We'd be okay with that."

"No." Will pursed his lips, the 'no' lingering for a moment. "I have no desire to live downstairs from James. And now that his husband is gone, the door between the two apartments is generally unlocked. I would not want to be the one to tell Jay the lock goes back into place and if I lived there I would insist upon it."

"Forgot about the husband. How'd he handle that?"

"There's nothing to handle yet. George has spoken with my father about going home but isn't willing to leave. He and James live apart, but they talk every now and then and are still arguing. Aisha tries to keep Jay out of it and she refuses to allow George to see him. So, we'll see."

"I hope they don't regret it."

"Why would they?"

"Because," Drew said, "everything happened so fast. If they'd intentionally taken a month to just stop being pissed off and for George to realize Jay got exactly what he needed, they might not have split. Stop fighting and just get over it."

George was not a person Will could be objective about. He would be happier if Finn took George home, so that he could pretend George no longer existed. "It's perhaps more complicated than I can say."

"Still. They were married a long time. That should count for something."

Perhaps it should, Will allowed, but it wasn't his problem and he had no intention of ever again speaking to James about George. He checked the time and told Drew he needed to get going; Jax expected him at City Hall in twenty minutes to act as a witness to a department hearing—which essentially meant two different government offices were arguing over their share of the toys—and the King wanted the Emperor on hand. He might want advice, he might want a simple witness, or he might want the intimidation factor of a glowering Emperor. It wasn't a matter of "if you can be there," it was a command.

'You *will* be there.'

"Feed Wick?" he asked as he headed for the door. "I gave him turkey for lunch. He hasn't forgiven me for it."

I jumped onto the kitchen counter to wait for Drew to make use of his thumbs and open a can. Will didn't like me eating up there any more than Jax did, but I could get away with it and Drew knew that.

"A year ago," Drew said as he dug into the cupboard for my food, "I would have had a panic attack at just the *idea* of being in this apartment. Being trusted enough to be here alone? You couldn't have convinced me that would ever happen. Then again, a year ago I wouldn't have been talking to you at all and I sure as hell didn't know Will could understand you."

Maybe you're asleep and this is all a dream.

I mean, you're talking to a cat, dude.

"That would suck. If I wake up and it's still a year ago and I've just fallen asleep on the roof, I'm gonna be pissed."

No war, no running off to the safe house, no trying to rescue Oz.

"No simulator, no Fluffy and Jeff."

No bouncing things with Oz.

"This better not be a damned dream then, Wick."

But you would still have that to look forward to.

He set my plate down. "But I'm just getting good at it!"

It's cute that you think so.

"Did Oz say something to you? Like, seriously. I don't think she would say anything to me. If I'm dropping the ball I want to know."

I would have answered him, but my mouth was full.

"Come on, Wick. This is important and you've, like, *been* there. If she's said something to you, you have to tell me."

If you only have one ball to drop, there's that. I dunno. I've never looked close enough to count.

"Jesus fucking—"

When we were playing pool, she said you were doing just fine.

He leaned his elbows on the counter so that he could see my face. "You have to tell me if you know she's not happy, all right? I don't know what else I can do, but I'll think of something."

She says 'oh god' a lot. That's a good thing.

"I suppose."

You worry too much.

"You started it!"

Only because you think you're getting good at it.

He huffed and set his head down on his folded arms.

You both suck.

He took my empty dish to the sink and rinsed it off. "All right. Fine."

You're too easy. Except for the whole weird whipped cream thing, I haven't really watched you together. Will says it's rude.

"You've been in the room."

I sleep through it. I only really like the after part, when people cuddle and say nice things to each other.

He softened a bit. "I'm a little partial to that, too."

I watched Will, though. I was afraid he was going to fall off.

"And?"

Not yet. But I think Aisha has been gentle with him. It's gonna happen, I know it is.

"I don't think that's a routine thing, Wick."

She's super enthusiastic. It's gonna happen. When it does, I'll come get you.

"Um, yeah, I don't think he'll need my help."

Sure, he will. Because when it does and he breaks a hip, she's gonna be laughing way too hard to take him to the ER. So, congrats. You're the designated naked Emperor lifter.

I don't think the idea thrilled him at all.

= = =

At ten o'clock, I was upstairs lounging on the sofa with the Queen tickling my armpits when the elevator pinged. Jax stomped out and headed for the kitchen where the beer lived, and Will strolled out, phone in hand. He tapped on the screen without really looking, and told Jax he was texting Drew. "'Upstairs *now*' should have them here in under a minute."

After he'd handed Will a beer, Jax shouted, "Zed!" and they sat down to wait. Jax took his favorite chair and Will took the other, and the Queen was asked to make no space for any of the kids to sit down. Jax wanted them standing and uncomfortable.

Zed grumbled that he was doing homework and had been jerked out of the zone, which would be a pain in the ass to get back into, but when he heard Drew and Oz scrambling up the stairs, he shut up. I flipped over, because I didn't want to be on my back and exposed if body parts went flying, and Jax's eyebrows were trying to shake hands so there was a chance he might cut something off someone.

They exchanged confused glances, especially when they realized that none of the old people were making way for them to sit.

"So," Jax started. "Forty-five minutes ago, we were in a meeting, when a member of the guard came in to inform me that I had a matter regarding one of my children, and while it wasn't an emergency, protocol stated I was to be notified immediately. I had to cut the meeting short and then listen as a very embarrassed twenty-five-year-old kid informed me that someone in this building had tripped the passive controls on our Internet account, and then had to show me the site that was being accessed."

"In English, Jackson," Aubrey said.

He waggled his pointy finger. "One of these three was trying to download porn."

Will tried to bite back a laugh but didn't quite succeed.

"Well?" Jax prodded.

"I've been studying all night," Zed said. "Check my laptop. The only thing I've been looking at are the equations Mrs. Okuda sent the class this afternoon." He glanced at Will. "Your girlfriend is mean, you know."

Oz folded her arms, a slight grin tugging at her mouth, and Drew stared at his feet. Jax waved Zed off—go finish your homework—and let Drew stew. He sat back in his chair and put his feet up, sipped at his beer, and waited for Drew to look up.

Oz nudged him with her elbow.

"I just—" He still couldn't look up. "I don't—"

"It wasn't really porn," Oz said. "We were just looking for proof that we're not completely inept in bed."

"Oh, lord," Aubrey sighed.

Jax remained silent. He rested the tip of the bottle against his bottom lip and stared until Drew finally looked up.

"I'm sorry," he said.

"Sorry you did it or sorry you got caught?" His eyes crinkled at the corners; he was trying to not laugh. "There is a difference."

"Honestly, really only sorry you know about it. We just wanted—" he exhaled sharply "—I think I suck and I just wanted to get a little better, all right?"

Aubrey muttered "oh, lord" again, but it was soft, and I think only Will and I heard.

"You don't suck," Oz said. "Well, not unless I ask."

"Oz!" Aubrey got up and jabbed her pointy finger in the King's direction. "Jackson, I swear. Leave them alone." She stomped down the hall, but he didn't leave them alone.

"The controls on the account are there for a reason," Jax told them. "Nothing you do online is private. Ever. Anyone snooping hard enough can find every site you visit, and they can connect it to your personal log-in. Do you really want to open the morning news and find a picture of Drew with a splash title hinting he'd viewed a video titled 'It's not like licking an ice cream cone?'"

"A *melting* ice cream cone," Oz corrected.

At that, Will laughed out loud.

I jumped off the sofa and went to sit at Drew's feet. He kept looking down, so I figured it was the best place to get his attention. *Sorry, dude. This is my fault. I didn't mean to get you in trouble. You don't suck.*

"It's not your fault, Wick," he said.

"Don't worry about him, Wick." Will got up and pointed at Drew. "You're coming with me."

"But—" His shoulders sagged as much as his ego. "I'll call you later."

I don't think he heard Jax chuckling under his breath when Oz kissed him and promised if he didn't call her, she would call him. I followed them down the stairs to Will's apartment; Drew shuffled along like he was about to be executed, so Will got there well ahead of him and waited at the door.

He's not in trouble for real, is he? It was my fault.

"You are truly not in trouble," Will said as he opened the door. "Frankly, Jax had forgotten that there were nanny controls on the account. But understand, he doesn't want to remove them until Zed is another year or two older. Where you were seeking information, Zed probably would look for porn and he'd likely find things he isn't ready for."

"I just—" He spread his hands helplessly. "I need to know."

"I understand. Sometimes I feel like I'm paddling the same canoe, Andrew. Most of the time I think I'm doing all right, but every now and then I wonder if Aisha simply isn't telling me when I fall short in order to spare my feelings."

Really. It was my fault.

I was teasing him.

I mean, I'll still tease you but I didn't want anyone to get in trouble.

"It wasn't your fault," Drew said again. "I mean, if anything it was a good thing. I decide to talk to Oz and tell her I was worried. We don't *know* if we're any good at it. We have fun, but we started wondering if there was more, you know? So we went online, but we weren't actually looking for porn. Just…ideas."

While Drew stood in the center of the living room and talked, Will pulled the router for his Internet connection out from under the bookcase and flipped it over, and then took a picture of the bottom of it with his phone. "Jax is not upset with you, Andrew. He was concerned that Zed was the guilty party and wasn't looking forward to that discussion, but he has no issue with you exploring."

He used his pointy finger to write on the picture he'd taken. "All right. I just sent you a picture that has a different account number on the bottom of my router, and I wrote the password on it. Connect online through that, and then delete the image."

"Your account?"

"I have unrestricted access and a much higher level of security. You can look at anything you want."

"I'm not sure I will."

Will sat down on the hearth and gestured to the sofa to get Drew to sit. "Jax is upstairs giving Oz access to his account. He understands your curiosity. And clearly, Oz has no problem admitting she shares that curiosity."

"I will never be able to look Mrs. B in the eye again."

Dude, if you don't, you'll be staring at her boobs.

That's kinda wrong.

"Andrew. Aubrey didn't leave the room because she thought you were doing something wrong. She left because she thought Jax was out of line."

"Seriously?"

"Oz turns nineteen in two weeks. You turn twenty-one in three months. You're fully committed to each other. This falls into the realm of being no one else's business. Jax understands that, but he was not passing up the chance to make you squirm."

Drew looked at the picture on his phone. "Personal question?"

Will nodded.

"Have you tested out this connection yet? I know you said before you'd never watched any porn, but your circumstances have changed."

"I still have not."

"That sounds like you're not still ruling it out."

He took a moment to weigh his words, and leaned forward

with his elbows on his knees, serious. "Like you, I wonder from time to time about my abilities, so to speak. And as you did with Oz, *if* I seek out anything online, it will be with Aisha. I don't currently find a purpose to viewing it alone."

Drew shrugged. "For the hell of it?"

"I don't need a visual aid. If Aisha isn't here with me, she's in my head. I'm not comfortable with the notion of using something impersonal and salacious for my own gratification."

"Human translation, you don't understand getting off to porn."

"In theory, I do. But in practice?" He took another beat. "You want a daughter someday. The women in those videos are someone's daughter, Andrew. Very few of them are engaged in the industry because it was a life goal. They fell into it and can't get out. Would you want that for your daughter? Or even for Oz? To be the anonymous body someone else uses for a few minutes of a masturbatory fantasy?"

"No," he said quietly.

"I choose to not go there. I would not judge you if you did."

"You would, a little."

"All right. I would endeavor to not judge. And I will never ask, not seriously."

Drew nodded.

"There's nothing wrong with being curious. I'm not sure that I wouldn't have done the same thing at your age, had my circumstances been different."

"I get it, Will. Use my own damn conscience."

"And try to not let Jax goad you so easily. Trust me, by the time he was your age he'd done much worse than search for instruction online."

That was something Drew didn't want to hear about. He thanked Will for the new log-in and the talk, and went to his own apartment to call Oz.

No Aisha tonight?

"I had to work late, and she has Jay tonight. I'll see her tomorrow."

Adulting sucks, doesn't it?

"Sometimes," he admitted, "but I am enjoying its perks."

Not enough to go looking for it online. Instead, he stretched out on his bed and called her, forgoing a video connection to lay in the dark and listen to her voice. I curled up on the spare pillow, and closed my eyes, only half listening while they said drippy, overly sweet things to each other. I made a mental note when he told her he was available to take Jay to a doctor's appointment in the morning and set my internal alarm, just in case he fell asleep without setting his own.

He slept more now; it was possible.

17

Will's fist was raised, ready to knock on the door. The thunder of size nine feet on the floor inside made him hesitate; he craned his neck so that he could see me, mumbled that it was going to be a fun day, and then knocked. Aisha's voice was far away, telling Jay to answer the door, and his was a loud squeak when he shouted that he was busy.

"A really fun day," Will muttered.

Nearly a minute later the door popped open, and she was apologizing before she'd even really seen him. "I am going to owe you so hard." She shoved computer tablets into her bag while trying to wiggle shoes onto her feet, and knocked the remnants of Jay's breakfast onto the floor. "Really, so, so hard."

"I've got it," Will said. He bent over to pick up the plate and toast pieces and then took them into the kitchen. "I'll get the rest, don't worry."

"Thank you. If he tries to tell you he needs to shower before you leave, he's lying. He took one an hour ago, but I'll be damned if he'll get dressed. It's been…a morning. Don't let him—"

"It'll be fine," he told her.

"He wants to postpone the appointment. I don't know why, but he's being a real pain in the ass about it."

"Go to work." He tossed the cleaning rag he'd picked up in the kitchen onto the table, kissed her, and then pointed her toward the door. "I'll get him to his appointment on time."

The bathroom door slammed shut at the same time he closed the front door behind her, and within seconds there was water rushing from the shower. He knocked on the door, loudly, and called out, "Five minutes, Jay, then we have to leave."

"I need, like, fifteen."

"In five minutes, I open the door. You might want to be dressed and ready to go."

"Door's locked, dumbass," he mumbled.

"Locked door will not stop me. Four minutes, thirty seconds. If you're not dressed, you're leaving in whatever you have on, and we're taking Zed's bike. It's cold out."

"How the hell do you think you'll open it? Kick it in? That'll piss my mom off."

Will ran his hand across the upper door jamb. There was a sturdy piece of wire there, and he inserted it into the tiny hole in the door knob, jiggled it, and listened for the click that told him he'd sprung the lock.

"It's now unlocked." He put the wire back. "Three minutes."

"Bullshit. It is not."

With a heavy sigh—this was Zed at thirteen all over again—he turned the knob and let the door open just enough for Jay to get the message.

The water cut off, and Will listened until he heard Jay scrambling to put his clothes on, and then went to wipe up the toast crumbs. With roughly ten seconds to spare, Jay bounded down the hall with his shoes in hand, asking for enough time to get them on.

Without answering, Will left the apartment. He took his time getting to the elevator, and when Jay slammed the apartment door and hopped down the hallway trying to wedge his shoes on, he didn't turn. He pressed the button and waited, hands clasped in front of himself. When Jay tripped on his own toes and landed with a nice splat, he grinned a bit but still didn't turn to look.

Once outside, he swung a leg over the air bike, took me off his shoulder and slipped me into the sweatshirt pouch, and fired it up. Jay had barely hopped on and grabbed onto Will's shirt before he pulled away and shot down the street, laughing under his breath.

= = =

"I really didn't need anyone to bring me here," Jay huffed as he settled into a waiting room chair. "It's like two miles. I could walk it on my own."

"When Zed offered use of his bike today, he mentioned that you still don't have your license and wouldn't mind getting it."

Jay wouldn't look at him. "So?"

"So, after your appointment we can take it out, and you can begin learning on it."

"You're going to teach me to ride Zed's bike."

If you quit being a dillhole.

"Zed would teach you himself, but he has a provisional license and can't legally act as an instructor. He thought that since I taught him to ride, you'd be open to allowing me to teach you as well."

"Huh. Okay, sure."

"Once you get the hang of the bike, you can learn to drive my car."

That made him finally turn in his seat and stop staring at the wall on the other side of the room. "Seriously? I mean yeah, I'd like that, but it's not like my mom or dad have a car. Or a bike. I'd just be learning to learn?"

Will reasoned that driving was a necessary skill and that Jay wouldn't be without a vehicle forever. Learn now before you absolutely need to. He refrained from mentioning that he didn't mind loaning his car for the occasional date or even for a joy ride.

I get to go home first, right?

I did not want to be on the bike while Jay was driving it. I didn't want to be on the bike at all. If I had realized it was the day's mode of transportation, I would have stayed home and watched Drew read.

After a quiet lull in the conversation, Jay dropped his voice to a near whisper and asked Will if he was going into the exam room with him. He sounded both worried and hopeful, and then admitted he was relieved his mother had not been the one with him because she would have wanted to be present for the exam and he had questions for the doctor he didn't want to share with her.

"She would have understood that."

"She would have wanted to know the questions."

"Well, now I want to know," Will teased. Then seriously, "Your father will answer anything he can, you do understand that?"

Jay grunted. "My dad is weirdly repressed, you know. He can't even say the word 'penis.' He just gestures to his crotch and says, 'you know.' I *tried* to talk to him. I think he thinks that by asking him anything about my body or sex, it means I'm gonna run out and jump the first girl who blinks twice. And it's bizarre as hell because he's seriously the guy who will fuck anything that moves."

Will ignored that slice of information. "Ah. My parents were the exact opposite. Perhaps your mother—"

"No!" He was horrified. "I am not telling her I keep getting random—just no."

"Erections?" Will guessed. "Happens to all of us. And she knows that."

He exhaled slowly, looking down at the floor. "Jesus."

"Unless you meant something else."

That was exactly what he meant. "It happens, like, *all* the time. I'm not even thinking about anything that should do it, but all the sudden, *boom*, there it is. I can't stop it. I don't even want to leave the house because it's gonna happen and there's no hiding it."

Don't laugh at him, dude. You were a walking erection for a couple of years.

"Sit up straight," Will told him. When Jay did, Will told him to plant his feet square on the floor, and then tighten his quads and abs as hard as he could. Concentrate on that. "It helps. Clenching those muscles as hard as you can helps divert the blood flow."

"Clench," Jay said as he tried it, gritting his teeth.

"But perhaps avoid making that face."

"No constipated facial expressions. Got it." He relaxed and sat back. "Now tell me what to do if I get back there and it happens during the exam. He's gonna be all up in my junk and touching stuff, and I don't think his being a guy will matter."

"Do nothing. If Mass even mentions it, it will only be to comment that your body functions normally. It's par for the course for him, I would imagine."

"I suppose it would be an opening to ask him other stuff." He glanced at Will sideways. "I'm kind of afraid I might, you know, break…it."

"It won't break," Will assured him.

"Yeah but it's new, so…I still haven't, you know…"

"Baby boys from the beginning of time have been tugging on theirs hard enough to make their mothers worry. Mine once admitted she'd been certain I would find a way to tie it into a knot. But ask him, Jay. He won't think twice about the question, and can tell you if you've healed up enough to begin normal activities."

"Normal," he snorted.

"To be clear, I also meant running, swimming, and perhaps karate. Oz and Drew are willing to begin your instruction."

"Sweet."

"But also ask him about that."

The door creaked open, and the nurse called Jay's name, even though he was the only patient waiting.

"I don't know if I can."

Once he was behind the closed door, Will pulled his phone out and sent a text.

You just sent a message to Mass, didn't you?

"Perhaps."

So that he would bring it up first?

"To make it easier on Jay. Who knows, maybe once he finally test-fires it, he'll stop being so moody."

You've been firing it off for over thirty years and that never helped you.

"Funny, Wick."

Maybe you need to get that website from Drew. It sounded educational.

"Wick."

You'd never look at an ice cream cone the same way again.

= = =

I found Drew and Oz on the living room floor, ignoring the perfectly good furniture. He was stretched out with his head resting against Jax's comfy chair and she was a few feet away using Aubrey's chair as a back rest, but their feet were close enough to touch. They were engrossed in the things they were reading; Drew squinted, as if the words on his tablet were trying to bite. Oz's eyebrows were knotted together, but it wasn't because she was reading as hard as he was. She looked like she was trying to talk herself out of a bad mood and was failing.

There was a spot right between them where I could see both of their tablets, so I stretched out and snooped; Drew was engrossed in an article on the future applications of nanobot technology and Oz was scrolling through the news. Every now and then her eyebrows relaxed and she snorted, softly so that she didn't bug him, until she hit upon an article she had to share.

She tapped his foot with hers to get his attention. "According to this, the Emperor ditched some poor girl for Aisha, and she wants to reclaim his attention because she's having his love child."

Drew twitched away from his article. "What? That's insane."

"Oh, and she *loves* him and doesn't understand why she was dumped for someone he only *just* met. If he doesn't step up soon, she's going to sue him for paternity."

"I wonder if he's seen that."

Don't text him about it. He's busy trying to not die on the back of Zed's bike while he teaches Jay to ride.

Drew agreed, it could wait. He tried to go back to his article, but she tapped his foot again. "Oh, and apparently, you're thinking about moving back to Chicago to overthrow Pacifica's acquisition of Midlam and then become King. Wouldn't you want to stay here to do that? This *is* where all the paperwork was filed. I suppose you could arm wrestle my dad for it."

"What the hell are you reading, Oz?"

"News, supposedly."

"I need to *visit* Chicago, but damn."

"Better get on it," she told him. "I want you here for my birthday, and then school starts. We damn well aren't missing it again."

"Maybe during a holiday," he said. "Thanksgiving?"

"As long as you're back for my mom's birthday."

After how last Thanksgiving turned out, you better be here.

"Good point, Wick," Drew said. "And we can't skip Christmas here because your family actually does Christmas. New Years?"

Oz set her tablet down and sat all the way up. "If you head to Chicago after Christmas, I'll be mad as hell, and your parents won't even be there."

"Why?" Then as it hit him, "Oh."

"You *forgot?*"

"No. I just wasn't thinking about that, I was trying to figure out a time to go see my parents."

Dude.

"And your own wedding wasn't even on your radar."

"Come on, Oz. It was a brain hiccup, that's all."

"A brain hiccup is forgetting that school starts on Tuesday instead of Monday. It's not contemplating going clear across the country the same week you're getting *married.*"

"Come on. I wasn't thinking."

"You do still want to get married?"

He scowled. "Of course, I do."

She stared at him, and her breath caught.

Oh, we're gonna fight now, aren't we?

"We're not fighting, Wick. I made a mistake, that's all."

"No shit." She got up and stomped out of the room, and three seconds later her bedroom door slammed shut.

Go get her.

"No. I didn't do anything wrong. I had a brain fart, that's all. She's reading way too much into it."

So?

"So, nothing. I'm not apologizing for trying to figure out a good time to go home."

You're home now.

"I meant to see my parents."

Well, there you go.

"Stop poking at me, Wick. This is my home now. But my parents, that's home, too, and the *only* thing I was thinking about was seeing them. I didn't forget our wedding."

She thinks you did.

He shrugged.

I'm surrounded by idiots.

I left him lying on the floor with his nanobot porn and crawled through the flap near Oz's bedroom door. She was on the window seat, staring out at the Square. I jumped up and crawled across her legs so that I could wedge myself between her and the window, because I could see her face from there.

Boys are idiots sometimes.

Her hand went to my head and she scratched right where I liked, but she didn't say anything.

Sometimes girls are, too, you know.

Her hand dropped into her lap.

I wind up in the middle. And all the kissing going on? You people could take a break for a while. Same thing with all the bouncy talk. It's been nothing but erections and licking things and bouncy bouncy bouncy. I miss when it was all stealthy spying on the Emperor and sitting near the water to look at the bridge and the ferry boats. Like, before your birthday last year. That's when it all started getting weird, when Drew kissed you.

"I'm allowed to be upset, Wick. He wanted a full wedding ceremony. It should matter to him. That's not the kind of thing that just slips your mind."

Stop letting him see you naked. If he knows he has to wait until then, he won't forget. It's kind of mean, but it would work.

"I'm the one who just wanted to have a small, quick thing. What the hell."

The hell is that you really do want the big wedding and you want him to want it as much, even if you're both all 'let's just run away and do it.'

"Don't you dare go tell him what I said. I miss being able to talk to you without knowing you can go tell the Emperor and now Drew."

I crawled onto her lap and touched my nose to her chin so she'd know that I wouldn't tell anyone. She kissed the top of my head and went back to staring out the window, and I sat upright on her legs, waiting for her to either cry or decide Drew wasn't being forgetful on purpose.

After a while, she got tired of staring at the people on the Square and rested her head against the window. I expected Drew to knock on the door, but we sat there for a long time and he didn't come in. We saw Will pull up on Zed's bike with Jay on the back, and a little bit later Aisha walked across the Square on her way to Will's, but Oz didn't move.

I wish you would tell me what's really wrong.

Maybe she wanted Drew to come after her and was still waiting, but by then he was probably downstairs in his own apartment, trying to figure out what he'd done. From the kitchen, I heard a skillet scrape across the top of the stove and then a sizzle, which meant Aubrey was home and cooking. Then Zed's footsteps on the stairs. Then the elevator pinged and Jax was home.

Oz had been at the window for hours, barely moving. She heard everyone on the other side of the door, too, and kept glancing at it, but I wasn't sure if that was because she wanted someone to come in and check on her, or if she was afraid they might.

Finally, she took a breath and said softly, "I'm late, Wick."

Dinner's not for another half hour, I think.

"You can't tell Drew that, either. I don't want him to know yet."

Okay, but chances are someone will come get you when it's time to set the table. I think it's your turn.

"Worse yet, I don't think he really wants to get married now. When I asked him, his colors shifted. He said 'of course,' but everything around him flared red. What do I do now, Wick?"

She twitched like she was going to get up, and I started to jump down, but instead of swinging her feet to the floor she pressed the side of her hand against that little space between her nose and her lip, and her breath hiccupped.

You want your mom? I can go get her.

Her eyes squeezed shut and she sucked in several deep, ragged breaths.

Or I can get Drew. Just tell me what to do.

When she opened her eyes, tears dipped over her eyelashes and down her face.

I'm sorry. I wish I could help.

"I'm going to lie down for a little while," she said, setting me on the floor. "Drew might still be here but if he's not, he'll be back soon. Tell him I fell asleep, all right? If they all think I fell asleep, they won't try to get me for dinner. And if he asks, I'm not sick. I was just sleepy."

You want me to lie.

"Please, Wick. I don't want to face anyone right now."

Okay. Drew will think you're mad at him, but okay.

I was right, too. When I told him that she was taking a nap and he needed to tell Aubrey, his first thought was that she was still mad at him. I tried to tell him she wasn't and she just wanted to take a nap, but he didn't believe me and couldn't figure out what he'd done wrong.

Halfway through dinner, Jax told him to just go talk to her already; he was tired of watching Drew scowl and push food around on his plate. Zed promised to do the dishes even though it was Drew's turn, but yeah, go do whatever he needed to stop moping around.

He knocked softly on her door and didn't wait for an answer before he went inside.

I hope he told her she's not in trouble for being late to dinner.

"No clue what you want, Wick," Zed said, "but you can supervise while I do dishes. If I miss a spot, holler."

He knew what I really wanted. After Jax and Aubrey left the dining room he set a gravy-covered plate to the side and didn't say anything when I licked it clean.

I think he washed it after I was done with it, but I wouldn't swear to it.

= = =

After he did the dishes, Zed dragged his homework down to Will's apartment and sat at the table with Jay, who was studying even though he wasn't taking any summer classes. He'd wanted to; he thought the summer would be boring with his mother teaching and best friend cramming an entire year's worth of math and history into two months. As far as Aisha was concerned, this was the compromise, since his surgery kept him out of school. He'd find things to read or study while Zed did homework, whether here at Will's, upstairs at home, or over at Aisha's apartment.

Will and Aisha were on the sofa and each had a tablet on their lap, but they weren't reading anything. When I jumped onto the hearth, they were talking quietly, so I waited for a lull in the conversation before stating my displeasure.

"Problem, Wick?" Will asked after I'd been staring a few minutes.

My whims are not being catered to.

"Did you have dinner? Or did you want to hunt the red dot?"

I could eat.

"I didn't ask that. I asked if you'd had dinner."

There was food.

Aisha patted her lap. "Come on, Mister Wick. I'll give you chin rubs."

"He's capable of amusing himself," Will said. "He chooses not to. If he was truly bored, he'd go pester Drew, because Drew cannot seem to tell him no."

Drew is unavailable and I shouldn't bother him.

"Do I want to know?"

Probably, but I promised Oz I wouldn't tell anyone that she's mad at Drew or that she was going to be late for dinner.

"Then clearly, you should not tell me that."

Then Drew didn't finish dinner and Jax made him go talk to Oz and I haven't seen them since. But she wasn't even late for dinner, she just didn't leave her room, so I don't really know what she's mad about.

"It's none of my business, Wick."

"What's the problem?" Aisha asked.

"They apparently had a fight," he replied. "Don't worry about them, Wick. They've got a lot on their plates and are probably a little stressed out."

But Oz didn't even have a plate. She's probably hungry now. Someone needs to bring some dinner to her.

"She'll be fine. She knows where the kitchen is." He reached over and took me from Aisha and then got up. "I'll get you a snack. That will make you feel better."

I feel fine, but okay.

"What about you two," Will asked Jay and Zed. "Hungry?"

Zed warned Jay that it was a trick question. "He has a fridge filled with protein-laden cardboard and little cubes of dairy-flavored despair."

"There's also a fruit platter," Will said. "And cheese."

I like cheese.

"It's a trick, I tell you," Zed whispered loudly. "It's probably mutant fruit injected with still more protein."

Aisha followed Will into the kitchen. "They're too busy studying to eat. Right?"

Zed tapped his finger onto his tablet. "Seriously. I have this bear of a math teacher and she's burying us in work that doesn't resemble anything she talks about in class. And why should I solve for x? Why can't x solve its own problems?"

"Oh, sweetie, your ex has more problems than anyone can solve," Aisha mumbled, reaching into the fridge for the fruit tray.

Oh, she went there.

Will leaned toward her and said, "Really?" at the same time Zed called out, "She's not my ex, she was never my girlfriend."

But that was still funny.

"I'm sorry, Zed, that was uncalled for." She set the tray in the center of the table. "But if you're stuck, just ask. I know your teacher, and I'm sure she won't mind if I help."

Zed was not offended; instead, he laughed and reached for a strawberry that was so big it might have actually been injected with protein. "It's fine. She was not one of my brighter moments. But I also need to ask…Sophia's coming for Oz's birthday, and I would really appreciate it if no one mentioned Rhonda. Or anyone else I've gone out with."

"Don't lie to her," Will said.

"I won't lie. She knows I've had girlfriends but I'm not ready to explain Rhonda, and the other girls that I really did date, I'll tell her about them eventually. I just don't want anyone telling her what a complete asshat I was. She'll figure that out on her own."

Will sat down at the table, leaning on his folded arms as he considered Zed. "Omission is still somewhat of a lie, Zed. Being unwilling to expose your truths can backfire horribly. Case in point, me."

"I won't let it get out of hand, Will. We're just not *there* yet. If we get there, and she asks about who and how much I've dated, I'll be honest with her."

"She's gotta understand the whole friends with benefits thing," Jay said.

"Except they weren't even friends," Will pointed out. "It's a point of character, and it may matter to her."

"Yeah, but Zed shouldn't lose a chance with Sophia because he made a mistake with Rhonda. She's kinda relentless. If she wants someone, she'll do whatever she has to in order to score. And I mean, like, score points, because it's all a game to her."

Zed pursed his lips; he knew what Will was doing, and in that moment decided to go along with it. "Will's all about integrity. He wants me to tell Sophia so that she can make an informed decision about me. Overlook what a douchenozzle I was, or assume I'm still an ass. And I get it, Will. Girls are not toys you take off the shelf when you want to play, even if they're the ones who start the game."

"Women can be quite forgiving if you're honest with them," Will told him.

"But they can also run like hell!" Jay sputtered. "Why should he take that chance?"

"Indeed. Why?"

"The sooner I tell her the better, I suppose," Zed said. "It wouldn't be fair to sleep with her and then tell her what a little slut I was. I swear, Will, I'll tell her before we get that far, but I still want to tell her when I'm ready, not when the rest of you are."

"Fair enough."

"And I also get that she's not just some girl from school. If I fuck up and hurt her, her father gets pissed, and if he gets pissed, it's a giant sinkhole in the road between Texas and Pacifica. And since that's a fifteen lane hyper-speed road, it would be a big freaking deal."

"Talk about complications," Aisha mused as she sat next to Will. "Do you ever get the chance to just be a kid?"

"Oz and I have to think ahead. Maybe not as far ahead as she and Drew did, but we have to consider the implications of the things we do. More now than even a couple of years ago, I suppose."

"Did they really decide to get married when they were like thirteen?" Jay asked.

"Started talking about it then," Zed said. "They didn't get super serious until last year, though. I don't think he even kissed her before then."

"On her birthday," Will said.

"And now they're fighting," Zed snorted. "Kinda wish she had come out for dinner so we could watch Drew melt in his chair and ooze onto the floor."

Hey. Oz was crying. Leave them alone.

"Remember that the first fight you have with Sophia," Jay said. "We'll pick on you, too."

"No, we won't," Aisha said. "Now, do you need some help, Zed, or do you understand the equation?"

"I got it. Or will by tomorrow morning."

She turned to Will. "Then we need to get going. One of us has to get up a whole lot earlier than she would like."

Zed started to pile his stuff up, but Will told him he was fine staying there to finish. He walked Aisha to the door and made Jay suffer while he kissed her good night. It was a long kiss, too, enough that Zed snorted and Jay sighed like it was the world's grossest display of affection.

He even rolled his eyes when Will said, "Love you," and she said it back.

When they were gone, he picked up his phone and texted Drew, and then told Zed he would be up on the roof, but he could stay as long as he wanted. He could even raid the fridge for cardboard flavored protein, or if he preferred, there were cookies in the pantry. "Aisha made them," he said.

Zed snorted. "Yeah, you want me to eat them so you don't have to."

"Saw right through that, didn't you?" Will grabbed a bottle from the freezer and then filled two glasses with ice. "I'll give them to Drew later. He'll eat anything. But feel free to raid the kitchen."

"I won't be long," Zed said. "Two more equations, then I'm done. I'll make sure the door is locked when I leave."

I followed Will up the stairs.

Why? It's not like anyone can get in the building and the Queen isn't going to sneak down here and steal your cardboard food.

"Common courtesy. Zed is trying to be considerate."

Drew was on the roof, flat on his back in the grass. It was the same way Will found him a year ago, right after Oz's birthday, when he was trying to figure out what Oz expected from him. This time, though, he'd obviously been crying.

Will sat next to him and filled the glasses. Reluctantly, Drew sat up, but he didn't say anything, even when Will held a glass out to him and said, "Cinnamon whiskey, ice cold." He took the glass and sipped at it, and sniffed a few times.

They sat together silently while they drank their whiskey; Will refilled Drew's glass twice, and then set the bottle out of his reach. Drew laid back again, hands folded across his stomach; he tried swallowing whatever was upsetting him, but he couldn't quite get it all down and one tear trickled from the corner of his eye. I don't think Will saw that. He had laid down, too, and was staring up at the sky.

"Look straight up, and then roughly twenty degrees left. Elysium. You're going to make that a reality again."

Drew wasn't going to talk, and Will knew it, so he kept right on going.

"Jax has only one title left to secure, and then it belongs to Pacifica. Everyone else has given up on it. Once you figure out the heat issue, we'll have the answer for the infrastructure that runs life support on Elysium. That will be your legacy, Andrew. Precision-cutting the final piece of the puzzle, the one everyone else gave up on.

"It wouldn't be limited to your work here and for Elysium. The Mars colony would benefit, as well. Improved control over their systems means they can expand. Deep space exploration—"

"Oz thinks she's pregnant."

He didn't look as happy about it as I thought he would be when they had their first sticky person. He looked like he was going to throw up.

"She also thinks I don't want to marry her."

Will sighed and sat up. "One issue at a time. Why does she think you no longer want to get married?"

Drew told him about their fight, his fixating on figuring out a good time to visit his parents and skipping right over the wedding part. "She asked me if I still wanted to get married and I said I did, but apparently the color around me changed, and that means more than what came out of my mouth."

"Perhaps at that moment, you didn't."

"Will, come on. I've wanted to marry her since we were kids."

"Were you angry?"

"A bit. But that doesn't mean I want to break up."

Will tilted his head a bit, looking at Drew as if he were a tiny bug scurrying across the grass. A tiny, non-thinking little bug. "No one said anything about breaking up, did they? You or Oz?"

"No."

"Then don't jump to conclusions. You had a momentary flare of anger because she accused you of forgetting your wedding, and in that sliver of a moment, for *only* that moment, you didn't want to get married. For less than a second. What she saw was anger, not a lie."

"Yeah, well, I have a different anger color, it seems. I hate this part of it all, Will. I can't lie to her. I can't have a bad moment to keep to myself. Every fucking feeling that I have, she knows almost before I do."

"You want to marry her."

"Of *course* I do!"

"Now, that sounds like you don't really want to. You're just mad about being called on it."

Drew sat up sharply. "I'm pissed off at everything right now, just let me have that. I don't know what to *do*."

"Wait until you've calmed down and then tell her you love her, and there's nothing that will stop you from marrying her. Not even a surprise pregnancy."

"Jesus. What the hell are we going to do? Or what the hell is *she* going to do, because Mr. B is going to kill me."

"He may be upset for a bit."

"He's going to be pissed. And Mrs. B will cry."

"And your own parents?"

He shrugged. "I haven't thought that far ahead."

"All right. But I can assure you, Jax won't kill you, and Aubrey will skip past the anger and go right to the part where she gets a grandchild."

"He already threatened to string me up by my balls. He's going to want to hurt me. All that will do is upset Oz, and right now that's the last thing she needs."

"I know him well enough, Andrew. Any anger will be fleeting. You may find yourself suddenly married by a King's Decree, but you're in no physical danger. Their disappointment will not last longer than it takes for reality to set in."

Maybe she made a mistake.

"Andrew?"

"She's going by the calendar, and she's never late," Drew said. "But it's not like either one of us can walk into a drug store and buy a test kit, not without it making every damned gossip site on the 'net. And going to the doctor? Did you know he's got a massive stick up his ass about anyone not married even *thinking* about having sex? Zed went to him for an implant, like, a year ago and he refused. It didn't matter to him that Zed was already having sex. He just outright refused and told Zed to stop being a little pervert and to get himself right with Jesus."

"Jacobsen?"

Drew nodded.

"Interesting. He had no qualms about mine."

"You're the Emperor. He doesn't dare tell you no."

"He wouldn't dare tell Zed no, either, if he realized what Jax's reaction would be. And will be when he finds out."

"Zed couldn't even go to another doctor. We're *stuck*, Will. None of us can just walk into a clinic or make an appointment with someone else. Zed even pays one of his friends to buy condoms, because he knows if he does it, some stupid cashier will tell someone, who tells someone else, and it goes public. The only way for any of us to see another doctor is to tell a parent, and we'd kind of like our privacy about this shit, you know?"

"I know." Then, as it occurred to him, "He wouldn't refill your implant, would he?"

Drew shook his head.

"Then this really shouldn't be a surprise, Andrew. If you've been having unprotected sex—"

"Not entirely unprotected. Condoms." He shrugged. "Zed shares."

Take him to see Mass. Mass will refill it.

"Jay's doctor?" Drew asked.

"And an old friend. It might not be that easy, Wick. Mass hasn't been vetted to treat the family, and his specialty would raise some eyebrows if they were seen going into his office."

Not if you all met in Finn's lab like a social thing. He could refill Drew and give Oz a test. No one else has to know. I won't tell the King.

"Will?" Drew sounded hopeful.

"I'll call him in the morning." He got up and then reached a hand out to help Drew stand. "You have my word, I won't say anything to Jax or Aubrey. Or Aisha. This is not mine to tell."

"I hate asking you to keep a secret," Drew said as Will pulled the roof door open. He was unsteady, so they rode the elevator all the way down instead of taking the stairs. I sat at Will's feet and Drew leaned against the back wall, staring up at the light in the ceiling. When the car pinged and the door opened, Will had to guide him out and toward the short staircase up to their apartments.

Drew's door was open and the lights were on. Oz was curled up on the sofa, her eyes puffy and nose red. As soon as she saw him she jumped up and ran at him; Will kept a hand on his back to keep him from tumbling backward, and told Oz, "He's a little bit tipsy. My fault."

To Drew, he said, "I'll call you in the morning after I speak to Mass."

When Oz let Drew go, Will reached for her.

"You're both allowed to have fleeting moments of uncertainty," he said to Oz, softly. "He loves you, no matter what color is swirling around him."

He closed the door gently, and I sat at their feet, waiting to see what would happen, hoping she wasn't still mad at him. She hugged him again and then kissed him, and didn't grumble when he pointed her toward the sofa.

"You taste like cinnamon," she sniffed. They sat together the way they did when they were on the window seat in her bedroom. He sat on the sofa sideways and she settled with her back against his chest, and pulled his arms around her.

She wasn't done crying, and he didn't tell her to stop, or that it would be okay.

I jumped onto the sofa and carefully crawled up her legs and then over Drew's arms. I let him support my weight while I pressed against her chest, my head on her shoulder, and I purred for her as hard as I could.

18

Mass sprayed the island in the lab with a disinfectant that made my nose hurt, and when it was dry, he told Drew to drop his pants and then hop up there. Before Drew could protest, Mass said, "I have penises in my face every damned day. Modesty is not allowed right now."

Drew didn't care. The only one there who hadn't seen him naked was Finn, and he had already slipped into his office and closed the door. Not that it mattered. All Drew wanted was to get the implant refilled and then find out if he was eight and a half months away from becoming a father.

Before Mass jabbed him with the needle, he placed a small red box on Drew's belly and ran it from his navel to his groin. "Checking the tube," he said. "No point in refilling it if it broke. If it's broken, then we have to do this in my office."

"It can break?"

"The tube that runs from the receptacle to the testicles can unseat sometimes. That's rare, though."

When he was satisfied that the entire implant was in working order, he rubbed Drew's belly with an orange ointment, and then slowly stuck a needle in. It took a couple of minutes, and the entire time Drew stared at the ceiling while Oz held his hand.

Drew grimaced just a little bit when the needle came out. Mass told him he could get up and put his pants on and then reminded him that it would take a few days to be fully effective.

"And now, Oz."

Mass pulled a tiny vial filled with a pale-yellow liquid out of his bag, along with a tiny needle. He swabbed Oz's finger with alcohol and then asked her if she was ready.

He poked her finger before she could say yes.

"Hey! That's cheating!"

He squeezed a drop of blood from her finger and let it drip into the vial, and then squeezed a little bit more. When he had as much as he wanted, he put a cap on the vial and shook it in his closed fist. Drew watched his hand as he shook the vial, but Oz closed her eyes.

"Ready?" Mass asked after a long minute.

She sucked in a deep breath and opened her eyes. He uncurled his fingers, the vial resting on his palm. The color had turned from yellow to blue, and she started crying again.

Mass had no idea how to handle that. He looked at Will helplessly, the vial still in his hand. Finn heard Oz and opened his office door; he nodded to Drew and then his office, giving them someplace to hide and settle with the news.

"I'm used to happy patients," Mass said as he slipped the vial into a pocket on his bag. "I get it, but still."

"Give them time," Will said. "It's been an emotional roller coaster."

"Let me know if I can do anything else," Mass said, clipping his bag shut. "And you might want to wipe that counter down with some bleach. No telling where that boy's ass has been."

While they gave Oz and Drew time to collect themselves, Finn and Will waited at the table on the other side of the room, as far away from Finn's office as they could get without leaving. There was coffee for them and cheese bites for me; I wasn't hungry—I was a little too upset because I didn't want Oz and Drew to be upset—but Finn went through all the trouble of cutting it into me-sized bites, so not eating it would have been rude.

"I don't suppose telling them this isn't the end of their lives would help much," Finn mused.

"Neither is telling them that this is proof that the timeline has changed. It should be five more years until Eli is born."

"So they start their family out of order."

"Or they never have him. We need to make sure we protect the lock on the Old Mint, Dad. If Eli isn't born, then you won't be here to invent it, and—"

"I didn't invent it."

Will's entire body twitched. "Explain. Because I was always told it was yours. Mom even thinks you invented it."

"Really now." He took a long sip of his coffee. One eyebrow was raised just a little bit, inviting Will to ask more, but not promising an answer.

"Dad, come on. That lock may be the single most important thing for the future. If you didn't invent it, then who did?"

Finn set the mug down and sat back in his chair. "First, it doesn't have to be invented again. It exists, it continues. Second... all the data for the time lock was left to me. It came sealed in a metallic blue box engraved with a word that was just enough to convince me to open it, and then take the contents seriously. I think you weren't quite two years old. It was before I found Wick, even."

"Who sent it?"

"It was delivered by your grandfather."

"That's not what I asked." He matched Finn's body language, sitting back, arms folded. "All right. What was the box engraved with? What made you want to open it?"

"Ozoo."

Oz and Drew!

"Ozoo," Will repeated. "Zed didn't anoint them with that name until the war, when we were hiding at the safe house. That didn't happen in your timeline."

Finn shrugged. "Doesn't mean he didn't come up with it later. But it was a beautiful blue box. You tried to take it from my office when you were four or five. You said you wanted to use it for your important secret things, which I gathered were toy cars and Wick's fallen whiskers."

The memory of being caught with the box made Will grin; he'd tried to hide it under his shirt, and he tip-toed down the hallway, feeling sneaky. Finn stopped him before he got to his bedroom and asked what the sudden growth on his tummy was; it looked serious, so he might need to go get that looked at. "But I don't want to," he sputtered. "I just want to go play."

Finn held his hand out and waited for Will to give him the box.

"Whatever happened to that box?" Will asked. "I don't think I've seen it since."

"Locked up several levels down. I don't want Drew to see it, either."

Will glanced at the closed office door. "He's going to be busier than either of us thought, then."

"Still planning on letting him tinker with his own hologram?"

Will nodded. "He was acutely interested in the simulator's holographic system. Rather than give him the information, I thought he would fare better if he discovered the steps on his own. So don't just hand him the answers, all right? He's the sort who will be far happier by creating something rather than having it dropped into his lap."

Finn grunted, but it was more of a chuckle than irritation.

"What?"

"Will, I'm not an idiot. And you don't know as much as you think you do." The chair squeaked against the floor as he got up. "Boot up the computer in my office when they're done with it, and look up the history of the simulator's creation. It's hidden in a shadow file. Look for a file listed in 'lunch codes.' Probably titled 'food that looks better than it tastes.'"

"Not under 'food my little shit of a son will eat'?"

"No, *that* file is a list of every location near the lab that has macaroni and cheese, pizza, and chicken fingers on the menu. I swear to God, Will, feeding you when you were little was the most aggravating exercise in patience a parent should ever go through."

"I was not a stubborn eater."

"Not as long as you had mac and cheese or chicken fingers." He headed for the door that led to his downstairs workspaces. "They can stay as long as they want. The air mattresses are in the closet, and the fridge is stocked. If they need an excuse to hide here for a day or so, tell Jax they're helping me take one of the gates apart."

"You'd lie for them."

He shrugged. "Unless they really want to help me take one apart, which I suppose we could do. They're my grandparents, Will. There's not much I wouldn't do for them."

= = =

They didn't want to stay in the lab. They wanted to get out, walk, run, do anything except go home. Oz felt like she would suffocate hiding in Drew's apartment and couldn't bear running into her mother. Drew was terrified of running into Jax. Will offered his car so that they could drive to the beach and watch the sun set, and told Drew that the back seat folded flat if they wanted to spend the night in it.

"But there are two conditions. One, call home and tell them you're going to dinner together and might stay out late. Don't make them worry."

Drew nodded.

"And two. Under no circumstances do you run off to get married. No knee jerk reactions. Just let it sit with you for a while. And I mean weeks, not hours."

A spark of defiance flashed in Oz's eyes, but she gave her word. There would be no eloping. They would walk around downtown for a while, then get his car and park somewhere.

"And no ditching your guards. That includes jumping through a portal."

She sighed hard. "Fine."

"Ozzie." He held his arms out to her, and then pulled them tight when she tumbled against him. "I promise you, it will be all right."

"I'll be fine," she mumbled against his chest. "Drew's the one who'll be swinging pantsless from a flag pole on Union Square."

He kissed them both, reminded them Finn said they could stay in the lab as long as they wanted, and then headed for the elevator. He still had work things to do, and only a couple of hours to do them.

"Come with me or go home," he said once we were at the Square's perimeter. "I can keep an eye on you from here if you want to go inside."

I decided to go with him, as long as he promised non-cheesy food soon. He bought me dead meaty things to nibble on and then let me ride on his shoulder all the way to the shelter's office. It was terribly exciting, and by exciting, I mean I was nearly bored into taking a nap; he signed his name to a dozen different documents—officially still "Emperor" as far as shelter things went—and then he met with a family who had arrived in the city in the middle of the night, people who had run from Florida, not understanding they were now free to come and go as they pleased.

He gave them a voucher to take to the immigration office, keys to an apartment in the Sunset neighborhood, and a card good for three months' worth of groceries. Neither the husband nor the wife wanted to accept any of it; they had only hoped for a night or two in a shelter and a lead on employment, and they left with a home and a promise that there were jobs waiting for them.

He signed a few more papers, and then took me to city hall to meet with the coordinator for the family's personal guards. He wanted eyes on Aisha and Jay, and wanted to meet with those chosen before they assumed the detail. He also wanted to be notified if Oz and Drew left the city, especially if they used his car.

The guard in charge of assignments didn't ask for reasons; he knew better. He did ask if they were under any sort of threat, and all Will would tell him was that they were young, impatient, and in love. If they went anywhere, he suspected it would be Las Vegas.

But they promised.

His shoes squeaked on the marble floor, quick little chirps as he made his way to the front of the building. It was already mid-afternoon and hot; he opted to not walk the three miles to Aisha's school because of the time and the chance I would get overheated. There was an underground train station half a block away, so he ran to that and we hopped on the subway.

It smelled like pee.

We rode for five minutes in silence. Everyone on the train was quiet, staring out windows into the darkness of the transit tube, seeing nothing, especially not each other.

Well, I wouldn't look at anyone else if I had peed on the train, either.

Five minutes before school let out, Will found a place to sit on the capstone of a giant planter that ran the length of a church across the street. He waited until kids were scrambling out of the building and the first teachers trailed after them, then pulled out his phone and sent a text.

'Hello, beautiful. Look up.'

Her phone pinged just as she stepped out, and she smiled before she spotted him.

That's the closest thing to a pet name you've ever called her, you know.

"It's not my forte, Wick."

She calls you sweetie and sweetheart all the time.

"She calls everyone sweetie and sweetheart."

Not sweetheart. Just you.

"And Jay."

Fine.

"Arguing with Wick again?" she asked as she reached him. Before he could answer, she grabbed the front of his shirt and pulled him close for a kiss, prompting the gaggle of nearby teenagers to make loud whooping sounds and someone with a deep voice shouted, "Hell yeah! Go, Mrs. Okuda!"

"I have *got* to change my name before the fall semester," she said after she let him go. "Hello, handsome. Did you come to walk me home?"

"I did. Unless being seen with me will cause scandalous gossip among your students."

"We can only hope."

We can call her Bob.

"What the hell, Wick?"

She wants to change her name. Let's call her Bob.

"That's not what she meant. And we're not calling her Bob."

She stopped at the corner, just before we turned away from the school. "Bob?"

"He misunderstood about changing your name."

"Ah." She cupped his face with her hands and made him kiss her again in front of all the kids walking in the same direction, which was roughly half the school. "Only you two can get away with that. And only if I get to call you Bilbo."

"I had a feeling that would stick," he sighed. "I don't mind, but I'm not calling you Bob."

Peter?

"Wick."

No, that's my name. She can't have that.

They held hands the rest of the way and ignored me.

John?

Luke?

Caesar?

Enzo?

That caught his attention. "Enzo."

Colonel Enzo if you want to get formal with her. She should outrank me, I think.

"I think I might like Enzo a bit more than Bob," she said on the ride up to her apartment. "Find some spray paint. We'll tag a building tonight. Bilbo and Enzo, with a heart around it."

"And when we get arrested? Which one of us gets to explain that to the King?"

"You do, sweetheart," she said as she opened her door. The apartment was quiet, and she went to the hallway and called for Jay.

"Note on the table," Will said.

She read it and said, "All right, his dad got home early, and they went to a movie. He'll call me later."

"Whose day is it?"

"James'. But Jay knew I expected him to be here when I got home. He gets a few points for the note." She wiggled her eyebrows at him. "The apartment is ours, no teenager stomping through here moaning about how horrible we are. No eyes rolling so hard you can hear them clear across the room if we kiss."

"Same thing in my apartment." When she let out an exasperated *hmpf*, he shrugged. "You have a rule. I won't break it."

"You've slept here before."

"Slept. And there were extenuating circumstances."

"And I told you then, I made the rule, I can change the rule."

"I respect the rule," he said.

"Is he always such a pain, Wick?" She plucked me off his shoulder and took me into the kitchen, where I was bribed into agreeing with her with bites of ham. While I munched on them, he leaned against the breakfast bar. She leaned on the other side, and they stared at each other. It didn't feel like either one of them was upset, but I had my face shoved in the plate and didn't really see.

"All right, Will. If you don't want to ravage my body, what do you want to do?"

"Save the ravaging for later. Take a long walk, get dinner on the Wharf. Watch the boats come in. Talk dirty to each other and then take a cab back to my place."

"Sounds like a very sweaty afternoon."

"I appreciate that you skipped right over the part where I have no skill in talking dirty."

Do I have to go home?

"Do you want to go home, Wick?"

I'll go home if you want privacy, but there are dead and delicious fishy things on the Wharf.

He didn't want to deny me any fishy treats. They took turns letting me ride on their shoulders—it was too hot for the sweatshirt, which I missed—and instead of going to a restaurant they bought fish baskets to go and had a picnic at the park behind Fort Mason. There was a family with several small children playing on the hill, and we watched as they ran partway up the slope and then rolled down.

The kids, not the parents. Though that would have been worth watching, too.

"All of the city to take in, and they're playing in a spot where the best thing they can readily see is a grocery store," Aisha mused after they'd watched for a while. "They're either locals who don't give a damn anymore or tourists staying on this end of the Wharf."

"Probably trying to wear them out so they sleep tonight." He looked over his shoulder and said, "Besides, they can see the Golden Gate from here."

They both chuckled when all the kids collided in a rolling mass halfway down the hill. No one cried; they got up and ran, yelling, "Do it again!"

That looks fun.

You should do that.

"I'm not rolling down the hill, Wick."

Fine. You need booze for things like that anyway, don't you?

"I'm not—" He tapped me on the top of my head with his finger. "We don't need alcohol to have some fun. Watching the kids is more fun than imitating them."

Yeah. You'd probably break a hip.

"Somehow, I don't think you're going to be talking dirty to me," Aisha said after a while. "Our delightful entertainment doesn't seem to lend itself to that."

"But they are cute."

"Cute little monsters who will be crying and whining in an hour because they're overly tired. And you've been a bit quiet in the last hour. Hard to talk dirty when you're not talking at all."

"Sorry. Long day."

"Things you can't talk about?"

"Just things," he said. "Today I met with a family that ran from Florida. They had no idea that they could simply pack up and move. They left everything behind to escape a government that no longer exists. I've been chewing on that a bit."

"How could they not know?"

He shrugged. "They left days after the war ended and have been making their way across Midlam and Pacifica since then. I imagine they became quite adept at hiding themselves from anyone who looked remotely official and didn't ask many questions along the way. You can imagine the fear and surprise when I mentioned I was both familiar and friendly with the First Minister."

"They assumed you meant Levi Munson."

"The gift that keeps on giving. In any case, I suspect that in a week or two they'll have learned more about Florida's current political climate and will return the apartment keys and vouchers so they can go home."

"So they get to walk back?"

"I'll get them on a shuttle," he said. "And there's another project. We need a dedicated shuttle between here and Florida now, at least weekly." He let out a tired sigh. "I loathe dealing with the department of transportation. I need a minion I can send in my stead."

"Is that really part of your job?"

"The government is like a pinball machine, and I'm the steel ball that bounces around. I keep a finger or toe in everything, my ear to the ground, my eye on…whatever. I'm running out of metaphors."

"When was the last time you took a week or two off?"

He thought about it. "Andrew, Zed, and I went hiking last year. Does that count?"

"No."

"There was the week in the simulator. We visited Oz and Drew. Jay's surgery. Mini-vacations?"

"Doesn't count. You need time to do nothing. Lay on a beach somewhere that isn't here, get a massage, and let some woman in skimpy clothing rub your back."

"Describe the skimpy clothing you'll be wearing."

"Very funny. You're allowed to see a real masseuse, Will. You're even allowed to enjoy it if said masseuse is female and only half dressed."

"I am not inclined to seek out rubbing of any sort from anyone else."

"You've never had a back rub, have you?" She didn't let him answer; she got up and reached for his hand. "Come on. We're stopping on the way back and getting some nice, fruity oils and anything else that looks fun."

= = =

Claiming he had no preferences about oil scents and harboring an uncertainty that I would be allowed inside the store, Will opted to wait with me on the sidewalk while Aisha shopped. Judging by the stiffness in his shoulders and the flush of pink that colored his cheeks, the truth was that he was too uncomfortable to shop for grown up playthings. We wandered down the street to sit on a bench where he could pretend she wasn't buying things to happily torment him with, and he made small talk with people who stopped to say hello. Worse, he allowed sticky people to pet me. When she came out of the store twenty minutes later, I was ready to get home.

At home, the fingers poking at me weren't covered in jelly or sugar or boogers.

I'm only reasonably certain about the jelly and sugar.

He didn't ask about what her purchases until we were in his apartment and she was kicking off her shoes. He started pulling things out of the bag, saying nothing about the blackberry oil, muttering that he thought he would enjoy the cherry, and then he blurted out, "What the hell?" when he pulled out a bottle of depilatory cream.

She took the bottle from him. "You're not a super hairy guy, Will, but you *were* thinking about trimming not too long ago."

The little scissors were still on the end table.

"I never said exactly what I was thinking about trimming."

"You didn't have to."

"How did we get from 'Will's never had a back rub' to 'I want Will's genitals as hairless as a baby's?'"

"We use the cream first," she said simply. "We wait a few minutes, then take a nice, long, hot shower together to rinse it off."

"Go on."

"Then Will gets his first ever back rub."

"I still don't see why I need to be utterly hairless for that."

"Because after the back rub comes the front rub, and sweetie, the oil is edible and *nicely* flavored." She pressed herself against him and whispered, "Use your imagination. My very warm, very soft tongue, your now very smooth ba—"

"All right, then."

She doesn't like flossing in the moment, dude.

It was a good thing I didn't rush to follow them down the hall or I would have been smothered by all the clothing that was discarded in the dash to get into the bedroom. By the time I got there, she was pushing him onto the bed with one hand and had snagged the waistband of his underwear with the other.

"Oh, good," she said, grabbing one of the bottles that had been tossed onto the bed. "The little emperor is getting out of my way. But I may need to move him around a bit, to get all your hair."

He was looking up at the ceiling. "As long as you don't try to bend him in half, you can do whatever you want." He sucked in a sudden, sharp breath. "That's cold."

"Five minutes or until it starts burning, there we go."

He half sat up. "Burning?"

"Relax. I made sure I bought the right cream. I'm just teasing you."

Tell that to the little emperor. He's trying to crawl back inside.

She stretched out next to him, head propped up with one hand, and she tapped the fingers of her other hand on his stomach. "We need interim music. Like on a game show. The tick-tock of a clock overlaid with some upbeat melody."

"This part is not as much fun as I had hoped."

"I'd make it fun, but I don't think the cream would taste very good. And you don't want me rubbing it in."

"I have an itch."

She laughed evilly and said, "*Suffah*."

"Why am I alone in this?"

"I keep my ladybits trimmed, Emperor. I'd hoped you noticed."

"And to whom shall I compare you? You do realize you're the only post-pubescent female I've seen naked, and as that came out of my mouth, I realize how utterly wrong it sounds."

"I know what you mean, sweetheart."

He blinked a few times and then closed his eyes. His jaw tightened and chest rose, and he held the breath a beat longer than normal. "That's not actually true, and I must admit, my libido just took a nosedive."

She checked the clock and sat up, reaching for his hand. "Go take a shower and get all the cream off."

"Aisha, I'm sorry."

"Bilbo, you don't have to explain. As soon as I said that I knew what you meant, I remembered what happened to Oz. Clean up and we'll cuddle. We have all night."

He really has had a long day, and you've been the only fun part of it.

"I'm not done with him, Wick. I just need to refocus his energy back to the moment."

That back rub might do it.

She stretched out and reached over to pet me. "You take very good care of him, don't you?"

I forgot about him for a long time. I still feel bad about that.

"I promise, I'll take good care of him, too, but I might need your help. I don't even want to imagine things without you here."

Yeah, well, if the oil starts flying, I'm leaving. You'll just have to make do.

"Give me a hint. If he's just tired because of a long day, roll over and I'll rub your chest. If he's as upset as I think he is, put your paw on my arm."

Putting my paw on her arm didn't feel like telling her something I promised I wouldn't. I wiggled closer and touched my paw to her wrist, and hoped she wouldn't press him to tell her what was bothering him.

By the time he was out of the shower, she had put her clothes back on and had gone into the living room. I waited for him on the bed, which turned out to be a good thing because he was surprised when she wasn't still in the bedroom and for a second or two he thought she'd left.

She said to get dressed and she's going to take you out for a drink or two or five or even pizza if you're hungry. And if you don't feel like being social, you don't have to be.

Also, clean underwear. You just showered.

"Fine, mom."

And, dude, that all looks really wrong. It's gonna itch when it grows out.

"Doesn't have to look right to you, Wick. As long as it makes her happy."

So she can make you happy. Got it.

"It's a perk."

We lapped Union Square a couple of times before heading to Fuzzy's. It was rapidly cooling off which meant I got to ride in the sweatshirt and Aisha got to walk close to him, his arm around her shoulder. It was warm and toasty riding in the pouch, so when we crossed the street and he pulled me out and put me on his shoulder, I complained.

Hey, you're making my useless nipples freeze.

Look at them. I have nipsicles.

He'd been looking ahead. Oz and Drew were half a block away and walking in our direction; they'd taken his car back to the parking garage and were headed home, and when he saw them he knew he was going to hug them both and didn't want to squish me while he did.

"Feeling any better?" he asked after they'd both been squeezed and kissed.

Drew nodded, and Oz said, "A lot. And thank you for letting us use your car. We spent a lot of time just driving around. Well, I did. Someone still needs to learn to drive."

"I have to be honest, I wasn't sure you'd stay in the city."

"We thought about it," Drew said. "I know what we promised, but…for about an hour, it made more sense than waiting."

Will gestured toward Fuzzy's entrance. "Come on. You don't have to drink, but I'm betting neither of you has eaten today."

They went in without argument; neither really wanted to go home yet, and he knew it. Will touched Aisha's arm—*thank you for not asking*—and led them to a table near the back, one of the private booths where they'd be away from other people. He ordered them each a virgin daiquiri and an extra-large pizza for the table and then sat back with his arm around Aisha.

"I had an idea I'd like to bounce off you," he said when it seemed like neither one of them wanted to talk. "The building we procured as a research center has more space than we need for the time being. There's an abundance of space for a private dojo. You could take the entire third floor."

"My instructor will never give his permission." Oz knew what he was doing, trying to get them to think of anything other than what was looming ahead like a giant soul-sucking shadow. "I haven't been a student of his for too long. I need to earn another degree at least, and I would need his cooperation."

"No, you really don't. You have the skills, and you were envisioning a rank-free system."

"And Will has the rank," Drew pointed out. "He's even willing to teach a few classes."

Oz managed a bit of a smile. "I'd like to keep students, not scare the hell out of them."

"I'll be gentle," Will said. "And this gives you the freedom to begin your own system. Ozoo-Ryu."

"Gesundheit."

"Pick any name you choose, then," Will said lightly.

"Maybe a year or two from now," she said.

He leaned forward, elbows on the table. "I will help you, Oz. With any part of it. Both of you."

"I know." She looked at Aisha and said, "It's not really about a karate school."

"I kind of figured."

"And we're not ready for our parents to know."

"Just found out?"

"This morning," Drew said. "I *want* to be excited—"

"Then be excited," Aisha urged. "Be happy. I know it's scary as hell, but you're going to be thrilled sooner rather than later. Jump over the dread and go right to excitement."

"They're worried about disappointing Jax and Aubrey," Will said.

"And about school and providing for a family and everything else that goes with it," Drew countered. "Realistically, if I keep my word to Mr. B and go to school, how much time will I have to be a good husband *and* a good father? I can see handling one of those, but not both. And dammit, I promised her I'd be both."

"You'll be amazing no matter what," Oz murmured.

Will sat back again. "You have a job, which for the time being is, frankly, doing well in school. The demands of that will be fairly limited for the next year. We've barely begun, Andrew. We have work space, but little equipment. No grant funding. Don't let this venture overwhelm you. I need you in school and studying. Otherwise you won't have the foundation necessary to make this a success. You will have the time you need, I promise. And the income."

"I'm not taking pay for work I'm not doing."

"Are you daft?" He was getting irritated, and his inner Scot popped out. "I'm no' handing over pay for nothing. School *is* your work. This is an investment, not just in your future but in *mine*, because I goddamn well finally have one. I'll coddle your ego only for a bit."

Drew flinched like Will had tried to slap him, but then nodded. "All right. I hadn't thought of it in broader terms."

"And you." He pointed at Oz; she was trying to not laugh because it sounded a lot like '*An ewe*,' which meant he was trying hard to not lose it. "You're no' so delicate you can't function well enough to stand in front of a few kids and tell them what to do. If you want to teach, then bloody well do it."

Drew turned to Oz. "Isn't 'bloody well' more of a British thing to say?"

"To be fair, Scotland was part of Britain for a good chunk of its history," she told him. "Maybe it's a carryover, like the way he drinks tea with his little finger stuck out."

"I do not," Will said.

"Yeah, you do." Drew laughed, and for the first time that day he didn't look like he expected someone to slap him. "Your giant hand and a tiny tea cup? You totally do."

"Grab that beer bottle," Oz said. "You do it then, too."

He started to pick the bottle up, and then said, "Shut up."

They poked at him while they had dinner—Drew ate nearly half the pizza and Oz ate two slices, which made Will happy—and they kept piling on through a couple games of pool that Will and Drew lost horribly. Midway through a game of nine ball he stopped playing to kiss Aisha; she raised an eyebrow, not because he kissed her but because he whispered something to her, asking her to join in. She let loose with a few of her own insults after that, making fun of the teenaged Emperor and his never-ending wardrobe of tight black t-shirts and jeans, and his beat-up guitar that he played only passably.

"Do you still play?" she asked.

"Not since—" He had to think about it. "Zed peed in it when he was two years old. I believe it was thrown out after that."

"What a shame. Have you heard him sing?" she asked them. "He was so-so on the guitar but he has a beautiful voice."

Will shook his head, lips pursed with *no I do not*.

He did, but he wasn't going to admit it. They mourned the death of his guitar and accepted his excuse that he was self-taught and she had only heard him in the beginning, and on the walk home Will asked if either of them knew whether or not Zed still practiced piano. He couldn't remember the last time he'd heard him play.

Oz didn't know but agreed, Zed needed to keep playing.

"Where I learned to play a few chords on the guitar and could pick out some of the notes, Zed innately finds the magic within the music," Will told Aisha. "One day we'll have to ask him to play 'Moonlight Sonata' for us. You'll cry."

Oz was near tears again as Drew punched in the code to open his door. Will reached for her and promised, "When you're ready to tell your parents, I will be there if you want me to. I can distract your father while your mother goes straight to how wonderful having a grandchild will be."

When we were back in Will's apartment, he stood with his back against the door for a minute. "Thank you," he said. "I know that being with them wasn't what you had in mind, but getting them to laugh made me feel a little better. And I'm sorry I couldn't tell you what was really bothering me. They're terrified, and I can't fix it for them."

She pulled him over to the sofa. "I get it. And I hope they get over being so worried soon. Jax and Aubrey might be upset for a bit, but for only ten minutes or so."

He still didn't think Aubrey would be upset. Jax was the one they were most worried about. "He was only half joking about stringing Drew up. He accepts that this relationship is happening and is somewhat comforted by the idea that I exist because of it, but he's certainly in no hurry for Oz to be married, much less to have a child."

"He probably wants them to have time to be a couple before they start having kids."

Will agreed him with, in theory. Accomplished fact could not be ignored, though, and he didn't want Oz or Drew to be frightened of either Jax or a tiny, squalling bundle that would keep them up all night.

"It's scary, Will. Hell, I was older, done with school, had a job, was married, and I was terrified. They're still so young."

"And they have an incredible support system available to them. I can tailor my work schedule to be available for child care while they're in school, and they have a place to live. None of us will let them starve. The only real fear is Jax, and they truly don't need to be afraid of what he'll do. Let him vent for ten minutes and then start calling him Grandpa. He'll get over it."

"They're allowed to be afraid."

You'd be afraid. Even if it happened now, you'd be afraid. Babies change everything.

"Babies change everything," he repeated. "I know, Wick."

You should stop talking about them. She still expects things from you.

"You know what?" he said as he reached for her. "Enough about them. My brain has been so cluttered that I don't think I ever asked you how your day went. Or how you were."

She wound up practically in his lap. "Your brain is a pretty big place. I know I'm in there."

"First thing I think of in the morning. Last thing I think of at night. If I sleep. I spend an incredible amount of time in between, thinking about you."

"Oh? And when I'm not here and you're thinking about me?"

"I touch myself inappropriately. With alarming frequency."

That made her laugh. "Yeah, mister, you don't think there's anything inappropriate about it. Come on, give me details. In the shower, in bed, here on the sofa?"

"Yes."

"Ah." She shifted until she was straddling him and her hands slipped between them, where I couldn't see them. "Tell me more. Do you start all soft and warm or are you already hard and hot?"

"Yes."

"Fast and furious or slow and gentle?"

"Yes."

"I'd worry about all the monosyllabic answers, but you're about to burst out of your jeans and I'd kind of like to help with that."

"Hell yes."

She barely broke eye contact as she unzipped his jeans and slid them over his hips, and she trailed kisses as she pushed them past his knees. He pulled his shirt off and started to reach for her, when she put a hand on his chest. "You stay right there, mister. I want to inspect how well the cream worked. We need to be sure there are no stray hairs."

"I think I got them all."

"But there might be tiny ones you can't see or even feel with your hand. I need to inspect closer."

"And how do you propose doing that?"

"With my tongue."

She checked so thoroughly that I thought he was going to pass out. But before he could, he begged her to stop so that he could catch his breath, and asked her to take it all off. Before he could get up and help, she was naked and jumped on him, which might have hurt a little because his eyes kind of rolled back in his head.

His brain must have stopped working, too, because she had to grab his hands and put them on her boobs, and he couldn't keep them there for very long. Next thing I knew they were on her hips, mostly to keep her from flying off.

Since she would have gone right into the fireplace, that was probably a wise choice.

On the upside, there was no fire going.

"Jesus. Fucking. Christ," Aisha moaned. She grabbed him by the neck and shoved his face between her boobs. "Will."

I blinked and they were desecrating my rug again.

At the rate they were going, I was going to have to ask for a new one for Christmas.

19

"You're the one who wanted to get into shape," Zed reminded Jay. "If you ask Will for help, it means early morning torture runs, and if he has a chance, it also means hiking for freaking forever."

"What about swimming?"

"That's more something he does with Drew. But I think he times it. The only time I ever swam with them, he just had me do as many laps as I could and he gave me hints about my form. But man, Drew is like a freaking fish, so don't ever try to race him."

We waited for Drew across the street from home, at Stupid O'clock on a Saturday morning, when there was barely enough light to see by. No one wanted to be out of bed much less ready to run, but this was the best time for Will and Jax to run together, so they peeled themselves up before the sun was even awake, just to run laps around Union Square.

Sticking to the Square was easiest for the guards—they could rim the perimeter to keep an eye on the streets, and not all of them had to run along with the King—and it was easiest for Will to figure out just how badly out of shape Jay and Aisha were.

"Hon," she told him when he reminded her she'd said she wanted to start running, "if I get down one block without having to stop, I'll call it a victory."

He didn't believe her because he didn't see anything about her body that suggested she was out of shape. He promised to stick by her whether she was running or walking, which got him a pointy finger to the stomach.

"Run with Jax or the boys. And no laughing if you lap me a dozen times."

He picked a median; he ran with Jax, and when he caught up to her on the next lap, he slowed down and jogged alongside her for a while. She was slow, but she wasn't gasping for air and she found a nice run-walk-run pace that kept her going.

"If I'm cheating, tough."

"It's not cheating," he assured her. "Marathon runners often use the same technique. Do whatever feels most comfortable."

"Sweetie, waiting at the bakery with a donut feels most comfortable."

Jay was sucking air halfway through the first lap.

After the second lap, he sat down on the steps, hard. I ran from my spot at the edge of the Square to make sure he was all right, because he practically had his head between his knees and I wanted to see if he was going to hurl.

You dying, dude?

"Balls bounce," he groaned when I stuck my head under his arm to get a look at his face. "Why didn't I think about that? Fucking hurts."

Drew slowed down as he passed to ask if Jay was all right, and when Jay nodded, he kept going.

When Zed ran past, he yelled, "Get up, loser!" and kept on going.

When Will and Jax approached, Will told Jax to go on and then stopped to make sure Jay was all right.

He just learned that balls bounce.

Will patted him on the shoulder and told him to stand up. "Side stitches and leg cramps ease up if you slow down. Walk for a while and it'll be fine."

Jay looked up, but he didn't stand. "Not that. I didn't dress for this," he said.

"We'll get you some compression shorts today," Will said. "Just walk for now, and if you feel like it, very light jogging. Don't let Zed push you harder than you're comfortable with."

He nodded and got up, and started jogging slowly. Will waited for Aisha to catch up, and then asked her to walk with him a bit. "Let him get ahead. I don't want to pass him too soon."

"He's not that out of shape, Will. He hasn't taken a gym class, but he's generally pretty active."

"That was before," he said. "He's moving with a different body now. It takes adjustment."

"Okay," she said uncertainly.

"I'll explain later."

I watched them walk off and then turned to look down the other end of the street. Jax had turned the corner, and Drew was not far behind, running hard. When he got close, Jax shouted, "Where the hell is my daughter? She should be out here suffering with the rest of us."

Drew passed him and shouted back, "I cooked for her last night. She *is* suffering."

"Stop running so fast!" Jax yelled. "You're making me feel old!"

"You *are* old!"

Drew lapped them all a couple of times, even Will, and on his last two laps he went so hard and fast that I thought he really would throw up. When Will caught up, he looked back to see where Jax was, and then asked Drew how Oz was feeling.

It had been a week, and they still hadn't told anyone else.

"She was going to run this morning until I told her Mr. B would be here."

"So, you lied."

"No, I really did cook for her last night, and we both paid the price until about three this morning. I feel like complete shit but figured I'd better be here."

"Do you need to call Mass? If she's ill—"

"She's not sick. Just dehydrated. Water and rest is all she needs." Drew sucked in a deep breath. "Nerves, too. She wants another day or two, but we're ready to tell them. We're over the shock, I think."

"And?"

"We want this kid, Will. I mean, *really* want it. I don't think I've ever loved anyone so hard and so fast before."

"Jax at your six," Will warned. "And I think I understand. That one—" he nodded toward Jay, who was rounding the corner at a very slow jog next to Aisha "—I am far more protective of than perhaps I should be. I realize it's not quite the same thing, but still. I have an inkling."

"Yeah, tell me about that later, after you've taken him and Zed and three of their friends to a movie. You might be ready to push him out of your car after that."

"Speaking of my car."

Jax came to a stop and waved his guards on. "You're making fun of me, aren't you? Old and slow, not worthy of your company?"

"It's so easy to do," Will said. "No, I was about to tell Drew that I'm taking Jay out for a driving lesson this afternoon, and he's welcome to come along. It's about time he learned to drive."

"Eh, I can already drive," Jax muttered. "Not that anyone lets me anymore." He headed toward home, leaving with a short wave.

"If Oz felt better, I would," Drew said. "Maybe next time."

She's gonna be hurling for the next three months, isn't she?

The Queen was nauseated for at least six months both times she was pregnant. If it was genetic, Oz had a lot of misery to look forward to. So did Drew, because there was no way she was suffering in silence. I think Will would have warned him about that, but Jay and Aisha were almost there and Zed was rapidly catching up.

"How many laps?" Will asked Zed.

"I was supposed to count?" he asked innocently. "Ten, I think. Three miles."

Jay was breathing hard. "I slowed him down. He walked with me a little bit."

"Fifteen," Drew said. "And screw you for lapping me."

"I don't think I did," Will said. "Now go home and throw up."

Zed watched Drew trot off. "He okay?"

"Mild food poisoning. He'll survive." He led them across the street and I followed, as close to his feet as I could without getting stepped on. Zed pressed the button for the elevator, but when Will frowned and said, "Really?" he relented and headed up the stairs.

It's food o'clock now, isn't it?

He opened his door and let Jay and Aisha in, but he didn't head for the kitchen.

I was promised post-run food. You ran, now I get food.

Jay headed for the guest bathroom to shower, and once the water was going, Aisha shoved Will toward his bedroom. They had plenty of time to take one together, she told him. "He lives in the shower now. If he's out in less than half an hour, it will only be to see if you and I are doing exactly what we'll be doing."

"He won't need to get out," Will said. "He'll hear you."

"Just me?"

He raised his eyebrow, just a little.

"All right, fine, I'm a lot louder than you are. I can be quiet."

I sat on the floor in the hallway, waiting to see who finished first, and part of me hoped it would be Jay, just to see how embarrassed they all got.

It was my first disappointment of the week. And certainly not the worst.

= = =

Three hours later, we were in a sporting goods store on the fringe of South San Francisco, where Aisha discovered there were a few things she was embarrassed about, and one of them was the underwear her son needed. While Will, Jay, and Zed discussed the merits of boxer briefs over regular briefs, and whether or not Jay would be more comfortable in tight briefs or compression shorts when he ran, she stood nearby with her arms crossed, waiting for this to be over with. When Zed asked Jay what he was working with—"You know, are we talking just an inconvenient handful, or like six floppy inches of wind resistance?"—she muttered that she would be over in swimwear, trying to find something reasonable.

Will told them to pick out a couple of each because he'd never know what he preferred until he tried it, then pointed them to men's swimwear and went to find Aisha. She was absently plucking through a rack of things that resembled bandages more than swim suits, her mind not on what she was looking at, and she startled when he came up behind her and said, "None of those are suitable for swimming."

"Jesus, Will." She pulled a tiny clump of red cloth from the rack and held it up. "This is not for swimming. This is for laying on the beach and soaking up the sun, and if I'm lucky, for watching a few well-built young men playing volleyball."

"No, this is for torturing Will and seeing how long he can avoid the inevitable erection when you walk past in it."

"Either way, I have fun."

"And if I sit on the beach next to you, ogling well-built young women?"

"Sweetie, you're allowed to look. I'm allowed to look. We're even allowed to point out people we find attractive. I'm damn well mentioning the tall brunette with hair down to her ass and boobs out to here to you. She's not a threat, and you'd enjoy looking."

"Perhaps."

"Perhaps, my ass. It's all right, you don't have to return the favor."

Do you even know when another dude is hot?

"Not really, Wick."

"What about you, Wick?" Aisha asked, holding the tiny suit up for me to see. "Hot or not?"

I don't think it's my size. But it's a lovely shade of red.

"As much as I would enjoy seeing you in that—" he pointed to the rack with suits made for actual swimming "—you might be more comfortable in one of those if you still intend to swim laps. Bear in mind, the kids use the pool often, and will likely be swimming at the same time."

"Killjoy."

She didn't put it back, but she started picking through the other rack. Jay poked his head over the rack that divided the men's from the women's sections and held up two suits. "I have no idea. What's a tech suit?"

"Generally intended for competitive swimming," Will told him. "You only need a regular suit."

"The selection here is awful." Aisha headed for men's. "Do they still make jammers? I could do laps in jammers and a swim shirt."

You should get matching suits. That would be adorable.

"That would be disgustingly sweet," Will said. "Besides, I have two that I prefer, custom fit. I don't need another."

"You have a custom fit swimsuit," Aisha said.

"Nearly everything I own is custom fit." He hesitated when he heard himself. "I realize how elitist that sounds, but I prefer to be comfortable, and the tailor is very good."

"Maybe a little elitist. But it does explain why those boxer briefs fit you *so* nicely."

There was a gagging sound behind her, and Jay groaned, "God, Mom."

"Sweetie, you might as well get used to it." She kissed Will on the cheek. "He's not going anywhere."

"Yeah, but I don't need to hear you contemplating his junk."

Zed laughed. "Why not? Everyone's been contemplating yours for weeks."

"But not like *that*."

"We'll try to be more considerate," Will said.

Consideration didn't necessarily extend to arguing, because they almost fought in the checkout line when Will handed over his bank card and Aisha balked because she didn't expect him to pay for any of it. He just as firmly insisted that it had been his idea; he wanted to spend more time with Jay, and going jogging and swimming laps with him was one way to do that.

She relented, but only because Jay visibly perked up when he heard Will say he wanted to spend more time with him. She and Will walked behind Zed and Jay on the way to the car, and he quietly apologized and then told her she could spring for lunch.

"Oh, sure. You ran them ragged this morning, and I get to refill their hollow legs."

He assured her that was his intention.

"All kidding aside, Will—you have no idea how much he eats now. He's hungry *all* the time. If he's going to start working out, I envision my grocery bill quadrupling."

"Puberty and testosterone," he said. "Push him away from the junk food. He won't be ravenous all the time if you load him up on protein and high-quality carbs."

"You tell him that. I don't think there's a greasy, salty, unhealthy thing out there he doesn't love."

Didn't he ask you about eating clean?

"He did ask me about clean eating, Wick. That doesn't mean he's ready to embrace it. Just wait a couple of weeks. If he's still struggling to run and sees Zed outpacing him too much, he'll be open to changing his diet."

"My fault, too," Aisha said. "I'm the one who does the shopping, and I cave to the things he adds to my shopping lists. Junk is an unfortunate staple in my pantry."

Trap him in a safe house. That's how you got Zed to eat better.

"There we go," Will chuckled. "We take the boys to the safe house in Denver where they're at our mercy. After a couple weeks of cardboard rations, decent food will taste far better than junk. It worked in getting Zed and Drew to eat better."

Zed spun around. "Did I hear that right? You want to go back to Denver?"

"I was joking, but are you interested?"

"Is it safe?"

"For recreational use, yes. It's no longer viable as a safe house, but we can go there for the hell of it."

"Camping?"

"If you like. I wouldn't press for a twenty-mile hike to the campsite this time. Perhaps something closer to the cabin. I might even let you explore the meadow you wanted to before."

Zed turned back around and began telling Jay about the safe house, and Aisha reached for Will's hand.

"You're taking them camping."

"Oh, hell no," he said. "You're coming, too. I took the kids there alone because I had to, but if I'm going back, you're suffering with me."

"This is how I know it's true love," she snorted. "You're willing to share the pain."

"Indeed."

= = =

Sharing the pain included teaching Jay how to drive. Aisha assumed she would go back to Will's apartment to bake cookies while she started cooking dinner for them, but he tugged her toward the car and told her she was coming, too. As Zed got into the driver's seat, Will whispered into Aisha's ear, "*Suffah!*"

Zed drove to Ocean Beach and parked at the bottom of the hill that led up to the Cliff House. After that, he switched places with Will and sat in the back seat with Aisha and me. He'd been the one to drive to the beach because Will hoped that if Jay saw how well Zed could drive and how confident he was, that it would calm any nerves he had.

Jay was probably the only relaxed one in the car.

"All right, so you can input an address, and the car can drive itself," Jay said. "I know that much. So why learn to drive it manually? Why not just let it take you where you want to go? Isn't that the point of self-driving vehicles?"

"You need to have the skills to pilot the car if the pilot program breaks down," Will answered.

"Plus, you can't get a license unless you can prove you know how to operate it without computer aid," Zed added. "They're oddly picky about that."

Will took a few minutes to explain the controls to him, and Jay listened even though he knew what they were. Throttle, air brakes, exterior traffic cameras, activity monitor, control wheel; Jay repeated everything Will pointed out, and when he was done explaining everything, he had Jay fire it up.

Aisha closed her eyes and clutched at her chest strap.

"This isn't much different than controlling the air bike," Will said. "The steering bar works the same as the handlebar on the bike. The biggest differences between the vehicles are the mass of the car and how it affects acceleration and deceleration. You'll feel the difference once we start moving, and you need to allow for more time to stop. You did well with the bike, so I don't anticipate it will be any different with the car."

Jay pressed the button that activated the air jets and aligned the magnets to the street, and slowly lifted the car. He inched along the parking lot, leaning forward and squinting as if his life depended on going slower than he could jog until he was on the Great Highway.

"Speed up a bit," Will told him. "Anticipate the vehicle ahead of you, but if you don't, the car will sense it and slow down."

Whether lack of control or that he took it as permission to open up, Jay pressed on the throttle, and we took off. There was no one ahead of us for the car to sense, so the speed increased rapidly, and Will did nothing to stop him. Even Zed was gritting his teeth, and he checked the safety harness around my plastic container twice.

Maybe we should have had lunch after this instead of before.
If I pee in here, you're cleaning it up.

"You're doing fine," Will said, without any of the histrionics I felt. "Ease back on the throttle a bit. There's a speed check zone ahead, and nine times out of ten there's an officer waiting."

"No kidding," Zed grumbled. "Five miles over, and *bam*, you have a ticket."

The car slowed considerably. "How much over was I going?"

"Speed limit here is one hundred miles per hour. You were going roughly one thirty."

"Damn. I'm sorry."

"Speed is displayed in the center of the activity monitor. Give it a glance every now and then."

"And never take my bike that fast," Zed said. "It'll get impounded."

"That'd be stupid," Jay said. "Besides, doesn't it have a limiter?"

Will turned to look at Zed. "It's supposed to."

"Eyes on the road, old man. You're teaching someone young and vulnerable to drive, and a butterfly might jump out in front of the car."

"I want a look at your bike when we get home," Will told him.

Zed tried to tell him he was pretty sure he'd bought the bike without it, but Will was the one who had inspected it before letting Zed hand his money over. He knew the speed limiter had been there. He let Zed worry about it for the next hour, while Jay went up and down the Great Highway, and then as he eased into traffic around the old zoo.

I think he worried about it until long after the car was in the parking garage and we were nearly home. As soon as we turned the corner, Will told him to go get the bike and then meet him out front—and to bring the limiter, which he'd better still have.

"How illegal is it to remove that?" Aisha asked as Zed and Jay ran off.

"Very, at his age. But the biggest thing he should worry about is what happens if Jax finds out."

"He'll take the bike?"

Will nodded. "He'll take it, scrap it, and make Zed save up for a new one. Presuming he allows him to replace it at all."

"And you're going to save the day."

"No. I'm putting the limiter back on, and then confiscating his bike."

She wondered if that wouldn't anger Jax and Aubrey; he thought it was possible, but he typically had free rein to discipline when necessary. "I could ground him and it would stick."

When Zed pulled up on the bike, he told Will he'd put the limiter back on, and then handed the key fob over. "I know, it's yours until you decide I've earned it back."

"And when your parents ask?"

He shrugged. "You caught me modifying it. That's not a lie."

"What else have you done?"

"Opened the air jets a little. I can get the bike a little higher that way."

"They'll be repaired by the time you get this back. You understand that?"

Will handed the shopping bags to Zed and told him to put everything in his apartment. They could stay there if they wanted, or go upstairs, but they were to remain in the building. He set me on the ground and told me to go inside, too, unless I wanted a ride on the bike.

I did not want to ride on the bike.

"So where are you going?" Jay asked.

"Wherever they want," Zed said. "It's charged up."

"I was just going to take it into the lab and lock it up there, but sure." He swung his leg over and patted the seat behind him. "Let's go for a ride. I might even give it back someday."

They watched as Will drove the bike away.

"Man, that was harsh," Jay said. "Sorry I brought the limiter up."

Zed shrugged. "That could have been so much worse. You have no idea how fucking lucky I am right now."

He had no idea how lucky he was, because two seconds after that came out of his mouth, Aubrey came out of the building, just missing hearing the number one word on her list.

They went to Will's apartment to dump the bags and then headed upstairs where there was better snack food, but since Aubrey wasn't there and Zed was not typically generous with treats, I went into Drew's apartment. At some point, if I stared at him long enough, he would give me cheese or ham. If he didn't, I could actually tell him I wanted some of the cheese and ham I knew was in his refrigerator.

That was the bonus to whatever had happened in the simulator that allowed him to understand me: he couldn't pretend to not know what I wanted, and I could wear him down if I was persistent enough.

He and Oz were on his living room floor, sitting with their backs against the sofa, making me wonder again if they were opposed to the proper use of furniture. She looked like she had recovered from his cooking and she wasn't sad anymore. Her eyes weren't puffy and red, and her eyebrows weren't battling for that little sliver of space over her nose.

I crossed the room and sat near their feet, intent on staring Drew into getting me something to eat, but they were talking about important things and it felt like I should wait.

"If we keep the wedding date, I'll be waddling down the aisle."

"We either go ahead and get married soon," Drew said, "or we push it back. Do we want to wait that long? After she's born?"

She did not. "Honestly, I'll be sad to give up getting married in the Cathedral, but I want it official before the little shit gets here."

"Getting married isn't exactly a prerequisite for having a baby, Oz."

"Maybe not for other people," she said. "We're expected to do things in a certain order, even if the dates don't quite add up. Besides, I'd like it that way. I want to be married to you before we have this baby."

"We can still have a big ceremony later," he said. "Maybe for an anniversary?"

Oz didn't think that would happen. They wanted the church wedding for their families, and she had let herself get excited about it, but once they were married, that was probably it. "We'll find reasons to put it off."

Drew slid his hand over her stomach. "And all of the reasons will probably be because of her," he said lightly. "We could use your family's position and get the Cathedral early, Oz. I know you hate doing that, but if we picked a weekday morning and not the weekend, we'd be less likely to ruin someone else's day."

She shook her head. "We did this, Drew. We'll accept the consequences."

Instead of being upset, he grinned. "Yeah, we did do this, didn't we? She's going to be amazing."

"Or he."

He scrunched his nose up. "Gut feeling. She. Are we ready to tell your parents, then?"

"Sunday dinner seems to be as good a time as any."

"There will be knives on the table, Oz."

"Duck."

"Sure, and your mom will be at the other end of the table in the line of fire. I'll let him chuck things at me until he stops being mad. Will is right, sooner or later he'll be happy. And your mom will be right from the start."

"If she's not, she'll hide it well."

"We're gonna be good at this, Oz," he said softly. "And I promise, I won't get lost in work the way my dad does or the way Finn does. I'll be here when you need me. And when she needs me."

"You're going to be a great dad." She leaned over to kiss him and then swore under her breath when Zed knocked on the door. He had a plate loaded down with sandwiches and Jay was behind him with an armload of soft drink bottles.

"Mom went out for a dinner meeting with Dad and some… someone, I dunno. The name sounded Swedish. She called and said to make food and bring it to you because Drew's face is always stuck in a book and you're always stuck to his side, and if we didn't feed you, one of you would shrivel up and die, and a funeral right now would be inconvenient."

She let him in. "She said all that?"

"I may be paraphrasing." He set the plate on the table. "They're not even plain cheese sandwiches. There's salami and ham and a couple of peanut butter."

"With pickle," Jay grunted.

"Mine," Drew said.

Shouldn't those be for Oz?

"You'll get fed, too," he said, ignoring the question. "You guys are eating with us, right? That's a hell of a lot of sandwiches."

"Well, since you invited us…" Zed reached for the sandwich on top and sat at the table. "Hey, if you guys have time later, can you help quiz the wonder kid here? He has a test in a few days. Well, we both do, really. It would help us both out."

"I thought you weren't taking a class this summer," Oz said to Jay.

"I'm not. I'm studying for the exit exam." His phone pinged, and he glanced at it but didn't answer. "But don't tell my mom."

"Seriously? You know it's three tests, right?" Oz asked.

"Yeah. First up is history. I know the stuff, but I have a bad track record of guessing the wrong thing that'll be on the tests. That explains my grades, anyway. Zed said you took the test and might know what I should focus on."

"It's a bitch of an exam," she warned him. "I left the room feeling like I was the stupidest person in Pacifica. Passed it, but still. I think I remember most of what was on the test, so if I can look at your study guide I should be able to highlight the important parts."

"Wait," Drew said. "You graduated with your class. Why'd you take the tests?"

"Ego. I wanted to see if I'd pass. What's your goal, Jay?"

The question seemed to puzzle him. "To…exit. School."

"Grundy got him a provisional acceptance to UC if he passes," Zed said.

"And really, don't tell my mom. I want it to be a surprise if I pass."

Zed snorted. "You pass, yeah, that'll be a surprise."

"Suck it, loser." His phone pinged again, and this time he didn't bother looking.

Drew pointed out that if he did pass, they would all start at UCSF at the same time. He also thought that with the extra classes he needed to add for his change in major, they might even graduate at the same time. That would be worthy of a huge grad party.

"Don't forget Sophia," Zed said, grinning. "Guess who's coming to UCSF?"

"Seriously?" Oz asked.

"She's coming out for your birthday and then looking for an apartment. I mean, she was accepted to thirteen schools, but her dad liked the idea of San Francisco since she'd be near friends."

"Friends," Jay chortled. *Ping.*

"Does her dad know you two have a long-distance thing going?" Drew asked.

Zed nodded. "I did the old-fashioned thing and talked to him about it and he seems okay with it. He figures if she's going away to school, he'd rather she came here where she knows people and has a social life waiting instead of going somewhere new and being scared and lonely. He seems to think I'm harmless."

Drew set his sandwich down. "Does Sophia know that you're not?"

"Come on," Zed huffed. "I'm not *dangerous*. And I'm not sleeping with her."

"Yet," Jay snorted.

They had the same conversation Zed had with Will, and he impressed me. Instead of stomping out in a huff, Zed was calm and rational. It was enough to convince Oz that Zed was serious and enough to get Drew to tell him that if he was planning on it, if Zed thought their relationship was leading to sex sooner rather than later, then he needed to talk to Will. "That dried up dust bunny of a doctor won't give you an implant, but Will can arrange it, and he won't give you any shit for it."

"Does *anything* embarrass him?" Jay asked. "He doesn't even raise an eyebrow when I ask him things that would make my dad dive out a window."

"I don't know if I've ever seen him embarrassed," Oz said. "Until last year we wouldn't have dared to ask him anything too personal, but we've always been able to ask him things we're too uncomfortable to ask anyone else. Hell, I begged him to buy tampons for me a few years ago because I was too embarrassed to do it myself. He came back with nearly a dozen different boxes, and didn't bat an eye." She laughed and added, "He even bought me three different kinds of chocolate, because he thought it might make me feel better."

"Did it?" Drew asked. "'Cause I'll go buy you chocolate. Anytime."

"It did, but not the way he thought it would. It also made me a little sad, because I couldn't hug him."

"We have a lot of hugs to make up for," Zed mused.

Jay was confused. "Why?"

You can't tell him.

"The Emperor has always had a little bit of a touch phobia," Drew said. "He was fine with picking us up and carrying us around when we were little, but once we hit, like, twelve and thirteen, he backed off. It's only been in the, what, last, year that he's been trying hard to not flinch when someone gets close."

"Huh. I thought it was just hand shaking he hated," Jay said.

"It's hard to explain," Zed told Jay. "It's not that he hated any of it. He just…couldn't. And don't be a prick, you don't have to ask him about it. Just accept that he always wished he could, and now he likes it when we hug him."

"He sure as hell seems to like my mom hanging all over him."

"Does that bother you?" Drew asked.

Jay's phone pinged again, and Oz finally had enough of it. "Really, just answer the damned phone already. Someone seriously wants to talk to you."

"It's just George." He set the phone on the table and looked at the screen, but he didn't pick up. "I want to answer, but it feels like if I do I'm stabbing my mom and dad in the back, you know? So I'm letting all his calls go to voice messaging."

"What's he saying?" Zed asked.

Jay didn't know. "I'm afraid if I listen, I won't be able to stop from calling him back. I know he probably just wants to say hello, but I can't help thinking maybe something is wrong and I should pick up."

Drew offered to take the phone into the bedroom and listen to the messages. "If there's anything important, I'll tell you, I swear. If he's just asking you to call back, I'll tell you."

"If he's being a fuckwad?" Zed prompted.

"We'll see." Jay handed him the phone, and he headed for the bedroom. I'm nosy; I went in with him and hopped up on the bed to listen. There were six messages from George, pleading with Jay to call him back. He still didn't understand but decided that what's done is done and he would work at being more accepting. In the next message, he promised to address him as Jay and use the proper pronouns, but also asked for forgiveness if he slipped up. Another message. He swore that he loved Jay, no matter what other people were telling him.

But the thing that bothered Drew was that in every message, he ended by asking Jay to not tell his parents that he'd called.

When he handed the phone back to Jay, he gave him a rundown on what George said, but brought up the point that it wasn't something he should hide from his parents. Tell them he's been calling. And for god's sake, don't meet him alone without telling them first. Don't meet him alone at all. "I'll go with you, or you can ask Will, if it would be too weird to meet George with either your mom or dad."

Jay promised he wouldn't see George on his own, but Oz was looking at him closely, and subtly shook her head when Drew looked at her.

Jay was lying.

Will is just outside the door. I heard Aisha laugh.

At the same time I said that to Drew, Jay heard her, too. "I better text her and tell her where we are. She might go upstairs looking for us."

While he was at it, he asked if he could spend the night. Aubrey had already said it was all right. Instead of answering him, Will knocked on the door and opened it when Drew called out that it was unlocked.

He tossed Zed's bike fob to him. "All right, you gave it up without an argument, and we enjoyed using it. I reset the air jets. But if you modify it again—"

"I won't," Zed promised. "And borrow it whenever you want." He looked past Will. "Fun?"

"More fun than it should have been," she said. "What are you kids up to tonight?"

"Jay and Zed made dinner for us," Drew said, holding up

a sandwich. "After this, we're helping Zed study for a test, then watching a video or something. Though we might go upstairs for that. Bigger monitor."

"History?" Aisha asked Zed.

"Exit exam. If I pass it, I don't have to finish the class. And then I can concentrate on math, which I need to because my teacher is just...well, you know." He shivered with feigned revulsion.

"You could take that part of the exit exam, too," she said. "I understand your teacher thinks her summer would go so much smoother if you did."

"Nah, she'd miss me too much."

"It's a risk she's willing to take." She bent over and kissed Jay on the top of his head. "You can spend the night, it's fine."

"Uh, the parents are not home," Oz said. "Mom knows he's staying over, but I don't think they'll be back until late."

"Jesus, Oz, we're not little kids," Zed groaned. "You grasp that I'm allowed to be outside, even at night? And that half the time I work in the middle of the night?"

"I grasp that you're seventeen, and two seventeen-year-old boys together can create really stupid havoc."

Aisha laughed. "It's still all right."

"Ah," Jay said. "She's staying in the building. So, it's kind of like having adult supervision. Distracted adult supervision, but still."

She kissed him again and said, "Be good," before turning around to leave.

"You heard her, Will!" Jay called out after them. "She expects good."

"Yeah, for sure none of us would have said something like that to him before last year," Zed said. "Can you imagine?"

"You would have gotten The Look," Oz said. "Arms folded, eyebrows knotted, and then the stare-down that makes you want to pee yourself, run, and then die."

Drew shrugged. "I just hid in the closet."

Oz pointed at Jay. "Your mom has been really great for him. So be nice to him."

Instant guilt. He grimaced and then sighed. "I may have pushed a few buttons already. Doors may have been slammed. I may have shouted that he wasn't my dad. And I called him a dumbass."

"Well, stop it," Drew said. "He's not going anywhere and they're happy together. There's no point in treating him like crap."

"I'm not. Well, not exactly. Not on purpose. I mean, I'm glad they're dating. My mom is really happy."

"Will won't hold it against him," Zed said. "Case in point— me in Denver last year. I was a huge dick to him."

"And you called him a dick," Oz reminded him.

"I think I said he was *kind* of a dick. And being there really sucked."

And yet he wants to go back there. And Will said yes.

"Back to Denver?" Drew asked.

"He was joking about taking us there, but I kind of want to go back. Camping for the hell of it instead of because we have to?" He looked at Drew. "Come on, if we hadn't been on the death march to find Oz, I think camping with Will would have been fun. And if we all go, I promise to not give you shit for sharing a sleeping bag."

"Depends on when," Drew said. "I'd love to go back without all that crap hanging over us, but school starts in a month, and Oz's birthday is next week. You still have summer school to finish. Finding the time might be a bitch."

"Semester break," Zed said. "It'll be cold, but we did just fine in the cold last year. And we could spend nights in the bunker if it got too chilly."

Oz pretended to consider it. "I'd love to go back, too. I think I need to face that place again. I still have nightmares—"

"Damn. I'm sorry," Zed said. "I wasn't thinking."

"No, it would be good. We need to go back and reclaim it as ours and face what happened. You, too. I don't think being there will be as easy as you think. But it really all comes down to timing."

"We're getting married during the break, Zed," Drew reminded him. "I'm not sure we want to spend our honeymoon camping with you guys."

"Sure you do. Take two days to go screw like rabid little bunnies, and then meet us there."

"Aren't they already doing that?" Jay said. "Who needs a honeymoon?"

"I do," Drew said. "And I don't want to spend it with you morons."

Oz allowed for the possibility—she knew it wouldn't happen and Drew knew it wouldn't happen—and then they all went upstairs to quiz Jay and Zed on the things that would be on the history test. Zed and Jay headed up first and Drew made me promise to not tell Will that Jay was studying for the test, because he might not want to withhold that from Aisha and it wasn't fair to ruin the surprise when he passed.

I didn't tell him Will already knew. Jay could, if he wanted.

Since I didn't need to study and there probably wouldn't be any food coming my way, I went into Will's apartment. There might not be any food there, either, but it would be quiet, and I could take a peaceful nap. The chances were pretty good that Aisha and Will had headed straight for his bedroom, so I could just stretch out on the sofa and snooze.

I should know better than to plan anything.

They were in the living room, lights were on, and there was music playing. The sofa had been shoved away from the fireplace until it was almost in the dining room, clearing the floor. My nap plans were thwarted by Will learning to dance.

Dude, I've seen you do that. You're hopeless.

"Hush, Wick. Aisha seems certain that I can improve."

I jumped onto the hearth to watch. This wasn't even a pretext to bouncing things; he was making an effort to move with her and the music, and they were plastered so close to each other that it looked like they were trying to soak each other up. And their clothes were still on.

Oh. Oz's birthday. There's gonna be dancing?

"She's not having a big party this year, but you know them. Chances are, there will be dancing."

Sophia Lopez is coming for the party.

"I know. Zed is excited to see her."

He says they're not going to bounce but I wouldn't bet money on that.

"I'm aware of Zed's proclivities, Wick. Give him credit for aspiring to self-restraint."

"A little more of what he's telling you would help," Aisha said. "I feel like I'm eavesdropping on a phone call."

"I'm sorry. I used to ignore everything he said when there was someone else present. The novelty of being able to converse with him in front of others still hasn't worn off, I suppose."

"I don't mind at all. But sometimes I need context."

You still haven't told her I think she has nice boobs. You should tell her they're magnificent.

All he did was grin, and then tried to dip her. He got her halfway down and then told her she had to kiss him before he'd pick her back up.

"I could sit my ass down and pull you onto your head," she said. "We're dancing here, mister. Save the smooching for later."

"As I have observed," he said, pulling her back up, "dancing like this invites a kiss or two. Jax and Aubrey. Oz and Drew. My parents. They used to dance in the living room when I was a little boy. I snuck out of my bedroom to watch from behind a chair, because they were always both calm and happy then. And without fail, at some point they would stop and my father would very gently kiss her. I hope they still do that now and again."

I stayed on the hearth and watched while they twirled across the floor. It was like the talking part that usually happened after all the bouncing things were done and they didn't want to fall asleep. Will was relaxed and happy and not afraid to talk in hushed whispers that sometimes ended in giggles.

You haven't farted in front of her, have you?

"What the hell, Wick?"

That's how you know it's true love.

"You can love someone and not ruin their evening with… flatulence."

"Oh my god," Aisha laughed. "You're arguing with your cat about farting."

"Apparently we're supposed to cement our relationship in odiferous ways. Only then will we know for sure that we'll last."

"Wick," she said to me, "we're saving that for a special occasion. Maybe on his next birthday. We'll commemorate our first kiss."

"As long as we keep it classy."

Will there be another party? You can dance and fart for each other right after you cut the cake.

I'm not sure why, but they decided they were done dancing right then and there, and then moved the sofa back into place. I thought Will was doing all right; he hadn't stepped on her toes, and he didn't drop her. He didn't even get all tangled up when she made him spin around a couple of times.

Can I get fed before you get naked? You'll forget once your pants are off.

"The kids didn't feed you?"

They had sandwiches. I didn't want a sandwich. I need real food. All I've really had today are snacks.

"Are you actually asking for cat food instead of steak or shrimp?"

Steak would be nice but I'm really hungry and don't want just a taste of something. I want a full tummy.

He opened a can for me, and after I had eaten I sat on the far end of the kitchen counter and watched them make dinner together. It was chicken and a lot of vegetables—normal for him, and I would be getting a bite of the meat—and they sat close to each other at the table, talking the entire time. They washed dishes together, which involved a lot of laughing and bubble flinging, and I figured that was it; they'd been fed, they cleaned up, so it was time for the clothes to come off, but instead, they sat on the sofa together and turned the video monitor on.

Will was not a consumer of mass entertainment. He watched the news and sometimes programs about ecology and space exploration and history, but his entertainment was usually found in books. Aisha wanted to watch a movie with him, though, so he sat down to watch a movie.

I jumped onto the back of the sofa and sniffed at him to make sure he wasn't oozing cooties and about to become violently ill.

You're not watching the news.

"Wick, you can stay here, but be quiet, all right?"

But it's not news.

"No, it's not the news."

You always watch the news.

"Tonight, I am not watching the news."

"It's an alien invasion movie," Aisha said. "Lots of weird looking creatures and things that go boom. I'm not torturing him too badly." She reached over his shoulder to rub under my chin. "We've been in space for what, five hundred years or so? Why haven't we had an actual alien encounter yet? We have a colony on Mars, we send people out into space for decades at a time, and zero alien contact."

"That we know of," Will said. "The odds of alien life being similar to ourselves are slim. There could be intelligent life the size of bacteria, and we simply haven't recognized it."

"Well, there goes my fantasy of finding some pointy-eared red guy for an afternoon of sweaty fun in a zero-gravity spaceship."

"Sorry to burst your bubble. It's not likely that we'll ever encounter a species we can actually mate with."

She shrugged lightly. "Who said anything about mating? As long as he has a tongue—"

Maybe I'm an alien.

"It would explain a lot about you, Wick."

Shave me. Maybe I'm red underneath.

He turned his head sharply, eyebrows knotted together. "Holy hell. You do realize the insinuation?"

She wants a pointy ear red dude to give her a bath. I wouldn't enjoy it because people taste like fleshy blobs of disappointment, but I would do it for her.

He turned back around. "She doesn't want a bath. Now either watch the movie or go upstairs and bug the kids."

I watched the movie.

The aliens looked just like people who had been painted blue and they used people-laser-guns to shoot at other people who had their own laser guns, and every ten minutes something exploded. There was a spaceship the size of all of San Francisco and it sucked people up off the ground and ate them, though Will thought it was less eating and more hostage-taking, and Aisha thought they were being used as slave labor. In the end, the people sent their own spaceship inside the alien one and it exploded, saving the world.

"Well, that's two hours we'll never get back," Aisha grumbled.

They blew up their own people with the aliens. That wasn't very nice.

"Sacrifice the few to save the many," Will said. "It's not an uncommon theme."

"Would that happen?" Aisha asked. "I mean, clearly not this claptrap of a scenario, but would we sacrifice some people to save the rest?"

"That's a soldier's life," he said simply.

"No, I meant average citizens. Put us in a war situation. Someone has a weapon, say a bioweapon, and if we could give up a thousand people in order to get that weapon neutralized, would we?"

"Ideally, we go after the weapon and neutralize it ourselves."

"And if that doesn't work? What happens?"

He scooted on the sofa a few inches and turned toward her. "Humanity under duress is capable of doing incredible things to save itself. People will sacrifice for the greater good. They'll do it by choice, knowing that what they leave behind will be secure."

"People under duress fight like crazy, Will. They scramble to be the ones who live."

He nodded. "The greedy, the elitist, sure. Some bury their heads in the sand and pretend the worst isn't about to consume them. But there are always those who step up and do everything they can, even when it costs them more than they can bear."

She reached out to touch his face. "Like sending their seventeen-year-old son away, knowing what his end will be."

He nodded. "It was so much more than that. And remind me in the morning to call my mother. I promised her I would make an effort and I'm not sure I've done a good enough job of that."

She glanced up at the clock and suggested it wasn't too late to call. "Ten o'clock. She would still be up, wouldn't she?"

"Midnight, she would still be up," he said, reaching for his phone. "Apple doesn't fall far from the tree."

Before he could call, though, his phone pinged.

"It's Mass," he said as he read the text. "He says he and Oz were at cross purposes and she misunderstood the test results."

"What?" She leaned over to look at the message. "Call him."

Ten minutes later, he clicked the phone off and sighed. "He thought she was upset because the test was negative. He had no idea she was upset because she thought it was positive, but Drew called him a few minutes ago, worried because she started bleeding."

"Oh no."

"I thought it was positive, too. The liquid in the tube changed color."

"Blue or brown?"

"Blue."

She got up. "It would have been brown if it were positive. Come on, let's go make sure she's all right."

The noises coming from upstairs indicated two things: someone was in pain, and it wasn't Oz, and something was obnoxiously funny. Will hesitated as he closed the door; he cocked an ear toward the sounds trickling down the stairwell from three floors up and was as confused as I was.

They bolted up the stairs because howling was never a good thing. When we got to the living room, Jay was curled up on the floor with his hands between his legs, and both Drew and Jay were laughing. Oz was amused, but sat in Jax's chair with her chin resting on the palm of her hand, and when she looked up, she sighed, "Boys."

Will got to Jay before Aisha could.

"He's fine," Drew said. "It was a learning experience."

"He sat on his balls," Zed explained. "Come on, get up, Jaybird. Your mom is worried."

Jay remained curled up, and squeaked, "She's never getting grandkids now."

"Yeah, but that's not because you did any damage. That's because no sane woman is ever having sex with you."

"I'll settle for a crazy one," he groaned.

Will left him curled up. "He's fine. Perhaps eliminate boxers from his wardrobe for the foreseeable future."

"Not wearing any," Jay said, a little less squeaky.

"Boxers?"

"Underwear."

Aisha opened her mouth to say something but then closed it because there really wasn't anything to say to that.

How big are they that he can sit on them?

Will bit his bottom lip to keep from laughing, then told Drew and Oz that he wanted to talk to them on the balcony. I was torn; if Jay did it again I wanted to be there to mock him, but I also wanted to make sure Oz was all right. I waited in the entryway where I could see the balcony and the living room. Aisha wanted to know why Jay was in a state of partial undress—it was because some of his clothes were in Will's dryer, he'd washed them after jogging—and when he got back onto the sofa he did it carefully, so there wasn't going to be anything to mock.

I went out onto the balcony.

"We couldn't exactly react with Zed and Jay in the next room," Drew said as I came through the cat flap.

"I'm just kind of…I don't know, stunned," Oz said. "I admit, I went into the bathroom and cried for a little bit. I wasn't exactly happy."

"But are you all right?" Will pressed.

Oz shrugged. "Half of me is relieved, but the other half wants to curl up on the bed and cry a little more."

"We were getting really excited, Will. I mean, just a couple of hours ago—" Drew's breath caught. "It was supposed to be amazing."

"It will be," Will said. "When the time is right. And now you know how badly you'll want a family together."

Oz's hand went to her stomach. "I know I didn't, but I feel like I lost something."

Will couldn't say that he understood because he really didn't, but he did think it was time for them to talk to Aubrey and Jax. If anyone would understand it was Aubrey, and Jax couldn't get too upset over a false alarm. "Take a night to get your bearings. But you need to tell them, Oz."

"They'll be so disappointed."

"No, they won't. And drive home the point that you couldn't get help from Dr. Jacobsen. He refused to help Drew, he refused to help Zed, and you didn't even try to because you knew what the answer would be."

"How much shit will you be in for getting Mass to see us?" Drew asked.

"That's my problem. But tell them everything. Including how disappointed you are."

"What's the point?" Oz asked. "It would upset them for no good reason. I'm not pregnant after all. Life goes on."

"Because if anyone can help you through the disappointment, it's your mother. They'll understand, Ozzie, I promise. And to be honest, if you're adult enough to be in this relationship, then you're adult enough to have uncomfortable discussions with them. Let them know what's going on in your life. You thought you were pregnant, you misunderstood the test result, and to find out you're not frankly hurts. They'll get that."

Oz should cry a lot. Jax can't get mad if she's crying.

I don't think she needed the advice. She was going to cry. So was Aubrey. Jax was doomed.

= = =

At five the next morning, Will slid out of bed and dressed in the living room so that he wouldn't wake Aisha. He was meeting Jax outside at six, to run laps around Union Square, because Jax wanted to go fast and hard, and it was easier to do that around the Square. His guards didn't have to keep up; half waited on the perimeter of the Square where they could look down on the street and make passersby uncomfortable.

I sat on the steps that were directly across from the front door, halfway up. They started slowly, but fifteen minutes in they were going at Will's comfortable speed and Jax's near-limit. At half an hour, Jax slowed down and told Will to go ahead while he caught his breath, which really meant sitting near me and staring up at the sky like he wanted it to swallow him whole.

Will sped up, running as hard as he could, and did three fast laps—a mile—while Jax was still trying to breathe evenly. They repeated it until Jax had run six miles. He wanted to stop before he hurled, and he dropped onto the step next to me while Will mocked him for his efforts.

"Run with Andrew some morning," he said. "Try to keep up. You'll be vomiting your toenails up."

"You want me to die young, don't you? I die, Oz takes the throne, and you become the power behind the crown."

"That job doesn't pay enough," Will said. "My job doesn't pay enough. We should discuss a raise."

"You probably have a hell of a lot more in the bank than I do. I know you earn more and you don't have teenagers to feed ten times a day."

"I feed your teenagers plenty."

"And you cheat. How many bank accounts have you opened twenty years in the past just for the interest growth? How many companies have you invested in, because you already know how they'll perform?"

"I would never violate securities laws, Jax."

"Not an answer." With a groan, he pushed himself up. "Wait. I gave you a couple hundred thousand bucks once, to invest for the kids. What happened to that?"

"Your children will be quite happy when they turn twenty-five and the trusts are released to them. Andrew, as well. If they handle the funds responsibly, they'll be able to indulge their passions without affecting their bottom line."

"I knew I kept you around for a reason."

He headed back inside, and with him, the guards left the Square. Will and I climbed the rest of the way up and made our way to a bench on the east side. He wanted to cool down before going home to shower, and I wanted to watch all the unhappy people who were beginning to head for work.

The corner bakery was open, and several of the tables were occupied by sleepy people clutching cups of coffee, ignoring the pastries sitting in front of them. One couple was less interested in their coffee than anyone else was in their donuts; James and George were at a table on the fringe, and Will spotted them a second after I did.

"James," he said, "is about to lose it. Whatever they're arguing about has the makings of becoming very ugly."

We could go say hello. I like James.

He had no desire to walk over there to make pleasantries but thought it would be all right if I did. I wanted to jump onto James' lap; it would make him feel better and would piss George off.

He doesn't like pets, remember?

"I do. If he makes any sort of motion toward you, run back to me as fast as you can."

That wasn't a suggestion, that was an order.

I didn't want to startle James by jumping on him when he didn't expect it, so I patted his leg and waited. He smiled when he saw me and said, "Well, hello Wick!" and then he looked to see if Will was nearby.

Will raised a hand to let him know that he was aware of where I was. James scooted back from the table and patted his lap, inviting me up. I gave him a good head bonk to his chin and then sat down. George was not, as predicted, happy to see me, and he grumbled about it.

"He's a friendly little guy," James told him. "He just wanted to say hello and to get a good head rub. He loves being scratched behind his ears."

"I don't care what the cat likes, James."

"I care, Wick," he said to me. "You're a good boy, aren't you?"

I forgave him for that; he didn't know better.

George leaned back, folding his arms. "Forget the cat. What about Jay? When can I see him?"

"Why would he want to see you?"

"Come on. I'd like to spend some time with him before I move back to Vegas. And if that goes well, I want to set up visitation."

James' fingers tensed on my back. "You're not entitled to visitation now, George. You're no longer one of Jay's parents. In another year, he can make up his own mind, but until then I want you to leave him alone."

"I'm making an effort here," George argued. "I'm still mad as hell that you went behind my back to get the surgery done and I don't think I'll ever understand why, but I love Jay, and I will try."

"George, if you'd gotten your way Jay would still be years away from his first surgery and it would have been fifty times more painful."

"Oh, come on."

"We did this because it meant a single operation, instead of three or four that it would take months to recover from. Look how well he's recovered. He's happy and healthy. He's *growing*, George. He's already taller than I am."

"How would I even know that? I saw him once, right afterward. I don't even know if I would recognize him if we passed on the street."

James had no idea but knew that it would take time. "Too much anger."

He was angry. He'd stopped petting me and his fingers were twitching against my back. George let out a long breath and unfolded his arms.

"What about us?" he asked. "I still love you."

The petting resumed, a bit too enthusiastically. "Jay overheard you, you know. When you referred to him as 'that freak kid' who would not be moving to Vegas." A little louder, "You called my son a freak. I can't get past that."

"Give Jay the decision to see me," George said, ignoring James' anger.

"No. The decision is mine to make, on his behalf."

Should I go? I feel like I should go.

"You know, I've forgiven a lot in our marriage. All the cheating? And don't deny it. I mean, I understood from the start that you play from both sides of the plate and have always been easily tempted, but I still forgave those betrayals. Forgive me mine."

"I can't." He held me a little closer and got up. "The ultimate betrayals in our marriage weren't against either you or me. They were against Jay. And honestly, he should be angrier with me than he is with anyone else, because I didn't have the balls to end our marriage years ago. And I should have, the day you walked out when Aisha and I agreed to raise him as a boy."

"You mean the week when you two fucked like animals? I knew about the affair, James. And even then, I came back, and I stayed."

"Well, you shouldn't have. Leave Jay alone, and go to Vegas already."

He carried me back to Will and set me on the bench. "Thank you," he said to Will. "A few minutes with Wick will be the highlight of my day."

When he was gone, Will looked over to George, who was vomiting into a trash can.

He was really pale and has dark circles under his eyes. He's lost a lot of weight, too.

Is it starting? Is time trying to smash him into dust?

"George needs to go home," he said, but he didn't get up and offer to take him there. Instead, he headed for home, to a hot shower and breakfast with Aisha.

20

"He wasn't mad," Drew told Will. "Stunned for a minute, maybe, but he was the first to reach for Oz and tell her how sorry he was. And it was super uncomfortable when he hugged me and said it would be all right before we knew it."

"Why was that uncomfortable?"

"Because I didn't think he was going to let go. It was like, here let me squeeze you until you pop like a zit."

We were on the roof, setting up for Oz's birthday. There was no big party planned this year; she wanted a quiet evening with family and extended family. Aisha and Jay were a given, and she invited Sophia and her friend, Kathy, who had come to San Francisco with her to share an apartment while they went to school. Oz wanted to grill burgers and hang out, complain when Zed and Jay began a burping contest, and maybe steal a sip or two of whiskey from her father, but Drew decided there would be lights strung over the grass lawn, loud music, and balloons.

Will helped string the lights and set the supporting poles at the lawn's edge. Drew went up and down the ladder while Will handed him the strings of white holiday lights that would hang between the tall poles around the lawn and one in the center. "A tent of lights," he told Will earlier. "She doesn't know she wants it, but she wants it."

"Why didn't you tell us they'd gone through nearly the same thing?" Drew asked as he clipped lights into place.

"For the same reason that I didn't tell them about what you and Oz were going through. It was not mine to tell."

"I don't think he's upset that you helped us, if it matters. If he is, he hid it well."

"He knows that I will keep to myself matters regarding his children that I deem private. You're adults now. You have a right to personal privacy."

"Yeah, well…" He climbed back down. "He wants to talk to you about Dr. Jacobsen. That, he was super pissed about."

"He should be. You and Oz are both of an age to consent to your own medical treatment. And by law, contraceptive rights were granted to anyone over fifteen several decades ago. He had no right to refuse treatment to any of you."

Drew dragged the ladder to the next pole. "Well, Zed needs to see someone soon. He and Sophia are intentionally not having sex, but I don't see that lasting long."

"He could stand to develop a bit more self-restraint."

"Him?" Drew snorted. "Three minutes after her shuttle landed, Sophia was fishing for his tonsils. Once she finds an apartment? Yeah. It's happening, and it's not all on him."

"Perhaps."

"Will, come on. I'm ninety per cent sure that if Oz had come on that strong when I was his age, I would have caved. I didn't decide to hold off on things until I knew I was moving here. The summer you told me I'd better respect her? I would have slept with her in a heartbeat if I thought she wanted to and I hadn't even kissed her yet."

"Yes, but you weren't of a majority age seeking to have sex with a minor. Sophia Lopez is twenty years old. Zed is seventeen. A reminder might be in order."

"A real reminder, or a fuck-with-them reminder? Because realistically, who the hell will press charges against her?"

"The latter would reinforce the former, I believe."

"Trying to be a dick?"

"Little bit, yeah."

"Good luck with that." He slid down the ladder and followed the length of the lighting cord and then plugged it in. "Nice. She'll like that."

It was a canopy of twinkling white lights that would irritate the neighbors who lived on upper floors across the street, but Oz would certainly enjoy it.

If anyone complained, they could be reminded of last year, when there were hover cars protecting the air space around the building. The lights, at least, were quiet.

= = =

Compared to Oz's eighteenth birthday, this one was dull. It was a happy kind of dull because there weren't fifty pairs of feet that could stomp on my tail, and neither Oz nor Drew were unhappy or scared. Everyone—except for Sophia and her friend, who were coming later because they'd found an apartment nearby and had to do something with it that didn't interest me at all, so I ignored ninety percent of what Zed had to say about it—was crowded around the fire pit, because as night time in San Francisco usually goes, even in summer, it was getting cold. There was a stack of sweatshirts piled up under one of the chairs for when the sun went down, and I had my choice of three that I could crawl into if I wanted to warm up.

The fire pit gave me a stellar view of everyone; I could walk around the rim, tease head rubs out of people, and it was easy to jump in laps from there. There wasn't a real fire in it—just a heater that blew hot air and had pretty lights shimmering under clear rocks—so my fur was not at risk. It was toasty on my missing hairballs, which was reason number three I liked it so much.

"Forty-four years ago," Finn said to Oz and Drew. "I sat here and saw your first kiss. If I'd had all my memories, I would have understood it was far more than what it appeared to be."

Drew looked puzzled.

"It was the beginning of everything that matters to me," Finn said.

Jax folded his arms and pretended to be hurt. "Aubrey and I had something to do with that, too, you know."

Finn snorted. "Yes, but you're old and had your first kiss back when men rode on dinosaurs and fairies farted moon dust. When I looked back on it and realized I had witnessed the onset of my grandparents' relationship? It stuck with me."

"Hopefully we still are your grandparents," Drew said. "Will seems pretty sure he murdered the timeline. Anything can happen now."

"He's right," Finn said. "Anything can, and you should embrace that. It no longer matters if I'm born. The Old Mint contains all the answers the future will need."

The mental gymnastics hurt Aisha's brain and she couldn't fathom how they kept things straight. Oz didn't even try; she knew that Finn had gone back hundreds of years several times, enlisting the help of his own ancestors, and that he'd become friends with her grandfather, but she avoided plotting everything out because it inevitably caused a brain cramp.

"Eli was the first to take me seriously," Finn said. "Your great, great, great grandfather was amused by the things I told him and allowed the lock to be placed on the Old Mint, but he didn't believe a word of it. By the time Eli was a young teenager, he'd heard enough stories about the odd man and his time-traveling fairy tales to connect the dots. He was the first one who was willing to step through a portal that he could not see, and when he did, any doubts he may have had vanished."

"What time period did you take him to?" Oz asked.

"Mine. I knew I needed to make an impact. When he stepped out onto Union Square and the first thing he saw was a line of commuters screaming past in jet packs, he was convinced. And when he met William, there wasn't a thing he wouldn't have done to help."

"He met me." Will's voice was tinged with disbelief. "I don't remember that. How old was I?"

"The first time? Eight or nine. He thought you had Donna's eyes. That's all it took, he would have done anything for you then. He saw you from time to time over the next few years, but I don't think he ever spoke to you. He didn't want to get in your way."

Will looked over the fire pit at Jax. "He knew who I was. The day on the bridge, he already knew who I was."

Did he know I was in the backpack? Because I'm still kind of annoyed about that. Who shoves a perfectly good cat into a backpack?

"That explains a lot," Jax said.

No wonder he accepted you so fast. It was more than saving Jax's life. He wanted to get his wife's eyes back.

"When I decided to stay here," Will said, mostly to Aisha, "he made sure I didn't lack for anything. My apartment? That was his doing. He tasked me with keeping an eye on Jax, which was my—" he used air quotes "—'job,' and while he let me believe I was wholly independent, truthfully he gently nudged me along in nearly every aspect of my life. He was a paternal figure, without being overly pushy about it."

"Your bonus dad," Oz said lightly.

"Indeed."

"Yeah, well, I wish your bonus dad would get his ass home," Jax said. "It's been years."

"He's coming for our wedding, Dad," Oz said.

"I'd like him to come sooner, and to stay."

Home was a painful place for the old King to be; every hall echoed his queen's name, and he could hear her whisper in every room. He'd made a life for himself in Scotland, which largely consisted of traveling Europe and drinking, and often getting into trouble with Will's maternal grandfather.

"Offer to get him a room at the Westin," Will said. "He won't come if he's expected to stay here."

"Or wait until he comes for the wedding, and then revoke his travel visa," Drew joked.

For a few seconds, I think Jax considered it as a serious option.

"Tell him I'm contesting his adoption of my only child," Jo said. "That will bring him home. We can fight for William."

The idea of that made Will laugh. "Hand to hand combat in a cage placed at the center of Union Square? You might win because he wouldn't dare hit you."

"Ah, sure he would," she said. "He's an evolved sort of man."

Jay screwed up his face. "I'm kind of lost here. But suppose that happened. Think of all the paperwork to change your name back."

Everyone turned to look at him.

"What? It would be a pain. First name 'The,' last name 'Emperor.'" He looked at Will. "Your legal name *was* the Emperor, right?"

"Just Emperor. However, since my father's name is Blackshear, I think I could just keep it."

"If you're all Blackshears, that means Drew has to change his name?"

"I don't have to, but that's the plan," Drew said. "Unless there are parental objections?"

"It's still the House of Blackshear no matter what name the two of you choose," Jax said. "I might object if Oz takes your name and then later officially changes the House, though. I don't think your grandfather ever got over your mother ending the House of Mor."

"He should have been less of a dick to her when she was growing up, then. And he should have considered that it was the House of Azaria before that. My grandmother changed it to Mor when she became Queen."

"Our house has never changed, has it?" Zed asked.

Jax shook his head. "From Pacifica's first king onward, it's been Blackshear. Some thought it would change with Queen Wyatt when she married Darius Ferguson, but he opted to take her name and she chose to not change anything. Precedent was set. Whoever ruled could keep the house name, even if they chose their spouse's surname for personal use."

"So I could someday change my name?" Zed asked.

"You could," Jax answered. "But why?"

He shrugged. "Why did Mom take your name? Why is Drew taking Oz's? If I marry someone it matters to, why wouldn't I?"

"Because 'Zed' sounds stupid with just about anything else," Jay said. "I mean, if I had a sister and you married her? It would sound like Zedo Kuda."

"Zedo," Zed repeated. "Zedo, Zedo. I could get used to that." His phone pinged, and he glanced at it and told Jay that Sophia and Kathy were downstairs. "We'll be back in a few minutes. They're afraid of opening the front door and having the guard flip his shit."

Aubrey sighed audibly. And yet, she had no idea how abused her Bad Word List really was.

"Sophia's been here before," Jax reminded him.

"Kathy hasn't, and she's a little freaked out by the bored teenager sitting at the desk inside. I think it's the gun."

"Aw, that's cute," Oz said as the door shut. "He says 'teenager' like he's not still one himself."

"And you're adorable," Jax said as he got up. "Like you don't still have another year there yourself."

"I embrace it. Another year of built in excuses for stupid mistakes."

"Lend me a hand," Jax said to Will. They each took one end of a cooler filled with ice and meat, and carried it over to the grill. I ran after them, because sometimes meat fell off the grill, and I wasn't above eating it off the ground.

"You could have managed this," Will pointed out. "It's not heavy."

"Could have, chose not to. Besides, it's not the cooler I need help with. I fired Jacobsen last night."

"Outright?"

"It wasn't just the kids he's been turning away. A quick survey of his staff suggested he denies treatment to anyone unmarried who he even thinks is engaging in sexual activity, as well as anyone he assumes to be gay, trans, or nonbinary. He tried to excuse it as his right to practice within the scope of his religious beliefs."

"When did he become religious?"

"No idea about his religion but he's always been a bastard. He refused to give me an implant when I was a teenager, but I thought that was because I was fourteen when I asked. I gave him the chance to retire, but the idiot dug his heels in. So, I fired him."

"And now you need a new physician."

"Your friend Mass might be a little long in the tooth, but if he would consider it and has colleagues he can drag along with him, I'm open to submitting him to vetting."

"He's a gender medicine specialist, Jax."

"So? He's a doctor foremost. If he can give me an annual physical and knows others he can bring into the practice, he's eligible."

"He's also going home."

He has a transponder. He's working in two Whens. He'll bounce back and forth.

"There's also that," Will said. "It wouldn't hurt to ask him. If he's not interested, he may have recommendations."

"Whether he accepts the offer or not, I would appreciate it if he could give Zed an implant. And Zed would be a lot more comfortable if you broached the subject. I mention sex, and he shuts down."

"That doesn't sound like Zed."

"I didn't handle the way he was treating that girl last year very well," Jax admitted. "I tried to shame him into better behavior, and it was the wrong thing to do."

"He got your message."

"But not the way I wanted him to, and now he won't talk to me about deeply personal things." He nodded toward the door. "Like Sophia. If I asked him about their relationship, he'd grunt and shrug. I only know she's moving here for school because Aubrey told me and then her father asked if we would keep an eye on her. I only knew she was coming tonight by hearing everyone else talking. He hasn't forgiven me yet."

"That's exactly why you need to be the one to approach him."

Jax tossed a couple of meat patties onto the grill a little too enthusiastically. "He'll assume I want him to get it because I don't trust him to keep it in his pants."

"You don't."

"Fucking hell, Will."

"You're presuming that's the direction their relationship will go."

"But that's not a matter of trust. It's accepting the inevitable. No, I don't like it, but the truth is that he tried to do the right thing to protect himself and was shot down by a narrow-minded bigot who took control of his reproductive rights. I'd be happier if he weren't having sex at all, not yet, but he's going to, and he's at least trying to be responsible."

When Will didn't say anything, Jax threw more meat down and said, "How long are you going to let me ramble on before you point out the obvious?"

"I already did. All of that is why you need to be the one to approach him. Tell him you learned that Jacobsen was deliberately throwing a roadblock in front of him and Drew, and you're furious. You don't have to tell him you think he's twenty minutes away from sleeping with Sophia. Just tell him you appreciate that he was being proactive and you're sorry he had nowhere else to turn. Then get him the damned implant."

He's going to kill the meat before it even gets to cook.

"Come on," Will said. "Out with it. You're irritated about more than just this issue."

He slammed the last burger down hard enough that it split and oozed through the grill slats.

"My daughter thought she was pregnant." His voice was somewhere between and hiss and a growl, and the only reason he hadn't raised it was because he didn't want anyone else to hear. "She was terrified out of her damned mind, and you didn't tell me. I get it, the kids confide in you, but when it's this big, you fucking tell me."

"When it's this big, I want them to tell you."

"Son of a bitch, Will, we could have helped them through this."

Will stared at him, unyielding.

"What?"

"When you were Oz's age, you were in their shoes. You begged me to not say a word to your parents because it was *your* problem. *Your* child. You wanted to come to terms with it before they found out. They wanted nothing less, Jax. They deserved the chance to get from being terrified to wanting that baby before they told anyone."

Jax exhaled sharply, and he looked up, scanning the sky for something that made sense.

"I will never," Will went on, "break their confidence unless it's for their own good. Telling you this would have been for your good, not theirs."

Aubrey is watching and I think she knows you're arguing.

"We're not arguing, Wick. We're discussing."

"Like hell," Jax spat. "I am fucking pissed off, Will. If my kids are hurting, I want to know."

"Tell them that. But I will not break their confidence."

"You know, if you were anyone else…"

"Fire me if it will make you feel better. I have other options. Hell, I still have my old apartment, I could be out of your hair tonight."

Whoa.

You can't move there. I'm not allowed to cross the street alone.

"Stop it. I'm not firing you and you're not moving out, especially not now."

"If I were anyone else, you'd fire me. That *was* the thought, wasn't it?"

"No." He closed the grill lid, and then let out a slight chuckle. "If you were anyone else, I'd have knocked you on your ass. Why would I fire you? I can't torment your sorry ass if you're gone."

"So take a swing. Make yourself feel better." He held his arms out from his sides and leaned his head back. "Come on. I won't even block it."

"Are you insane? Aubrey would hurt *me* if I hit you. I'm not stupid."

"Fine." He uprighted himself. "And why am I not moving out right now?"

"Why the hell can't you just let me be pissed off for a while?" Jax let out an exasperated sigh. "The guest suites have been used once in the last several years, so we're remodeling them. With Oz and Drew getting married, it seemed like a good time to get it done, before they actually do start a family."

"His apartment is small," Will agreed. "It was barely big enough for me when I lived in it, and I owned very little. They'd be thrilled to get one of the suites."

"Not them," Jax said. "We're offering it to you. The footprint is nearly identical to the official family apartment, which gives you a lot of space. You can spread some of those books out. Hell, you can choose the final layout, even."

"I have no need to live in a five-bedroom apartment, Jax."

"You'll need more space if Aisha and Jay move in with you. And you're clearly headed that way."

Will mused that if it happened, he might move in with her.

"With her ex living upstairs? And to be honest, I need you to be close. If you take the first remodel, Drew and Oz can take your place. Think about it. You could give Aisha her dream home. Cut the bedroom numbers down, make the master bigger, put in a shower stall with a dozen heads or a tub big enough for group activities… whatever you want."

"Activities." Will glanced over at Aisha. She and Aubrey were laughing about something, and it looked like whatever it was,

Jo started it. Jo's hand was on Aisha's arm, and she'd covered her mouth with her other hand as she laughed. Quietly, "We would do well where I live now, Jax. There's plenty of space, and I could put my books in storage."

"I know. Aubrey and I were fine in that apartment, even after the kids were born. And if you don't take it, we'll offer it to Oz, but…"

"You want them to move into the first apartment where you felt like your mother approved of your marriage."

"It was instantly home. And I swear, we're not trying to push you out. Aubrey would be upset if you left. The kids would be upset. I *might* notice you were gone."

Will thought Aisha might not be willing to move. The whole point of where she lived was to keep Jay close to his dad.

"It's a mile away. We'll get him an air bike. He'll still see his father. And it's months away, Will. The plans haven't been formalized yet, only the concept."

You should do it. You sleep when she's with you. You're content.
"Indeed."

Jax wanted to know what I said. Will told him that in the weeks he'd been with her, he'd been sleeping. More than an hour or two; he was sleeping six hours at a time.

"You're happy as hell, too. Aubrey says you look—"
Will finished, "Content? Wick said the same thing."
It's not too soon? It's only been a couple of months.
"I don't know if it's too soon, Wick."

"What if it is?" Jax said. "You're not getting any younger, you know."

Will was still watching her, and the corners of his mouth were turned up in a very slight smile. "Don't mention it to her yet, all right? I'll talk to her later tonight."

"The suite is yours regardless."

"If I don't take it, give it to the kids. Start a new tradition."

"Meh. They have to earn it. Finish school, find a purpose, pop out a grandkid." He looked past Will to the fire pit, where Oz and Drew were talking excitedly with Sophia. "In that order."

Not long after the burgers were consumed and the grill was cooling down, the lights over the grass clicked on. Oz reminded Drew that they had danced together on her last birthday, so they were dancing on this one, and every birthday after that. No matter where they were or what they were doing, she wanted to dance with him on every birthday from then on. She invited everyone else to join them—the old people were less inclined to get up at that point—and then Zed turned the music up.

It wasn't too loud, but it was fast, drum-driven music with noisy guitars and screeching singers. It begged for wild, unbridled movement, and Sophia and Zed jumped right in while Jay and Kathy tried hard to imitate them, but Oz and Drew danced slowly. They weren't uncomfortably close; there was enough space between them to satisfy parental comfort, and they didn't wrap their arms around each other. Instead, Oz took his hands and they found a beat in the music that was their own, and after a moment Drew set his forehead against hers.

They look sad. I thought they were done with sad.

"I think they're still a little bit sad," Will said, quietly.

"It's a painful mixture of sorrow and relief," Aubrey said. "A little bit of guilt for feeling relieved. They'll be all right."

Jax blinked against his own sorrow and relief. He watched them dance, squinting against the lights, and he sucked in a deep breath.

"What?" Aubrey asked. "What is it you see?"

"I don't think I've ever seen this before." His voice was soft, almost reverent. "The colors around them have intertwined. I don't mean they've just merged where they're touching, either. Her colors have thinned and wrapped around him, and his are virtually the same. And more than anything else, they're happy."

"But?"

"Genuine longing. I rarely see that in anyone. But they both have it. And I don't mean in a ditch-the-parents, go make out kind of way. This is—I can't explain it. They have zero doubts about each other."

Maybe they just want music that doesn't sound like torture porn.

"How do you know what torture porn sounds like, Wick?"

I'm listening to it.

Will changed the music to something that didn't hurt my ears and then took Aisha onto the lawn. They danced closer than Oz and Drew, which Jo admitted still made her a little bit uncomfortable because she had a tough time shaking off the idea that Will shouldn't touch anyone, even though she was excited about them being together. They were amused at Jay, who was staring at his feet because he was afraid of stomping on Kathy's toes, and Jax wondered out loud if he should go growl at Zed and Sophia.

"Just to keep some space between them."

It was boring. I left them and climbed Will's leg so I could sit on his shoulder. It was as close to dancing as I would get, and I could be reasonably certain that as long as he was with Aisha, he wasn't going to start that spastic up and down hopping thing he did at summer parties when he wanted to make Oz and Zed's friends laugh.

Don't get much closer.

"Why's that?" he asked.

Everyone is watching.

"He's concerned that everyone is watching us. They've seen us dance before, Wick."

At your party. She kissed you.

"Indeed. It was a wonderful kiss. So why is it a problem now?"

Because now you get this close to her and she makes your dick twitch. They'll notice.

"Holy hell, Wick."

Drew laughed and buried his face against Oz's shoulder to make himself stop.

Well, I'm not wrong.

She promised to not do anything that would lead to his embarrassment, not at Oz's birthday party. "There will be plenty of other chances for that."

"When we're old and gray, you'll still be making me twitch," he said. "And I mean that in Wick's way, not in a nervous tick sort of way."

"Very old and gray. I hope so."

He stopped moving. "Old and gray, and impossibly wrinkled. I love you, an insane amount. If anyone had asked me just two months ago, I'd have told them I was sure I loved you, but it was going to take time. And yet, I knew. I even told you I knew."

"Knew what?"

"What this is all leading to."

She took a step back, and then set a hand on his chest. "Are you asking, Will? Because I still had it in my head that I would. I've just been trying to figure out a way to make you feel like a princess."

"I can do without feeling like a princess," he chuckled. He lifted her hand from his chest and kissed her fingers. "I love your son, too. I was surprised by how quickly that came, but I would do just about anything for him."

"Will. Wait."

Drew and Oz stopped moving and were deliberately trying to not stare.

"I'll wait as long as you want me to, but—"

She took a step back. His muscles tensed under my feet and he took in a short, tight breath, waiting for her to tell him to back the hell off. It was too soon. And not right then, on Oz's birthday with her son watching. He braced himself against it.

Aisha dropped to one knee.

"I'll match your insanity, Will. I love your entire, weird, inexplicable life and I want to be a part of it right up to the last squeak of my rocking chair. I want you to be my Emperor until the last time my eyes close." She cocked her head a touch and grinned. "It doesn't have to be soon. Next year maybe. But William Blackshear, I'm *not* letting you get away again. Will you marry me?"

Behind us, Aubrey squealed.

If you don't say yes, I will. We have to marry her.

He reached for her hand and pulled her up. "In a heartbeat," he said.

"That's a yes?"

"Damn right, that's a yes." He managed to kiss her before the kids piled on; they fell over in a massive lump of hugs and I leaped for safety, landing near Aisha's feet. It took a minute to shake them off, and when he got to his feet, he was facing the wrong direction. He grumbled and told them he was bruised beyond belief and they owed him, and then braced for Jax and Finn, just in case.

They didn't jump on him, though. Will turned around, and his mother and father were with Aisha, arms wrapped around her. Oz came up beside him and whispered, "Every color I see there? Joy. Nothing but joy."

What about Jay?

Jay had jumped on him with the others but was now hanging back, watching his mother get the stuffing hugged out of her. Will whispered in Oz's ear and she glanced at him.

"He's happy. And a little bit afraid."

He's been bit in the ass by his dad's marriage. He doesn't want to get bit again.

Will stepped over to him. "I love her very much," he said softly, so that only Jay and I could hear him. "I promise you, I'll take care of her. And I swear to you, I will never try to step between you and your parents."

Jay looked up at him and nodded.

"I love you, too, and that promise is for you as well. Whatever you need me to be, I will endeavor to never let you down."

Jay stood up a little straighter and looked Will in the eyes. He'd grown taller; at the start of summer he barely reached Will's chest, and now the top of his head was just past Will's nose. He'd filled out some and had wild peach fuzz, and was trying hard to look his age. "Just treat her all right, you know? Do that and you and I are fine."

He held his hand out to Will, and as they shook, Jay's phone pinged.

He tried to ignore it, but it pinged again.

"Take a look," Will said. "If it's George, turn your phone off. If it's not, do whatever you need to." He went to Aisha, to rescue her from his parents.

"Zed," Jay hissed. He shook his phone at him. "Grundy."

"*Now?*"

"Seriously." He stared at his phone, thumb poised to tap on it. Oz and Drew noticed them staring at it, and came over to check. "Grundy sent me a link. The exam results posted."

"So look!" Drew urged.

"What if I didn't pass? My mom *just* asked your weird-ass uncle to marry her, and everyone is fucking happy. If I blew even one of the tests, my mood is going to go south, fast, and I don't want to wreck this for her. I mean, fuck, look at her. I can't do that—"

"Your mood is going to nosedive if you *don't* look," Oz said. "You'll be preoccupied with it. Check the results, and if it's not what you want, you'll fake it for a while, and then we'll get you out of here. We can go to Drew's and play video games or down the street to get ice cream."

He took a deep breath, closed his eyes, and pressed his thumb down on the screen.

"I can't look," he said.

Zed took the phone from him. "Damn, dude," he said. "I am really sorry."

Jay exhaled slowly and then opened his eyes.

"Seriously," Zed went on. "These scores mean you only have about three weeks to scrape up some major, university-level tuition." He held the phone so that they could all see the screen. "You're done with high school, Jaybird. You barely squeaked by, but a squeak still gets you out the door."

When they erupted in another happy noise that had the potential to become another pile of people, I ran over to Will.

Jay's got news.

"Jay?" he called out. "What happened?"

Jay handed the phone to Aisha, and let her read the screen.

"What's this? Test scores?" She peered at them closely. "Liberal arts and English, history, and math?"

He grinned and shrugged at the same time.

"I need some context, Jay."

Zed shouted from across the lawn, "Exit exam results!"

Her eyes went wide. "You took the exit exam? Jay!" She looked at Aubrey. "He took the exit exam!"

"And I passed!"

The phone went from person to person, and I wasn't sure Jay was ever getting it back.

"Um, there's more," he said. He shoved his hands into his pockets and gave another slight shrug. "Before I took the tests,

Grundy got me a provisional acceptance into UCSF. Since I passed, I can take up to three classes this term. I mean, if you allow me to. I'm kinda done with high school, Mom." His voice cracked. "I don't want to go back."

She cupped his chin with her hand. "I know, sweetheart. You don't have to."

"And I know it's short notice and the tuition—"

"Your dad and I planned for school, Jay. Don't worry about it."

He half-turned and gave Zed two thumbs up. After that, Oz and Drew offered to take Jay and Zed for ice cream—"yeah, morons, we know you're not ten anymore, but it's not like we can go to a bar"—and left the old people to finish the party on the roof.

Two hours later it was just Will and Aisha. They left the lights on and turned the music down, and danced in two-inch increments with their arms wrapped a little too tightly around each other. I lounged on the grass, wiggling on my back because that's what grass is for.

You're really getting married?

"I assumed you would be in favor of it."

I am. She's good for us. And once you do, we should spend some time apart.

"Why would we do that?"

Because I need to know that she's your new anchor. I need to know that if something happens to me, you'll be okay.

"Wick, even if she is, I won't be okay if something happens to you. None of us will."

You'll be sad, and everyone else will be all right eventually. I need to know.

He gave Aisha a quick kiss, and then picked me up. He held me close and then kissed the top of my head. "I love you, Wick. Just know that."

"What's he worried about?" Aisha asked.

"He wants to resign as my anchor."

She reached over to pet me and said I wasn't allowed to do that. "You need to stick around, Mister Wick. He'll need you when I'm gone."

"No, don't."

"Come on. We both know the odds. And I'm fine with that, as long as I have you right up to the end. I want my last words to be for you, even if I can only whisper 'Bilbo' to you."

Hey. Hey. Hey. Remember when she said she was dropping her married name? Maybe because back then she was thinking about taking yours.

"She doesn't have to take my name at all, Wick."

"Oh, I'm taking your name, mister."

He leaned back and pretended to consider it. "All right, but you don't really look like a William."

Maybe if she lets that mustache grow.

He laughed but refused to repeat it.

Will. It's Oz's birthday.

"I'm aware of that. I hope she didn't mind the mid-party proposal."

She liked that. But it's almost midnight. You're supposed to meet old Oz and old Drew at midnight.

They scrambled to get to the elevator, and all the way down Will bounced on his toes, wishing they'd taken the stairs, even though the elevator was still faster. He kept me tucked under an arm so that I wouldn't bounce too much as they ran across the street and up the stairs. He skittered to a stop near the portal, where old Oz and Drew waited.

Along with young Oz and Drew.

Before he could say anything, Oz, our Oz, reminded him that he'd done exactly the same thing before. He'd gone back to talk to his younger self more than once.

"To make sure the timeline was preserved," he argued.

"And you don't have ownership rights to that," she said. "They had things to tell us. Stuff I needed to hear."

Old Oz agreed. "It occurred to me, when you visited. This Oz and this Drew will have a different life than we've had. So why not meet? I hoped that like we did, on her nineteenth birthday they would end up on Union Square, fretting about their wedding."

Will moved closer. "To what end?"

"To let them see with their own eyes," she said. "I wanted them to know that they'll still be together in thirty years. The love isn't going to fade away, and it's not a mistake."

"There were doubts?"

Old Drew, "We were *so* young…of course we had doubts."

"Man, I am so tempted to reach out and kinda poke you with one finger," Drew said to his older self.

Old Drew laughed. "But what if we explode?"

Will sighed. "I touched myself plenty, Drew."

"Um, yeah," Drew said with a forced grimace. "I don't want to hear about your solo sex life."

He doesn't have to do that anymore. But he does anyway.

"Dammit, Wick," Will sputtered.

Drew laughed. "It's a guy thing, I think."

Old Drew twitched. "You understand him?"

"It's a lucky remnant from a time traveling mistake," Drew said. "Which kinda makes me feel not bad at all about making the mistake. Wick is one of my favorite people."

And to think I used to smell wet dog every time I was around you.

Will held up a hand to stop them. "Look, ground rules. No questions about what you studied, what your work became, nothing about kids." To old Drew he said, "Volunteer nothing. Your lives may be on different trajectories, but as much of it as possible needs to be preserved."

"Then wouldn't it help to know?" Oz asked. "It usually helps to have some kind of navigation program when you're headed somewhere unknown."

Old Oz shook her head. "You'd think so, but he's usually right, isn't he?"

Oz looked at Will. "Don't rob us of the joy of greeting the firsts for the actual first time, right?"

"Indeed," he said. "And to that end, allow me to switch gears from friend to uncle, and tell you it's time to go home and go to bed. Mistakes won't be made if you're not here to ask the wrong questions."

Old Oz asked them to wait a moment. There was a purpose to this visit, other than to show them that they would still be together. She looked specifically at Oz. "A request. Really, I'm begging you. Don't end the monarchy. If I could change only one thing that I did in the name of Pacifica, that would be it. It was a mistake."

"How?" Oz wanted to know. "You brought back democracy. A government by and for the people."

"And with it," old Oz said, "we brought back all the partisan infighting. Government rapidly became the playground of rich old men making laws to benefit themselves and their equally rich friends, all while stripping rights from the middle class and the poor. I can see the class system bearing down on us again, as strong as ever, and those who aren't at the top are going to suffer the most. We're rapidly heading into an oligarchy, and I no longer have the power to stop it. In a few short years, I've watched the Emperor's Paradigm crumble, the protections my father and grandfather put in place are eroding, and there's nothing I can do. The number of homeless is skyrocketing, and the medical safety net is gone. But if you hold onto the throne? Unite the country, but not at its own expense. No one will be more kind to the people than you and Drew."

Oz had no idea how to keep a united Pacifica yet still give people more of a voice. "We rule as we reign," she said. "There's got to be a better way."

"And the United States," Drew said.

Old Oz nodded. "Unite as much of the old U.S. as you can. Bring Florida back into the fold. As Red ages, he'll look to Pacifica for help, and he'll be more willing to become part of it. There was so little left of it after the war—you have all of Florida still. Bring them back, Red will accept the help. Invite New England, everyone except for Texas, which will never again yield its Republic. You can bring back the United States without bringing back a system that once fell apart just short of civil war."

"Every ideal we had as kids," old Drew said with a sigh. "The intentions were good, but we didn't pay enough attention to history. She's right. The two of you will be far more compassionate than the oligarchs, and you'll protect the people."

Drew asked about their heir. "No specifics, but how do we assure he or she will continue our work?"

"Choose wisely," old Oz said, smiling.

Will pointed toward home. "Now, go home and go to bed."

Oz took Drew's hand. "You heard the man. Take me to bed."

"That's not what I said."

As they walked away, Drew called out, "Too late, old man. You've condemned her to a night of disappointment. Your fault."

Oz punched his arm. "Stop it."

Old Oz turned to old Drew. "We never stopped that, did we?"

"Probably because I never got any better."

She poked at him, then turned to Will and Aisha and apologized. "He also never grew up."

"How long has it been for you since we saw you?"

"A few days," she replied. "Just long enough to confer with Finn. He didn't think there would be any problems, but…"

"But you couldn't resist picking a time when you knew you would see yourselves. Were you really that uncertain?"

"Most of the time, no," Drew said. "But late at night, when our guard came down and we were honest? We were *so* young, Emperor. We wanted to be together more than anything, but there was that fear that we were rushing into it when there was no reason to. We wanted them to see that their fears are unfounded because those two have been chewing on whether or not they should wait."

"And they shouldn't," Oz said.

"Why would they?" Aisha asked. "They're young, but still."

"The Emperor is clear that the timeline has changed. But if they wait—"

"Eli," Will said. "If they vary from the timeline too much, there won't be an Eli."

"No Eli, no Finn," Drew said. "No Finn, no Emperor."

It didn't matter, Will told them. He led them over to the bakery at the Square's corner, and they sat at the closest table while he explained the protections in place. He reminded Drew of the Old Mint, and told him he wasn't sure how—and to not tell him—but he was aware that Finn wasn't the one who invented the time lock. It would get done, and all the information contained inside would be protected.

"Regardless of how many children they have, or when, every scrap of data is there and available. Backups are being made. If they don't have Eli or he never leaves his home to move forward, it won't matter. We'll make sure of it."

"No Eli," Drew sighed. "I can't imagine."

"They'll have him," Oz said. "Time wouldn't be that cruel."

Time's a bitch, though. It wants Will dead.

"Time just wants me to go back where I came from, Wick. If it really wanted me dead, I wouldn't have survived this long."

"Maybe this is your When now." Oz smiled at Aisha. "You beat it at its own game. So now you get the reward. They told us you proposed to him. I wish we could have seen that."

"Tell your parents," Will said. "Make them happy."

"Ah, tell them yourself," she said. "Dad is already talking about his birthday, hoping you'll be there. He has a bottle of eighty-year-old scotch and won't open it without you."

"I'll be there."

"Four o'clock, on the roof." She and Drew got up, and we headed for the center of the Square. "He'd hate me for telling you this, but every year he sits by your memorial with two glasses, and toasts you. He drinks his, repeats your last words, then drinks yours."

That gave Will pause. "My last words. What were they?"

Drew smiled warmly. "Aubrey was reading to you, and you closed your eyes, listening. We hoped you'd actually fallen asleep, but then your eyes flew open and you spurted out 'What the hell, Wick.' Another breath, your eyes closed, and you were gone."

Will laughed and then asked if that was recorded as a matter of record.

"Emperor," Oz said, "not only was it recorded, but it's also engraved on the plaque in your memorial display."

Drew said, "I always hoped it was because you were seeing him, and he was telling you something inappropriate. Or asking you if you'd brought any cheese with you because he missed his cheese."

They stepped through the portal, and Aisha reached for me. "Your last thoughts were of him."

"And I was annoyed."

I was probably sitting in the afterlife waiting for you, leg hiked up, licking myself.

"You are a bendy one, Mister Wick," Will said.

Aisha reached for his hand, tugging him in the direction of the building. "Speaking of bendy."

He didn't move but instead tugged her back toward him. "You know, today this incredibly wonderful woman asked me to marry her, and she said it didn't have to be soon. But I keep thinking, why not? Why wait?"

"It depends on the kind of wedding you want, Emperor. Are there protocols for the royal family?"

"Not for me. The people will want to see Oz and Drew's wedding, but I don't think they're entitled to ours. And I'm more interested in the wedding that *you* want. Do you want to top the drunk drag queen and have a formal ceremony?"

"There's no topping a drunk drag queen," she said lightly. "That was weird and fun, but something you only do once. I want something very small and informal. Family only."

"If you truly don't want the ceremony, we could ask the King for a decree."

Aisha wasn't sure what that meant.

"We stand before the King and ask for his formal declaration of our union. Our family can be there. It requires someone stand with you, and someone stand with me, as official witnesses. He signs the paperwork, and it's done. There are varying degrees of formality depending on what the couple wants, but it's essentially marriage by royal command. And it's irrevocable. If we wed by decree, you're stuck with me. Jax has never reversed a marital decree."

"I'm not letting you wiggle loose no matter what. Is the Queen allowed to stand as a witness?"

Will nodded. "I would ask Drew to stand with me."

Can I be there? I'm part of the package. She's really marrying us, not just you.

"Indeed, Wick. I expect you to be right next to me." To Aisha, "Typically, when people ask this of Jax, it's only the couple and their witnesses, but when their families join in, he'll add requests to his decree."

She wanted to know what he would add.

"I will never try to take James' place as Jay's father, and I will never place the two of you in the position you were in with George. But I would like Jay to be part of the decree, for Jax to acknowledge, as King, that I'm taking your son as my own, as if he were my firstborn, with all the rights and inheritances that come with that."

Surprised, she asked, "You want to name him as your heir?"

He nodded. "If—and I understand it's a huge if—we have a child together, they'll share equally in my estate. But if we don't, I want no questions left to public inquiry. A decree by the King will do that. He will legally be my firstborn, and if I outlive him, his children become my heirs."

She slipped her arms around him and said she knew he would likely outlive Jay. "But it will mean everything to him to know you truly do want him in your life."

"Indeed, I do. But I also want him to know I have no intention of pushing James out of the picture or belittling their relationship. If I have to become close friends with James, I will. Anything to make Jay feel loved and wanted all the way around."

"God, I love you."

Will kissed her, then, "A decree by the King? We could literally do it tomorrow if everyone has time."

With a slip of a laugh, she suggested they give people some notice. Jay especially.

"How well will he accept doing this soon? Because it means moving here, at least until I retire."

She was sure he wouldn't mind living downstairs from his best friend. James wouldn't be happy but she refused to live her life around him anymore. "But I think we need a couple of weeks. I want informal, but I still want it to feel like a celebration."

"Do you mind if I pick the location?"

Her hands went to his face, and she sighed before she kissed him again. "I will follow you anywhere, Bilbo Blackshear. If you want to get married by the King while we all stand ankle deep in the water at Crissy Field, I'll be there."

I really hoped he wouldn't choose that.

"All right, then it will be casual-formal. Afterward, we can spend some time with family, and then go off and celebrate, just the two of us."

She tickled me under my chin and said it would be the three of us.

No. Just the two of you. You need that.

"You're a good man, Wick."

Take her to twenty-one-thirty, something like that. Spend a couple of weeks. Let her be your anchor.

Will repeated what I said. "If I need Wick, it's a quick trip back."

"And the future is off the table? No showing me more of the San Francisco of your youth?"

"If that's what you'd like to do, I'd be willing. There are a few things I would like you to see. It doesn't feel as foreboding as it once did."

"Tomorrow morning, talk to Jax. I'll talk to Jay."

"I'll also speak with security again. I've already started the process, but it's time for your detail to be assigned."

"A guard? For what?"

"You're taking Pacifica's most mysterious bachelor off the market. People might be upset with you."

Aisha sighed. "Aubrey was right. You think you're funny."

21

Will woke up at six in the morning, alone. It took him a minute or two to orient himself, and he rolled over to look at the empty side of the bed before it clicked in his brain: he'd slept, alone. Aisha had papers to grade and a test to create, and he had early appointments, so they decided to be all grown up and spend the night apart.

The bigger surprise to him, though, was the fact that he'd slept well. He went to bed at midnight and was asleep within minutes, and barely moved all night.

A few more days. You won't wake up alone anymore.

Sleepily, he sat up and said, "I'm counting down, Wick."

He fed me before he showered, and when I was done eating I told him I would go nap on top of Drew; his appointments didn't interest me and scaring the crap out of Drew did.

Unlike Will, Drew wasn't sleeping alone. He was flat on his back with Oz's foot on his stomach, and he'd flung his arm over his eyes. On the nightstand, his phone was buzzing insistently. It quieted for a moment and then buzzed again, so I stretched from my spot on the mattress to see who it was.

Jay.

Jay wouldn't call Drew at stupid o'clock unless it was important. I head butted his chin, tapped his mouth with my paw, and when that didn't work, I leaped up and landed on his junk.

That woke him up. His massive *oof* woke Oz, too.

Jay is trying to call you. Answer him.

He picked up when the phone buzzed again; before he could grunt, "What?" Jay started talking and Drew couldn't get a word in.

"I know I promised and this is really stupid but George called me last night and asked me to meet him for coffee at seven-thirty and I said yes and I wasn't going to tell anyone but now I'm worried because this will piss off my parents and I feel super crappy about it, and is there any chance you can meet me there, just in case?"

No lectures; Drew grunted that they would be there by seven-fifteen and then nudged Oz. "Take me to breakfast, gorgeous. The coffee shop has muffins and scones, right?"

"Are we drinking coffee now?"

"Tea," he said, sliding out of bed. "An homage to the Queen. Of England. Like, five hundred years ago."

"That makes no sense."

"I've had four hours sleep. Cut me some slack."

Jay was already there when we arrived at ten after seven. He sat at an outside table, dressed in shorts and a sweatshirt and was hugging himself against the cold, foggy morning air. Oz went inside and bought tea for her and Drew and hot chocolate for Jay, and they sat quietly for a few minutes.

"I know it's a bad idea," Jay said. "I know I should have told my mom. But I want to hear what he has to say, you know?"

They did know. Drew assured him that calling them was the right thing to do; Aisha might still get mad, but knowing they'd been there to keep an eye on things would smooth it over. She would appreciate that he'd thought to call for backup, even if it wasn't her.

We would be at the table next to them, no matter what George wanted or how big a tantrum he threw.

"You're not leaving here with him," Oz said firmly. "I want that clear. If he tries to convince you to go or I think you're twitching in that direction, I'll signal my guards."

Jay turned in his seat, looking for them.

"You won't find them," Drew said. "That's the point. But they know her signal."

A few minutes before George was supposed to show up, Jay moved to the adjacent table, where they could see him while keeping an eye on George, and Oz reminded him they didn't care if it annoyed George. "We're here for *you*. I don't give a flying fuck what he thinks. If he complains about us and wants us to leave, you're coming with us. All right?"

"I got it…Mom."

"Big sister," Oz said. "If I were anywhere near the level of either of our moms, I'd be dragging your ass home right now."

"Why aren't you?"

"Because," she sighed, "I get it. And I can take him. Seriously."

I stretched out on the table so that I could see both of them. George looked worse; his hair was nearly gone and what was left was thin and patchy, and the black circles under his eyes sagged. His face was thin, his eyes were watery, and his hands trembled.

He looks like he's a hundred years old now.

The first thing George said to Jay was that he looked good; he was surprised at how tall Jay was and how broad his shoulders had gotten. He brushed a finger over his peach fuzz and told him it suited him, and then commented that he needed a haircut. It was all perfectly normal, the things a teenager would endure after connecting with an uncle following a long absence.

There was nothing worrisome—small talk about what Jay's summer plans were, and about the video games they once played together, which eased into a project George was working on that had potential to be re-tooled into a game—and Drew relaxed, until George told Jay he was going to make sure that he'd be able to visit once he moved to Las Vegas. He promised to not give up; he'd fight until his parents agreed. He had a lawyer, and if they refused visitation, he would file with the court.

"You didn't want me moving to Vegas with you in the first place," Jay pointed out. "Why would you want me to visit? You told your boss I was a freak."

"I did," he admitted. "The whole thing is bizarre to me, Jay. I can't fathom why you couldn't wait a few more years to see the person you'd become before making such a big decision. By the time you hit your mid-twenties, you'd have probably realized you were fine and happy the way you were. You shouldn't have rushed."

"Sure. And when was it you decided you were gay? How many women did you fuck before you decided you liked the taste of dick more?"

Whoa. Dude. You have a point, but…dude.

"Come on. That's not something you decide, and you know it. It's just who you are."

Jay folded his arms and leaned back, waiting for George to hear himself.

He didn't. He was confused; Jay sighed and unfolded his arms, giving up. "You look like shit," he said. "Like, total shit. Are you even eating? I think you weigh less than I do now."

"Stress. Hard to eat or sleep when everything is crashing around you." His chair scraped along the cement as he got up. "I get it, I upset you. We can do this another time. But next time, don't bring your bodyguards."

Oz popped up. "Until Aisha says it's all right, Jay's going to have someone with him. Me, Drew, or Will."

"Mind your own fucking business, Princess. This is between Jay and me."

"Nope, it's not that at all. And it's too bad you can't see that."

"You really don't want to get in my way," George growled.

At that, Drew laughed and finally got up. "One, Oz could beat you into a bag of broken bones before you could even blink twice. Two, her guards would kill you before you got the hand on her that would give her the permission she needed to turn you into a rattling meat bag."

"Not likely," he said, though he didn't sound certain.

Oz reminded him that he'd already taken a swing at her father, and the guards all knew it. "You attack another member of the royal family, and they won't hesitate. They won't go easy on you. You know that. You were warned about that."

It was news to Jay; he'd been floating in orange goo at the time.

"You tried to hit Mr. B?" he sputtered. "For what?"

"I lost my cool," George stammered. "Jay, he ripped away my rights as your parent. No one asked me to consider *anything*. He signed the damn papers that took you away from me."

"So?"

"So? Doing that *ruined* you, Jay. Now you don't have a choice in who you become. You're so much less than you could have been." He jabbed a finger in Oz's direction. "This is really your Emperor's fault. He started all of this and treated me with unnecessary brutality. He damn near broke my arm."

"He protected his King," Oz said evenly. "And you're lucky he didn't break your neck."

"You're blaming Will?" Jay flinched at the idea, and he sounded small.

"That freak should either be locked up or killed for what he is, not roaming near normal people and certainly not fucking your mother. These people are not good for you. That man is just—"

"Shut up." Jay turned to Oz and Drew. "I won't do this again, I swear. I just want to go home."

"Yeah, no, you're going home with us." Drew picked me up and skirted around the table. "There's no way we're sending you to your Mom's right now, not alone."

"We're still talking here," George spat.

"No, we're not." Jay shoved his hands into his pocket and started to follow Oz. "We're done, George. Just…done."

= = =

"Don't think about your mother," Drew said to Will. "Think about Aisha. Her eyes, her smile, her—"

"That won't work on me, Andrew," Will said as they waited for Mrs. Kovlov's machines to warm up. "But by all means, keep trying."

"If I hit on the right combination of words, it'll work."

"No, you misunderstand. It might work, but I don't care. You can put any image you want into my head, and the end result won't bother me at all. The rest of you might be horrified, but I'll own it and won't apologize for it."

Will, Drew, Zed, and Jay were standing in a line, waiting in tight red shorts while Oz stood off to the side, amused. They were getting fit for wedding suits; Will could have worn his intimidation tux, but Aisha wanted the men in regular, navy blue suits, and what she wanted, he wanted. "I'll show up in a cocktail dress if that will make you happy," he told her. "Slit right up the thigh."

She enjoyed the idea but didn't want him to look prettier in a dress than she did.

"What the hell are you two talking about?" Zed asked.

"Just tormenting Will," Drew said. "He refuses to take the bait."

"Remind Drew what he was doing in here almost a year ago," Oz said. She stepped up behind him and slipped her arms around his waist. "First dressing room on the right. Poor Wick screaming at us."

"Please don't," he said.

Her fingers flicked the waistband of his shorts. "Are you sure? I can help you change clothes after you're done here. Finish what Will interrupted last time."

"Jesus, Oz."

"How's that medicine taste, Andrew?" Will chuckled.

"Really, what the hell are you talking about?" Zed asked.

"Boners," Jay said. "Who cares?"

"We're not that close, Jaybird. I really don't want to see it."

Drew tried to peel Oz's hands off him. "Then someone needs to get her out of here before this becomes a memorable occasion that we'd all like to forget."

Mrs. Kovlov crooked her finger; she didn't care which one, but someone was getting into the giant glass jar to get measured. Jay shrugged and stepped forward, then placed his feet where she told him, his arms held out from his sides.

"All right, now I feel inadequate," Zed mumbled. "How freaking long did they leave him in that tank, and can I go for a dunk?"

"Why are you checking him out?" Drew asked. "That's kind of disturbing."

"Yeah, there's no hiding in these shorts. I don't *have* to check him out. This was a hell of a lot easier when I was ten, and Dad was the only one with me."

Will went next, and while he stood in the jar, Jay asked about his tattoos. "Those are kind of badass," he said. "What's the big one?"

His entire chest and stomach were taken up by a tattoo of Icarus and Daedalus, a story Jo told him frequently when he was a little boy. He started the process of getting it when he was twenty and finished when he was twenty-five, but no one had seen it until the last time they'd been at the Kovlov's being fitted for suits. He also had portraits of Finn and Jo on his ribs on one side—the real reason he'd kept his ink hidden—and on his other side he had two crowns and two baby footprints, shaped to form a heart.

He's getting the tattoos removed. Except for the crowns and feet.

"I know, Wick. This afternoon, even." Drew said.

Don't tell Aisha. It's a surprise. She doesn't like tattoos very much. And Jo won't like it if she sees her face on him.

"All right, I won't tell anyone." To the others, he said, "Don't ask, I can't repeat it."

"Do you ever get used to that?" Jay asked Zed.

"Them talking to Wick? Yeah, it took a while. Just roll with the punches. This is not a normal family, and you're about to be part of it."

He didn't seem to mind. He'd lived a different kind of family life long enough that they seemed like a nice, quiet bunch. "All those years of walking on eggshells with George? I'll take your weird-ass time traveling freak show over that anytime."

I tapped at his bare leg with my paw.

We like you. I'm glad we get to keep you.

He squatted so that he could give me head rubs when Drew told him what I'd said. "Me, too, Wick. I'm even more glad that my mom is happy. Seriously," he said as he stood back up, "you guys have no idea."

"How's your dad taking it?" Zed asked. "They're pretty close still, it might sting."

"You should have seen him when I told him that Mom proposed to Will. He literally clapped his fingers together and bounced on his toes and squealed. It was the gayest thing I've ever seen him do. For real, I don't think I've ever been so happy to see him play out a stereotype."

"Huh." Zed half shrugged. "I thought he would be a little upset. I always had the feeling that if he could, he'd try to get her back."

"Yeah, no, they love each other, but not like that."

"I wonder if she'd ever told him about Will," Oz said.

"No clue. All I know is he's super happy for her. He's not thrilled with me moving, but it's close enough that we can see each other when we want and it's not going to screw up their custody schedule."

"Get your license, and you can borrow my bike sometimes," Zed offered.

Will stepped out of the jar. Drew was up next, and he pleaded with Oz to not grab her own boobs or make kissy faces at him while he was up there.

"Close your eyes," Will said. "Why are we lending out Zed's bike?"

"So Jay can ride it to see his dad."

"It's a mile," Will said. "You can walk that, you know."

"It's incentive to make him get his license," Zed said. "He might want a bike of his own sooner or later. School and all, you know."

Jay mused that Zed could just give him a ride. Leaving the same house, heading for the same place, why not?

"We might not have the same schedule, and I have to work after classes sometimes. Get a license."

"Indeed," Will agreed. "Get your license, Jay. If needed, you can use my car."

You're getting him a bike, aren't you?

He didn't answer me. Instead, he asked Oz to keep an eye on me and went to change his clothes. Jay watched as the changing room door closed, and then turned to Oz.

"I need an idea of something to get him as a wedding gift. The only thing I know he likes is books, but those are super expensive."

I have an idea. Get him another guitar. Aisha wants him to play and sing for her.

Zed looked down at me. "Yeah, you need to wait for Drew. You either know, or you want food. Or both."

Well, both.

"Tell Drew when Will isn't around. But don't tell Will, all right? Bump my leg if you get it."

That's kind of beneath me, but all right.

I head-bumped his leg.

Will came out of the dressing room as Zed went into the jar. "I need your help this afternoon if you have time. Considerable time."

Drew said yes without hesitating, Oz wanted to know what for.

"Both spare rooms in my apartment need to be cleared out. All the books boxed for storage, and the bed donated to the shelter. I'll pay you in pizza and soft drinks."

Drew was horrified. "You're getting rid of your books? Why?"

"I'm only storing them until the new apartment is ready," he said. "Once the rooms are cleared and cleaned, Jay can pick one, and the other will become an office. Aisha and I both need work space."

"I want the room that's not even close to yours," Jay said. "Nothing personal."

"You don't think they'll be *loud*, do you?" Oz asked, laughing.

"Are they loud, Wick?" Drew asked.

They talk to God a lot. She keeps asking God to make him lose weight.

"Stop it, Wick." Will scooped me up, kissed the top of my head, and handed me to Oz. "You will no' ask him anythin' else about that. Take him home when your clothes are done, and I'll be there in about four hours. There are already empty boxes stacked in the living room."

Drew nodded and said he would take Will's suit home, too.

"He got all Scottish," Oz snorted. "What did Wick say?"

"Apparently, Aisha wants God to make Will lose weight," Drew said.

"What the hell? From where?"

Drew bent over to look me in the eye. "But that's not what you meant, is it? It was more like 'Oh, god, you're big.'"

Huge. She said huge. But you're not supposed to ask me.

"Heh. Go, Will," Drew chuckled.

Jay screwed up his face. "Come on. He's doing my *mom*. I don't need to know that about him."

"I wonder what she considers huge," Oz said.

"Oh my god!" Jay took a step back. "Seriously."

"I wonder what most people consider big," Drew said. "I'd like to know how I stack up."

Oz stretched up her toes to kiss him, even though he wasn't that much taller. "I have no complaints."

"Fuck it, geez, just look it up online or something." Jay crossed his arms like he was holding the disgust in.

"Ah, he doesn't know about the controls on the Internet at home," Oz said. "Fair warning, don't find out the way we did. You can't look up anything that resembles porn. Search for information of the sexual kind, and alarms go off and guards track my dad down, and then you wind up standing in the living room explaining why you're trying to find videos on oral sex."

"Oh my god, no."

Drew laughed and nodded. "Yeah, don't make that mistake. I think you can look for educational things, just not…porn."

"Don't panic. You can find pictures of naked women," Oz said. "Or men, whatever floats your boat. Just not if they're doing anything."

"I'm not gay. It's not genetic."

"And just because your dad is doesn't mean you're not. Who you're attracted to isn't something I ever gave any thought to. Wasn't going to presume."

Jay sighed. "Yeah, that came out snottier than I meant. It's just that I think my mom thought I was gay for a long time, but I'm not."

"Not what?" Zed asked, coming out of the jar.

"Gay," Jay said.

Zed put his hands on his hips and pouted. "Well, now I can't ask you to the prom, and I was going to. I had *plans*, Jaybird."

"You can still ask," Jay said. "I mean, I'd go with you, but I'm not having sex with you at the end of the night. Not even a little bit."

"Your loss. Besides, I think we lose access to the prom by leaving school now. I'll have to find another way to get Sophia under the gym bleachers."

She has an apartment, dude. Class it up some.

They headed for the dressing room, and I waited with Oz. While we stood there, Mr. Kovlov wandered over to pet me and handed Oz a small package.

"The Emperor asked for this," he said. "A new collar for Mister Wick to wear to his wedding." He rubbed my head and added, "You'll be handsome in purple. Make sure someone takes a picture of you so I can put it on the wall here."

Finally, a custom collar.

It was about time.

I was going to look fabulous.

"This room stinks," Jay said under his breath. "What the hell?"

Drew ran a cloth over the spines on a row of books, blowing the dust away from his face as it floated toward him. "I'm not sure why, but he keeps it closed off most of the time. It's just stale air and dust."

Dust is dead people skin flakes.

Maybe there's a body behind one of the bookcases.

Zed taped boxes together while Drew and Jay filled them. More than once Drew reminded them to be careful, because these were practically the only things Will cared about that weren't people.

"Has he read them all?" Jay asked. "There are a ton of them."

"Probably more than once," Drew said. "And seriously, be careful. They're ridiculously expensive. He probably won't say anything if a cover gets bent or torn, but it will matter to him."

There were bookcases on every wall, and several in the middle of the room, lined up so that he could store books on each side and get between them when he wanted to look for something specific. Some of the books were gifts, and his favorites were thin volumes of poetry and short stories that Oz and Zed had given him for no reason other than they wanted to surprise him.

Drew was the one who appreciated Will's library the most. His computer tablet was loaded with books that he'd already read, and some of the hardest decisions he had to make were about which book to read next or read again. He loved classic science fiction, so when he realized the shelf he was cleaning was an entire row of old sci-fi, he let out a surprised squeak.

"Heinlein," he murmured.

Dude, are your hands shaking?

"Probably. I've never seen Heinlein in print, Wick. It's probably, like, the one millionth print run, but still."

Zed stuck his head out the door and yelled. "Will! Drew's about to have inappropriate relations with one of your books!"

He came into the room and took the book from Drew. "Ah, that's right. He's your hero." He handed it back and said, "Here. It's yours."

Drew's eyes went wide. "I can't," he squeaked. "This is, like, way too valuable."

"Take care of it, then." He nodded toward one of the bookcases. "In fact, if you want to haul a couple of these into your apartment, you could borrow as many books as will fill them. Someone might as well enjoy them instead of keeping them in storage. But that one is yours to keep."

He's gonna hyperventilate.

I don't think he was that excited about bouncy things.

"I expected sex sooner or later," he said, staring at the book. "Never this."

Will told Zed to help Drew move some of the bookcases, and went back to the other bedroom where Oz was helping him box up odds and ends. Most of it was going to the shelter—the bed, the dresser, and all the linens—but he had a few personal things to keep. He wanted to clear it all out so that Jay could decorate it the way he wanted, and he didn't think Jay wanted pictures of old San Francisco on the walls.

"You may hate me," he told Oz. "Drew is taking a few of the bookcases and books to store in his apartment for me."

"He had an orgasm when you told him, didn't he?"

"Possibly," Will said, amused. "But remind me to lay some ground rules for handling them. Clothing must be worn at all times, and no bodily fluids are allowed anywhere near them."

"I'll be the book police," she said. "And thank you. He's always wanted a printed book. Storing yours is just as good."

"I gave him one." He wasn't ready when she jumped at him with an attack hug and stumbled back a couple of steps. "It's just a book."

"Bullshit. You know that ancient Steinbeck you've been known to visit now and then at *Ex Libris* on Market?"

"My ultimate temptation? Yes. But that's more than three years' salary, Oz. I will remain tempted."

"Any single book you could give him means that much to him. He'll be terrified to read it, but he'll treasure it, always."

He told her to remind him about that near Drew's birthday, and then pointed her toward the box she'd been filling. The room was nearly empty, boxes lining the hall, waiting for the van from the shelter to get it all; the boxes going into storage were stacked in the living room.

"Are you really ready for this?" Oz asked. "You've lived alone for a long time."

"I'll adjust. I would rather endure the frustrations of suddenly being accountable to two people than wait until I feel completely ready."

"King's decree," she said, as if it were a reminder of something potentially ominous.

"A leap of faith, for sure. I have no doubts, Oz. There's no part of me that worries this is the wrong thing or too soon. I trust in the decree because we *will* stay together."

She looked at the colors surrounding him. They didn't change, not even a flicker. "It's more than that," she said. "It's Jay, too. You won't just be living with a woman. You're becoming a parent."

"He may occasionally be a challenge, but I've had a glimpse of what's to come with you and Zed. I suspect he will bring more joy to my life than frustration."

"He's a good kid."

"You're all good kids. The sad part is that you're no longer kids. I'll miss that."

"Grandkids," she said. "Bonus dad gets to become bonus grandpa."

The idea made him smile, but he thought she needed to find another name for him. "I will take nothing from your parents, and the title belongs to them."

"Uncle Willie," she said. "There, I knew I'd get to use that one day."

"No."

"I suppose coming out of a toddler's mouth it would sound more like 'Unca Wiwie.' That works, too."

"No. It does not."

"This will be so much fun. Unca Wiwie. I can't wait."

"That works both ways. It wouldn't take much to convince a child to call you 'Australia.' Consider how *that* will sound coming from a three-year-old."

Bob. Teach him to call her Bob.

"You really want to name someone Bob, don't you, Wick?"

"What happened to the kitten he wanted?" she asked. "He can name the newby 'Bob.'"

"How about it?" Will asked. "You can still have a kitten if you want."

It wouldn't be Fluffy and I would always want it to be Fluffy. And I'm not sure I have time to raise one properly. I'm still raising you.

"Are you sure? You've always wanted a minion."

I have Drew. That's good enough for now.

22

"Right here," Will said. "On this spot. I have stood here many times, soaked in regret, and I want to change what it means to me."

"Sweetheart, this spot changed the minute I decided to go to your birthday party with Jay."

"Still. I picked this spot because it was where we fell apart. I want it to be where we come together. I want to stand here and soak in every micro-moment as you walk toward me, and hopefully write over the memory you have of watching me walk away."

That earned him a long kiss. When she let him up for air, he nodded toward the bakery and offered to buy her a drink and a donut. She offered to take him home and do things to him, but he stole another kiss and said the donut would have to do for now. He would even make himself eat one.

Can I have a bite? I don't remember what a donut tastes like. It's been years.

"It's been weeks, Wick."

That's kind of the same thing.

"A tiny bite." He reached for Aisha's hand and turned toward the corner bakery. "I think they have bacon for their breakfast sandwiches. I'll ask if they'll sell me a slice for you."

That would be awesome, thanks, but I'm still getting a bite of your donut.

I sat on his shoulder while they waited in line, turning every few seconds to get a new view. There weren't many people in line, and only one table outside was taken; across the Square there was a couple sitting together on the bench, but they were busy checking each other for tonsils and faulty taste buds, and staring at them felt like invading someone's privacy.

I turned again to see behind Will on the other side and spotted Jay heading for the royal house. He wasn't looking where he was going, exactly, and I didn't think he realized that George was not far behind, trailing him.

Jay's over there, near the lab. So is George.

Will glanced over his shoulder. He told Aisha he'd be right back—don't forget Wick's bacon—and slipped out of the line. He kept one hand on me and walked swiftly toward Jay, who was twenty feet from the elevator. When George caught up to Jay, he grabbed him by the wrist, which made Will break into a run while shouting things off the Queen's list.

"Let him go," Will seethed.

"This is none of your business, Emperor. I just want to see my kid."

He had declined even more in the three days since Jay met him at the coffee shop. He was a sickly sort of gaunt and he twitched uncontrollably, and with his free hand swatted at things only he could see.

He's about to collapse.

I strained to listen.

He's really bad off. His heart is going lub-lub with a long pause in between. His lungs are whistling and something in his gut is crying. Keep him talking long enough and he'll croak right here.

"George," Will said, trying to calm himself, "you're dying. You're dying, and you can't even see it. You need to go home."

"I will. And I'm taking Jay with me."

"You know what I mean."

Through gnashed teeth, George growled, "He's coming home with me."

Jay remained calm. He didn't try to pull away, even though his hand was turning red from the pressure on his wrist. He gave George a pitied look, and sighed, but didn't fight against the hold George had on him.

"Just for a few days, Jay," George pleaded. "Give me a chance."

"Fucking let go and maybe we can talk."

"If I let go, he'll kill me. I promise, you'll be fine, just come with me."

He's not gonna let go, not without some incentive.

Will stuck his fist in the air and raised his pinkie finger. "That will never happen. Just let him go, and I'll take you home. You'll start to feel better within minutes."

"Home," George spat. "What the hell is there at *home?* No family, no job, no place to live, nothing. This is my goddamned home, Emperor."

"It can't be, not anymore. You can feel it, you know what will happen if you don't let me take you home now."

"We can have more than one anchor, Emperor. I had one before James, I'll find another. Just get out of our way. I won't hurt him." His voice withered a bit, and he started to whine. "I wouldn't. He's my kid. Mine, not yours. Just let me take him home."

"I'm not your son, George," Jay said. "I was never your daughter, either."

"I don't care about that anymore. I love you," he hissed.

Jay let out another tired sigh. "Yeah, I get that. I believe you. But I'm not yours and I never was. Man, I care about you, but I don't like you and there's no way in hell I'm going anywhere with you. Not home, not Vegas. And unless you change a fucking hell of a lot, I'm not visiting."

"I have the right—" He stumbled back half a step, but didn't let go of Jay's wrist.

"Look around," Will said.

Without moving, George glanced to his left and his right. Three guards had quietly stepped out of the shadows and had weapons trained on him. Will and George were both so focused on the guards and each other that neither heard Aisha's soft footsteps as she circled to George's back, and the guards weren't giving her away.

I decided not to, either.

"I won't allow you to leave with him," Will went on.

"You will." George pulled a small handgun from the waistband of his pants, and we were surrounded by the click of weapons being readied. Will held a hand up to stop them from firing; George's gun was aimed at him, not Jay, and as he took a few steps closer, he said evenly, "This won't work. Don't be stupid. They will *kill* you."

"Then I'm taking you with me."

"As long as you don't harm him, that's a chance I'm willing to take. Just let him go, George. Don't risk hurting Jay."

Will's eyes were on the gun. It was old, centuries old, a small caliber handgun that fired bullets and not lasers. If George pulled the trigger, given its condition and the likely age of its ammunition, it might explode in his hand. If it fired, the tremors in his hand guaranteed he wouldn't hit his intended target.

He thought the most likely thing that would happen was nothing. If George pulled the trigger, he would hear a frustrating click, and then what? He was mentally loopy and physically broken, making him unpredictable.

Will could now see Aisha sneaking up behind George, but with the gun on him and Jay's wrist still in a death grip, there was nothing he could easily do. If he took another step, George might shoot. If he faltered, he might hit Jay. Will mentally went through his options, praying that George didn't hear Aisha behind him, but there was nothing he could do.

He couldn't rush George.

He couldn't warn Aisha off.

He couldn't grab Jay.

He couldn't give the signal for the guards to fire because he refused to risk the one percent chance that Jay might get hit.

We were less than two feet from him, and Aisha was less than an arm's length away. Someone was going to get hurt, and I wanted it to be George.

I leaped from Will's shoulder onto George's face, my claws and teeth bared. I felt my back claws sink in first, dragging down his cheeks, and then felt his warm breath on my belly as I grabbed the top of his head and pulled it toward my mouth.

Just as I bit down, I heard him scream and waited for him to begin thrashing back and forth as he tried to dislodge my claws from his head, but I didn't expect the sudden jolt of being yanked forward, nor the quick flash of pink mist.

I dug in harder and held on. We were falling, but I didn't want to let go until I had to.

George landed on Aisha, and I landed on my feet, flicking chunks of his scalp out of my mouth with my tongue. She jumped up, no worse for the wear, and as I looked up to make sure she wasn't bleeding, I noticed that there was a curious woman in a jet pack lurking ten feet overhead. She called out to make sure we were all right, and when Aisha gave her a thumbs-up, she flew off.

George was still on his back, moaning. I heard more footsteps rushing toward us and ran to Aisha, just in case.

"Y'all fall through?" a young man asked. He peered at George and added, "Or, hell, did y'all blast your way through?"

"I jerked his ass through," she said.

"Ah." He whipped out from his pocket a device no bigger than an ice cube, squeezed it, and spoke to it. "Hey, Finn? We have hoppers. One of 'ems injured."

"Finn?" Aisha asked. "He's here?"

"He bounces around a lot. You know him? What's your name?"

"If we're in synch, he knows me. Aisha."

He squeezed the cube again. "One of 'em might know you. Her name is Aisha."

Thirty seconds later, he was running from the lab, calling her name. "Aisha! Where's Will?" He stopped when he noticed George. "Oh. You."

George slowly rolled over and struggled to his knees. "What the hell did you do?" he groaned.

"I took your sorry ass home," Aisha spat. "What the hell did you think you were doing? You pulled a gun on Will with Jay *right there?* Why? What the fuck is *wrong* with you?"

We don't have that kind of time. You'll miss your wedding if you stand here and listen to it all.

He tried to get to his feet, but couldn't. Blood was running down his face and his neck, and there was a flap of skin that had torn away just under his right eye. He could barely see and had no more strength to fight.

"I just wanted time with Jay," he said, just before he vomited. It was blood and bile and reeked of death.

"You probably got him here at the last minute," Finn told her. "Another hour or two, a day if he was lucky, and he would have been dead." He looked down at George. "You were warned. Don't expect any sympathy for this."

"You should have let me die," George moaned. "I have nothing left. Nothing here."

"I don't care what you don't have," she screamed. "You tried to take my son, and you pulled a gun near him! You could have killed him!"

He struggled to speak, his words strung out with long pauses. "Jay was safe. I would have only shot the Emperor. The world needs to be rid of that freak."

"That freak is my son," Finn growled.

I don't know if George heard that because as Finn spoke, Aisha kicked George right in the junk. He folded over and landed in his own vomit, out cold.

"I don't give a damn what happens to him," she said, pulling me close. "Let him lay there and…oh, goddammit. Can you make sure he gets some help, Finn?"

"I'll call for a medic. We'll see if we can't find someone in his family to take him in."

"Hey." She leaned over and kissed him on the cheek. "You better be home in time for the wedding. He can rot in hell if helping him means you'd miss it."

"She still doesn't get it, does she?" Finn asked me. "Take her home, Wick. Since Will isn't here already, I'm betting he's waiting for her on the other side."

"I'm honestly surprised he didn't barrel through after me to break George's neck," Aisha said. "I know he wants to."

He was right there on the other side of the portal, hands on his hips, head tilted, an amused smile on his face. The guards were behind him, weapons down, mouths gaped open in surprise. Jay was rubbing his wrist but grinned when he saw her.

"That's the second time you've saved my life, Enzo," Will said. "I think I need to keep you."

Oh look! You called her Enzo!

She reached for Jay's arm, making sure he was all right. "What did George say to you? Did he give you any idea what he was doing?"

"Said I was leaving with him, like it or not. He didn't want his kid anywhere near…"

"Me," Will finished for him.

"Yeah, I'm sorry. But there was something seriously wrong with him. It was like looking at a scared, rabid dog."

"Apt description," Will said. He turned as one of the guards approached him to ask how he should report the incident. "Write your report exactly as you witnessed. Publicly, however, this was a training exercise."

The guard gestured to the portal he couldn't see. "How do I explain that?"

"You don't. I suggest you write the report and then forget about it. I'll fill in any blanks with your superior."

As the guard picked George's gun off the ground and bagged it, Jay asked what had happened, and wanted to know why she jerked George through the portal.

"I took George home," Aisha told Jay. "And Finn was on the other side. He'll make sure George gets the help he needs."

You two have some explaining to do. He didn't know about George, did he?

"He should be feeling better in a few days," Will said. "He'll sleep for a week and should be back to normal in two to three. I'm guessing." He clucked me under the chin. "What about you, Wick. Were you injured?"

No. But I have a whole lot of George aftertaste in my mouth, and it's awful. Something dead and delicious would help get rid of it.

We went back to the bakery, and Will convinced the kid at the counter to give me two slices of bacon. While he broke them into Wick-sized pieces, they explained his connection to George, how they knew each other and why he was rapidly sliding downhill.

"When he and your father separated, the connection between them severed, and there was nothing to keep George here," Will explained. "Time knew it. He either needed a new anchor, which I suspect he was counting on you for, or he needed to go home. Otherwise, he was dead."

"Be clear," Aisha said, "I don't think I'd have mourned if he'd died here. But when I saw he was right in front of a portal and had no clue, I realized there was nothing he could do to stop me from pulling him into it. Wick jumping on him was a surprise."

"A fortunate surprise," Will said, sliding the plate with the bacon to me. "It's why George let go of Jay's arm and why he dropped the gun."

"It's also why George couldn't fight back," Aisha said. "Wick tore his face up. The best he could do was get to his knees, and I think he was waiting for you to pop through to finish the job."

"I didn't follow because I was certain you'd be back in a minute or two. If you hadn't, then I'd have followed and been there within seconds. But you're pretty badass—I didn't think you needed my help."

She kicked him in the nuts.

"You kicked George in the groin," he repeated. "And stopped there? No one would have faulted you for doing more."

"A lesson learned from Oz when she faced Tobias in the simulator. Grace before homicide. No matter how badly I wanted to hurt him before I killed him—and your father would have let me—I couldn't be that person."

"Like I said, badass."

"Remember that, Bilbo." She leaned over and kissed him. "I am seriously badass."

Jay snorted. "No shit. But why was Finn there? I thought he was here."

"He spends time in both Whens. He has work both here and there to keep him occupied." Will considered it for another moment. "This is family legacy, essentially. We exist in that space between Whens, Jay. The Blackshears' lives are tangled up in both here and there, and often straddle timelines. I assume that eventually, you'll also learn to navigate through time."

"What do we tell Dad?" Jay asked. "He won't believe that Mom jerked George's ass into the future. And he's not going to buy it that George is *from* the future. We can't tell him any of that, I know it."

Will wanted to speak to the King first, but his choice would be to have George declared dead, while privately explaining to James that he'd simply been relocated. He'd witnessed it when George tried to punch the King; it wasn't a stretch to think he'd done something else equally stupid. Relocating rather than executing him would seem to be a kindness.

"But why tell everyone else he's dead?"

"A while back," Aisha said, "when he was first offered the chance to go home, he said he wanted to be dead to the world so that your dad would be the beneficiary of his insurance and receive all his property and holdings. He knew their marriage was over, but he still wanted to take care of you both."

Jay was amazed that the same guy who wanted to kill Will and run off with him would even think of that.

"Really," Will said. "Out of all of us, you're the one who perhaps shouldn't be surprised. It was clear to me that you understood he was deeply flawed and needed forgiveness, and you knew that he loved you. What happened today was the act of someone very ill. Hold onto that forgiveness, because you truly are the better man."

23

"Wait. We *just* moved in, and you're sleeping across the hall?" Aisha tossed her things on the sofa. Her purse bounced and wound up on the floor, spilling her wallet and a disturbing number of breath mints onto my still-not-washed rug. "You're sleeping on Drew's couch?"

I wouldn't eat those now. I've seen what's gotten onto that rug.

"Air mattress on the floor," Will said.

Then again, you've had a lot of it in your mouth before, anyway. But still. Gross.

"Start explaining, Bilbo. I've had a bitch of a day with teenagers who want the term to be over today and not tomorrow, and I have forty tests to grade tonight."

Yeah, you're a spitter. I know you don't want to eat those now.

He kept the sofa between them. "I think we should sleep apart until the wedding. I'll spend the night at Drew's to save you from all of this." He waved his hands from his shoulders to his thighs. "Reduce the temptation."

"Seriously, Will?" She sighed hard. "I won't see you until the wedding?"

"I didn't mean that. I just meant that we're keeping our clothes on and our hands to ourselves."

"Is this because of Jay? Will, he knows we're sleeping together."

"I am aware."

"You realize we haven't had sex in about a week as it is? I was looking forward to spending the night with you."

He grinned and shrugged.

"You're mean, Bilbo. I love you, but you're mean."

= = =

"Why do we need a rehearsal dinner when we didn't rehearse anything?" Jay flopped his head on the sofa back and sighed dramatically. "Instead of getting all dressed up to go eat expensive food that no one can pronounce, why not just go get pizza? It's not like this is some weird royal thing requiring bowing and calling Mr. B 'your majesty.'"

Will felt the same way; the simple, short ceremony of a King's Decree had turned into a Real Wedding, and leading the way was a Queen with explosive excitement over her best friends tying the knot. What he and Aisha thought would be fifteen minutes followed by a small party with friends now had a complement of the royal guard, news cameras, a public announcement and closure of streets, and a rehearsal dinner.

He leaned over the back of the sofa, elbows sinking into the cushion. "This is important to your mother and to the Queen, so we'll do it without complaint. All right? It's a small thing to ask of us."

"Easy for you. Your suit fits."

Jay's wedding suit fit; the only other one he owned, however, was several inches too short in the legs and the jacket wouldn't go on at all.

"Is your suit your only complaint? That can be fixed with a phone call."

"I don't want to look like a dork, Will. If I could wear jeans, it would be fine. Then it would just be a family dinner with someone else doing the dishes at the end." He grabbed the suit pants from the end of the sofa and held them up; they didn't cover his ankles.

A minute later Will was on the phone with Mrs. Kovlov, who assured him she could take Jay's recent measurements and have a proper suit finished by the time he arrived to pick it up. "We have three hours until we have to leave for the restaurant," Will told him. "Fifteen minutes to walk there, fifteen back, and leave yourself time to shower. If it's all too cumbersome to carry, take a cab home, but be specific when you call for one. It has to be one permitted to drop off at the royal house."

"Wait, really? Just like that?"

"Just like that. She'll have two pairs of slacks, a jacket, and two dress shirts. Ask her to select a few ties to match. Please tell me you have dress shoes."

"Just the ones for the wedding. But my regular shoes are black, and you can't really tell."

"That'll do. Now go."

Jay darted out of the apartment at the same time Aisha came in. She paused at the door and watched him scamper down the stairs and outside. "Who lit a fire under him?"

"He picked now to inform me that he didn't have suitable clothing for tonight."

"He has a suit."

"I saw the suit. Do you realize how much he's grown in the last six weeks? He started here—" Will held his hand at his nipple line "—and he's now here." He moved his hand to the bridge of his nose. "He's on his way to meet with Mrs. Kovlov. She assured me that not only will she have clothing ready for him, but she'll make sure everything can be altered later to accommodate his growth."

She winced. "That sounds expensive."

"He needs semi-formal attire. Tonight is not the only time he'll need a suit that fits. By the end of the year, there will be at least two more occasions requiring he wear one."

"Oz's wedding. What else?"

"Likely a reception or two. Jax hosts at least one a year, depending on which dignitaries are visiting Pacifica."

"We're expected to go to those?"

"It would look odd if you didn't."

She looked almost panicked. "I didn't really think about that part of all this," she said.

"You're becoming a part of the royal family," he reminded her. "You won't be expected to take on official duties or make appearances unless you choose to, but events such as receptions that I am required to attend—"

"I get it." She crossed the room to give him a kiss. "I'll panic, but I'll do it."

"They're nothing to worry about. And Jay will have the other kids with him. They tend to turn receptions into parties. They're both entertainment and comic relief."

"Let's just get through this," she said, taking a deep breath. "How did this get so involved?"

"You asked Aubrey to help. That's all it takes."

= = =

The rehearsal dinner was held in a small restaurant on the Embarcadero. We rode in one of the official cars, and Will made me walk on a leash from the house to the car to minimize the amount of fur I decorated his suit with. There was a seat designated for me, covered with a soft, fuzzy blanket and a there was a thin plastic cage that clicked into place to keep me safe if the driver wrecked.

Jay came home with three complete suits and everything he needed to go with them. "Mr. Kovlov said anything you didn't want, I could bring back. And whichever suit you want me to keep, they left long hems in so you don't have to keep replacing it."

Will told him to hang them up; he was keeping them all.

Jay's choice for the rehearsal dinner was an off-white jacket with black slacks and a black shirt, which made Aisha weepy because he looked so grown up. I'm not sure he felt all that grown up because he kept tugging at his shirt collar in the car, even though it wasn't tight.

"You get used to it," Zed told him. "And you should have shaved. It's not even peach fuzz now, Jaybird. You have the freshman goatee starter kit going on."

His hand went to his chin. "I didn't even think—"

"You look fine," Will said. "This is just family tonight, and no one will care."

"Except Mom," he said, glancing sideways at her.

She waved it off; she wanted him clean-shaven for the wedding, but after that, if he wanted to let it grow, fine. She patted Will on the leg and said that applied to him, too. "I don't want stubble in any photos tomorrow, but what you do after that is up to you."

"There will be photographs tonight," he reminded her. "Up front warning. There will be photographers posted outside the restaurant, but they are not paparazzi. Pretend they're not there, and go inside."

"Where there will be another photographer, maybe two," Zed said. "The ones outside, Mom's doing?"

Will nodded. "Mostly to keep the actual paparazzi at bay."

"Poor bastards have probably been there all day to keep anyone else from being able to get too close." He leaned forward so that he could see out the windshield. "Why are there so many guards?"

Will slid over so that he could see, too. There were twice the number of royal guards he expected; they were three deep on each side of the entrance and formed lines behind the photographers. "As far as I know there have been no issues requiring more than the usual complement of guards," he said. "This is likely a scheduling hiccup."

They're too organized for that.

He pulled out his phone and called the King. "Jax?"

He'd noticed from the car behind us. Neither he nor Aubrey had requested additional protection and told them to stay in the car until he checked with General Myer.

Two minutes later the General opened the car door and stuck his head in. "Not a mistake, and nothing to worry about. We had more volunteers than needed and no reason to turn anyone down for the assignment."

Will didn't believe it but gestured for Zed and Jay to get out, reminding Jay to pretend that none of the photographers or guard were there. He freed me from the cage and handed me out to Zed, and the reached a hand down to help Aisha get out.

That's when all the cameras started going off.

"Close your eyes, Wick," he told me.

I narrowed them to slits instead. I didn't want to miss it if he tripped on a shoelace.

"All right," Zed said once we were inside. "I've never seen that many people taking pictures *or* that many guards in one spot."

"What the hell?" Drew sputtered when he and Oz came in. He blinked rapidly against the spots he was seeing and barely registered when Finn and Jo came out of the dining room.

"Glad we got here before the madness began," Finn said. "There are six guards in the dining room."

"And none of the other diners seem to care."

Oz peered around the corner. "That's because they're all guards."

Will had no idea, and when Jax and Aubrey were finally inside, he asked what the hell was going on.

"Myers swears there's no threat, so everyone can relax," Jax said. "This is a fluff assignment with free food and booze after we leave, so everyone wanted it."

Will still wasn't buying it, but he let it go. The host was waiting to show us to our table, and he really wanted to go to the bar and get a drink.

Our table was a giant round one in the middle of the room, with all the other tables pushed away from it. They were also round, but tiny, with two diners at each one, and the people were picking at the food in front of them. No one looked up in surprise to see the royal family. No one leaned to whisper to their dining partner.

There were eyes on the door, eyes on the windows, and eyes on the kitchen. The bar was in the far corner, and I recognized the bartender. He was the one who always worked when the family went to Kaluto's; I wasn't going to be surprised if the servers working were also from Kaluto's. Everyone there was already vetted and approved to be around food for the royal family.

Order off-menu and see if their heads explode.

"I don't think you'll have to stay in a high chair tonight," Will told me. "But stick close to Drew or to me, all right? I don't think anyone here will complain about your presence, but I don't want you getting lost."

If anything happens, you mean.

Can I sit on your shoulder for now?

He grabbed a cloth napkin from the table and draped it over his left shoulder—no fuzzing up the suit so early—and took me to the bar. Aisha was busy talking to Aubrey and Jo so she wasn't going to miss him, and Jax followed.

"Something's going on," Will said, his voice lowered. "Tell me you know what it is."

"I have to take Myers at his word. If there were a threat, he would tell me."

Maybe he's just hyper because of last year.

"If he's being overly cautious because of the events of last year, he should be forthright about it," Will said.

"The building is covered, Will. Relax and enjoy this. You're only doing it once."

"I will not relax," he said. "I will, however, fake it so that Aisha and Jay are not alarmed." He waved Drew over, and when he was near, he ordered a cinnamon whiskey on ice for him. "You don't have to drink it. Just stand here with it in hand. In fact, don't drink it. I want you alert."

"So something is definitely up?"

The pretend diners were taking small bites of their food, and a couple of them were even laughing.

"Not a clue. But I want your eyes on Oz and Zed for the most part. Peripherally, keep an eye on my parents, but don't make them think you're watching on purpose."

Pretend you're me, and everyone else is doing bouncy things. Look for what's not happening, not what is.

"Don't be hypervigilant," Jax said. "Seriously, Will, relax and enjoy the evening with Aisha. There are more guards than we need. Everything's fine." He asked the bartender to bring soft drinks and bottles of booze to the table and then prodded them to go back and join everyone else. "We can't stand here at the bar. It displeases the Queen. If the Queen is displeased, then my night will be self-serve."

Drew grimaced. "Really, Mr. B?"

"Like your bedroom wouldn't glow if we waved around a black light in it."

Everyone was clustered near the table, talking over each other. I looked around the room; half of the other customers were making an effort to look like they were there for dinner, and the other half were looking over each other's shoulders. A few minutes later, they swapped.

After the bartender brought the drinks and bottles to the table, Jax asked a passing server to bring menus to the table, and she nodded, but she headed into the kitchen and not to the host stand up front where they were stacked behind the podium. He tensed then, his jaw grinding together, and Will noticed it, too. But before he could ask Jax what set him off, the head guard and his minion stepped into the dining room. They stood on either side of the entryway and snapped to attention.

I heard the front door open, and with it came the clicking of cameras and a tidal wave of murmuring. I leaned toward Will and was going to tell him, but every fake diner stood up and snapped to attention, too, and the head guard took a deep breath. He was about to announce, and I didn't want to distract Will.

I wanted to see the look on his face.

"King Eli Blackshear," the guard barked. He then took another deep breath, which was more like a resigned sigh. "Retired, but not too tired."

I heard his booming laugh from around the corner. He stopped in the entryway; he was no longer the hunched over, grieving widower who left for Scotland when the pain became more than he could bear, and he no longer looked like he wanted the world to swallow him whole. He was grinning, and his eyes looked as happy as his mouth. He was thinner than when he'd left home and not nearly as pale, even though he had spent most of his time in Scotland. His hair had turned silver and there were no more flecks of black, his face had fine lines, and his eyes crinkled more than they had before.

He was happy.

"Well?" he said when it seemed they were all too stunned to speak. "Did you miss me? Daddy's home."

24

They're going to break him. He's old. Something's going to snap.

Jax was the first to get to the old king, and he hugged his father so hard that he lifted him a foot off the ground. That hug was going to make the news, as was the piling-on that followed. Jax hugged him, Aubrey hugged them both, and then Oz and Zed practically jumped at them, which made me listen closely for the sound of cracking bones and popping joints.

"How long has it been?" Aisha asked Will while Eli was still under siege. "Has he ever come back?"

"A few times, but never for long. It's been a good five years since the kids last saw him." He turned to Finn. "You did this, didn't you?"

"I may have suggested that your grandfather remind Eli that none of us are getting any younger. He would have come, too, but—"

"I know."

Will's grandmother, Jo's mother, was frail and couldn't travel. He usually went to see them every six months, but because of the war, it had been over a year. As part of their honeymoon, he planned on taking Aisha to meet them.

When Oz and Zed finally peeled off the top of the break-the-king-pile, Will was the first person Eli went to. "You finally got the girl," he said. "It's about damned time, Emperor."

Will stood stiffly, his hands clasped behind his back. "Yes, sir. It is."

"Oh, no, you don't." He looked at Finn. "He knows now. You told me he knows."

"Eh." Finn wobbled his hand back and forth, a "sort-of" gesture.

"William Jackson Blackshear, you are my second son and my distant grandson, and I refuse to accept your stodgy formality any longer. You call me by name, and you damn well relax. You also have only three seconds to hug me, or I'll turn around and go back to Glasgow and drag your Gran into bail-worthy shenanigans." He jabbed his pointy finger. "I know you've prepared for that."

Will wasn't stupid. He hugged the old king and started to relax. "Eli," he said as they parted, "This is Aisha, my—"

"I remember you," he said warmly, leaning in to kiss her cheek. "The one who got away and made him utterly useless for a good six months."

"And her son, Jay," Will said, nodding in his direction.

"We met on a video chat with Zed!" Eli boomed, reaching to shake Jay's hand. "You've grown a bit since then, son. Nice to meet you in person."

Jay was too flustered to say anything, but he was saved by the King and Queen. Jax wanted to know why he hadn't told them he was coming, and Aubrey chastised Jax because no matter what, she was just happy he'd come.

Someone needs to tell the head guard he can relax before he passes out.

Everyone was still standing, and the head guard and his partner were stuck at attention. "Stand down," Will said. "Also, apologies for his theatrics."

Before they all sat down, while Will was setting me in the high chair he'd said I didn't have to use but apparently did because I wasn't allowed on the table, Eli went over to Drew and stood in front of him. His eyebrows were knotted together and he stared intently, until he finally said, "What the hell are you doing with my granddaughter, Prince Andrew?"

"You want a list?"

Eli let out a bark of a laugh and hugged Drew before taking his seat. Dinner was loud, which made me think it was a good thing that all the other customers were there to guard the family and not to have fun because they were obnoxious and annoying and the noise level was fatiguing.

There were four conversations going on at the same time, and laughter riding over everything; I gave up trying to figure out who was saying what or to whom, and concentrated on the bites of meat I was getting from Will simply by patting his arm.

By the time the plates had been cleared from the table and more drinks were consumed, they had quieted and were speaking at volumes that didn't make my ears hurt. Eli leaned back in his chair and told them he almost hadn't come. "The attention belongs to the bride, and somewhat to the groom," he said. "I didn't want to overshadow that. But then this one—" he jutted his thumb toward Finn "—suggested surprising you tonight. The damned photographers and gossip mongers would get their fill, I would get to see how surprised you were, and then the wedding would be all about the happy couple. As it should be."

"I'm grateful that you came," Will said. "And Dad, thank you. Not just for me, but for everyone. Jax and Aubrey have missed him terribly."

"A boy's second father should not miss his son's wedding," Finn said lightly.

Jay leaned toward Zed and whispered loudly, "What the hell does that mean?"

"Grandad adopted Will last year, after we found out who he was. Keep up, Jaybird. It's gonna get a lot more confusing the longer you're in this family."

"That means you're a prince?" Jay asked Will.

"No. Simply the made-up title of Emperor."

"Bullshit." Eli slapped at the table, which made me jump. "I didn't sign a figurative document, William. You are literally, legally, my son. Like it or not, you are Prince William." He turned to Finn and Jo. "Not to step on your toes. But you don't legally exist, and a boy needs a parent."

They both laughed, and Jo told him it was all right. She appreciated that he had looked after Will when he was too young to really be on his own.

"I am not a prince," Will argued.

"And I have paperwork that says otherwise," Eli insisted.

"Don't argue with him," Jax said. "He'll sit here and bicker all night if he has to. Accept the title, and we'll keep your official duties to a minimum."

Will stuck his pointy finger in Jax's direction. "I have enough to do, Jax. You add anything else, and I might quit. I told you before, I have other options. I have no issue with becoming a kept man."

Jax turned to his father. "He gets double duty, doesn't he? As both the Emperor and the Prince?"

"I should think so."

"It's your own damned fault," Jax said before Will could complain again. "You're the one who showed up claiming to be the Emperor. If you'd just introduced yourself as Will, you'd only have half the official things to do. And hell, if you'd just been adopted earlier, when you were older than I was, you could be the king now and I could be the errand boy. I think I'd like that."

"No, thank you."

"It's a shame we can't access the timeline coming up behind us," Oz said. "I mean, its future. Because in that one, you're totally going to be king."

Will picked his glass up. "Well then. I'll start drinking now, for that poor bastard's sake."

= = =

Will was not, Aubrey declared, seeing the bride before the wedding. She made him get his clothing and anything else he thought he would need, and told him he was sleeping upstairs. It didn't matter if he'd planned on sleeping on Drew's floor again; the proximity was too convenient, he might see Aisha accidentally on purpose, and she reserved the right, as Queen, to make this decision. After the rehearsal dinner, he was given enough time to collect his things, kiss Aisha good night, which went on long enough to make her think about going against the Queen's wishes, and then Jax and Drew forced him up the stairs.

He only grumbled a little bit, complaints that were for Aisha's sake. Most of the tattoos were gone, and he wanted it to be a wedding night surprise. She could have promised him all kinds of kinky things and he would have said no. He would have hated himself for it, but he was sleeping elsewhere no matter what.

Aubrey had no idea and thought she was being a little bit mean, but he was relieved to have the decision taken from him.

Staying upstairs also meant being able to sit out on the balcony with Jax and Eli and a bottle of old scotch the old king had brought with him from Glasgow. Will didn't expect to sleep much that night, so a night in the cool air with fine liquor and better company was welcome. He dropped his stuff on Oz's bed, and then headed outside, where they were already waiting.

Eli was watching the activity on Union Square; he missed it, missed evenings spent winding down from a long day while snooping on people who were going about their business without a clue that they were entertainment for the King. Now he watched as guards ushered people away so that ropes could be put in place to block anyone from accessing the Square while it was being decorated.

They were all standing too close to the edge, and I didn't want to see it if one of them went over, so I hid under one of the chairs.

"Ah, it's fine, Wick," Will said. "You'd be happy if the barrier went back up, though, wouldn't you?"

I'd be even happier if Jax banned pigeons from Pacifica.

"I've considered it," Jax said. He finally sat down, which prompted Eli and Will to follow. "It's a security risk, not having one. But if I order it put back?"

"No one will use the balcony," Will said.

"The kids love sitting out here. Oz and Drew in particular."

"So did you," Eli said. "The two of you practically lived out here with the beer you stole."

"You knew about that?" Jax asked.

Eli looked at him as if he'd grown an extra nose. "During the summer I lost four bottles of beer a day, how could I *not* notice that? And you cleaned out the staff refrigerator at least every other week. I'd hoped that when you became serious with Aubrey that she'd buy your beer and I'd get to keep some, but no."

"She refused to contribute to his delinquencies," Will chortled.

"Any that involved alcohol, sure," Jax said. "The rest, she was more than happy to help with."

"You," Eli said, pointing at Will. "You contributed far more than I liked. Giving him excuses, telling his mother he was with you when I damn well knew he was with Aubrey."

"His mother minded his dalliances. You did not."

Eli grinned. "Not one bit. She was good for you, right from the start, Jackson. Any fool could see that."

"Except Mom."

"She saw, but it was something she wanted for you a few more years down the line. And she envied the two of you, son, she envied you horribly and hated herself for it."

"Why?"

He pressed himself into the chair, hands folded across his stomach. He took a moment to scoop up his thoughts. "Your mother was my breath, Jackson. And yet to the rest of the world, we were at arms' length. At home, with you present, we were less stodgy, but still…she was not comfortable with demonstrations of affection. Privately?" He grinned again. "She wanted to be warmer, especially around you, but she simply didn't know how and I never pressed the point. And right from the beginning, you were open and free with your affections for Aubrey, and the closer you two became and the more intimacy you allowed others to see, she recognized her own inability to be openly affectionate."

"Dad, she had to know. I knew she loved you and I knew she loved me."

He nodded. "I know. She wanted to show it, regardless. And I think somewhere deep down she resented me a bit for not pulling it out of her. I didn't know how. I only knew that no matter how reserved she was to the world, she was warm and loving with me." He took another deep breath, this one ragged. "I miss her still, Jackson. I came out of that elevator, and I swear I heard her down the hall, complaining because you'd peed on the bathroom floor again." He lifted an eyebrow and said to Will, "He was seventeen, mind you."

"Stop it, Dad," Jax snorted. "I was not."

"Fine. Eighteen, then. Before Aubrey got her hands on you and convinced you not to be such an animal." He took a long sip of his drink and then spun the ice cubes around in the glass. "I hope that you die before Aubrey does, son."

"Um. Thank you for that?"

The ice cubes swooshed around the glass, and when they stopped, he let Will refill it. He took another sip, letting the scotch breathe on his tongue, sucking air through his teeth.

"Donna was my breath," he said again. "Aubrey is your breath and your heartbeat and every blink of your eyes. I have been *broken* missing your mother. If you lost Aubrey, I imagine it would destroy you, only life is not so kind as to take you with her. You would shatter, and you would stop living, but you wouldn't die."

Jax nodded, just slightly, and they fell quiet for a while. I wiggled out from under the chair and jumped into Will's lap, just in case I needed to purr for one of them.

"I felt cheated," Eli said, breaking the silence. "I avoid coming home because she's in every corner of this house, and I can't bear it for long. I miss you all, terribly, but…she was too young, it wasn't fair, and when she died, I'm not sure she realized how much I loved her."

"Dad. She knew."

"We had our moments, Jax. There was distance between us in the end. I should have been by her side through every horrible moment, and I wasn't. I needed more hours in the day to see to Pacifica and still be there for her."

"Being King sucks," Jax said.

"Aye. It robbed us of time. I always thought there was one more day that I would have to spend with her, to make her comfortable. To tell her. To ask forgiveness for being…me."

Will shifted forward in his chair. "Give me your hand," he said to Eli. When the old king hesitated, he added, "Trust me."

He carefully set his hand on Will's, and then closed his eyes as the images sped into his brain. Will let Eli see everything he'd given to the queen the week before she died, and everything he'd heard in her mind, including the moment of perfect understanding, when she saw how much Eli had done for Will and why. He gave Eli her most treasured thoughts, which were of him, the joy she felt with him, and the deep forgiving and understanding love she felt for him.

"She was terrified of me," Will explained when he was finished. "Selfishly, I wanted her to understand. What I took from her was how much love she had, and how much love she felt. She knew, Eli. She knew it as well as she knew anything."

Eli's eyes reddened, and he croaked, "Fuck you for that, William." He pushed himself out of the chair and patted Will on the shoulder as he passed. "And thank you. Now excuse me, I'm going to pester my beautiful daughter-in-law."

Is he mad?

"No, Wick. He's not mad."

Jax leaned forward, elbows on his knees. "You touched my mother before she died. Why didn't I know?"

"Because it was private. She agonized against everything she would never know, and I had the answers, Jax. The things I let her see, and the things I took, were hers alone."

He nodded. "And I wouldn't have understood. I didn't know why you never touched anyone, just that you didn't." He suddenly sat up. "Wait. You didn't hear anything inside his head just now, did you?"

"I have much better control than I did then. I can share and not listen."

"Damn. I really wanted to know if he's all right."

His laughter boomed at us from the kitchen.

"Okay," Jax said. "I suppose he is. Good. Now, what about you? Ready?"

"I don't feel like I want to throw up, so yes." He set me on the chair next to his and got up to peer down at the Square. "We truly would have been content with a very simple union, Jax. Family on the Square, you tell us we're married, my mother cries, then we all go out and get drunk."

Jax got up and looked with him. "Your fault for bringing Aubrey into it."

Will huffed a laugh through his nose. "Indeed. And I think in the end, Aisha will be happier for it, too."

Jax is no drunk drag queen, though.

"Why Union Square?" Jax asked.

"It's where I left her standing so many years ago," he explained simply. "I want it to be where we come together again. And I wanted the decree as proof to her. I will not run, never again. I'm not certain I'll be terribly good at being accountable to someone else, but no more excuses. That spot on the Square is my promise to her."

"Ah, you didn't need a decree for that. If you run again, I'm having you shot on sight. Problem solved."

25

Rows of white chairs lined a narrow red carpet that ran from the elevator doors to the center of Union Square. At the end of the carpet was a round rug with tiny marks where everyone was supposed to stand, and there were dozens of guards protecting everything from the pigeon gangs that were bent on destroying it before the start of the wedding.

Everyone—except for Will and Drew—waited in Finn's lab. They'd taken their clothes with them and planned on fighting for the best spots to change in. Aisha got Finn's office because the bride gets the most spacious place, but everyone else was on their own. Even King Eli was told he'd probably wind up taking his pants off in a broom closet because no one was going to make the groom's mother or the Queen use it.

Zed and Jay had no problem changing in the middle of the common room. "If you don't know what I've got by now," Zed said, "that's your problem."

Jay reasoned that at least thirty people had scoped out his junk in the last three months. What was a few more?

James came by in the morning, before Aisha and Jay left for the lab. He brought a bottle of wine for the bride and groom, and a new shaver for Jay. He stood in the bathroom doorway and coached Jay on how to shave with plasma and not burn off any skin, and before he left, he kissed Aisha on the cheek and said he was more than just a little bit happy for her. He was overjoyed, and after everything she'd put up with, she deserved the fairy tale ending.

"He squealed when I told him you'd proposed to Will," Jay said. "He's not lying."

Instead of following everyone else to the lab, I stayed with

Will and Drew and walked from the royal house to the Square on a leash clipped to my stunning new purple collar. Drew fastened a tiny red bow tie to it because weddings require ties, and I was not exempt. There was a plush blue carpet that ran from the door, across the street, and up the stairs, and a line of guards formed a path for us, all dressed in formal uniforms with shiny things dangling from their chests. Each had a laser rifle resting on their shoulders, held perfectly by white-gloved hands.

"No, they're not planning on shooting anyone," Will said when I asked. "It's for show."

"Yeah," Drew said, "but I bet every one of those rifles has a full ammo pack, and they're all sharp shooters."

Jax said he would have you shot if you ran.

"I will never run again, Wick. You have my word."

The entire Square was protected, armed men and women at each corner and each set of stairs, and without looking, I knew every rooftop surrounding the block was lined with armed soldiers. The streets were blocked to taxis and delivery vans, but people were permitted to walk past and to watch if they wanted.

By the time we'd made it up the stairs, nearly every window facing Union Square was open, with people crowding around them to watch.

Will and Drew waited off to the side, not far from the largest of the cameras that would broadcast the ceremony and record it for posterity. He was a bit annoyed by them but hadn't argued when Aubrey insisted, because arguing was pointless, and he admitted that one day he would appreciate having the recording to look back on. "This was supposed to be a small, uncomplicated event," he said to Drew, who laughed because that was not possible when Mrs. B was given even a little rein in planning things.

"Nervous?" Drew asked.

"Not even a little bit."

"Liar."

"I am awash in anticipation, and I am absurdly eager for this to begin, but I truly am not nervous."

"All right. Excited."

"Indeed. The only thing I want right now is for those elevator doors to open, and for her to come out."

I hear a camera.

"We have photographers here, Wick. They'll be discreet."

"Did you really give Mrs. B permission to choose the official photo?" Drew asked.

Will nodded. "She felt it should be released before we returned and neither of us wants to spend any part of our honeymoon looking through a thousand images to find the right one."

Aisha asked her to make sure it was a good one. "The one to crush ten thousand hopeful hearts. He's mine, boys and girls."

"Does she know about the tattoos?" Drew asked. "I damn near blew it when you left Kovlov's. I almost said something to Oz in front of Jay."

"No, and keeping that from her has been…difficult." He put his hand to his chest. "And somewhat painful. But as far as I can tell looking in the mirror, there's no trace left."

"You kept Oz and Zed's footprints, right?"

"Of course. I told my parents about their portraits before the removal, and neither felt I should keep them. Oddly, as much as she objects to permanently modifying one's body, my mother was in favor of keeping the footprints."

"And she hopes you'll add to that soon."

"Truly," Will said. "She's already hinted several times that whatever reservations she once had are gone and that she would, indeed, like to be a grandmother. She may need to accept that future footprints will belong to those of your children, Zed's, and Jay's."

"I still say you'd be a great dad," Drew said.

"And perhaps a better uncle."

"Grandfather," Drew said. "If Jay has kids, you're going to be a grandfather."

Will let that sink in and said, "Step."

"Step, nothing. Jay already likes the whole bonus dad thing and he's trying to figure out something to call you other than by your name. You're gonna be a *grandpa,* old man."

There was no time for Will to absorb that. Guests had arrived and the seats were filling. Sophia and her friend Kathy were seated in the second row—the first had been left open for family—and Aisha's friends were scattered throughout. James was in the third row, right on the aisle where he had a good view; Aisha invited him and refused to accept that it would be awkward.

"Be there for Jay. Let him see how all right you really are with this."

There was no groom's side or bride's side; people chose where they wanted to be. "Pick a seat, not a side," Aisha had said. I worried she wanted it that way because Will didn't have enough friends to fill an entire side, but he tapped me on the head with his pointy finger and said that was mean; he had friends, but most of them were also colleagues, so I hadn't met them.

By the time we were ready to start, all the seats were filled, and guests were standing to either side, half way to the steps.

Lots of people like Aisha.

"You really think I'm antisocial, don't you?"

Everyone thinks you're antisocial. And grumpy.

Soft music began to play and the elevator opened, which prompted Will and Drew to take their places on the round rug. His parents were the first out, with Oz and Zed stepping out right behind them. Jo and Finn held hands as they made their way down the carpet; Oz and Zed did not, though he offered her his arm and she slipped a hand near his elbow.

She didn't hit him. That's almost disappointing.

Will collected kisses from them, and they sat in the front row while the elevator went back down, and next up was the old King and the Queen.

When Eli stepped out, a roar went up from onlookers. There was a chant—*Eli, Eli, Eli*—that he pretended to not notice as he shook Will's hand and offered his best wishes. He gave a slight wave as he turned, mostly to shut people up, and then sat next to Jo; he immediately started flirting with her, which prompted Finn to wag his pointy finger while reminding Eli that Jo was taken.

Aubrey stood with Will and Drew, her hand protectively on Will's arm after she finished hugging him.

"You look beautiful today," he said. "The tiara, though? A bit understated, don't you think?"

"No one outshines the bride, sweetheart, not even the Queen."

Jax exited the elevator alone. A murmur floated on the air; I didn't know if that was because no one expected him to make a solo trip down the red carpet, or because he walked with his hands at his waist, his crown in hand and not on his head.

It also might have been because he was ridiculously happy and had to exercise restraint to keep himself from skipping toward his wife.

I'd forgotten that he had an official uniform. I'd only seen it once, on the day Eli abdicated and Jax took the throne. There were other occasions he considered to be important enough to wear it, but I either hadn't paid attention or was spending my time in Will's apartment and missed it. It closely resembled Pacifica's military dress uniform, with crisply ironed blue slacks with a red stripe, but his jacket was brilliant white instead of blue, and in place of the dangling shiny things he wore a red sash. It was, he said, just stuffy enough without being overly pretentious, and worthy of being worn on the day he declared his only brother wed.

When he reached the round rug, after shaking Will's hand and kissing Aubrey, he moved to the spot furthest from everyone else and slipped his crown on. It still didn't fit right and tilted a touch to the right, but he didn't care. He gave a short nod to someone off to the side, and the head guard and his minion stood at attention on either side of the elevator door.

As it slid open, new music swelled from all four corners of the Square. Aisha and Jay stepped out, and I heard Will take in a short, tight breath.

She wore a simple, strapless, white linen dress that flowed around her and trailed a bit behind. She paused to take in everything; all the people watching from windows surrounding the Square, the brightly colored flowers and soft music, and the guards in formal attire, standing at attention. She kissed Jay on his cheek, and then focused on Will. When she smiled, I thought he was going to melt, and when she took Jay's hand and began walking toward him, I heard him sniff.

He held his fist to his mouth, and his eyes filled. When his breath hitched, Drew leaned toward him and whispered, "Man, I would cry, too. There's your bride. And she's amazing."

Breathe, dude.

By the time Jay let go of her hand, setting it on Will's, he had mostly composed himself. She reached her free hand to his face to brush a tear from the corner of his eye and smiled again, mouthing, "I love you, mister."

Jax tapped a tiny button on his lapel, and as he began to speak, his voice boomed from speakers placed around the Square, loud enough that even people watching from upper-story windows could hear.

"Normally I would do this at city hall, and it would be over in a minute or two, a simple, no frills decree, with no fanfare and no audience. These are not simple circumstances. I remind all who are watching and listening that the Emperor has been the protector of the people since he was just a boy. He's dedicated his life to taking care of others, and once sacrificed a chance at happiness with this very woman when he was young enough, that were he made of lesser things, he would have chosen his own happiness over the needs of the city. Instead, he honored his commitment to the people, to protect the vulnerable and to guard their safety. He has provided many of you with homes and jobs. He's made sure you were welcomed into this city, and he fed your children, sometimes at his own expense.

"It's time to give him the freedom to see to himself, to his own happiness, to protect the family he always wanted and to guard the love he's offering to his bride and her son. This is a promise we make to him; as much as he has protected the citizens of San Francisco and Pacifica, we will honor his choice to pursue a life for himself, and we will protect his union from our own self-interests.

"The Emperor is, in every way that matters, my brother. He helped raise my children, and they are better for it. He helped me to be a better father and husband and challenges me daily to be a better man. And I hope that now I can be those things for him. Aisha has been a sister to my wife, a treasured friend who holds a place so near to her heart that even distance and time failed to create shadows. She brings a light to this family that it cannot live without.

"She also brings to the Emperor a son whom he loves as his own, and from this day forward declares James Jordan Okuda, Junior to be his firstborn and his heir."

He beckoned Jay to the center of the round rug and asked him to face Will.

"My promise to you," Will said. "I will take nothing from your mother or father, and I will never stand between you and them. I respect your relationship with them, and the relationship they've formed, and the choices they make as your parents. I will always honor that. But you are a son of my heart, and I ask you to accept, with or without the King's decree, to be my heir, and to be my firstborn, understanding that this survives both your mother and myself. Your rights to me will not end with my death, nor with your mother's. What I have, and what I am, is yours."

He smiled warmly. "I do love you, more than I thought possible. You're bringing into my life something I was unaware that I needed until it came to me with slammed doors and stomped feet. With your consent, I name you as my own, and I declare you as my heir."

"Is consent given?" Jax asked.

"Hell, yeah," Jay said. "Yes. Yes, sir."

Will let go of Aisha's hand to scoop Jay up in a tight hug, and kissed him on his cheek before letting him sit back down. "I mean it, Jay. I love you, and I will do whatever is necessary to be what you need me to be."

Jax gestured for Will and Aisha to hold hands and face each other. "I was witness to the proposal of marriage, on the day when Aisha Salazar asked for the hand of William Blackshear and was witness to his affirmation. Their vows to each other are confirmed by their own declaration, to honor the commitment they have made to love one another and to respect each other and their union. Their consent was given in their request that this marriage take place by decree. Therefore, by my irrevocable order, they are duly married husband and wife, witnessed this day by Prince Andrew Van Hoff and Queen Aubrey Blackshear, and celebrated by the House of Blackshear."

Their kiss went on for a long time. I could no longer stand being at his feet; I climbed his leg to sit on his shoulder so that when they parted I could stretch forward and give Aisha a kiss of my own.

I married her, too, Will. Move over.

Jax took off his sash, his official duties over. Everyone was on their feet, and the family surrounded the happy couple. Jax grabbed Will and planted a long kiss on his cheek and then hugged him. "Son of a bitch, I am happy for you."

Will kissed him back, then turned to his mother and said, "The King just called you a bitch."

= = =

The reception was held in the same place as Will's birthday party, one floor down from the roof of the house. It was louder than his birthday; music blared from massive speakers set up on the stage, and while it was decorated tastefully there was no mistaking what it was going to turn into: a party ruled by teenagers.

That was exactly what Aisha and Will wanted.

Oz, Zed, and Jay's friends were invited because they all liked the Emperor and wanted to celebrate along with him, and because he and Aisha thought that if needed, they could use a mass of sweaty, dancing teenagers as cover for when they wanted to slip out.

On the far end of the room, a bar had been set up, with their favorite bartender from Kaluto's manning it. At some point the room had divided; most of the younger guests were near the loud, thumping speakers, and almost everyone over thirty was congregating around the bar and near the food. The lone exception was Eli, who had taken to the dance floor with Oz. He didn't care if he looked foolish; he moved in a tiny circle, swinging his arms while snapping his fingers. He only cared that he had fun, and made her laugh.

He danced worse than Will; she was laughing, all right.

I was perched on Will's shoulder, though he'd taken off the leash and given it to Drew. I was free to wander if I wanted, but there were too many feet in the room, and I wanted to be where I could see everything. From his spot at the bar, the entire room was visible. Aisha was at a table with Aubrey and Jo, and they were laughing hard enough that they had to be making fun of Will. Finn was talking to people I didn't know, and he was waving his arms the way he did when he was excited, so they were probably work friends or his personal minions. He'd hired several people to take on some of his research because Will threatened him with bodily harm if he kept ignoring Jo.

He showed Finn what happened to the future Jo and Finn, and it rattled him so hard that his knees nearly buckled and he had to sit down. He promised, no more long weeks lost in the lab. He agreed to a schedule that he would only break sometimes, and only if he'd warned her first.

Jo was happy enough with his promise that touching and smooching began and Will was uncomfortable enough to leave them alone, though he did part with the thing that had been thrown at him several times over the last week: *I wouldn't mind a little brother or sister.*

Jax stood at the bar with Will, watching his father dance with his daughter. "He's going back day after tomorrow," he said wistfully. "I can't get him to promise to come home before Oz's wedding."

"It's my Gram," Will said. "She's near the end and he doesn't want to leave my grandfather alone too long, just in case." Jo and Finn were traveling to Glasgow with Eli and thought they might stay a while. It had been decades since she had seen her parents, and video chatting did not count. "Aisha and I will be there in a few days. I'll remind him about what he has waiting at home. Sometimes he needs to be nudged."

Drew left the dance floor—Eli wasn't giving Oz up just yet—and asked Will to get him a drink. "The cinnamon stuff."

"Has he turned you into a drinker?" Jax asked.

"Only on occasion. For the things that matter." He held his glass out to Will. "To the smartest damned thing you've ever done, or ever will do."

"I will, indeed, drink to that. And you're next."

"After today Oz is going to change her mind about what she wants. I know it. She'll want a quick royal decree."

Jax sipped at his drink and then said, "And I'll refuse."

Drew's face pinched.

"You saw how many people were there today, crowding in windows and standing on their toes to see," Jax said. "They were excited and happy that this wedding was shared with them, and when it comes to their princess, they'll hope for the whole show. I was wrong before. It really is more than just your wedding. The two of you will be promising the people as well as each other."

"Besides," Will added, "*I* want you to have the wedding. How many people get to be there when their great grandparents tie the knot?"

Drew accepted that. "And how many people stand as their great grandfather's best man?"

Will blinked. "What?"

"I want you to be my best man, Will. I don't want anyone else standing with me when I marry her."

"Carter—"

"Is my brother, but not my best man. He understands."

"Then I would be honored."

"Where's the honeymoon?" Jax asked. He was watching Aisha and Aubrey, still laughing. "If Scotland is a few days away, I presume you're going somewhere else first."

"Home," Will said. "Well, my childhood home. There are some things she would like to see, and one place in particular I would like to share with her."

"The park with the bubble over it and the northern lights inside?" Drew asked.

"The very same," Will said. To Jax, "I allowed Drew a small glimpse of my birth When using a holographic computer. He holds out hope that one day I'll allow him to portal forward to visit it."

"That'll happen," Jax snorted.

"It might. I'm finding fewer reasons to withhold information, Jax. As I told Drew, your future is no longer limited by my history. I am willing to use what I know to create something better. Honeymoon first, though. And I am frankly surprised at how much I'm looking forward to going there."

Jax set his drink on the bar and reached into his jacket. "Almost forgot. Your new travel visas."

"We have visas, Jax."

"Not updated ones."

Will pulled the engraved metal cards from the envelope Jax handed him. "Prince William Blackshear of Pacifica. Princess Aisha Blackshear of Pacifica. This was your father's idea, wasn't it?"

"Aubrey's, actually."

Will couldn't help but smile. "This means you'll all stop calling me 'Emperor?'"

"Hell, no," Drew said.

Jax nodded. "Not a chance. But none of us will mean it the way Aisha does."

"Meaning?"

"Hell, she screams it at three in the morning, doesn't she?"

No. Now she screams 'Bilbo.'

Will turned a lovely shade of pink.

Jax looked over at Aubrey again, and after a moment said, "Dammit, I have to know which one of us they're laughing at."

He left Drew and Will alone.

"You have a Mrs. Blackshear now. How awesome is that?"

"Indeed."

"Happy?"

"Little bit, yeah."

"Then go get her and leave. This isn't a family night out. This is your wedding day and it's starting to creep into your wedding night. Grab your wife, and go."

Will set his drink down on the bar. "In a bit, Grandpa. We'd like you and Oz and Zed and Jay to come downstairs for a few minutes." He leaned forward and whispered in Drew's ear, softly so that I couldn't hear it.

It took half an hour of enduring kisses and well wishes before he and Aisha could get to the elevator. Drew rounded up the others and we followed, and during the ride down they pestered him to tell him what was up, but he wouldn't say. They were also excited because they would get there just a minute after Will and Aisha, and would get to see them discover the gift they had chipped in on and left on the fireplace hearth.

Will had the guitar in hand when we walked into the apartment. "This is wonderful," he said. "It even looks like the one Zed peed in."

Jay picked a box off the end table and handed it to his mother. "This is your part of the present."

She opened it and laughed, "A custom ear plug kit."

"We figured you might need those until he gets better at playing."

"I'm insulted, and thank you," Will said. "I promise, I will play for her, even if it hurts." He set it down carefully and asked Drew to put me on the hearth. "We keep talking about declaring a day to be Wick's birthday and still haven't done it. So, if it's all right with you, Mister Wick, Aisha and I would like to share today with you."

I get a birthday and a wedding day?

"Indeed. From now on, this date will be both our anniversary and your birthday. That way we'll never forget."

He kneeled and stuck his hand under the sofa, and pulled a long, flat box out. "It's not a birthday without a gift. And since you decided you weren't ready for a kitten, we thought you might like this instead."

Will pulled the top off and pulled from the box a brand new, thin, bright and shiny hover cart. "Now, there are rules. You never take it on the roof or the balcony, and you don't leave the house on it unless you're with Drew or me. All right?"

I didn't know what to say.

It was beautiful.

"You're gonna be stylin', Wick," Zed said.

I love it. Thank you. Turn it on?

Will pressed a button and it hummed to life, lifting a few feet from the floor. He set me on it, and they watched as I got oriented, and then zoomed around the apartment. When I'd gone up and down the hall a few times, Will showed me how to land it—something I'd never done—and how to turn it off.

"Is it fully charged?" Zed asked. "We can take him back to the reception and let him float around, flirt with the girls."

Can I stay here? I think I've had enough partying tonight. I'd like to nap.

"Of course you can stay here," Will said. "After we leave, though, go to Drew's. He's going to feed you while I'm gone. Make sure you give him the same nightly attention you've been giving me, all right?"

He needs help?

"Yes, he does, and a lot of it."

After the kids left—there was a lot of kissing and hugging—I jumped back on the hover cart and turned it on. I lifted it until I was at Will's chest height, and gave him a head bonk on his chin.

Show Aisha what you did. It's your wedding night now. Show her.

"Is that why you stayed behind, Wick? To see her reaction?"

Yep.

"I did something," he explained as he tossed his suit jacket to the sofa, and began unbuttoning his shirt. "I really hope you like it."

She wiggled her eyebrows at him. "Got your nipples pierced?"

"Ow. No. Close your eyes."

It took her a few seconds, but she did. He took his shirt off and tossed it on top of the jacket, and then shoved his hands into his pockets. "All right. You can look now."

It took a couple seconds for it to register. Icarus and Daedalus were gone.

"Will," she breathed. "What did you do?"

"Started over," he said. She set her hand on his bare chest where Icarus' wing tips used to be and brushed her fingers over his skin. "I told my parents about the tattoos. And as expected, my mother was horrified, but not for the reasons I thought, and she practically demanded I removed their faces, at the very least."

"But why?" Her hand slipped to his ribs, where the portraits used to be. "Sweetheart, I honestly never expected this. I was serious when I said I didn't want you to change for me."

"I know. But it was time. And her reasoning made me decide it was a good idea."

"Why?"

"She said, and I quote, 'every time you're in bed with her, she'll see my face. What woman wants to have her mother-in-law staring back in the middle of sex?'"

That made her laugh.

"I kept the crowns and the baby feet," he said. "Truthfully, I couldn't bear to have them removed."

"And I would never want you to." Her hands slipped from his chest to his belt, and she started to unbuckle it. "Any other hidden surprises?"

"Maybe." He grabbed her hands. "But don't we have a portal to walk through?"

"Don't we have a marriage to consummate? The portal will be there later."

"Indeed, it will." He let go of her hands and pulled her close. "Do you have any idea how much I love you, Enzo Blackshear?"

"Almost as much as I love you, Bilbo Blackshear."

Oh, barf. Really. I'm going to hurl from here, and paint the floor in a splash of chunky chicken and ham that I ate off the old king's plate.

I lowered the hover cart and turned it off. When they headed for the bedroom, I jumped onto the sofa and curled up, because it was a good time to snooze. I needed to be refreshed later, when it was time to wake Drew up and tell him everything he was doing wrong in bed.

Four in the morning seemed like the right time to explain about pudding and handcuffs.

I decided I could sleep in the living room. Will didn't need my help anymore, and I was sure I wouldn't have to run and find Drew to pick him up from the floor. The living room was quiet and the bedroom surely was not. I closed my eyes and sucked in a deep breath, and was almost asleep when I heard it.

Thud.

Dammit.

I am a writer living in Northern California with a couple of people known as The Man and The Woman; there was a Younger Human but he moved out and now lives with That Damned Dog Butters and his canine sister Lady. Oh, and I live with Buddah Pest, a furry, constant pain in my asterisk. You can find me online at my blog, The Psychokitty Speaks Out, or on Facebook. And if you've made it this far and are still reading, GO YOU!!! - *Max Thompson*

www.ingramcontent.com/pod-product-compliance
Lightning Source LLC
Chambersburg PA
CBHW070800030726
47504CB00003B/626